SINS OF OMISSION

Candace Flynt

SINS OF
OMISSION

Random House   New York

11/1984
Am. Lit.

Library of Congress Cataloging in Publication Data

Flynt, Candace, 1947-
Sins of omission.

I. Title.
PS3556.L95S5   1984   813'.54   84-42629
ISBN 0-394-53955-9

Manufactured in the United States of America

24689753

To my father
and to Mary Carpenter

SINS OF OMISSION

Chapter One

SO SHE was reading the want ads. Tough. They rarely had customers late Thursday afternoons, none today, so why shouldn't she? Because boredom reigned at the pancake house, and Ruth, her fellow worker, expected her to quit reading and make something happen. It wasn't enough that this place would soon be crawling with basketball fans. Nor that three more waitresses should arrive any minute, willing to provide whatever conversation Ruth might want. Nor even that, according to the radio in the kitchen, Wake Forest was clobbering Carolina for once in the opening game of the Big Four basketball tournament played each December at the Greensboro Coliseum. No, no one could entertain Ruth, pesky Ruth, but Suzanne. It was about to drive her crazy.

Suzanne was hostess at the pancake house; Ruth was cashier. When the restaurant was busy, either of them was expected to wait tables, hence their ridiculous pinafored waitress uniforms. The further insult of doilies, which Bennie their boss said made them look cute, sat atop their heads, Suzanne's starched to attention, Ruth's lifeless against her skull. Suzanne was ready for *no* doily and more sophisticated clothes, a skirt and sweater, for instance, which might camouflage her skinniness and upgrade this place a little. One reason she'd taken a job at a pancake house in the first place—didn't it make sense?—was to fatten herself up. But that had been a year ago, a year of enduring Ruth and Bennie, and she hadn't gained a pound.

A whole restaurant of empty booths, lit by the late afternoon sun, stretched behind her. To her right was the swinging door that led to the kitchen. To her left slumped her best friend on a backless stool before the cash register. At forty, twice her own age, Ruth had alert eyes and an enthusiastic smile that showed a set of false teeth, surface-shiny like dime store pearls. As Suzanne watched without watching, Ruth straightened her back and flexed her hands as if the numbers on the cash register were keys to a musical instrument she was about to play.

For some time now Suzanne had been thinking of Ruth almost as a sister. They enjoyed the same jokes; they were offended by the same kind of women; they both even laughed at men. Or so it had seemed. As a result, Suzanne had begun to share what she did—those efforts she made to dig up and expose the world's facts—with Ruth. Ruth was receptive, especially pleased when Suzanne managed to get one of the waitresses, Rita Byerly, fired. But Ruth had wanted Rita fired, she later found out, because Rita couldn't add up the checks right, not for the same reason Suzanne did. Bennie was hers and no one else's. To insure that, she had had to convince him that Rita was stealing. If she and Ruth were like sisters, shouldn't Ruth want the same things she did?

Even in one of her smallest campaigns—the plan not to wear a waitress uniform anymore—Ruth complained that she was being unreasonable. This morning, while Suzanne was dressing for work in the slinky skirt and sweater she'd carefully selected, Ruth's general hesitancy had finally affected her. She actually changed clothes. And now here she sat, dressed like she never intended to be dressed, in a tacky waitress uniform.

She had hoped for a companion in this work of hers. Had hoped to find someone who cared as much about the truth as she did. But not only did Ruth not understand, she had come close to thwarting Suzanne's sense of mission. Today was the day Suzanne was to decide whether or not they were going to share an apartment. The answer had to be no.

She continued to peruse the want ads. Ruth's impatience could almost be heard. Each time Suzanne shifted her weight, the springs of the booth creaked noisily, giving her friend an excuse to keep glancing in her direction.

Finally, Ruth broke. "Are you looking for a new job?" she whined, straightening her back when she spoke and then slumping to shapelessness again. The least Bennie could do, Suzanne thought, would be to get her a decent stool to sit on.

Suzanne did not answer. No, she wasn't looking for another job, only some excitement. A trip over Greensboro in a helicopter, a free kitten, music lessons, a $50 scalper's ticket—which on her pay she could only inquire about—to see Elvis Presley on his comeback tour. Whom might she meet, choosing any one of those? She had met a very nice doctor once when she'd answered an ad in the newspaper soliciting thirty people with cold hands for an experiment. She'd had cold hands all her life, cold skinny hands. But it wasn't simply that she had no fat insulating her body, she'd found out. She suffered from Raynaud's Phenomenon: whenever she was nervous her hands got cold. By the time the experiment ended, she had learned how to warm them up by willing her blood vessels to expand. What the good doctor had learned was less scientific: a man should not initiate a relationship he wasn't willing to see through.

Ruth was watching her again. With a red pencil from behind her ear, Suzanne bent to the page of ads and boldly circled one. For a brief moment she lifted her eyes from the column and stared wistfully ahead. Don't worry, Ruth, she thought. I have no plan to better myself. All I want is to be a hostess/sometimes waitress in this lousy hole for the rest of my life.

"This job not good enough for you?" Ruth interrupted again.

"It's good enough," she answered, using her red pencil to circle another item, guitar lessons.

"What are all the circles for?" Ruth checked the parking lot for potential customers and then arose, arching her back in an exaggerated motion that showed off her large breasts. She came to stand at Suzanne's shoulder, but Suzanne quickly folded the newspaper.

"None of your business."

Ruth lowered herself into the opposite side of the booth, making the springs groan. "Are you bored? Why won't you talk to me? Have you forgotten all your jokes?"

Suzanne gazed idly at the front page.

"Let me see your paper a minute." Ruth's small eyes darted aggressively. Grabbing the top corner of the newspaper, she began swiveling it around on the orange Formica table top. Suzanne grabbed it back. "Can't I see what's at the movies?" Ruth whined.

"No, you can't." What Ruth wanted to know was what Suzanne had circled. One house for sale, although the house was just to throw Ruth off, and guitar lessons, which were beginning to seem like a good idea.

Suzanne pulled out a cigarette, creating, as if she didn't have enough already, more evidence for herself. Sure enough, before she could even light up, Ruth said, "Should you be smoking?" Ruth wasn't worried about Suzanne's health; she was worried about Bennie's rule that his girls were not to smoke in uniform. Ruth would intrude into her life horribly. There was just no question about it. Only by herself, Suzanne finally realized, could she live the life she wanted. Only alone could what she said and did maintain its meaning. Like the water in that teapot in the kitchen, she felt herself shrieking for escape. Too much time had passed in her life without anything of value happening.

Ruth crossed her arms emphatically on the table. Suzanne had helped her dye her hair a ruddy brown that looked incongruous, although she had never said so, beside Ruth's gray eyebrows. "Why won't you share anything?" Ruth asked in the tired tone of an ignored mother. "It's not normal to have so many secrets."

With an earnest stare Suzanne locked Ruth's eyes into her own. "I *do* share myself," she said in a low serious voice. "I have someone that I share all my thoughts with. All my wild imaginings," she added with a trace of irony that Ruth did not register. "It's just not you."

Ruth hesitated. Her brown eyes crinkled; her mouth curled into a sort of disbelieving smile. "Well, good, Suzie," she finally said. "Good." Ruth knew how much she hated that nickname but used it anyway. "I'm glad you have somebody. Thanks for telling me about them. Now you don't have to talk to me anymore at all." She arose from the booth, a sense of dignity steadying the pained expression on her face. "I'm going to get some coffee cake," she said.

"Bring me a piece," Suzanne called brightly. Ruth nodded, her eyes averted, giving up without a fight. If only she would persist, she might pull Suzanne back. Suzanne stared challengingly at her friend's slowly moving figure, hoping to will her to turn around, but Ruth only pushed through the swinging door, her shoulders slumped in defeat. Where was her natural tenacity?

When she heard a conversation under way in the kitchen, Suzanne found the ad for guitar lessons again and committed the telephone number of one Robert Carter to memory. Pulling the cash register lever, she held the drawer so that Ruth wouldn't hear it *ping* open. She helped herself to several dimes in case she wanted to call him more than once. After all, if Bennie chose not to provide a private phone for his employees, he had a responsibility to pay for their calls. At the pay phone located near the front door (another humiliation) she dialed the number. A single ring and then a strong "Hello." He had a deep bass voice. She could tell by the single word that he was a young man who had not experienced much.

"I'm calling about your ad for guitar lessons. Do you still have openings?"

"Sure do," he answered. "I'm Robert Carter. May I ask your name?" She heard him opening a drawer.

"*The* Robert Carter?" Why she said that she had no idea, but he chuckled.

"A Robert Carter," he said. "Is there somebody named Robert Carter who's famous?"

"I don't know. I just said that. It was a joke." She hurried past the remark, hoping he wouldn't pay much attention. "I'd like to ask you a few questions before I give my name," she said.

"Shoot. Anything." He sounded open, eager, as if no question would be out of line.

"How old are you?"

"Twenty-one."

"Same as me," she murmured thoughtfully, although she was twenty. "Is this what you do all the time?"

Ruth was backing through the door from the kitchen with two servings of cake and coffee on a tray. Her lips drew back in a sort of mirthless grin.

"I'm a voice major at the university," her teacher-to-be was saying. "I'll graduate this coming spring, and I'm supposed to go to Juilliard."

"Who will I take from then?"

"By then you'll know how to play," he said, adding, "honest."

Ruth sat down in the booth. She pulled napkins out of the holder for each of them. She offered a cup to Suzanne, but Suzanne, waving one negative hand, turned her back. The harassed springs of the booth announced that Ruth was bringing the coffee anyway. Her hand over the receiver, Suzanne turned and whispered furiously, "Not now."

"What's Juilliard?" she asked Robert Carter, fiercely calm.

"Just a school," he said. "A graduate school everybody wants me to go to." After a slight hesitation he added, "My plans are to sing professionally."

Suzanne waited to hear what other information he might volunteer, but instead he asked, "What kind of musical background do you have?"

"None."

"You want to take for fun?"

She was silent.

"That's not exactly what I meant. I meant, are you interested in folk or classical?"

"I've got to go," she said. Her coffee was getting cold. Besides, Ruth was listening to every word. Without saying goodbye, she hung up.

"Who was that?" Ruth asked.

"Who was who?"

At her place sat her coffee, the sugar bowl and creamer pushed close. Ruth reached across the table before Suzanne could sit down. "Two-and-a-half teaspoons. Right?" she smiled, dumping the sugar into Suzanne's cup. "A thimble of cream," she continued, pouring a thread of milk. "The person you were talking to. Who was she?"

Did even Ruth think she was not capable of having a man? Suzanne drank while standing, watching her friend down the sides of the porcelain mug. By dilating her eyes, she could see two Ruths. She finished the hot coffee without flinching and smacked the cup hard on the table for someone else to take care of. As if she weren't hungry, she pushed away her plate of coffee cake. With almost no hesitation, Ruth began to eat the second piece. Larry, the cook, studied when they didn't have customers, but today Suzanne was going to interrupt him. She had to escape Ruth before she started screaming.

"Come back," Ruth called. "I'll stop asking so many questions. Suzie," she said, plaintively drawing out the hated nickname. Suzanne pushed hard through the swinging door.

In a kitchen where grease was a way of life, Larry was actually trying to do his drafting homework. He'd erected plastic walls around a section of counter top. He peered at her through grease-spotted glasses when she called his name. He had heavy black hair and a nose that dominated his face. The radio blared the Wake Forest-Carolina game, which was tight with two minutes to go. Carolina was staging a comeback, but they were still six points behind.

"There's more coffee cake over there," he motioned with his nose. Through the plastic she could see him engaged with his slide rule and pencil.

She walked over and lifted the flap.

"Do you have a customer?" he asked, anxiously looking over her shoulder. He wore a clean apron on top of the one he'd cooked in earlier.

"Yeah. Me," she said. "I'm starved."

"I don't have time to cook for you." He turned his back.

"Please," she said, but there was no sense of the word in her tone.

"Help yourself to anything," he called. "You can use the stove.

Or I'll be glad to fix you something when I start cooking for some customers."

"I can't eat if I'm waiting tables," she said flatly.

"You've done it before. Please, Suzanne, *you* cook. I've got to finish my project."

"Do you work here or not?" she began in a rapid-fire voice. "Are you paid or not? Shall I report you to Bennie or not?" The "or nots" reminded her of heels clicking together.

Larry emerged from the plastic room as from a cocoon, his nose as shiny as if he'd basted it with grease. "What do you want, goddamnit?"

"Absolutely nothing," she said breezily. She leaned back against a counter with her arms folded and stared at the space above Larry's head, a stance that had always enraged her father. He took off his clean apron and wadded it into a ball.

"You're going to eat. If you don't decide what, I will."

All she'd wanted was an omelet, but suddenly she realized that she was famished, so she would have pigs-in-blankets and hash browns, too. When she gave him the order, he looked at her with contempt.

"Go ask Ruth what she wants," he ordered, as if he didn't mind cooking after all. But what he wanted was to get her out of his way. How ineffectual men were. Not many would slug you unless you were their wife or daughter, so what power did they have? She retreated to the restaurant—only a tactical move—and found Ruth examining her newspaper. While the spying irritated her, at the moment she was angrier at Larry.

"The cook's cooking," she announced. "Want anything?"

Ruth shook her head. The second piece of coffee cake had disappeared. The corners of Ruth's mouth were tucked into her cheeks as if she were trying to hold back tears. "Are you really thinking of buying a house? Are you, Suzanne? Because if you are . . . I am really hurt."

"Come on, Ruth, have something to eat. I just talked Larry into cooking for us." Ruth's eyes closed tightly as she began to cry. "I'm not buying a house," Suzanne said. "That was a joke. Omelet? Blueberry pancakes? Decide."

"I'm not hungry," Ruth said halfheartedly. "Oh, yes, I am. Do you promise? If you promise, I'll have the western omelet."

Suzanne rolled her eyes in exasperation. "I promise."

"Then you *are* going to move in with me?" Ruth's small eyes shone. For the last week they had been making lists of the money they would save and the things they could share. Ruth had a car; Suzanne had a stereo. Ruth had a small inheritance; Suzanne had a wealth of knowledge about the world.

It might as well be now. Slowly, Suzanne shook her head.

"No?" Ruth said in disbelief. "You're really saying no?"

"I'm really saying no," Suzanne said. She turned her back to walk to the kitchen, not wanting to observe the pitiful sight. No, no, no, she thought to herself, wondering if it was the word she said best.

In the kitchen Larry had assembled his ingredients and turned up the radio. Only thirty seconds left in the game. Wake led by one.

"That's more like it," Suzanne said loudly so he could hear. She leaned against the door-facing to watch. "Bennie will be happy to know how well you take care of his girls," she added.

Larry raised his eyes from the grill, where the hash browns were already sizzling. The odor pulled at her stomach. "Be sure and tell him," he said with a smile that appeared to be directed inward rather than at her. Was he patronizing her? Suddenly he became genuinely engrossed in cooking, almost as engrossed as he had been in his drafting assignment. He didn't look up again, and in a few seconds, mission accomplished, she left.

A small passageway connected the kitchen and the restaurant. Here Suzanne stood, trying to decide whether or not she could face Ruth again. She wasn't going to share living quarters and that was final. Perhaps her subconscious had told her to circle the house for sale so Ruth would begin to get the idea. There were still no customers, no waitresses either, and it was past four. Soon that would change. Ruth had set the table for their meal and done something with Suzanne's newspaper. Out of sight, she must hope, out of mind, but Suzanne was not so easily distracted as most people. Ruth's face still drooped with disappointment. When Suzanne entered the dining room a green light began flashing over the waitress's station.

"Go get our meals," she said, moving toward the telephone. Ruth hesitated, hoping to stay and listen, but Suzanne waited like a statue with her dime poised above the slot. "Go," she said. As Ruth rose from the booth like an old woman and slowly crossed the restaurant, Suzanne dialed the last digit.

"Hello?"

"It's me again," she said.

"Yes?" His voice sounded more tentative than it had before.

"I'm sorry I had to hang up so abruptly a little while ago, but my boss walked in."

"I figured something like that happened," he said.

"He thinks he owns me," Suzanne said. "He pays me a dollar an hour, lets me keep my tips, and thinks he owns me."

"There was a mistake in the newspaper ad," Robert said. "The lessons are three apiece instead of four."

"I can afford a four-dollar lesson," she said.

"I'm sure you can, but the lessons are three."

"Can I pay you four?"

He sighed. "You can pay four if you want to pay four."

"I have a couple more things to ask."

"Shoot."

She paused before the essential question, the one that would determine what she did next. If she had to guess, she would say no, he wasn't married because he'd so easily reduced his fee. "Are you married?"

"Yes," he said.

"What does your wife do?"

"She works for the newspaper," he said, his politeness growing strained. "Anything else?"

"No. Are you angry?"

"Why should I be?"

"Would you rather not have me as a student?"

"I'd like to have you as a student," he said with great deliberateness. "I'd like to have your name and I'd like to set up a time."

She needed to be easier to get along with. Besides, Ruth was walking through the door with their food. She didn't want to start out as adversaries, but from his first mention of Juilliard, he'd seemed so smug. The whole world didn't know about fancy music schools even if she did.

Robert was going to begin teaching a week from Saturday, which gave her ten days to reconsider or to make plans. First she had to meet his wife. They agreed to have her first lesson at five o'clock in a practice room at the university.

Now the rush was on. Carolina had nipped Wake by two. Glassy-eyed college students, claiming a victory they had nothing to do with as their own, fumbled through the doors. Drunk from the narrow victory and the booze they had smuggled into the coliseum, they tried to by-pass their hostess and take the table they wanted, but Suzanne spoke sharply to the lead blond of this particular group.

"I'll have to seat you, sir."

He smiled chummily. "Wherever you want me, sweetheart." She could tell that the only thing he'd determined about her was that she was female.

"How about your car?"

The young man leered, thinking this was an offer, until his eyes actually focused on her critical face. "This way," she said briskly before he could make some rude remark. The group of four, all dressed in baby-blue and white school colors, followed. "Who won?" she asked, wanting to hear what they'd say.

"We smeared them," one of them said. "We," he continued. "The University of North Carolina at Chapel Hill. Heard of us, haven't you?" He jutted his chin into her face. She stuck a menu against his stomach.

"Vaguely," she said. All these assholes were the same, she thought, aware that with these drunks she could say those very words. But she had too much on her mind right now to bother. She was wondering what Robert Carter was like. From the breadth of his voice she had the impression that he was a large man. If he wanted a professional career, or if someone wanted one for him, he must be attractive. What kind of professional career? she wondered. Like Frank Sinatra?

When the next lull came, she telephoned him again. "I just wanted to let you know how much I'm looking forward to my lessons," she said.

"Same here," he replied, but already there was distance in his voice.

In the background she heard someone ask who it was.

Half covering the receiver, Robert said, "A new student, honey."

The "honey" cut through Suzanne's heart like a razor blade. He was married. She'd found that out already, of course, but now it was real.

"Can I call you back?" Robert asked. "My supper is on the table."

"Are you the cook?" she asked.

"Let me call you back." He hung up without letting her say anything else.

Chapter Two

W HILE the poky elevator—bane of the newspaper staff—descended to the lobby, Molly Carter put on her gloves, hat, and scarf and buttoned her coat close around her neck. She left her heavy waist-length hair tucked inside both for the insulation it would give and to avoid the stares it often drew. As the elevator creaked past the second floor, she thought, as she had many times, about its incongruousness at a newspaper office. How many deadline stories had it thwarted? Every morning it made her late for her job as a headline writer. It made her late returning from lunch. It was going to make her miss her bus home, which was why she'd already prepared herself to walk. Sure enough, as metal scraped against metal, the unaligned door opened and she emerged to the braying sound of an engine and a swell of black smoke. But the bus itself was gone.

In the glass exit door she could see her reflection. She looked more logical without her long hair showing but not that much more logical. A simple haircut was not the answer. Like everyone else these days, Molly wore very short skirts. But whenever she looked in a mirror, something was wrong. Her lengths were off: her hair was as long as her skirts were, and then her legs were long, too, and she looked odd. Even though her legs were her best feature and the more of them that showed, she supposed, the better, she hoped that styles would soon change. Legs that felt perfectly normal in an office full of reporters almost guaranteed rudeness out on the street.

By eating a packaged sandwich from the canteen, she'd managed not to leave the office for lunch. But at two o'clock an interview for her weekly column—the only bit of writing she did so far—had come through, so she'd had to face the out-of-doors. There came a day in every winter when the sun didn't make a difference anymore: today was that day. She had braved the cold anyway to learn the distinction between hard- and soft-core pornography—something she could have lived her life without knowing—and now she had to brave it again to get home. Somehow it seemed that since she had worked hard all day, she deserved not to face the miserable elements.

She put on a pair of huge sunglasses, which made her look as if she were going for a ride in a convertible but were meant solely to keep street grit out of her contact lenses. Not long ago she'd had a car, not a convertible, of course, but the U-AAS or You-Ass, her pet name (thanks to Ralph Nader's book *Unsafe at Any Speed*) for the Corvair her father had given her when she started college. Now she walked or rode the bus because starting in September, her husband, Robert, had said he needed the car more. Classes for his senior year had begun, and while she usually sat at a desk all day, he had to travel constantly between home and the university. She'd wanted to ask why he couldn't hang around school between classes like most students, but she hadn't. For one thing, she thought it was a test: would she give up her favorite material possession for love of him? For another, she thought he would eventually change his mind: because she didn't have a car she wasn't able to dash home at lunch for a "nooner" on days he didn't have class. The car was hers and she wanted to drive it, but how could she tell anyone but her parents and not sound terribly selfish?

Although she was embarrassed to admit this, only seven months ago Molly had looked upon marriage not as giving and taking but primarily as the right to make love legally. Her wedding day had brought great relief: no longer would she have to sneak Robert into her childhood bed when her parents were out of town and never again would she have to park down those dangerous country lanes. She had thought marriage would be sort of like living in a dormitory room: you took care of your side and your roommate took care of hers (his). A fifty-fifty proposition. But it didn't seem to be like that at all. She guessed she ought to remember that Robert was as used to having a car as she. But he'd sold his to buy her engagement ring, which now seemed foolish in light of the fact that most people skipped diamonds these days in favor of wide gold bands.

She moved through the swinging glass door, waving and smiling at Allie, the switchboard operator, before she put on her walking home expression. The air was so chill that for a moment she couldn't breathe. In the last hour the sky had turned a dense gray, and although nothing was falling yet, Molly could feel particles of ice in the air she breathed.

Stepping quickly into the meager flow of people, she held her head first up and then down—never at eye level—like a woman walking alone in New York City. Although she hadn't been to New York since her high school scout troop's trip, she'd never forgotten the models—as tall as ladders—with their eyes so literally and figuratively beyond reach of her own. If Molly had fallen dead at one of their handsome pairs of feet, she knew that the model would have simply stepped over and gone on her way. All those bewitching eyes that never saw you, really did. They knew your sex, your threat potential, how far away you were from them, what they would say if you moved too close. She walked briskly, tuning her ears to cars approaching from behind. She thought of herself as practicing for the day—only a year off— when she and Robert became citizens of the greatest city in the world.

If she stretched things, perhaps she could tell Robert that walking on the street scared her. Having been in a motor vehicle every day from her sixteenth birthday until three months ago, she certainly knew what drivers were like. They got stung by bees, they dropped lit cigarettes in their laps, and if they wore contact lenses, sometimes both lenses would flick out of their eyes at once. Then they ran off the road and killed somebody. Didn't he remember how she herself had balanced a bowl of cereal on the steering wheel when she used to drive to work? Sometimes keeping the milk from spilling could make her run off the side of the road. But maybe this was an argument for staying away from roads altogether.

Probably the only argument Robert would accept was for sex. After all, the main reason they'd gone ahead and gotten married instead of waiting for him to finish his senior year, as her father had strongly suggested, was that neither of them had the forbearance to spend another twelve months without a regular dose of it. It remained a point of pride with Robert that if people their age copulated four times a week (knowing her dutiful girlfriends from college, she was sure those figures were exaggerated), *they* would copulate six. But didn't Robert want to double the national average, like they'd done a few times? She suddenly wondered if she'd been having too much sex. She'd never thought the word "copulate" in her life. Was she growing less romantic?

I am *selfish*, she thought, as she waited for the WALK sign. I am young and selfish, but during my marriage I will grow old and become generous. Especially when we have enough money to afford two cars, she added, teasing herself. The truth was, she hardly thought about the car anymore unless it was a day like this, overwhelmingly cold. But then she thought about it exclusively. Maybe Robert would agree for her to take the car on days that the temperature was below thirty-two.

It was too dark for sunglasses so she paused in front of Montaldo's to put hers away. Inside the cozy store window a mannequin dressed for winter held some kind of black fur muff. What poor animal was black? All she could think of was a Burmese, but she was certain they didn't make fur objects out of domestic cats.

She paused longer at the next window, where three more mannequins showed off sleek chiffon party dresses for the upcoming holidays. She admired exotic clothes but almost always refused to wear them. Once for a special weekend during college, she had let her mother dress her, and she'd looked as silly as one of those outfitted pet poodles. Not that there was anything wrong with her mother's taste. With the same taste that made Molly feel ridiculous, her mother looked stunning.

Molly especially disliked clothes that had parts of themselves missing, such as one-shouldered or strapless gowns, bathing suits without middles, and backless dresses. The navy dress her mother had chosen for her to wear that weekend to the Governor's Mansion for tea had long sleeves, a huge white bib collar, and no back. There was something obscene about the way her spinal column was exposed to everybody in the world while her arms were so carefully covered.

This mauve dress would look elegant on her mother's statuesque frame, but if she told her about it, she ran the risk of being accused of taking her own first step toward becoming a woman of style. It was not. After all these years, her mother still chose not to understand that no matter how old Molly got or even how famous she became, she would still be her plain old self in her socks and moccasins and hand-tooled leather belts and knapsack-style pocketbooks—purses, her mother would correct—like the one she was carrying now. She would never wear eye-makeup or lipstick: one irritated her contact lenses; the other she chewed off. She would never cut her hair, the way her mother said all young women did in their twenties. She was different from all young women. Although she would never publicly give this as an example of how, sometimes she skipped a day taking a bath if she hadn't done anything to make herself sweat.

She canceled some of her thoughts. Not the part about the hair, but maybe the clothes, and for as long as it would stay on, the lipstick. If Robert ever sang with the Metropolitan Opera, she'd dress up for that. If she won a Pulitzer Prize for her newspaper reporting, she'd dress up for that too.

She moved beyond the protection of the Montaldo's building. The wind careening down Friendly Avenue blew up her skirt, chilling her through and through. Walking toward her half a block away was a tall, thin black man wearing an Army-green jacket. The wind spread the tail of it out behind him so that she could see it wasn't buttoned. As they drew closer to each other she thought he might not be wearing a shirt, or if he was, it was a shirt the exact color of his skin. Was he crazy, in this cold? He had closely cropped hair or might even be bald. Beyond him at the far end of the block, she could see a policeman. Not that she was afraid. She just liked to know where everyone was. As he drew closer she had to quit staring; one thing she had no idea of was his age.

Because of the policeman then, she was not looking directly at the black man, and because of politeness, not even using her peripheral vision to see if he *was* half naked, when he stepped into her path.

"Shake," he said, thrusting forth his hand so that it almost touched her stomach. He wore no shirt. Muscles rippled across his chest. "Shake a black man's hand." His arms were so long that she thought they could wrap around her twice. "Shake," he said again, his voice louder and now menacing. The side of the bank building loomed above his head.

Before she could think clearly she took his hand lightly in hers, pumped it down, up, down. Of course, she would shake a black man's hand, she thought indignantly. She would *date* a black man if she wasn't married and one asked her. Not one like him, of course. She couldn't tell if he was drunk or crazy or whether he just hated all white people. She was one of them he shouldn't hate. She was a Frank Porter Graham supporter. Should she say so? He was too tall for her to see the policeman.

She tried to free her hand, but he wouldn't let go. Like a vicious dog he clenched his teeth and curled his lips at her, showing gums as red as raspberries. He emitted a low hum, maybe a growl. She tried to jerk her hand away by sliding it out of her glove, but he bore down harder. The pain around her college ring was excruciating.

He pulled her hand toward his fly. He was going to make her touch it. She yanked back as hard as she could. All five of her fingers felt as if they had been squeezed inside her ring. She could not break free. Her eyes closed from the pain.

"Stop," she moaned. "Please, stop." The "please" made tears start seeping out of her eyes.

Suddenly he stopped, although for a moment she didn't realize it because her fingers were numb. She didn't know whether he'd made her touch his fly or not, but if he had, she was disgusted. Whirling around, she couldn't even find him. All around her the world had turned white, sudden walls of her pain. Then she realized that it had begun snowing. Hard.

She relocated the man finally, vanishing around a corner of the bank, and ran after him a few steps. She turned back to hail the policeman, but he had disappeared. She tore off her glove to look at her injured fingers. She wanted to cry, but the cold air shooting down her throat made her cough instead. Needing some support, she leaned against one of the marble columns that held up the bank.

Who was he? Why had he run off? Why wasn't he fully dressed? Why had he let go when he did? Had he let go *in time?* Would she ever even know? Did it really matter what she'd touched? she asked herself, suddenly becoming realistic again. The person she was angriest at, it occurred to her, was not the black man, but Robert for being so selfish about the car and making this happen. She wiggled her fingers, hoping that something would at least be sprained, but the wiggling only made her hand feel better. The dent marks on her fingers were already going away.

Suddenly her body wrenched sideways without her even knowing why. Then her eyes focused. Standing before her was a girl about her age who seemed to have materialized out of the driving snow. She had short beige-colored hair with bangs and wasn't as tall as Molly. There was something hawklike about the way her eyebrows protruded too far over her eyes. Molly attempted a smile.

"What happened?" the girl asked, her voice cold but strangely pampering, like fresh snow when you lie in it. The way she stood at a distance seemed somehow reproachful. Molly forced herself to think clearly. Somebody was only trying to help. She must not be recovering as quickly as she'd thought.

"I'm fine. I'm okay. Uh—thanks. A man frightened me, but he's gone." Managing a faint smile in the girl's direction, she pushed herself away from the marble column. The girl shied briefly, then regained control almost as if she'd been afraid Molly might touch her. Not wanting her to see her hand, Molly put her glove back on.

"Can I walk you somewhere?" the girl asked. Flakes of snow powdered her hair and her protruding eyebrows.

"No, really, I'm all right," Molly said. "I just needed a minute or two." She took off her hat and scarf for rearranging. In her periphery she noticed that the girl was giving her legs a critical look. Could she think Molly had invited the attack? "He was a total stranger," she blurted.

The girl began to back away. "I know," she said, watching Molly's face with fresh interest.

Molly again thought that she might have misjudged. "Thanks for stopping," she called. The girl had turned around and was watching her over her shoulder.

"Anytime." The curtness of her voice said that she hadn't been appreciated enough. Noiselessly, she moved down the street. When once she looked back, Molly made a show of beating the snow from her hat and shaking her scarf in the wind. Normally in such a setting she would have felt instant kinship with a helpful stranger. The black man, after all, could have chosen her if she'd happened along first. But, no, he wouldn't have. She was fairly sure he wouldn't have chosen that girl.

As she looped the cold scarf back around her neck, she realized how much her hand did ache. Removing her glove, she saw that the dents on her fingers were almost gone. She had an intense desire to rush over to Robert's biology lab while her hand still looked injured, while she was cold and frightened, while she might still cry if she talked about what happened. But the walk was too far. The sidewalk was growing icy, and already she was having to pick her way beside the slick path that the girl had made. If only her finger were fractured. Then Robert could not minimize what had happened. Not that he necessarily would. But if *she* was the one who wanted to keep driving the car in the face of someone hurting *him*, she would certainly claim that lightning never struck twice or that maybe the man didn't mean anything by it—he just shook hands too hard.

She became aware of something large and stubborn growing

inside her. She knew it was only a reaction, but it felt as real as a rock jammed in among her vital organs. It was fear and anger and ownership and selfishness and three months of giving up something she didn't want to give up all rolled into one. She loved Robert more than any woman had ever loved a man, but the You-Ass shouldn't be used as a test. Or if it was a test, why wasn't he showing his love by letting *her* drive? It wasn't a question of whether work or school was more important. Because, of course, work was. Nor a question of which of them was more cold-natured. It was a question of safety. Where lightning struck once, it could strike again. No laws of nature said the opposite. In the back of her mind she wondered if Robert would think to ask her how she was going to manage in New York City if she was scared in Greensboro.

They could divide the car up: she could use it when she had to go to the office; he could use it when he had to go to the university to teach. Last week he had advertised for and taken on seven guitar students. Although he was enrolled in fifteen hours of courses, he'd said he wanted to begin saving to pay back her father's loan for his education as soon as possible. She had the niggling feeling that he wanted to buy a second car. Whatever his motive, she admired him. But they could not afford two cars.

She guessed she ought to tell Robert about the black man first, but in this snow there was no way she could get to him. The person she really wanted to call was her mother, who would be the only one to understand how afraid she'd been and yet not afraid. Already it was as if the black man had happened to someone else. Not her Good Samaritan, but the person who used to be her but wasn't anymore. It was hard to explain, but her mother would understand.

She would not be able to tell her father about this encounter at all. He would insist on her providing a description to take to the police department. The episode might even wind up being written about by the newspaper, a possibility too embarrassing for words. She could not work there and be a subject for inquiry, too.

He was tall, Daddy, maybe six feet, and thin, with hardly more than crayon scrawl for hair. He wore an Army fatigue jacket—unbuttoned—and no shirt. And he was cold. I know he was cold because I saw his hard coffee-colored nipples. I'm not being obscene, Daddy, I'm telling you what I saw. I remember the most about his mouth—thin lips that moved with the suppleness of chicken snakes. And he had stained teeth. Gums as red as raspberries.

A black man *offered* to shake her hand today . . . *made* her shake his hand . . . *dared* her (yes, in a sense) to shake his hand and, when she did, wouldn't let go. She would have been just as upset if he'd been white. No, then she would have never offered her hand.

Until today she could have lived without the car. A discussion last week with her mother had half convinced her that men needed cars, partly as penis extensions (*not* her mother's words). She could have kept defending Robert against her father's unarticulated charge that he was a gold digger. Robert couldn't help it that his father was dead and his mother had run out of money to put him through school. Besides, what Daddy didn't know was that she thought of herself as a sort of gold digger too. One of the things she loved most about Robert was what he was going to do with his life. She would still love him if he decided, for example, to be a policeman; but she loved him more because he was going to sing in the opera someday. Maybe she thought of him as someone she could get into the big time with. Whatever the big time was. It was in New York City—that, at least, she was sure of. But maybe if Robert didn't give her back the car, he *was* a gold digger. The stakes didn't seem too impressive, a hazardous Corvair, but maybe they were higher than she thought.

She trudged up the last hill before home, not wanting to go the extra blocks to the grocery. Robert would have to eat an omelet tonight. Far ahead of her, the girl she had been watching turned left on Mendenhall Street where Molly usually turned right. Occasionally, Molly would stay on Friendly Avenue to walk past the First Baptist Church. Today would be a good day to take her shortcut through the church parking lot and at the same time thank God she hadn't been hurt.

For the weeks she'd walked this way she'd been trying to figure out what was wrong with the architecture of the First Baptist Church, and now that it came into view, she thought she knew. It reminded you of every small-town brick church you'd ever seen—gleaming Doric columns, steeple bells, a boxwood-lined walkway—only First Baptist was ten times as large. The front walk took a twenty-foot-wide bite of the grass, the steeple stretched bigger in diameter than any redwood tree, and three sets of double doors were poised to welcome the masses that Molly imagined didn't exist. First Baptist was not like a European cathedral: majestic enough to make everybody feel equally poor. It was just grand enough to make you think you needed to have a lot of money to go inside.

She stopped when she reached the steps, raising her eyes to follow the line of the steeple where it pointed toward God. She hadn't felt religion since she was in high school, and what she'd felt then, she knew, was too mixed up with her boyfriend to be pure belief. Never in high school or college had she actually denied God, but she didn't have this passion for Christ—Christ, in particular—that she knew you had to have to be a Christian. Her high school boyfriend, Al, had had a passion for Christ that he'd wanted to rub off on her, taking her Saturday night after Saturday night to the War Memorial Auditorium, where blazing Youth for Christ rallies were held and then taking her out parking. Perhaps because she'd faked religion then for Al's sake, she would never have it again.

For long moments she looked at the three sets of doors, any of which could usher her into the kingdom of heaven. Should she say thank you, God, for not letting her get hurt? Did she have the right to thank someone she wasn't sure she believed in? How much and exactly what did you have to believe to try to talk to God? If the black man had happened to kill her twenty minutes ago, she'd be burning in hell right this minute, that was for sure. Should she therefore *pretend* to believe, hedge her bets against a future of lightning striking twice?

Even in the snow this was not a graceful church, but certainly she couldn't blame man for not being creative enough to properly reflect the glory of God. Nor could she blame God for not giving man the tools to express the inexpressible. It was no one's fault, as it was not hers, that she felt as much a stranger to religion as she felt, this minute anyway, to desegregation.

Chapter Three

MOLLY put their breakfasts inside the oven to keep warm, kneeing the door so that it closed audibly. Without avoiding spots where the floor creaked, she walked around the corner of their L-shaped apartment to where the bed sat against the far wall. Despite the fact that the bed was located in the living room, the place was airy and pleasant. Over the summer Robert's mother had helped her make curtains and a bedspread out of Cannon sheeting. Her parents had donated two handsome wing chairs from the furniture company that her father represented.

Robert remained dead to the world, none of her surreptitious noises having done their job. She wanted to show him her class ring. Examining it this morning, she found that the black man's handshake had bent it slightly out of shape. Which must mean something. Last night Robert had looked at her fingers and asked how something so traumatic could result in no injury. Frankly, she wondered the same thing, but it was an insult that he had put it into words. She'd been thinking that she might tell her father after all. She wanted a little sympathy. A little male sympathy. When she'd described the scene to her mother, she'd made the mistake of including her discovery of the dress at Montaldo's, so as soon as her mother found out she was all right, she'd wanted to know the color of the dress. Part of the problem of her story was the shaking hands part, Molly realized. It seemed so civilized. The next time she described what happened, she was going to introduce it differently.

Earlier she had placed her ring in an ashtray on Robert's bedside table, hoping he might notice it when he smoked his waking-up cigarette. In addition, she had wrapped two Band-Aids—the new colorful type that admitted all skin was not pink—around her ring finger, a visible reminder of her encounter in case Robert pretended to forget. There was some irony in her recent choice as a consumer, she knew, but she still thought purple, orange, and green Band-Aids were not only hilarious but also a deserved slap at all the people who thought flesh was just one color.

Sidling across the sheets, she curled close to Robert as if she hadn't been up. The cuddling was intended to seem romantic, the movement of an unconscious lover, but it also reminded her that several parts of her body still ached, namely her hand, but also the muscles up and down the right side of her body that she'd used to try to get away. Even though she'd been unusually tired last night she hadn't been able to sleep late. Her body had a self-winding alarm that woke her on the weekends the same time it woke her the other days. Besides, she wanted to enjoy her Saturday, even the early moments of it, which weren't so early anymore.

Their sausages and waffles were waiting—it would seem like magic when she opened the oven door. The sun had ushered forth a sparkling blue sky in brilliant contrast to yesterday's snowstorm. According to the radio in the bathroom that she had let play softly at first and then a little louder, the single inch of accumulation would be slush by the time the stores opened. Last night they had agreed to spend the day Christmas shopping before he had to teach his new roster of students beginning midafternoon. She slipped out of her robe, lay her naked body directly against Robert's back, and sighed distinctly. Would he please get up?

Suddenly he moved away from her with a disturbed flurry. She wished she could sleep the way he could. But one of them had to meet the day alongside the rest of the world, and already she knew it would never be him. Sometimes when she called him after her last deadline at noon, he would still be asleep, having missed his eleven o'clock voice lesson. She was learning firsthand about the artistic temperament—an excuse to be spoiled, spoiled, spoiled. It just showed, like his mother said, how much he needed a wife.

"Breakfast is ready," she whispered. His face lay in her direction now, indented by the sheets he seemed able to abandon himself to. His blond curls stuck out in all directions. He had thick eyebrows, a darker blond than his hair, and peach-colored skin. Maybe the innocence of his face was that of sleep rather than his own special innocence, but still it summoned protective feelings within her.

"Are you awake?" she asked, a little louder, so eager for the day to begin that she was willing to take a chance at ruining it. She started to get out of bed again, but wordlessly he enfolded her in his arms.

"Be quiet," he said. "Let me sleep." Gently she tried to move out of his arms. He had trapped her like this before and refused to let go, which maddened her when she was awake and ready to move. Suddenly he insisted on a deep tongue-touching kiss. She should have slipped away sooner. She was not in the mood for this before she ate. He pressed his chest against hers. He was not a breast worshipper, which she was thankful for. Al, in high school, had dealt with her breasts as if they were all there was to her, his eyes always searching out her eyes from too far away because his lips were always on one of those mounds of flesh. After a while it began to feel undignified. Somehow her breasts didn't really seem like her. At least not the part of her that she'd wanted Al to love. Kiss *me*, meaning her lips, she'd told him more than a few times.

Suddenly she felt Robert's brain rising to consciousness. She opened her eyes to check his, but they were tightly shut. The room had grown hard with the early light. "Robert?" she whispered.

"Yes," he answered in a perfectly normal voice.

"Are you ready to get up?"

"In a few minutes." His eyes were strained tighter shut than they needed to be. His lips moved against her neck. "I had a horrible dream," he said, hugging her closer. She relaxed more in his arms.

"What about?"

"I can't tell you."

"Did it have to do with what happened to me yesterday?" she asked softly.

"No. Well, sort of. I said I can't tell you."

"What time did you come to bed?"

"I don't remember." He squeezed her and then turned away as if he wanted to stop the conversation.

"I just had to go to sleep early," she said, letting her voice take on the quality of total wakefulness, a quality that tells any married person he's supposed to wake up too. "That thing yesterday zapped my energy. Did I tell you that someone stopped to help me?"

He didn't answer.

"It was a girl. I mean, I think she stopped to help me. She kind of stared at me for a while. For some reason I was scared of her too."

"Christ," Robert said. He rose up menacingly, the covers draping his shoulders like wings, before he slammed back against the springs. "Will you please let me sleep?"

She felt unfairly misled. "I'm tired of you sleeping our lives away," she said. It was a line straight from her father's critical file on Robert. She grabbed her robe from off the floor. "I'm going to eat breakfast and go shopping by myself."

The cold linoleum of the kitchen reminded her that her slippers lay by the bed. She opened the oven and took out one of the pretty plates she'd prepared. Sitting down, she propped her bare feet on the open door near the heat coil. Before she could take her first bite, Robert appeared around the corner.

"I'm sorry," he said. "But you know how I am in the morning. You ought to, anyway. The dream wasn't even about me. It was about you."

"It's easy to make a bad dream go away," she said matter-of-factly. "All you have to do is get up." She started to put a bite of sausage in her mouth, but his apologetic face made her reach for the second dinette chair and turn it around to face the oven. "Get a fork," she said, nodding toward the drainboard. She'd already had time to wash last night's dishes. "Dreams don't mean anything." Suddenly she remembered her ring. Robert had not taken time for a cigarette, so he hadn't noticed it. "My ring is bent," she said.

"Your what?"

"My class ring," she said, irritation returning instantly to her voice. How could he pretend not to know what she was talking about? "The class ring I was wearing yesterday when I almost got raped."

"You did not almost get raped," Robert said. She had meant to shock him into a greater concern, but his tone was reproachful. In a dramatic way, she stood up with her plate and walked across the room to his bedside table.

"Look," she said, holding the ring in the air.

"I can't see it from here."

"Do you even care?" she asked, feeling immense self-pity.

"Of course, I care."

"No, you don't." She put the ring in her robe pocket and sat down on the bed, eating there instead of next to him.

"I want to see it."

"Not until you take me seriously."

"I'm taking you seriously," he said. "All I said was that you didn't almost get raped. Be honest. You know how you exaggerate."

"I don't exaggerate," she said. She crossed the room, pulled the ring out of her pocket, and handed it to Robert. "Do you know how hard you'd have to squeeze somebody's hand to bend a class ring?"

He gave the ring careful scrutiny. "It's bent," he agreed. "Barely."

She snatched it out of his hand, put it on her finger, and gave her entire attention to her plate. She felt that her experience had been totally underestimated, both by Robert and her mother. How could they not realize the danger she'd been in? But there was something deliberate about Robert's response that she suspected had to do with the You-Ass.

"I know he scared you," Robert offered.

"Thanks," she said.

"But I don't know what you want me to do about it."

"Nothing. Nothing at all. I just wanted you to know what's happening in my life."

He stepped over her legs to refill his coffee cup. Mechanically she chewed another bite of waffle, watching his large muscular back under the terry robe her parents had given him for his birthday. Perhaps she was taking herself too seriously. The kitchen had grown warm, and the smell of butter and syrup began to tantalize her mood. Maybe Robert would get so famous in New York that they would go everywhere in taxis.

Still eating, she followed him to the closet, where he was pulling out trousers and a plaid shirt. Although she'd said she wanted to go shopping right away, she hoped they could first make love and soothe this edginess each of them felt. She put her plate on the bedside table and took off her robe. As if absently, she sent her arms into a feline stretch. "I love Saturdays," she said, her voice coaxing.

In this stage of Robert's life he couldn't spend a whole day with her without starting to touch. And once he started—no matter where they were—there was no relief until they made love. Anyway, she'd rather not be in Sears when the urge came upon Robert. It would just mean they'd have to come all the way home, do it, dress, and go back out again.

"If you're going with me, you'd better get ready," he said. His eyes had lingered on her body, but now he whipped his clothes off the hangers, not looking at her.

"Why don't we stay here awhile?"

He turned his back, hitching a leg to step into his trousers. "I'm not in the mood," he said.

"Well, I am," she said. He bent to lace his boots.

"I told you that my dream upset me," he said. "You didn't even pay attention. All you want to talk about is yourself. Dreams can be like real life," he added darkly.

"Just what happened?" she asked. "Did I die? Did somebody murder me?"

"I'm not going to talk about it. I've said too much already. It didn't even happen here." Nobody had ever refused to tell her a dream because what happened to *her* was too horrible for words. She had a right to know.

"Where did it happen?"

"It happened a long way away from here. That's why you don't have to worry about it."

"Where, Robert?" she demanded.

"We had just moved to New York. But it's nothing to worry about. We may not ever move there." What did he mean by that? "I don't know why I told you. It was so horrible I guess I needed to get it off my chest."

"You haven't answered whether I got murdered," she said dryly, thinking she understood what he was getting at.

"Just attacked," he said. "I don't mean 'just' attacked," he corrected. "It was worse than what happened to you yesterday. I meant that you weren't murdered."

"That's a relief." She waited to see if he would ask how she was going to manage in New York City if she couldn't manage in Greensboro. But he continued dressing, his face dark and taut as if genuinely troubled by his disclosure. Had he really dreamed that? Did someone else's dream about you have a better chance of coming true than your own? Was Robert really so upset that he couldn't make love to her? There was a sick feeling in her chest. She felt almost sicker about the dream than she felt about what happened yesterday. Robert had seen her so bloodied and battered that he was extremely distressed. Had he tried to save her? If she hadn't been murdered, she must have been raped. She pictured her unconscious body lying on a stretch of bare ground, probably in Central Park. Her hair was tangled, her clothes torn; blood dripped out of one corner of her mouth. A black man stood over her prostrate figure. Leaning down, he grabbed her chest and shook her. "Wake up," he said wickedly. "Wake up and see what I got to show you." Robert was standing by a tree. At first she thought he was alone, but then she saw that another man held a knife at his throat.

"Did they beat you up when they finished with me?" she asked in a soulful voice. Now at least she had her own version of his dream.

"You're trying to trick me into telling you what happened," he said. "Stop it. I'm not going to say another word. Stop. Okay?"

"I have one more question," she said.

"No more questions."

"I promise I won't ask anything else if you'll answer this one." She wanted to ask if he thought his dream had anything to do with who drove the You-Ass.

"Get dressed," he said.

"I'll leave you alone," she promised. "I'll stop bothering you. I'll never bring it up again. Just answer me."

"No." He started toward the door. "I'm leaving."

"Wait," she said. "I'll be ready in a second. Pour me one more cup of coffee." Having won, he went to do as she asked while she hurried into her jeans.

He'd say just enough to frighten her but not enough to make himself feel ashamed. Just enough to make her feel like she should be brave, that she should learn to face the world, so that he could keep the car. Just enough to make her think that their move to New York City might not be so certain as she thought. Every once in a while, he still mentioned that at heart he felt he was an outdoorsman, that he'd like to be a forest ranger or even a fishing guide but that he was going to be a singer because it would be criminal not to be one. His mother had told her not to worry: he'd been saying the same thing for five years.

They reached the door at the same time, and he handed her

a cup of coffee. Outside, yesterday's snow remained only in patches in the woods. All around, birds were chirping. It seemed almost like the beginning of spring rather than the beginning of winter.

"Want me to drive?" she asked. Robert was tossing the keys to the You-Ass into the air and catching them.

"Nah, I like to," he said.

She thought, I like to, too.

Isabel's car, an MG Midget, was parked beside theirs. The house above their basement apartment was dark, as if their landlady was still asleep. How could people waste so much time? When she got to her side of the car, instead of opening the door, she leaned against the roof, crossing her wrists under her chin. Robert took a long look down the driveway before returning his eyes to meet hers. The worldly blue of them seemed to know what she was going to say.

Over the smooth white roof of the You-Ass, she spoke. "I don't feel safe walking home from work anymore."

"I guess that guy really scared you."

She waited, still hoping that he loved her enough to offer instead of making her take. "It's been so cold for people who are cold-natured," she said. "Even my mohair gloves don't keep my hands warm." He had not commented yet on her funny-colored Band-Aids, although with her hands lying on the white roof, they were very obvious. "The almanac predicts this winter is going to be a rough one."

"If anybody knows, the farmers do." His mouth was a stubborn, waiting line.

Molly took a deep breath. "If it's okay with you, Robert, I'd like to have the You-Ass back." Not at all the way she'd meant to say it. She wanted to share the car not take it, but something kept her from saying more.

He got in the car and started the engine. Had she not opened her door immediately, she thought he would have pulled away without her. He backed out of the driveway, his hand clenching the wheel. She told herself not to lose her temper: if she could be an adult about this, maybe he could too. At the very least, it was her *turn* to use the car.

It was not like Christmas shopping ought to be. Pensive and deliberate, Robert led the way up and down the Sears aisles, asking in a perfunctory way what she thought about his choices. Fortunately he made selections only for his last year's roommate Mark, who'd joined the Marines, and the uncle who had helped out Robert and his mother until her father had taken over. Once, when he was examining a toaster oven for his mother, she said firmly, "That costs too much." It was the only time during the entire excursion that he looked directly into her eyes. Since she was the one who made the money, she had veto power over how it was spent. "You *know* it's too much," she said softly. But he only stalked to the next aisle.

When they arrived home with plenty of time to make love before the first scheduled lesson of his new series of classes, she thought they might make up. But he told her that he had to leave right away in order to walk to the university in time.

"Don't be ridiculous," she said. "You can take the car. I only want it when I have to go to work." He was unlocking the basement door to get his guitar.

"It's your car," he said, his back to her as he fussed with the key. "Your daddy bought it for you. Enjoy yourself."

"I don't want it all the time, Robert. I just want it when I have to go to work. Please don't be this way." She felt inclined to offer the You-Ass back, full-time. Perhaps, like her mother had said, a man without a car felt emasculated. She didn't *have* to drive. If she was truly scared, she could wait for the bus instead of martyring herself by walking. Or she could catch a ride with her friend Gisella. She could even try her bicycle again, although she had discovered that she was not a deft rider in traffic. Plus, when she got to the office, she was sweaty.

Had she not felt pain when she stretched her arms into the back seat to pick up the pile of presents, she would have begged him to take the car, at least on this Saturday afternoon. But it rippled to her elbow and then on to her shoulder, an echo from yesterday's frightening confrontation that Robert had ignored. If New York City proved to be as great a threat as Robert was trying to tell her, she'd just take a cab. Certainly she would not go for a walk in Central Park. She did not speak as he passed, his guitar case hanging from his fingers, nor did he.

Chapter Four

H IS VOICE had made him sound attractive, but sometimes you could be fooled. Only sometimes. Through the small window in the door of the university practice room where he'd asked her to come for her lesson, Suzanne observed her new guitar teacher. He sat at the piano, his hands repeating a phrase, adding a few notes, pausing, as if he was composing. He looked about six feet tall, blond with thick corkscrew curls, a vivid profile: deep forehead, straight nose, and full lips, singer's lips. He was taller than any man she'd ever been out with, which opened up in her mind a whole new set of questions. Where would her face hit, for example, when they made love? He had a generous look about him that indicated he'd shared himself with a lot of women. At least he could share himself with her. His guitar case stood in a corner of the tiny studio. It was probably against university rules for him to teach here. She opened the door. Maybe if she reported him, he would have to teach her at her apartment.

"There you are," he said, pointing his hand at her like a pistol. He closed the piano hastily, losing forever the song he was composing. "Glad to meet you, Suzanne." He held out one graceful hand. He had a smile that had a faint touch of sadness to it and handsome blue eyes with lashes as curly as his hair. She liked his easiness. She liked his lingering summer tan and the lack of seriousness in his looks. Most students she'd met were more intense than he and smaller physically. Robert could have been a guard on a college basketball team.

"I'm looking forward to this," she said, extending her hand to meet his.

"Me too," he said in what she thought was a complimentary way. Suddenly she wished she could make him fall in love with her. But how? He squeezed her hand instead of shaking it and motioned her to a slatted chair on the far side of the piano. "This isn't the best place in the world to have a lesson," he apologized, taking the bench. "But my wife and I live in a one-room apartment, which can get a little crowded." The negative words warmed her: Molly must not give him enough breathing space. "At least here we have a piano when the guitars go out of tune." He glanced behind her. "Where's your instrument?"

"I haven't bought it yet," she said, her eyes focusing on her lap. "I thought you might know where I could find something inexpensive."

"How inexpensive?" He seemed to be disappointed that she wasn't ready that moment to start playing.

With an expression of suffering honesty she said, "I have about fifty dollars. I've been to the pawnshop and that's almost enough, but I wasn't sure which guitar to buy. Would you have time to go there with me after this lesson? Or during it?" she added hastily.

Robert looked at his watch. "I have another student scheduled in an hour," he said.

"I'm sorry to have to ask you to do this. I should have called."

"Do you have a car?" he asked. She shook her head. "I don't have mine with me today. In fact, I'm not sure when I'll have it again." He seemed to feel absolved of any duty to help her.

"There's the bus," she suggested. She could tell from the suspicious way Robert glanced up that the bus was not the usual way he traveled about. Who drove the car? she wondered. Molly walked home from work, at least she'd been walking yesterday when Suzanne followed her home from the newspaper office. "A bus stops right up the corner from here in five minutes," she continued. "The pawn shop is open until seven. I already checked." Despite the clarity of her plan, Robert did not appear ready to seize on it. "Look, I'll pay you for the lesson," she said.

"That's not it." He quickly drew himself to his feet. The way he towered over her took her breath away. She felt a tremendous urge to move against him, to press her face into his stomach, to lock her arms around his waist, to massage his ass with her capable fingers. Did Molly want him in the same way? Did every woman who met him?

"Do you want to wait until you have a car?"

"I may not have a car," he said shortly.

"Ever?"

"Do you think we can be back by six?" he asked.

"I know we can."

Picking up his guitar case, he opened the door and gestured, a little too grandly, for her to move through. The tension across his cheekbones gave tight emphasis to his eyes.

"Can't you leave your guitar here?" she asked. It seemed such an encumbrance.

"I could, but I'm not." At the coatrack he stopped beside her but apart from her as they put on their coats. "It might get stolen," he offered in a less abrasive tone.

Out in the cold she swung along ahead of him up the long rising sidewalk to the bus stop, taking care to keep purposefulness in both her posture and her pace. She was no more interested in being his companion than he was interested in being hers, if anyone wanted to know. They were on a business trip, so to speak. She wondered if he noticed her slight doll-like figure, ever so much more appealing than Molly's gangly one. Did he imagine how powerful she could make him feel? At the bus stop he looked up and down the street. He leaned his guitar case against a telephone pole and stood apart from her just enough so it would continue to appear that they weren't together.

"I don't see why you're mad," she said in an intimate voice. "I'm going to pay you."

"You should have told me earlier," he said. He lit a cigarette. "This is a waste of time."

"I don't smoke," she commented.

"Good, it's bad for you." Still, he didn't offer her one, but she decided not to pull out her own pack.

"I called you, but you were eating supper," she said. "You *promised* you'd call me back."

He blew out smoke in a long steady stream.

"This is not a waste of time," she continued. "It seems to me that the right instrument is a key part of learning how to play."

"There's no need for me to go with you." His disinterested eyes stared up the street.

"You're my teacher. I know nothing about guitars." Her voice climbed in intensity. "What do you expect me to know before I come for my first lesson?"

He responded to her outburst, which she immediately knew had been too vehement, with a curious, assessing look. She turned her attention to the bus, which was lumbering down the street toward them. Since so many students were aimlessly milling about, she signaled. The carriage lurched forward as the driver put on brakes; it continued rocking as Suzanne climbed the steps. She looked over her shoulder at Robert.

"Forget it," she said. "Just go on back." She was the same height as he now; her small chin protruded in the air between them. But he followed so closely that she could feel the heat of his body, could smell the odor of his clothes. Her token clinked down the box. The driver noted it and sent it to the bowels of the bus, safe from thieves. She chose a seat halfway back.

"How much?" she heard Robert ask.

"Twenty-five." The driver, a man as big around as his huge steering wheel, tripped the gears and started rolling.

"Whoa!" Robert said, grabbing a pole to keep from falling. Still holding on, he reached into his pocket for change, counting a coin at a time into the box. He guided himself down the swaying aisle by grabbing the backs of seats.

"You're tough," he said when he sat down.

"Because I know how to ride a bus?"

"Not just that," he said, without elaborating.

She gazed out the window at the brick administration building, the chancellor's house, the Yum-Yum ice cream shop. The bus would travel to Aycock Street before it turned back toward town. Reflected in her window she could see a vague picture of Robert.

In her periphery she noticed that his knees touched the back of the seat in front of them, making her a virtual prisoner here. She turned toward him, her own bare knee, as small as a child's, grazing the soft fabric of his khakis.

"The pawnshop has a used Aria folk guitar for seventy-five dollars," she said. "I'll bet you can get it for fifty."

"That's a good choice. But you already knew that," he added shrewdly. "Why would I get a better price?" For the first time he really looked at her, and she felt her heart floating inside her chest like a cork on a fishing line waiting to be dragged beneath the surface. His eyes were sensual, full of the music that must be so much a part of him. A melodious shiver traveled through her collarbones.

"A woman runs the pawnshop," she said, her voice carefully tender. "You'll get a better price because a woman runs it."

"Well, maybe," he said. As if discomfited, he began looking around the bus. "But don't count on it." Her mind was whirling at the journey they'd begun. The fingers of his left hand, the hand nearest her, drummed a steady rhythm on his knee.

"You're nice to come with me."

"Sure," he said, implying that despite all his resistance, a short bus trip was no big deal.

"I've wanted to learn how to play the guitar for a long time."

"Yeah?"

"Forever. I always thought my hands were too small."

He surprised her by taking her right hand out of her lap. Her hand burned like fire; an unexpected flush crossed her cheeks. "Dainty," he said. She'd always thought of them as stubby. He brushed her fingertips across his palm. She felt an almost uncontrollable impulse to snatch her hand away. "I can tell you've worked with them," he was saying. She'd given herself a nice manicure so that he might not notice the roughness, but he noticed anyway. His own skin was surprisingly coarse; the tips of his fingers felt like plastic. He let go of her hand. She was tempted to let it drop to his thigh but resisted.

"You'll need to work with your guitar every day to get your

fingers used to the strings," he said. "The people who quit usually quit in the first two weeks. They can't stand the discomfort."

"Are my hands too small?" she asked, spreading her right hand in the air like a fan. Her knobby joints made it look undernourished.

"One of the best guitarists I ever knew had the hands of a child," he said. "It's dexterity that matters."

Suzanne smiled. "I've got plenty of that."

"Good," Robert said blandly, as if he didn't catch her drift. "To play well, though, you're going to have to get rid of those nails."

"I can't," she said.

"You have to."

Because he found some problems with the bridge, which he said he could fix, the pawnshop lady sold the guitar for $60, which seemed to please him as much as it did Suzanne. She paid with money she'd borrowed from Ruth while Robert examined an array of shotguns and rifles.

"Going hunting?" she asked over her shoulder.

"Someday." His voice had turned private again.

The pawnshop lady, who stood leaning forward in order to balance her huge ass, looked up from the transaction she was recording. "Let me unlock those," she said, moving like an ostrich around the counter. "You have to sight a gun to tell anything about it."

Robert waved her back to her work. "Not today," he said, but he reached forward to touch the stock of one of the weapons. "Nice," he said.

"You're awfully interested not to be interested," the woman purred. She opened a padlock and freed the guns by removing the thick wire that snaked through the triggers. "Doesn't hurt to look," she said.

"Sometimes it does," Robert said. Leaving him alone with the guns, the woman returned to finish writing up the bill for the guitar.

"Why?" Suzanne asked, her voice arch and friendly at the

same time. It had just occurred to her that the pawnshop lady probably thought they were a couple. Without answering, Robert picked up the gun he had previously fondled and aimed toward the sky.

As soon as they left the store, Suzanne flagged a bus. She plunked two tokens in the box, telling Robert that the least she could do was give him a free ride. The bus was full of people going home from work, so they had to stand with their guitars propped beside them.

"What do you go after?" she asked. He looked uncomprehendingly at her. "When you hunt. Birds? Squirrels?" Her father used to sit on the front porch of their house and shoot whatever kind of animal came within range, including stray dogs. Shortly before she'd left home, he'd even warned that he might shoot her if she kept jumping out in front of him unannounced.

"Deer," Robert said. Her father had never managed to shoot a deer, although once when he was drunk and hunting, he had killed a neighbor's cow.

"I'm impressed," she said. She corrected herself: "I'm impressed if you've ever killed one."

"Be impressed," he said, his expression coming alive. "I got my first deer last October in Montgomery County."

"Buck or doe?" she asked.

"What do you think?"

"I think you can kill just about anything with a .30–30 rifle." She knew she sounded haughty and knowledgeable at the same time.

"You're probably right about that. I use a bow and arrow," he said, pride pumping in his voice. "I tracked him for two days before I got my first shot."

She gave him a skeptical look, but he didn't seem to notice. "I just thought of something," she said.

"What?" he asked absently, the memory of his kill apparently uppermost in his mind.

"I went to a flea market last weekend and bought two boxes of music. I wondered if you'd look through them—it won't take long—and tell me what I'll be able to use. This bus takes us right by my apartment. You can run in and look at the music and be on your way in less than five minutes." She briefly touched an insistent hand to his wrist. "I only live two blocks from the university," she added. Actually, she lived five blocks away, but he was such an athlete he'd never notice.

A resigned tone in his voice, Robert asked, "What time is it?" With the familiarity of a girlfriend she turned his wrist over to find out for both of them. "Five-forty," she said. "We're almost there. I'll have you in and out in five minutes. I promise." I promise to love you, comfort you, honor and keep you, she thought. She kept the eager look on her face although Robert was frowning. "I'll pay you," she muttered out of one corner of her mouth like a gangster. He grinned: finally there was a joke between them.

He followed her brisk climb up the steep steps to her apartment, which was located in an old Victorian house. She asked if he was born in Montgomery County, but he said, no, he was from Wake County. Quickly she unlocked the door, tossed her new guitar carelessly—maybe too carelessly—on the sofa, and lugged two boxes of music from under the table where her stereo sat. "Look through these," she said efficiently. "Excuse me while you do." She vanished purposefully through her bedroom door, her shoes clicking against the wood floor, as if she were making a trip to the lavatory. Standing before her mirror, she tousled her short hair and pinched her cheeks until she looked breathless. She did not turn back the bed covers, so it would seem less planned.

She could hear him flipping through the music. "Can you come here a minute, Robert?" she called, her voice firm for the last time. One lamp burned softly away from the bed.

He appeared in the doorway. He was so tall—that was what she adored about him. His tallness made her feel like a doll. She wished she could take a razor and remold her own features, reshape her bold forehead, eliminate the eyebrows she plucked and plucked but never seemed to reduce.

"What are you doing?" he asked. Even though his eyes had

adjusted to the light and he knew very well what she was doing, he looked confused.

"Come here. I'll show you." She lay on the bedspread, her dress raised to her belt, her breasts falling out of her open shirt-waist. "Come here," she said again, the demand in her voice rising.

He stepped forward as if to see more clearly. One of his hands grasped the door frame as if it was a life preserver. Suzanne gently swayed open her legs. Waves of desire swirled through her. She drew her knees together and then parted them again. "I told you I'd pay you," she coaxed. "Come on."

"You're crazy," he said incredulously. But he moved toward the bed, staring at her. In that practiced manner he began un-buckling his belt.

"Get over here," she said in a ragged voice.

He pushed his trousers barely to his thighs. He knelt to the bed, an aroused but curious expression in his eyes.

"Do it," she pleaded. He lowered his pelvis to her frantic body. Like an angel he hung suspended over her, his smooth stomach just above her face. "Move," she ordered. He thrust harshly into her. She moaned. He told her to shut up. She tried to bite the hand that was over her mouth, but he pressed harder, gagging her. He pulled out as if he were going to stop, looking down at her in disgust, but then he reentered, moving with pragmatic speed. Moments later he pulled out again, but this time he had finished. A sheet of perspiration slicked his face. He began to raise himself off the bed.

"Hold me," she said, grabbing his shoulders and pulling them toward her own.

"*Hold* you?" he asked, wrestling out of her grasp. He stood up beside the bed and began reorganizing his outer appearance, a shameful look on his face. But it was too late for shame. Pushing her skirt down to her knees, she propped herself on her elbows to watch him zip his pants.

"Why did you do this?" he asked.

She lay back down on the bed, arms and legs weightless, as

she reimmersed herself in the surges of pleasure still echoing through her body. "You took me shopping," she said in a dreamy voice. "I promised I'd make it worth your while." Although her eyes were closed, she could feel the anger in Robert's body. This was genuine distress now, not like his petulance over the trip to the pawnshop. She imagined his eyes glaring fire, his nose shooting out smoke. Suddenly—she couldn't help herself—she giggled. It was because his sperm was swimming in her fluid, tickling her interior walls like a feather.

The air suddenly sharpened as if he were about to hit her. Exercising amazing willpower, she did not open her eyes. She wrestled with her face, which was trying to shy away from the blow. When she had won, she pushed her chin higher in the air to make herself an easier target. The moment passed. He walked away from the bed, and she propped herself on her elbows again.

"I can't give you guitar lessons," he said from the doorway, waiting for some acknowledgment.

"Please teach me," she said in a false tone.

"Absolutely no." He turned to leave.

"Robert," she called, so earnestly that it brought him back to the door. "I'll see you next Saturday. If not before."

She heard him cross the living room for his guitar. He reappeared, the case held before him like a shield.

"This is just not a good idea," he said. "I'm married. You know I'm married." There was a new uneasiness in his voice.

He left, not waiting for her answer, which she did not intend to give anyway. The door opened and closed quietly, secretly. She lay on the bed for some time, feeling the heat ebb slowly out of her body until her skin actually felt cold to her own touch. She arose and dressed and went to the kitchen to whip the meringue for the lemon pie she'd made for Robert if he'd cared enough about her to stay. She was ravenous. An exotic dessert was an appropriate dinner, she thought, as she gorged herself. She ate the pie in bed so she could keep her pelvis tilted upward, aiding the life Robert had given her.

About nine she called his house.

"Mrs. Carter? Hello. My name is Suzanne Cox. I'm one of Mr. Carter's new students. Is he there?"

He had not returned from the university, Molly said, although she expected him any minute. Suzanne thought of the shocked expression she'd seen on Molly's face yesterday and wondered if she should say something to re-create that look. Not yet.

"We were just together for my first lesson," she said instead. "I have some things I need to talk to him about. Could you have him call me?" Molly not only took down her numbers at home and work, she repeated them for accuracy. They hung up with goodbyes that were almost fondly spoken.

Robert did not do her the courtesy of returning her call that night or the next day. By the time the Sunday brunch crowd at the pancake house had left, she felt he'd had time enough.

"Please leave me alone," he said when he realized it was her. She had not bothered to identify herself. The fact was, he should be able to recognize her simply when she breathed. Molly must not be within hearing distance.

"I can't go away," she said. "I love you." She imagined his huge suffering body. How pitiful it was to see a large man break down. Ruth sat at the cash register only a few feet away. Now she'd believe she didn't know everything there was to know about Suzanne.

"Stop it," Robert said. Ruth busied herself filling the toothpick holder.

"I love you. Let me love you."

"Look, Suzanne, I don't even know you. The whole thing was a big mistake. I don't know where my mind was."

As if he was generally too intelligent to mess around with someone like her. She motioned Ruth toward a group of people who had just come in, and with a pained expression, Ruth went. "Your mind—sweet man—was on my cunt. And don't you ever forget it."

"That's not true," Robert said feebly, and then he hung up the phone. Immediately she called back and slammed the receiver down in his ear.

Bennie came in late that afternoon, and Suzanne told him she thought Ruth was a lesbian and that she wanted to go on the night shift. They sat together in a booth in the section that opened to the public last. Bennie was a small-shouldered round man who ate pancakes at least once a day because he thought he should set an example. No matter that hardly anyone knew he was the owner. His teeth were brown like the syrup he gobbled up. He had small eyes and thin red hair that he'd let grow too long on top, hoping for a thickness that had not resulted.

"That's the craziest thing I ever heard of," he said, although he always needed girls to work at night. "I thought you and Ruth were buddies."

"We were until she—" Suzanne rolled her eyes.

"Tried something?" Bennie fought the horror that was growing in his features. What was wrong with a little perversion, he seemed to be trying to think.

"I'm not going into the details," she said before he gathered the courage to ask. "You need to get Ruth a stool with a back."

In disbelief Bennie turned around to look at Ruth as if the suggestion had something to do with her alleged lesbianism. "What for?" he whispered hoarsely.

"Her back hurts, you fool," Suzanne whispered back.

"What do you care about her back?"

"I care about her back," she said evenly. "I don't hate her for something she can't help. But I need to make a change. You either put me on the night cycle or I quit."

"Quit," Bennie said. He took such big bites that syrup got all over his face.

"Wipe your mouth," she said. He did. "I think Adele's one of the nicest people," she added politely.

At the mention of his wife, Bennie gave Suzanne a startled look. "You can't be the hostess. You'll have to go back to waitressing. I already have a nighttime hostess." It was amazing to her that Bennie imagined he had any control over her at all.

"I don't want to be the hostess," she said, although it meant she would have to keep wearing a waitress uniform.

He sighed. "Godalmighty, I guess so." He signaled to Kathy, who came over to the table. "Coffee," he said. Without waiting for Kathy to get out of earshot, he asked, "What time are you getting up tomorrow?" Kathy threw a smirky look over her shoulder. If Bennie didn't watch out, he'd lose control over her, too.

"None of your business."

"Come on, Suzanne."

She waited until Kathy was gone. "I'm not going to do that with you anymore."

"The hell you say."

"I'm not."

"Honey . . ." he said.

"You wouldn't give me air in a jar."

"What are you talking about? I just gave you a new shift." Bennie leaned into the table, trying to look bigger than he was.

Suzanne pulled out a cigarette and handed him her lighter. "You didn't have much choice, now did you, doll baby?" she purred.

Walking home after sixteen hours of work, she felt the growing hum of adventure that had sounded in her body almost like a single bee a couple of weeks ago. That bee happened to be a queen summoning her drones and her workers. And now Suzanne's whole body, except for her mind, seemed to be affected by a sort of vibrato tingling. Her mind she held away from the excitement so that it could always make rational decisions.

Bennie had thought he was exacting penance by making her work a back-to-back shift, but she was the one who'd felt a need to exhaust this growing current that would sometimes surge so fully that she thought her body might not be able to keep it contained. She thought of Ruth, but Ruth seemed insignificant in view of what was happening to her now. Ruth would be hurt when she found out Suzanne had changed shifts, but Ruth would also be there when she came back. The best thing about the new shift was that now she was free all day to watch over Robert and Molly Carter.

She slept the next morning until a telephone call from Bennie awakened her.

"Can I bring you some lunch?" he asked.

"Do you want to?" She was groggy, without her normal defenses, and no was not the first answer to come to her mind.

"I sure do, sweetheart."

When she fully awoke, she was sorry that she'd told him he could come over. She called the restaurant, prepared to disguise her voice in case Ruth answered, but a voice she didn't recognize was on the other end. Bennie had already left.

She scribbled a note on the back of an envelope: "Dear Bennie, An emergency. A friend of mine was in a car accident, and I've rushed to the hospital to see him. Maybe tomorrow. Love, Suzanne."

She was bathing when she heard him knock. In a rare slip she'd refastened the chain, so if he used his key, he'd know she was there. The thought of keys gave her an idea. She would send Robert a key to her apartment. Soon he'd get over the shock of having a lover, if he was really shocked at all, and come to visit. Bennie kept knocking. He'd probably forgotten he even had a key, she hadn't let him use it in so long. She suddenly felt lucky that she didn't have an Adele or a Molly like Bennie and Robert did. No husband, no parents, no children. For no matter how much wrath she provoked now and for the rest of her life, no one could ever squeal on her to anyone else. There was a certain safety in that.

Chapter Five

I T WAS either the last moment of a dream or her first semiconscious thought, she wasn't sure which. But the idea jabbed her fully awake: she should write about her experience with the black man. It was a perfect subject for her *Viewpoint* column. In a recent survey subscribers had asked for more exposure of personalities in the articles they read. Now all the columnists were writing about their vacations, their children, their problems with in-laws, even their love of such things as creecy greens. To Molly it had already become boring. But maybe this story wasn't. Most people loved to experience danger vicariously.

Although she wasn't scheduled to work this Sunday, she decided she would go to the newspaper office while Robert was still asleep. Generally, she was limited in her exposure to the city because she didn't have a beat, so she got her column ideas by combing the stories other reporters had written, by reading the personals, by knowing what celebrity was appearing where, and when. The idea to interview the porn star had come from a movie ad.

Now something newsworthy had happened to her. She'd been exposed to the city with what she might describe as a vengeance. Furthermore, a Good Samaritan of sorts had come to her aid. Only last week Charlie her editor had asked that the six regular columnists help him build up a backlog of *Viewpoints*. Although he'd said he didn't expect her help, since she wasn't a full-time reporter, she was going to be the first contributor. She might be the only contributor: no one liked to write a timeless column for fear that it would never be used. Furthermore, helping out might cause him to transfer her to the news side sooner.

She slipped stealthily out of bed. Robert lay swathed in covers from the waist down: his young bare chest brought a tightness to her throat. Last night he had come home from teaching thoroughly ashamed that he'd been so difficult about the car. He'd had an attack of selfishness, he said. Of *course*, she should drive to work; he would walk over to the university. She'd been so gratified by his change of heart that she suggested they try letting him take her to work and pick her up. He would not even agree to that, but after he walked a few days next week, she was sure she could convince him.

Making up, they had gradually slipped into a rhythmic movement, but before they could undress, Robert broke away, saying he had to study for a music theory test that was being given Monday. She reminded him, her hand inside his trousers, that he had all day tomorrow, but he persisted in saying he needed to get started now. He had still been sitting at his desk when she fell asleep.

She hastened into her clothes, filled a bowl with cereal and milk, felt the dark length of the kitchen counter for her car keys, and left without his stirring. Going to work on a Sunday, when she didn't have to, gave her a strange sense of elation. Out on the porch she ate from the cold cereal bowl for as long as her hands could stand it. Then she set the leftover milk beside the door for Isabel's cat. With a surge of affection she started the You-Ass. So what if it was a dangerous car? That was only if you had a wreck, Ralph Nader, and she wasn't going to have one.

She'd expected to be the lone traveler at such an early hour, but the roads were surprisingly filled with cars. More people than she would have thought must go to early church. She imagined the massive doors of First Baptist opening for a stream of automobiles—church at the drive-in. Under such circumstances even she might make a visit. Despite the thoughts that had gone through her mind on Friday, she realized that she still had plenty of time to get to know God. She often worked on Sunday, or thought she might from now on. That was why she couldn't be a regular in the House of God.

At the office she chose her friend Gisella's desk to work at because it was tucked in an out-of-sight corner. If she was seen, nonguild members would come nosing around to see what scoop she was working on; guild members, who were pressing her to join them, would want to know why she was working overtime for free. She hoped not to have to explain to anybody.

She was eager to get her story written before she rationalized it out of existence. Her first reaction had been to give up on black people. Then yesterday morning she'd realized that one person didn't represent an entire race. Her thinking today was that if anyone was to blame, it was she, an attitude that, at the least, would enable her to write sympathetically about everyone involved. But it was true too. She'd offered her hand. The black man—unknowingly, of course—was a sort of natural sociologist, testing various white women to see if they would shake his hand, and then doing to them what they always expected from black men: a little harm. Could she translate all that to paper?

She got a legal pad out of Gisella's desk, planning to write down her story and then type it. But this was a good, pressureless opportunity to try to compose at the typewriter. If she happened to become a reporter next week, she would not be able to perform that most elemental function.

She needed to make this story fairly timeless for Charlie's bank: a snowy day, Greensboro, North Carolina. A black man shakes the hand of a young white woman and then won't let go. But was she opening a can of worms? she suddenly wondered. Race relations here were stable after several years of confrontation, some rioting, and one murder of a student at A&T State University in the aftermath of Martin Luther King's assassination. Did it even matter that the man was black? Was it enough that he was a man? Maybe, since it was near Christmas, the thrust of this story should be the Good Samaritan. The girl had meant to help her. Molly's mind had not been operating properly when they stood before each other by the bank building. Why else would she have stopped? She began typing:

> *Leaving her office to walk home from work on what was surely, so far, the coldest day of the year, the young woman gazed toward the heavy gray sky, wondering if she could complete her journey before the predicted snow became fact. It seemed not, she thought. Pulling her scarf up around the lower half of her face, she became aware of how warm the inside of her body must be compared to the outside. Passing a department store, she saw an array of mannequins, smilingly oblivious to the winter air. One held a black fur muff, which the young woman wished she owned. Her thick wool gloves were not doing their job.*

Why was she concentrating so much on the cold? Molly wondered. It had nothing to do with the story she was trying to write. She pulled the sheet out of the typewriter and began again.

> *A handshake, that gesture of friendliness that we all find ourselves quite willing to respond to, became a way to express rage, this female reporter found out recently on her way home from work. She was walking near the corner of Elm and Friendly avenues when from not far away she noticed a tall, thin man approaching her. When he drew close, he held out his hand, and she, thinking that she must know him or that he was just being friendly on this very cold day, took it to shake. But she didn't know the man, who by now she clearly saw did not have on a shirt, only a loose jacket and some tattered pants. Did he want money? Was he in some sort of trouble? Did she look like the sort of person who might help him? Was he simply cold, like her?*

Molly knew she was giving herself too much credit, but she *might* have thought all those questions if she'd had time. Besides, unlike other areas of reporting, columns could be part fiction.

> *Instead of shaking her hand, though, the man began squeezing it tightly. Her bones began to scrape against each*

other. This was not a friendly gesture. She tried to break
free, but the man only held tighter. He had no weapon. He
seemed intent only on crushing her fingers.

Until this moment Molly had forgotten about the man trying
to make her touch his fly. Should she allude to that? No, she
couldn't. Everyone would want to know if he'd succeeded. And
she didn't know the answer. Slanting the story toward sex would
reduce it anyway. Rage was not the same as kinky sexual drive.
Maybe she should not mention motive at all. Who knew why
people did things? Maybe it was time to bring in the Good Samaritan.

A second young woman emerged from the bank, where she
had just made a deposit of her weekly earnings. Two people
stood on the sidewalk not ten feet away from her, performing
a strange dance. One was a woman; the other, a tall, slender
man. Neither of them made any sound. Did they know each
other? Was this a personal argument? Was it an argument
at all? Should she yell for help? She walked toward them.
The man gave the woman's hand a last hurtful wrench and
then ran around the side of the building. The woman swayed
and then turned to run after him, not noticing the person
who had frightened him away. But it was still unclear whether
they were in love or he had stolen from her.
This newspaper reporter bent at the waist in pain. The
woman moved closer, hoping to offer at least a word of
comfort, at most a helping arm. When the reporter finally
saw the woman, she gave an awful start, as if the man
himself had come back. She had only begun to realize that
someone was actually trying to help her. After a short but
kind inquiry the woman went on her way.

Molly counted her lines. So far she had eight inches. But she
hadn't said anything yet, only described a brief and not very
frightening incident. It was still the shaking hands part. Never-
theless, she needed to make a point.

A growing thought in many people's minds these days is not whether they will become a victim of random violence but whether anyone will come to their aid. Take heart. I was too frightened to learn the Good Samaritan's name, so I'm using this column to thank her. We will always suffer, as do the great cities, from random attacks on our citizens, but we have something that Detroit, Los Angeles, and New York don't, namely, involved people who care. Our city will never be a place where a man might faint on the street and someone pass him by. Nor will our citizens shout "Jump!" to someone intent on leaping off the parking garage. Each of us prays that the numbers will go our way, that we won't become a victim. If we do, though, the next best thing to have nearby is people who care. Thanks to all the Good Samaritans, present and future.

The story sounded flat. Was it because she was working at a typewriter and not with a pencil and paper. Did all Good Samaritan stories sound the same? Or was it because she had altered the facts? Should she possibly be writing about how her feelings of prejudice had flared up and then subsided? Certainly Charlie could not print a story with that theme. He might not even print the story she'd written. Would it sound as dull to him as it did to her?

She reread the story, noting all her lies. She'd claimed to feel safety in numbers. She did not. In fact, she still wasn't sure that the girl had intended to help her. Deep down, Molly thought that she'd stopped just to give her short skirt a dirty look. But no one would do that. The black man had run away when the Good Samaritan approached. What other explanation made sense?

She tried again to see things from the Samaritan's point of view. When she herself observed an unexpected event, what did she make of it? First, she tried to fit the event into a normal pattern. Then if it didn't fit, she tried to understand what was different. Only slowly had she ever been able to determine that someone might actually be doing something wrong. Like once when she'd seen a woman putting cheese in her pocket at the grocery. She had not been sure that the black man meant any harm until several seconds after he'd started squeezing her hand. Only slowly, therefore, could one person come to another's aid. Of course, the woman had tried to help. If she read this column, she would see that Molly knew that. Perhaps Molly should add a sentence, asking the woman to telephone. This could become the newspaper's search for one more Good Samaritan. Kind of hokey, but just the thing her editor liked.

She read the column again, suddenly feeling confident enough to leave it on Charlie's desk as a surprise. Normally, she would review and reconsider, at least until she came to work tomorrow. Charlie and a skeletal staff would be here before long to work on Monday's newspaper, but she would be gone. She wanted to spend some time with Robert.

She pasted the pages together, rereading. Could the column be too naïve? Often she was aware of her youth showing through in what she wrote. It was present here, this naïveté, but naïveté was at least part of the reason she'd been hired. Management liked the freshness of youth. For one thing, Molly and the other young reporters hadn't turned into Republicans yet. For another, they were cheap talent. People her age were willing to work for $100 a week, take home $86.50.

Her thoughts were interrupted by the arrival of Jake Johnson, a reporter, loaded with two Thermoses and work he had taken home. He hurried into the room in time to let what he was carrying slip out of his hands onto his desk instead of the floor. Jake had thick fish-gray hair, parted in the middle and held in place by his own personal hair oil. In his clothes he affected the tweedy professorial look so common to older male reporters. The young ones wore blue jeans and ties. He did not seem to notice her.

The guild was after Jake as well, but it was because he worked so many extra hours without pay. He claimed to be a slow writer, thus owing the company extra time. He refused to join any group that had what he called a collective opinion. Molly admired him for standing his ground, although she thought he should be paid for his extra work. If she ever hoped to be hired by the New York *Times* or even the *Daily News*, she should consider working as hard as he did. Today was a start.

Jake righted his Thermoses and straightened his file folders. "Whatcha working on?" he asked, without looking her way. He always knew what any reporter on either paper was writing about. His bulging gray eyes roamed people's desks when he stopped by to chat, and Molly imagined that he might even go through trash cans.

"I thought I'd get my column out of the way," she said. Reporters always talked low-key about stories they were working on, whether it was an exposé on school busing or a story about the Girl Scouts.

"Anything interesting?" Jake brought coffee *and* tea to work, alternating all day between them. He opened one of his Thermoses and poured the top of it full of . . . coffee, her olfactory sense told her. Cup in hand, he began wandering not exactly toward her but in her direction.

"Just an encounter I had," she said. The finished article lay face-up in soft pasted folds on her desk. It seemed silly to turn it over, but as Jake sidled ambiguously closer, she wanted to. The decorative copy hook that her mother had bought when Molly first got her job sat empty on Gisella's desk. Just as Jake arrived she spiked the story upside down. Being the amateur she was, she would like to have his approval, but she was not ready for his more likely criticism.

"Can I look?" he asked, pulling the story off its sacred spot.

"You already are," she said.

Jake respiked her work, jerking his hands away in a mocking fashion. "Didn't know you minded," he said.

She hesitated. "I guess I don't. It's nothing earthshattering." She felt her confidence seeping away. "It's not even very good." But maybe he would like the column; maybe it wasn't as weak as she suddenly thought.

He took the story off the hook, letting it drop open from his eyes to his knees. She wished she hadn't sounded as if she were begging for a compliment. She began picking the dried-up glue off the mouth of her paste pot. Jake scanned the story quicker than she would have thought possible, folded it, and respiked it without saying anything.

He ambled toward his desk. "Black man," he said over his shoulder, his voice as penetrating as thunder.

"What?" Molly asked. A sort of squeal tinged her voice.

"Why else would you have written the story?" He drank his coffee without looking at her.

"I didn't want to sound like a racist," she said.

"What's racist about it?" He took his cover off his typewriter and rolled in a sheet of paper as if he was too busy to discuss this with her.

"He was black and I'm white. That's about as race-oriented as you can get."

Jake's horsey mouth showed a grin of triumph. "And since you're scared of all black men—which means, in fact, that you *are* a racist—you thought you'd leave that vital fact out of the story."

"I'm not a racist," Molly stammered. "It's just a little made-up column." She was not exactly defending herself well.

"It's not your job to alter the truth," he said.

"It's not your job to edit what I write," she retorted.

An immediate irrevocable silence fell. Jake cursed his coffee under his breath, poured what was left of it back into his Thermos, and opened the second Thermos of tea. Molly alternated between feeling insulted and feeling like a hardhead. Jake had been accurate in what he'd guessed, after all. Was the column no good unless the man was black? Did all newspaper stories have to be literal or could they be illustrative? Paying no attention to her, Jake began typing in uninterrupted rhythm. How could he compose so smoothly? Molly's typewriter worked by fits and starts. Maybe she should be trying to learn from someone who obviously knew more than she.

Garland Frost, the wire editor, who was her primary boss, and

Charlie Elks, the city editor, who was her secondary boss, walked in the door together. She'd have to seek out Jake later. Upon seeing her, Charlie, a small sloppy man given to newsroom dramatics, pretended to swoon. "What are *you* doing here?" he called across the room. He gave his ambiguous smile that Molly was never sure meant approval or disapproval.

"Writing some letters," she said. Jake's typewriter did not miss a stroke.

"On your day off?"

"I don't have a typewriter at home," she explained.

Garland, a pleasant balding man, went to the wire room to collect the national and international stories that had been transmitted overnight. She expected Charlie to go to his desk, but suddenly he was crossing the room in her direction, rapping his knuckles on the top of Jake's typewriter as he passed. She jerked her column off the copy hook and opened the bottom drawer of Gisella's desk, but it was too late.

"Letters," he said, standing before her with his hands on his hips. "Let's see that long letter you just crammed inside that desk." Molly could claim no privacy from Charlie, as she could from Jake. As city editor, he had the right to sit on her shoulder and read her words as she committed them one by one to paper if he wanted. But this story was a lie. Charlie would be able to tell as surely as Jake had.

She set her foot against the drawer handle. "I've got some work to do on this," she said. "It won't be ready until tomorrow. I already gave you my column for this coming week anyway."

"It's pasted up," Charlie declared. "It was on your hook." He rubbed his thumb greedily against his fingers. "Just let me see it."

"It needs some work. I don't want you to read a rough draft." Her face began to flame as she thought how Jake must be gloating.

Charlie stared at her, his fingers ominously poised.

"Why can't you wait?" she asked in a soft voice. Might this ruin her chances of becoming a full-time reporter?

When she reached into the deep desk drawer, she felt as if she were reaching into her own grave. If she didn't give Charlie the story, she might ruin her chances of becoming a reporter. If she gave it to him, he might wonder if she deserved the job. Thinking he might see her stricken face and relent, she offered him the copy, which he took quickly out of her hands. With a deeply felt lassitude she covered Gisella's typewriter. When she crossed in front of Charlie's desk on her way to the ladies' room, he held up a finger to stop her while he finished reading.

"Nice story," he said. "But I want to use it tomorrow. Top of B-1, though, not as a *Viewpoint*." He liked the column, her confused mind registered. "The longer we wait, the less timely it is," he continued. "Even if I ran it for your Wednesday column and held the porn story for next week, it would be too late." He began editing the copy, not waiting for her input. "Let's use it tomorrow," he said. "You know how strapped for news we always are on Mondays." Decision made.

"It was for the bank," she said. "It was for when I couldn't come up with an idea." She was trying to decide if Charlie needed to know that the man was black.

He looked over the downward-pointing rims of his glasses. "This isn't the kind of story you hold, Molly. This is news. This happened. You're not really worried about coming up with ideas, are you?"

"Of course not," she said. "I just thought you wanted to build up a bank of columns."

"I do," he said. "But not with this."

She went to the canteen for a Coke, still trying to decide whether or not to tell. What if Jake tattled? He wouldn't. What if the Good Samaritan called and announced the truth? She bought Charlie a soda, although he hadn't asked for one, and when she returned to the newsroom, she set it on his desk.

"That man was black," she muttered.

Charlie's chin shot up, his lips curling inside his mouth as he contemplated the new information. "I think we'll leave that out," he said slowly. "No need to fan dying coals. This is a story about a Good Samaritan, don't you think?"

"That's what I thought," she said, deciding not to mention that Jake thought differently. "I didn't see any need—"

"Agreed," he interrupted.

She flashed a look toward Jake, who appeared to be taking notes from someone over the telephone. Whom did he have the nerve to call on Sunday morning? Both Thermos tops sat empty on his desk: it was a wonder he didn't spend half his day in the bathroom. His criticism had simply been wrong, she thought. Charlie, the editor, should know what he was doing. Still, a doubt nagged her: what story would Charlie have to play on top of B-1 if he yanked hers? The lead story on most Mondays was who had been killed in traffic accidents in North Carolina over the weekend.

When she drove past Montaldo's she noticed that the dress she wanted her father to buy for her mother was no longer on display. They were to meet Wednesday at her lunch break to consider it. She hoped it hadn't been sold. When she turned at the First Baptist Church she glanced at it, too, thinking how, from this distance, the church looked less overwhelming. Maybe the reason its lines were stark and cold was so it wouldn't appear to be competing with God. Maybe the architect was simply showing humility. Maybe she should withdraw her story and take the consequences.

Chapter Six

S HE WORE the same dress she'd worn Saturday evening when Robert made love to her. Not that she thought she'd see him, but there was always a chance. He and Molly lived ten or so blocks away from her in the old section behind the First Baptist Church. The house number in the phone book was 309¹/₂, so she assumed they had a garage apartment, or, like her, part of an old house. It was an easy walk to where they lived, but she preferred something more circuitous, something that might let her see Molly again. Telephoning the bus dispatcher this morning, she'd found out that to get to their house, she should catch one bus downtown and transfer in front of the newspaper building to the shopping center line.

She'd already ridden one complete circle so she could learn the entire route, which, incidentally, passed the university. Now once more she waited inside the vehicle, staring out the filthy window at the front door of the Greensboro Daily News-Record building in case Molly was a member of the group that appeared to be returning from lunch. She didn't *have* to see her again right now, but it would be interesting to observe if the look of brash innocence Suzanne had seen on her face on Friday had altered in any way. Not that she thought Robert would have told. But she wanted to find out if she looked at Molly in some new way.

"Miss your stop, lady?" the bus driver asked her.

She paused before she answered, feigning a daydream. She'd thought he hadn't noticed her. "Did we pass the Forest stop?"

He reached his arm behind him as if he were yawning. "You'll have to pay another nickle," he said, wiggling his fleshy palm for the money.

"It was an accident," she muttered darkly.

He shrugged. "Suit yourself." He opened the door for two passengers, neither of whom had come from the direction of the newspaper building, revved his engines, and started the route again.

She had no real plans yet, but as in any exploration, she'd gathered a few things she might need: tape, a pad of paper, a small transistor radio in case she found herself waiting longer than she anticipated, an apple, a ham sandwich, and enough change for several trips on the bus. The weather had remained cold all weekend, but an early morning rain had warmed things up. Now the skies were clear although the streets were still wet. This time, without her even pulling the cord, the driver stopped where she wanted to be let off. She disembarked with her head held high. Was he being nice or making sure that she didn't get another free trip?

The streets in this neighborhood were curvy, laid out to fit the flow of the land. Houses varied widely in style; yards, in the attention paid them. She turned the corner onto Forest Street, wondering what she would find. Already she had certain expectations about the kind of people Molly and Robert were. She didn't want things fixed too rigidly in her mind, but from the little she'd seen, she thought she could predict how they lived with each other. Neither of them would ever believe it, but they needed her: to shake them out of their complacency, to show them how cruel the world was, to make them appreciate their future more than they had their past. She wondered what kind of things they owned. Probably not much more than she unless they were still under the wings of their parents, a possibility she hadn't ruled out.

She walked past four houses before she reached 309, a ranch-style residence that sat half on a hill to allow for a basement apartment, labeled 309½, on the right-hand side. Because the property was so heavily wooded, the only approach to the house was by way of a graveled driveway. An old red sports car, an MG Midget, Suzanne believed, sat up close to the house, its convertible hardtop lying on the grass. It was a nicer car than she'd expected them to own. Was Robert getting ready to go for a ride this very minute? The top to his car would make a nice trophy for her living room. She wondered if the bus driver would help her lift it up the steps.

She walked to the basement door and knocked firmly, but there was no answer. Above her at the main front door she heard someone jiggling keys. A steep stairway rose from the driveway to the main entrance of the house. Stepping back, she looked up a bank of periwinkle and called, "Hello."

"Yes?" answered a middle-aged woman who wore tight slacks, a scarf, and a short fur coat.

"Am I at the right address? Robert Carter's?"

"You are," she said. "What is this—Monday? Robert comes home either at four or six today. I'm not sure which." She turned to lock her door. The MG was obviously hers. Could she be Robert's mother? Or Molly's? As she descended the steps, she asked if she could take a message.

"I'm supposed to meet him here for a guitar lesson," Suzanne said. "I didn't realize I was early." She would appear more convincing if she had brought her guitar, but this woman still might let her in.

"You're welcome to wait," the woman said. "There's a nice sunny spot around back, a picnic table and some benches." She gazed down the driveway to the street, where there was no visitor's car. "I'm sorry I can't let you in, but I don't have a key."

Liar, Suzanne thought. "He'll be here," she said with a faint note of possessiveness that she thought was not lost on the woman.

Without more conversation the woman, evidently only Molly and Robert's landlady, got into her car, undergoing—to Suzanne's eyes—a remarkable transformation. She'd been a rather stiff middle-aged woman, but now she had a young eager look about her as if she were on her way to discover some sort of situation that would change her life. Impulsively, Suzanne waved goodbye when she turned out of the driveway. Isabel Gant—she quickly found out her name from a letter in her mailbox—saw her and waved back.

Hurrying up the cement steps the landlady had just descended, she peered through the picture window into the living room. She corrected her impression that the woman was a divorcée: over the fireplace hung an oil painting of a man. But perhaps Mrs. Gant was a widow. She didn't quite look like a married woman. Another wall showed pictures of two boys, evidently her sons, neither of whom was Robert. Something in the room moved, startling her, but it was only a cat. The cat hopped onto the sofa and then onto the window sill, where it proceeded to rub itself against the cool glass. Making her hands into claws, Suzanne jumped at the animal, but it paid no attention. She knocked hard on the glass, but the cat acted as if she weren't there. Why was she wasting so much time?

She hurried down the steps and around the basement to the backyard, looking for windows. The rear of the apartment had a sliding glass door, but a drawn curtain prevented her from seeing in. Propped against the house was a girl's bicycle, which she got on and rode over to the picnic table, where she left it. She returned to the high rectangular window she remembered seeing in the front, but it was too far off the ground for her to see inside.

The picnic table was too heavy to move but not the bicycle. She rode it down the driveway to see if anyone was coming and then returned to park it under the window. Standing on the narrow seat was tricky, but she managed to grab hold of the window sill and pull herself carefully up.

The sun was playing tricks: all she could see were black spots, but then her eyes began to focus. They lived in one large room, as Robert had mentioned, more done-up than she'd anticipated. Their unmade bed, toward which she felt intense resentment, was tucked in a corner to the left of the window. Had Robert made love to Molly since he'd made love to her? Two chintz-covered wing chairs sat more or less facing the bed. Bright, framed travel posters—one from Ireland, another from Greece—decorated the walls. A bookcase fashioned of bricks and boards held a stereo system and lots of books that looked like college texts. The telephone hung at a point toward the rear, where the room became a kitchen. Along the near wall were located a door, which must lead to their bathroom, and two unfinished wood desks and chairs. In the kitchen there was a dinette set big enough for two.

She returned her attention to the unmade bed. There was no need to make it up, she might mention to Molly, considering how often Robert used it while she was at work. Had Molly noticed how youthful Mrs. Gant had been looking these days? Suzanne saw on the floor a polka dot bedspread with the same pattern as the ruffle at this window she was looking through. But they weren't polka dots, she suddenly realized; they were hearts. She felt a sudden anger at this sickening display. Forgetting where she stood, she curled her body pretending she was going to vomit. Unexpectedly, the bicycle began rolling forward. She tried quickly to steady it with her feet, but it was already falling. Her chin hit the window sill with a *thunk*. Her hands and forehead scraped the brick wall. She landed sprawled on top of the bike, the seat wedged against her stomach.

The abrasions on her forehead and one of her hands burned. The abrasion on her other hand was covered with black mud, which soothed the pain. The ham sandwich in her coat pocket had been flattened. She stood up, angrily brushing trash off her clothes. Now she didn't care if they caught her here. Now, if Molly drove up, she would simply announce that she was having an affair with her husband. She knew the kind of girl Molly was: the type she'd known in high school who had everything . . . who was so arrogant, for example, that she would even rearrange history if it suited her purposes. Louise Sherrill, in particular, was whom she was thinking of.

She picked up the bicycle, rolling it forward a few feet to see if it was damaged, but the fall had not hurt it at all. On the other hand, *she* might miscarry. She threw down the bike and walked around the apartment to the sliding glass door to see from her reflection what damage had been done. Pushing aside her bangs, she gingerly touched a large lump of bruised flesh. She knew that her body had been strained in ways that were going to make it ache.

She sat down at the picnic table to eat her smushed sandwich and her apple. No, she wasn't ready to be caught here, she realized, not this soon, but she'd leave one clue. She put her sandwich back in her pocket and returned to the bicycle, walking it halfway down the driveway, where she let it fall. Then she held aside some saplings and stepped into the woods, prepared to wait as long as it took for one of those fools to come home.

Louise Sherrill. She had not thought of her in months, but now that she had, she instantly understood why she felt such distaste for Molly. It wasn't simply because she'd shaken a nigger's hand, as she thought at first. It wasn't because she used hearts to decorate her apartment. It was the lie behind those gestures. Louise and Molly were two of a kind. Now that she had observed Molly, now that she had seen inside this apartment, she knew it was true.

Football season of Suzanne's senior year in high school had stretched on past its normal ten weeks because the team was headed for the state championship. Louise Sherrill, short, brunette, bouncy, had been the head cheerleader; her halfback boyfriend Bo ran most of the touchdowns. Monday after the final victory, Louise came to school with an announcement, which she couldn't have made earlier without being thrown off the cheering squad. She surrounded herself in the cafeteria with all the girls who were interested in hearing first hand "the biggest news of the year—next to the state championship." Her parents had said it was time to tell, and Louise wanted her friends at school to be the first to know.

"The truth was we just couldn't wait any longer," Louise began. She made individual eye contact with each of the girls to assure them of the gravity and honesty of what she was saying. "Bo is a very moral person, and he felt that we should get married before—" She giggled and the whole group of girls giggled too. Suzanne, who was eating lunch at a nearby table, thought she might get sick. "So the weekend that the Beta Club went to the beach, we slipped away and were married. We weren't going to tell anybody, but then I accidentally got pregnant so we had to." Almost every girl surrounding Louise had shrieked at that last bit of information.

Not the lies themselves, but the parading of them was what had so disgusted Suzanne. All Louise's parents had done was print a marriage announcement with a favorable date and send their daughter to school with the story.

Three months after Louise's announcement, on a cold, wind-swept day in March, Suzanne told her mother that *she* was expecting. They were in the car on the way to the drugstore to pick up some pills for her father's stomach. Louise Sherrill Gibson was finishing her senior year through the home-bound program, normally reserved for handicapped students, but allowed by unanimous vote of the school board on which Louise's father served. Bo had moved into Louise's house, into Louise's room. He'd gained enormous stature at school because at eighteen he was legally sleeping with someone.

Without a word her mother had pulled over to the curb, both hands clutching the steering wheel. She was a skinny unattractive woman with gray wiry hair and skin ruined by pigment splotches. Her skittish eyes, set close together, never settled for more than an instant on anything; Suzanne didn't understand how she was even able to drive. When she talked, it was in a high-pitched, nervous voice.

"I think you ought to get out of the car," she'd said, touching everything in the car with her eyes but her daughter. "I'll meet you at home." Suzanne had acquiesced, but only because she wanted to follow this strange drama created by her mother instead of making one of her own. Her mother had turned the car around and sped off. Suzanne had begun walking, thinking about how unfair it was to be made to walk when you were pregnant and it was cold. She burrowed her hands into the pockets of her coat, but they were so numb that it made no difference. She had not learned how to will them to be warm yet. Not knowing how to respond to the news, her mother had hurried away to ask her father what to think.

Suzanne hadn't gone home, of course. Instead, she went to a pay phone outside the Seven-Eleven and called her boyfriend Jerry. Actually, Jerry wasn't her boyfriend, but they had done it in the woods behind the gym during the Valentine's dance. They hadn't gone to the dance together, but she had noticed him and a couple of other guys sneaking away to the parking lot for drinks from the trunk of a car. When he finally went out alone, she followed. She wasn't even sure he knew who she was until it was over.

Jerry came and picked her up, and they drove around the high school complex for a while. Finally, they parked on the dirt road behind the stadium. The brisk wind made the pulley chains on the empty flagpoles tinkle like off-key bells. She let him kiss her some, his eyes closed, while she observed his pointed ears and freckled face and the strange wrinkles in his cheeks. He wrestled in the 123–pound class for the school team. When they graduated, he'd drunkenly told her on Valentine's night, he wanted to sell insurance like his uncle, who was a member of the Million Dollar Round Table. His father was in a tuberculosis sanitorium.

After a particularly delicious kiss, she pulled away. "I want to talk to you," she said. He had one hand caught inside her blouse because he hadn't bothered to unfasten the buttons.

"Can I keep my hand here?" he asked sweetly.

"Sure, but I think I'm pregnant." His wrestler's grip had grown still against her breast. Its sudden dampness caused her nipple to shrivel.

"I thought you used something," he said.

"What made you think that?"

"Have you told anybody?"

"My parents." She figured that by now her father knew.

"What did they say?"

"They think we ought to get married."

With his free hand he unbuttoned one of her buttons so he could slide his hand out. "I don't even know you," he said.

"That's not exactly true," she answered.

Anyway, she hadn't been pregnant at all, but she wanted to see what would happen if she said she was. What happened was that Jerry's uncle called her mother the next day, saying that he would pay for the cost of the birth or the abortion (he knew a place in New York where she could get one), whichever they decided on, as long as the baby would be given away if she decided to have it.

While she stood in the hallway listening, her mother accepted gratefully. "I really regret my daughter's behavior," she'd told Jerry's uncle in her high uncertain voice. Suzanne slipped out of the shadows so her mother could see her. "I really regret it," she repeated, but this time she looked directly at Suzanne.

He'd never said much to her in the first place, but then her father stopped speaking to her at all. That was why she started jumping out in front of him: to startle him into some kind of response. But he seemed to know what she wanted, and no matter where she surprised him, leaping out of the pantry or from behind a door or even from behind the coal pile in the basement, he never uttered a sound. Finally, he did say something: he might shoot her if she didn't stop. His sunken eyes were bloodshot, his hair oily and ragged, his hefty shoulders stooped. For the first time she realized how much she was affecting him. "I swear to God, if you don't stop, I'm going to kill you," he repeated. They looked at each other, and she laughed, and then he laughed too, but it was like they were both screaming in a muffled way. She did not try to frighten him again.

In May, two months after she'd made her announcement, she told Jerry and her parents that she'd miscarried. Jerry was delighted, but neither he nor her parents asked when it had happened or if it had hurt. The night of high school graduation she packed her clothes and walked out the front door. Her parents were watching television in the kitchen. There was no reason to stay. Even before her announcement that she was pregnant, her father had told her that when she graduated she was on her own. She'd decided not to wait for them to kick her out.

It wasn't exactly the same thing—the way Molly had tried to alter history by shaking hands with a nigger—but it was similar. Gestures like hers, like Louise's, would not change anything. You could not put an innocent face on a century of hatred, just like you could not pretend you were a virgin when you weren't one. You could not pretend you had true love by decorating your apartment with hearts. You had to face life's facts.

It was after four-thirty. When her legs had grown tired of squatting, she uncovered some dry leaves to sit on. Finally, about quarter to five, a white Corvair headed up the driveway. Suzanne peered through tree limbs. The car stopped behind the bicycle that she'd thrown in the middle of the driveway. Out of the car stepped Molly, who picked up the bike, examined it, and rolled it toward the house. There was no questioning look about who had left the bike in such an unusual spot, Suzanne observed as she passed. Just blind acceptance. Although Molly didn't remind her much of Louise Sherrill, Suzanne could almost impose the petite high school girl's figure on the one she was watching now. But was that even necessary? Could she not simply despise Molly Carter for who she was: a haughty, foolish child inexperienced in the ways of the world . . . but not for long. Molly returned to the car and drove it close to her front door, leaving room for Mrs. Gant to park beside her.

She began unloading the car in what Suzanne thought was an inefficient way. First she took three bags of groceries, a pile of file folders, and a hanging basket of greenery out of the car. Then she picked up everything and sat it by the front door. Finally, she unlocked the door and took everything inside. When she came out for the last load she leaned against the basement wall, catching her breath. Her own fault. Robert could be helping. But where was Robert? She waited to see if Molly went to get him, but Molly closed the door and turned on a light that beamed out of the window where Suzanne had fallen. Evidently, she was making him walk.

Slipping from her hiding place, Suzanne walked with the normal amount of noise down the gravel driveway. Even now if

Molly saw her, she wouldn't know who she was. She felt a simultaneous attraction and revulsion toward her new enemy. What she hated about Molly was how, like Louise Sherrill, she'd been protected all her life. How the protection had made her a coward, prevented her from developing a sense of perspective, given her no sense of what was true and what was false. On the other hand, what she liked about Molly was the same sort of intimacy she felt with anybody she'd ever spied upon: the intimacy born of watching a person behave like a human being. She had observed Molly hurt. Now she was observing her in everyday life. She would even stop by the newspaper one day and watch her work. How else could she feel but intimate?

She moved quickly down the street, her tennis shoes thudding against the sidewalk. The MG came whirring by, but if Mrs. Gant saw her, she didn't acknowledge it. Suzanne's knees and elbows hurt. She sat down on the curb waiting for Robert or the bus, whichever appeared first. After fifteen minutes the bus arrived, her same driver at the wheel. Clouds of exhaust rushed forward when he stopped. She stood on the bottom step, coughing.

"You gonna get on, lady, or you gonna stand there?" He didn't seem to recognize her from their earlier encounter.

"You choked me," she said. "Your exhaust."

"All you got to do is get in when I open the door, and you'll miss the exhaust," he said. "You stood there waiting for it." His tone turned patronizing. "You getting on or are you gonna waste the rest of these good people's afternoon?"

She heaved up the steps and saw that the bus was empty. "What people?" she asked. She was tired and sorry that she hadn't seen Robert. "You asshole," she said. But it was his fault; he'd picked on her.

The driver had a determined smile on his face as he stood, took her firmly by the elbow, and guided her back down the steps. "This is my bus, lady," he said. "When you clean up your mouth, you can get back on it."

She could have walked, but she decided instead to wait the twenty minutes it took the man to drive his circuit. Dusk had fallen when next he stopped, carrying about twenty passengers, mostly maids. She started up the steps. Brushing past her, face averted, Robert moved like a criminal. She turned to follow but changed her mind. She'd let him wonder what she'd been doing at his house. What she'd been telling his tired little wife. She moved back to the bottom step. "Sorry I missed you," she called, but the slamming rubber muscled her words back into the bus.

The driver took off without giving her a chance to sit down. She'd think of a way to pay him back. She bent her head, watching Robert lope down the sidewalk, feeling proud that she was the one who'd taught him to ride buses.

A piece of paper taped to her apartment door raised her hopes until she discovered it was the note she had left this morning for Bennie. Scrawled across the bottom was a message she hadn't noticed when she'd left. Bennie wanted to see her tomorrow for breakfast. He'd deliver, she didn't even have to feed him. She'd better answer the door this time or she was fired. If she had any funny ideas about threatening him through Adele, he'd wring her neck.

She picked up the afternoon newspaper, knowing that Molly's column appeared on Wednesdays but looking anyway. Today's *Viewpoint* writer was Rebecca Rimmer. But then she noticed the headline all the way across the top of the page: YOUNG REPORTER SAVED BY GREENSBORO'S MYSTERY SAMARITAN. She scanned the story quickly. It had been her opinion that Molly would sense who she was, *not who* she was, but that she was an enemy, the way Suzanne would have known about Molly if their roles were reversed. But Molly was writing about her as if she were a hero. She reread the article slowly, astonished that Molly's assumptions about her were so wrong. Something else was wrong with the story, too, she realized. Nowhere did Molly say that the man who attacked her was colored. Could they print lies like this?

She let herself into the morning mess, sorry that she hadn't cleaned up before she'd left, and telephoned the pancake house.

"Bennie's not here," Jemma, the night hostess, said. "Can I do something for you?" Nosy Jemma.

"Is this Jemma?" she asked.

"Yes.This is Suzanne, isn't it?"

"Am I scheduled to work tonight?"

"Is this Suzanne?" Jemma repeated.

"Who do you goddamn think it is?" she yelled. She felt near the point of exploding.

Like a good manager Jemma did not raise her voice. "You're on the chart to be here at seven," she said calmly.

"Well, I'm sick."

"You don't sound sick."

"Call Bennie and tell him I won't be there."

"Call him yourself."

She decided to go to work because she'd found in only two days that she liked the night shift more than she ever thought she would. Tips were better. The way male customers looked at her became more suggestive. The way she looked back was more bitter.There was, of course, the heightened sexual tension caused by it simply being night. The men always thought that their eyes were getting away with something, especially if their wives were with them. But if they went too far—for instance, if one of them "accidentally" brushed against her—she knew what to say. Sometimes one would leave his table to go take a leak and ask her on the way if he could pick her up after work. She always said no. She was the one who chose a man: she did not let herself be chosen. Ever.

As if she had foreseen the future, she began feeling sick after all. She willed the blood vessels in her hands to open up, but her hands would not get warm. In the ladies' room she washed them in hot water, trying to rid herself of the chills she was having. She felt that she had already worked once today, sleuthing around Robert and Molly's house, being stranded by an asshole bus driver. She didn't want to work anymore at all. But it was always like this for a person of total commitment. When she became involved with people, her desire was to devote every waking moment to the fact of them and every sleeping moment to the dream of them. She'd made one mistake today. This afternoon she'd had the opportunity to see Robert again. Once the bus had driven away, they would have been alone on the street. But she had let her anger at Molly get in her way. She shouldn't be angry with Robert, at least not yet. She hadn't really given him a chance.

She finished work at two. Once around midnight the pay phone had rung and she answered, but the person on the other end hung up. He might be trying to call her but not know what to say. As she walked home, the hum of the bees filled her body. She had her usual early morning headache, but excitement rolled through her head, massaging the pain. She was no longer tired. Pacing her apartment, she wondered if she might wake up the old bitch who lived below, but she didn't really care. By turns she felt elation and anger. Sometimes the force of her excitement was so intense that she wanted to scream. At last she saw what she must do. The way flooded her like a deep, painful, poisonous sting.

Except for the *shub-shub-shub* of her bedroom slippers, the apartment was quiet, although out on the street she heard some early morning traffic. She found a classical music station on the radio in the kitchen. She had hoped for, had demanded, a television set from Bennie, but he'd kept putting off buying her one.

Some sort of long piano piece was being played. She didn't normally listen to this kind of music, but maybe if she did, it would impress Robert. The melody seemed wild to her with great runs up and down the keyboard. She lay her chest across the breakfast table so that her breasts seemed to dig into the wood, not to sleep but to listen. Her arms stretched to each side as if she were a sacrifice. Her mind began to run with the music. When it was over, she raised her head, rubbing her eyes with her fists as if she'd been asleep a long time. She wrote a short letter, which she sealed and stamped, and then she labored over letters to the department of motor vehicles and the department of vital statistics.

At four o'clock she put on her coat and walked downtown to the post office. An occasional lone individual in a car drove past, peering out his windshield to see if she was female. When he found out yes, he would honk or wave, and she would freeze into a statue: she had to protect herself now. Not knowing what to make of this strange motionless creature, the driver moved on.

At the central mailbox she found that a pickup had just occurred and that another was scheduled in two hours. Robert would not receive her plea until Wednesday. Without hesitation she opened the box and tossed the letter in.

Chapter Seven

S HE CALLED Robert after her first edition deadline in case he hadn't woken up for his eleven o'clock class. After deciding last night that he wanted to take her to work so he'd have the car, this morning he'd flung her arm away when she shook his shoulder. "Honey?" she half whispered into the receiver that Garland had stretched across the big copy desk to her. None of the other editors seemed to be listening in, but still she felt embarrassed that her husband was asleep when all these husbands had been at work for hours. Freedom from responsibility was something that people who no longer had it would not forgive. Herself included, sometimes. He hadn't spoken yet. "I thought I'd let you know what time it is," she said. "I guess you realize I have the car." She wanted to ask if he wished she'd tried harder this morning to wake him up. She wanted to tell him he'd better hurry now because it was already quarter to eleven. But she didn't want to say those things in front of her fellow junior editors. One thing she hadn't realized until now was that if she took the car every day, Robert might miss more classes than he should. "If you want me to, I'll pick you up in front of the music building at four-thirty," she said.

In a quiet voice that seemed intended not to rouse himself any more than her call already had, he said, "That'll be fine."

Although she couldn't hear it happening, she suddenly knew he was hanging up the phone. "Robert," she called sharply. Now everyone at the desk was listening.

"What?" he answered irritably.

In a whisper she asked, "Will you be there?"

"Probably." She heard him strike a match which must mean that he planned to get up.

After lunch at the canteen, she used the automatic part of her mind to lay out inside pages for tomorrow's paper while the conscious part considered ideas for her next column. She was breathing easier than she'd been this morning. The more time that passed, the less likely she was to hear from the Good Samaritan about her story. Yesterday, when she checked the final proof for typographical errors, she had hoped that the story would read better than the day she'd written it. But all the lies were still there. The black man was not black, and, more than ever, she knew that the Good Samaritan was not a Good Samaritan.

Midway through the afternoon Charlie called her to his desk to show her an editing change he'd made in her porn story, which was supposed to appear tomorrow. The column had already been set in type, which meant that unless it was serious nothing could be changed. Where she had used the term "sexual intercourse" in describing the difference between soft- and hard-core skin flicks, Charlie had substituted "what goes on between the covers."

" 'What goes on between the covers'?" she repeated in a horrified undertone.

"Do you have a better suggestion?" The look on his face was not as patient as the look he'd given her Sunday when she'd resisted him.

"You're making my *column* pornographic," she said. " 'Sexual intercourse' has no connotation. 'What goes on between the covers' sounds dirty."

Charlie spiked the column for its return trip to the composing room and began editing another story.

"Will you let me try to think of something else?" she asked. "Please?" She wanted to take the column off the spike but knew she dared not. If she challenged Charlie every day, he wasn't going to want her on his staff. But at the same time, how could she let such a phrase appear under her by-line?

Without looking at her, Charlie lifted the column off the spike.

"You've got ten minutes to come up with something better. But I will not use 'sexual intercourse.' Not in a column written by a twenty-two-year-old girl." She wanted to shout "double standard" in his face, but he was adding, "Not in a column written by anyone here."

Turning her back on his stupidity, she hurried downstairs to the morgue to look up some rape cases, hoping to find either a precedent for the use of "sexual intercourse" or a decent euphemism. What she found was that "rape" was used over and over again: alleged rape, forcible rape, attempted rape, convicted rape. The only euphemism she could find was in a story about a local sex counselor who called it "having sex," but she didn't like that either. Surely, when the Kinsey report had come out, this newspaper had not substituted "what goes on between the covers." She quickly found the file. "Sexual intercourse" was used in the story, but it was a national story, not "a story written by a twenty-two-year-old girl." Woman, she might remind Charlie.

As she slowly climbed the stairs she realized she had only one weapon: she could insist that Charlie take her by-line off the story, rendering it unusable as a column. But that would keep her working on the copy desk forever.

"Any luck?" he called as she trudged in the door.

"Nope." The look he gave her said he didn't want another argument. The look she gave him said he had won this round.

Ten minutes later she returned to his desk.

"Yes?" he said, his always tired eyes looking over his glasses. This time his mouth curled wryly at her. She realized that it was possible he felt sympathetic to her position but was following orders from above.

"Do you think 'having sex' would be better?" she asked.

"Better than what?" he asked, choking with laughter. She smiled as if she thought it were funny. "Seriously," he said, rubbing his eyes with his thumbs. "It might be, but I already sent back the proof."

She knew he could ask for another proof. "Charlie," she said, waiting for the seriousness of her tone to capture his attention. "I can't bear to have 'what goes on between the covers' appear under my by-line."

"Are you saying you want me to pull the column?" She thought she had been more subtle than that.

"Do you have something else you could use?"

He pushed his glasses up his nose, a brittle barrier between their eyes. "I don't have a backup, if that's what you're asking, but I can sit here and write something. I've done it before and I guess I'll have to do it again." For troublemakers like her, she thought.

"Good heavens, no," she said. "It's no big deal. I want you to use the column. I understand that there are certain policies. I also understand that you're the editor and I'm the writer," she added to show she knew her place. "I was just curious about what happens if you have to pull a column and there's no bank to go to." This was a subtle reminder of her earlier effort to make the first deposit in his bank.

But Charlie was onto her. "Are you trying to tell me something?"

She flushed deeply. "I can't say *anything*," she pouted, turning her back on him and more or less flouncing to the copy desk. When she turned to her typewriter, which faced his desk, she kept her eyes lowered.

"The column goes?" he asked across the ten feet of space that separated them. Without looking up, she nodded, and since he didn't repeat the question, she figured he'd seen her answer.

She'd spent so much time arguing with Charlie that unless she bore down now she wouldn't be through soon enough to pick up Robert. She hurried through the long takes of Associated Press stories, which at least were easier to edit than the dense copy they got from the Los Angeles *Times*-Washington *Post* News Service. It amazed her, if it was true, that Charlie could have written a substitute column this afternoon without having to go anywhere or interview anyone. That was something for her to work toward:

having a brain bursting with ideas and the information to back them up.

She left at four-thirty, heading in the direction of the university to pick up Robert. He was leaning against a telephone pole in front of the music building smoking a cigarette. Before she completely stopped the car, he opened the door and swung inside. "Hi," he said, grabbing her bare knee with his cold hand. She pressed it further into his palm, aware of how the shortness of her skirt made an easy approach to her body possible. All this talk about sexual intercourse must have worked on her subconscious. His blue eyes gleamed like glass.

"I've figured it out," he said.

"What now?" she asked, his enthusiasm simultaneously delighting and warning her.

"We'll buy another car."

"You're out of your mind," she blurted. His hand came off her knee like he'd been burned, the eager face closing against her. She wished she'd said it in a nicer way. "Honey, we can't afford another car." She touched his knee with the little finger of her hand that was changing gears.

"We'll buy on time and pay with the money I make teaching," he said.

"That money's to pay off what Daddy loaned us," she protested.

"He doesn't need our money. He said we could pay him whenever it was convenient." Because her father had preferred it that way, she had done the negotiating regarding the loan for Robert's education, which had included signing a legal IOU. For next year they were expecting a partial scholarship from Juilliard. Robert was right: her father had told her not to think of paying back the loan until they both had jobs. But that didn't mean they could afford two cars.

"We can't pay the *insurance* on two cars," she said.

"It's not that much more," said the man who didn't pay the bills. "Not for adding a second car."

"Do you know how much I make, Robert? Do you know that we've never paid insurance the first time? Daddy added you to the policy he had on me for the rest of this year. But in January he said we had to take over the payments. That's a hundred and fifty dollars right there."

Robert's jaw was locked defiantly, his mind made up. Unless she convinced him of what a foolish step it would be, he'd come home with a second car within a week. "I won't sign," she said, her own sensibleness growing like a dark cloud. "You don't have a job: the bank won't accept your signature."

"They'll accept it."

"Don't embarrass yourself, Robert. They won't." She hated herself for talking down to him, but there was no other way to make him understand. How much she sounded like her father. How much Robert sounded like her ever-pressuring mother. "When we get home, let's make a list of our income and a list of our expenses," she said in a conciliatory tone. "Then you'll understand." She ought to turn over her paycheck to him and let him pay the bills.

When she turned in the driveway, the crunching of tires on gravel was like a snare drum in the quiet car. She'd give the You-Ass back before she'd agree to this overextension. Maybe that was his intention in the first place. No, she thought, glancing at his intent profile. He'd decided he was going to buy his own car.

His feelings still hurt, Robert preceded her through the door while she stopped at the mailbox, which was chock-full of Christmas cards. She was glad for this intermission. The return name on the top letter was that of one of Robert's new students, Suzanne Cox, who'd called Saturday evening to talk to Robert. Had he ever called her back? She'd given him the message, she was sure. She held out the letter for him while she tore eagerly into the card from her college roommate, who now lived in Richmond.

"Pat's already gotten a promotion," she crowed. "And a big raise!" Maybe the working world had enough rewards that you forgot about your earlier freedom. "She's coming through on the twenty-third and wants to spend the night." She felt undeservedly grown up, thinking of welcoming friends into her home, even though it was just an apartment. There was also a letter from Robert's former roommate Mark, who had joined the Marines and who wanted to spend the night of the twenty-third too. "We'll have to borrow sleeping bags," she said. "Do you think we should put them up at my parents'? No. Then it won't be nearly as much fun. They won't care—sleeping on the floor—do you think?" She was letting this fresh subject change the air between them.

With a beer in his hand Robert looked less single-minded. Perhaps he would be easier to redirect than she'd imagined. The tight coil in her chest began to relax.

Nostalgia for her college days, when she didn't have to worry about money, flooded her, which was silly because those days had had their own struggles. She'd been struggling then for her self-image: the same old questions—who was she and why was she here. Now that she was married and going to work every day, she felt she had a niche. She was a soon-to-be newspaper reporter married to a student named Robert Carter.

"One of your new students has written you a love note," she teased. Robert chug-a-lugged his beer. She stood before him with the envelope, openly admiring his jaunty body. "Want me to read it to you?"

Robert tossed the can toward the trash. "Sure," he said, but he held out his hand. She offered him the card and he stuck it in his back pocket.

"What's wrong?"

"Nothing."

"Why don't you open the letter?"

"I will." He got down on his knees beside the bed and began pulling out the Christmas presents they had already bought. "I want to see if this golf bag for your dad looks as good as it did last summer." When they'd agreed that the inexpensive canvas bag still looked good, he slid it back under the bed. He spent time rearranging the dust ruffle, although the bed wasn't even made. The letter poked out of his back pocket like a lollipop.

"Is there something wrong?" Molly asked.

"No." He pulled the envelope from his pocket and with deliberateness tore open the card, which showed a reproduction of a Renaissance Madonna and Child. At an angle she couldn't see, he scanned the message. "She's not going to take lessons anymore," he said, a strange smile flickering across his face. He pressed the card back into his pocket and started for the kitchen.

"I guess that settles that," she said.

"Settles what?" he asked, opening the refrigerator for another beer.

"You won't be able to afford another car."

When he realized she was kidding, he smiled, but it was a nervous smile that did nothing but turn up the corners of his mouth.

"You called her back, didn't you?" He looked blankly at her. "I gave you a message when you came home Saturday night. She said she'd misled you on something."

"She's a nut. I'm just as glad she quit."

"Did you call her though?"

"Nah."

"Is she quitting because you didn't call her?"

"I don't know why she's quitting."

"Can I see the letter?" The question hung in the air like a gunshot. She wasn't even sure why she'd asked it. She preferred that they not have secrets from each other, but she'd rather not probe into something so insignificant as a letter from a student he'd met once, even though she thought there was a lie involved in what Robert was telling her.

"You won't understand it." She cocked her head to the side. "She made up some things. What she wrote isn't true, so I'd rather you not read it. Just . . . just accept what I'm saying."

"You think I won't believe you?" she asked. "You think I don't trust you?"

Robert took a long swallow of his beer. Then he said, "It's always been easy to believe me. There hasn't been anything hard to believe."

"And now there is?"

"Yeah. This girl's a mental case. I'm not going to have anything else to do with her, so I'd rather you not get involved."

"Involved in what?"

"Not involved," he said. He struggled for words: "It's . . . it's just . . . just not significant. It may hurt your feelings. Trust me."

"What did she say?" Molly asked. "Come on, tell me."

"I'd rather not."

"You have to. You've got to trust me too. You've got to trust me to believe in you. Haven't I always believed everything you've said?"

"Molly."

She knew she should stop, but the logic of what she was saying pushed her on. "If we don't trust each other, we can't stay married." Robert's eyes glared angrily at her. "That's not a threat, it's just a fact." She thought of her mother and knew it wasn't a fact for everybody. "I'll believe whatever you tell me. What does that letter say?"

Suddenly he turned his back, offering her the pocket that held the envelope. "It's a lie," he said. "I want you to read it knowing it's a lie."

"I will," she said. Taking the letter from his pocket, she thought it seemed less like a tempting lollipop. In fact, the more she'd worked at convincing him, the more unconvinced she'd become. Maybe she should prove her trust by throwing the letter away. Waiting for her to read, he stood close as if he was going to take her in his arms when she finished. She felt like part of a drama that she wanted to interrupt. Yet she was also a member of the audience, and would be angry if the play was not completed. Almost against her will, she opened the card and read Suzanne's letter.

Dear Robert:

Merry Christmas, I guess.

I've been thinking about your decision about us, and I want you to know that I think I understand. Unlike your wife, I cannot exactly be considered a resource. I can continue

*to be your lover, though, so if you change your mind, you
know where to find me. I love you terribly. I always will.*

*By the way, I really wish you'd reconsider about giving
me a picture of you. That's the only thing I've asked
for . . . which I think is more than fair.*

> All my love,
> Suzanne

Robert reached to take her in his arms, but she stepped away.
The letter fell to the floor. He kept coming toward her, but,
backing away, she held both arms straight at the level of his chest.
Finally, her legs against the bed, nowhere left to escape, she
struck his shoulders with her palms.

"You said you trusted me," he cried, a betrayed look on his
face.

"Did you make love to somebody else?"

"Of course not."

"Did you have *sexual intercourse* with Suzanne Cox?" The
phrase "what goes on between the covers" sang idiotically in her
mind.

His eyes bored into her. "How many times are you going
to ask?"

"Just answer," she said contemptuously.

"I said no. I said no the first time." He reached to take her
hand, but she still wouldn't allow him to touch her. "Good God,
Molly. I told you it wasn't true before you read the letter, and
you promised you'd believe me. I told you she was *crazy*."

She stooped to pick up the letter, but he moved more quickly,
tearing the card into fours. "Don't do that," she demanded. "I
want to read it again."

"I'll tell you what it says," he said bitterly. He took her by the
elbow and guided her back to the bed. This time she did not
resist. This time she felt a weakness in her stomach as he tightened
his grip on her arm when she stumbled over a bedroom slipper.
The ache in her chest was from fear, but it was also a longing
ache because of the way he was holding her. The bed sank under

their weights as if with relief. She allowed him to put his arm around her.

"I should have told you on Saturday what happened," he said. "But you were still upset about that black man shaking your hand." She let the hand that Robert was massaging go limp to indicate she preferred not to hear him again minimize what had happened to her. "She . . . she took off all her clothes," he continued in an uncertain rush of words.

"She what?" Molly pulled her shoulder out from under his so she could look him in the eyes. She felt a flush of shame that she herself had once done the same thing this horrible person had done. Before they were married, Molly and Robert had made love in his practice room. But how could Suzanne have taken off her clothes with Robert right there? "In the practice room?" she asked.

"No," Robert said. He looked uncertain about how to proceed. "I'd better tell the whole story from the beginning. She came to her lesson without a guitar and asked if I would go downtown with her to the pawn shop to buy one. My five-thirty student won't be starting his lessons until next week. So I had the time."

"You went in her car . . . ?"

"She doesn't have a car. We rode the bus."

Suddenly Molly's skepticism returned in full force. "She took off her clothes in the bus? Or did she take them off in the pawnshop?" No one would make up anything like this. How long had Robert known Suzanne? With a flurry she reached for the pieces of the letter that he had laid in an ashtray on his bedside table. It indicated that they'd known each other for some time.

"Don't look at that again," he said. "Let me tell you what happened."

"Maybe I don't want to do it your way." Unfolding the pieces and placing them side by side on the bed, she felt a sudden estrangement from him that she doubted would ever go away. It surprised her that he did things she didn't know about. She thought of him on a daily basis as sleeping until ten, rushing off to class without breakfast, arriving home either just before or just after her, depending on who had the car. It never occurred to her that he might be someplace she didn't know about. Like riding a bus with another woman or visiting a pawnshop. Whether he'd been unfaithful to her or not, this was the first time she'd realized he had the opportunity to be. In a way, it ruined everything.

"We went on the bus to the pawnshop," Robert said in a dominant, overruling voice. "I selected a guitar for her, she paid for it, we got on the bus to come back to the music building."

"So where did she take off her clothes?"

"In her apartment," he snapped.

Gathering the pieces of the card, she jumped up from the bed, but he grabbed her arm. "I can't believe this."

"Sit down," he said. "Sit back down."

Angry tears welled in her eyes. "Why don't you lie to me?"

"Because nothing happened. Maybe I should say that the letter came out of the blue, that she had a perfectly normal guitar lesson and then went home and wrote that." He made an ineffectual swipe at the torn pieces. "Would you believe me?"

The answer came to her slowly: no, she wouldn't. With simple dignity she unhooked his arm from around her elbow. Looking down on him, she said, "I'm listening." He returned her steady gaze.

"We were riding back to school on the bus"—he paused for the comment that had risen to her lips, but she shook her head, indicating that she would not make it—"when she asked if I would look through a couple of boxes of music that she'd bought at a yard sale. She thought I might be able to teach her from some of the books so she wouldn't have to buy any."

Molly looked skeptical.

"She's a waitress, Molly. She doesn't make much money."

"I work for a newspaper. Contrary to popular belief, I don't make much either."

"You have access to money. She doesn't."

Molly remembered with resentment that Suzanne had called her a resource. "Would you tell the story?" she asked.

"Honestly, she's poor."

"I don't *care* how much *money* she *makes,*" she said in a rising voice. "*Tell* the *story.*"

"We got off the bus at her apartment and went inside. I started looking through her music, which was music for piano instead of guitar."

"What did you expect?"

Ignoring her remark, he continued. "She excused herself to go to the bathroom. A few minutes later she called my name. I went to the bedroom door. She had taken off her clothes and was lying on the bed. She said she wanted to pay me for my time. I walked out, went back to school, taught my other students, and came home."

Molly sank slowly to the bed.

"She was furious at me for leaving. That's why she wrote the letter—to get even. The last thing I said to her was I wouldn't give her guitar lessons. She said I was wrong. I guess her plan was to blackmail me into teaching her with this letter. She didn't realize you would read it first thing." Molly heard the slight rebuke in his voice. "She's ugly, Molly. God. She's ugly. I wish you could see how ugly she is. You'd never have another doubt if you could just see her."

"She talked like you've known each other a long time," Molly said, fitting the pieces of the letter together.

"I met her on Saturday."

"Did she ask you for a picture then?"

"No."

"Why didn't you tell me about it sooner? Why didn't you tell me when you got home?"

"I didn't think it would be necessary. I didn't think I'd ever hear from her again."

"Even when she said you *were* going to teach her?" She read the letter again.

"I just won't be there."

"What if she waits?"

"She won't," he said. But Molly could tell he hadn't considered the possibility.

"Maybe you can change where you teach."

"Maybe so."

She told him she was hungry, which she thought would indicate she believed him without overstating how she felt. She wanted time to think through what he had told her, to recall the phone conversation she had had with Suzanne, to rethink what had happened after he had come home. Already she remembered that he hadn't wanted to make love to her, had instead wanted to study for a test, something he had never before done on a Saturday night. Could he explain? Could everything she knew fit together logically?

It was easy enough for things to stay the same, she thought, as she kneaded the ingredients for a meat loaf into a single mass. She could accept Robert's explanation and never mention Suzanne Cox again. Later she might even view this frightening experience as one that had helped their marriage by showing them its fragility. As she set the table she realized that rising within her was the need, now that they both were subdued, to ask again a question she'd asked earlier in extreme anguish. She needed a straight, unemotional affirmation. At his desk, where Robert was doing music theory homework, she stopped his moving pencil with her hand.

"I've got to ask you this one more time," she said.

Without raising his eyes Robert said, "I already answered." Why did he not understand that she needed to hear it again?

"Did you screw Suzanne Cox?" she asked.

He shook his head, but she thought it was a shake of sadness rather than a no.

"Is that your answer?" she persisted.

"I told you nothing happened."

"Supper's ready," she said. The insignificant words connoted suspicion, but Robert didn't seem to notice. At the table he talked about his voice teacher, Elizabeth Loewenstein, who was threatening not to recommend him to graduate school at Juilliard unless he quit smoking. His words were at first tentative, as if testing her interest, and then evocative of the lowliness of being a student.

"You can teach here," she offered, changing the subject back to what they were both thinking about. It was less an offer to visit Isabel while he gave a lesson than her indication to him that the subject was still broachable. Neither of them should be scared to mention Suzanne Cox.

"I'll figure it out," he said in a tone that banished the subject from the rest of the evening's conversation.

After supper Robert left her at the table with her coffee and began cleaning up, something he never did. While he was wrapping the leftover meat loaf in tin foil, the phone rang. She downed a last cool swallow and went to answer, but the caller hung up. A minute later the phone rang again. "Hello?" she said. This time the caller waited a few seconds before hanging up. When the phone rang a third time, she told Robert to answer. The caller hung up again.

They looked at each other across the counter that divided the living area from the kitchen. Robert's normally ruddy complexion looked wrung out, but she put her hands on her hips in obvious irritation.

"She can't keep this up," he said, identifying for them both that this was probably Suzanne. Just then the phone rang again. This time Robert lifted the receiver without speaking. There was a long pause, longer than the others, as if the silence was what was being used to communicate. Finally the caller disconnected, the click as loud as a key in a lock.

"Take it off the hook," Molly said. He let the receiver hang by its cord to the floor. They continued looking at each other as if waiting for the phone to ring again. A minute passed and then another. Molly felt the stirrings of a sort of sympathy for Robert. They both recoiled visibly when they heard a phone begin ringing but then simultaneously grinned with relief as they realized that the phone was Isabel's, upstairs. They heard their landlady walk across her kitchen to where the phone was located. The ringing stopped, but then a moment later it began again. The same process was repeated.

"Could she be calling Isabel?" Molly asked in a stunned voice. Isabel's phone was ringing for a third time.

"There's one way to find out." He leaned over to retrieve the receiver. A few minutes later their phone instead of Isabel's began ringing again.

Rather than have Suzanne disturb their landlady anymore, they took turns answering on the first ring for the next two hours. At nine o'clock the ringing stopped and Robert and Molly fell into bed, too exhausted even to kiss each other good night.

Chapter Eight

NOW SHE might have to write again about the Good Samaritan. The girl to whom Molly had expediently assigned hero status had apparently telephoned at noon. Knowing that Molly was on deadline, the switchboard operator had sent the call up to her friend Gisella. The girl had refused to identify herself, but she'd left Molly a message: Weren't there some factual errors in the story Molly had written?

"Something weird's going on," Gisella came to tell her as soon as the dummy pages had been sent to the composing room. "The Good Samaritan called you, but she wouldn't say who she was." Gisella, a petite, lively girl, spoke in an unaffected but distinctly Charlestonian accent. She twisted her long black hair into a sloppy knot on top of her head in a failed attempt to make herself look older. She coated her olive complexion with cheap makeup, which Molly had decided to mention one day very soon. Like Molly, she had bravely majored in English, not taking the courses that would lead to a teaching career. Also like Molly, she was just married, although her husband was five years older and had a regular job.

Charlie, who sat only a few feet away, quickly rounded his desk and sandwiched himself between them. "What's happening?" he asked.

Molly flashed her friend a warning glance. Although Charlie knew her attacker wasn't white, he didn't know her Good Samaritan wasn't a Good Samaritan.

Gisella said, "The Good Samaritan called Molly but because

of deadline, Allie sent the call up to me. I think she'll probably call back this afternoon."

Charlie waited, his face toward the floor, the way he always listened, but Gisella had started back to her desk. He looked up, first at her retreating figure, then at Molly. At that moment the pneumatic system that connected the news room with the composing room spit out a tube. His pipe in his mouth, Garland, who was nearest, pulled out the blue layout page. "Your dummy just came back," he said to Charlie. How did he know whose page it was? But he was right, and for the moment, she and Gisella had been rescued. Charlie snatched the page out of Garland's hands.

"Those idiots," he said, referring to someone in the composing room who'd been unable to decipher his scribble. He hurried to his desk and began working furiously on the page, which was now four minutes late. In his boss voice he called across the news room to Gisella, "Don't leave for lunch until I talk to you." He cut his eyes to Molly, who was looking at him over her typewriter. In a less tyrannical tone he said, "You either." She was glad this new confrontation with Charlie included her friend. Gisella had joined the staff a year before Molly and in that brief time had already won a statewide contest for a feature story describing her experiences as a shoplifter. Gisella was valued on the staff—tested and proved, unlike Molly.

After the local page was put to bed, Charlie asked them to bring chairs to his desk. The news room had been quickly vacated except for Garland, who spent the lunch hour in the wire room checking for breaking stories. "Now, what's going on?" he asked in a voice that attempted to be paternal. He'd made sure they talked to him before they had a chance to talk to each other.

"Nothing," Gisella said. "A woman called Molly on deadline and Allie forwarded the call to me. All she said was to tell Molly that the Good Samaritan was glad to have been of service. She didn't say whether she herself was the Good Samaritan or whether she was speaking for the Good Samaritan. That's all I know."

Charlie "hmmmed" skeptically.

"Did she leave a number?" Molly asked. "Did she act like she wanted to talk to me?"

Gisella shook her head.

"I thought you said she was going to call back," Charlie said.

"I said she might."

He shrugged. Now that the excitement of deadline had passed, he was less interested in an anonymous phone call. "Got a column idea for next week?" he asked Molly. She was due another afternoon off the desk today to write.

"Not yet."

"Now you do." He waited for her to identify what he was thinking about.

"An anonymous phone call?" she asked, pretending disinterest. The idea made her uneasy. Suzanne Cox might be reading her column now. "Nobody's interested in that."

"Not one anonymous phone call," he said in a patronizing tone. "All of them. You can call Southern Bell. Find out what kinds of tracing devices they have. Ask them about their most interesting cases of phone abuse." He smiled beneficently: the donation of an idea was clearly the most charitable act in a news room.

"Okay," Molly said halfheartedly. "If I can't think of anything else."

Charlie smiled at her in a way she could not interpret. "Do the story," he suddenly ordered, the smile disappearing. Sighing audibly over his heavy-handedness, Gisella left them to return to her desk. Tears of embarrassment sprang to Molly's eyes but she forced them back down their paths with a fierce "Okay." At least she wasn't going to have to write about the Good Samaritan. She should be grateful.

She was supposed to meet her father at Montaldo's to look at the dress during her lunch break, but she quickly phoned his office to try to catch him before he left. Charlie had not made a simple suggestion; he'd ordered her to write a story for which she had to do all the investigation this afternoon. As soon as they were connected, her father asked why she hadn't told him what happened to her on Friday. He'd opened his mail this morning to find a letter from his insurance agent that enclosed the story. He'd even had a couple of phone calls.

"What are people going to think when I don't know what's happened to my own daughter?" he asked.

"It wasn't that important," she said. Why had she decided not to tell him? She couldn't remember now.

"It was important enough to be in the paper. Important enough to terrify your mother—"

"Mother? Terrified?" she interjected.

"Your mother hid the paper from me because she was upset." Although she wanted to, Molly dared not laugh. Instead she concentrated on his cooing sounds of relief that she was safe.

"I'm sorry, Daddy. I had no idea Mother wouldn't tell you. I would have called myself, but some other things came up. More important."

"What?" he asked in a voice that insisted on being told this after not being told the other. She was skirting near explanations that she did not want to give, but at the same time the danger gave her a feeling of getting even with Robert. Her husband had followed a woman into her apartment. Wasn't that a sort of betrayal? Now she was letting her father know that something was wrong. Didn't that serve Robert right? Perhaps she should go ahead and tell Daddy about Suzanne Cox. Would it help to laugh off her crazy accusation? Something held her back. Perhaps because of his own past, her father would think Robert was lying.

"I don't want to talk about it, Daddy." Her mind searched for a neutral excuse while a hurt silence came from his end. "It's just something I'm not ready to discuss—with you or Mother." She felt the tension let up. As long as he wasn't left out of something, he wouldn't be too hurt.

"Nothing serious, I hope," he said stiffly.

"Not really." Maybe soon she would confide in him. He'd been so concerned about her confrontation, the only one to whom she didn't have to say "near-rape" to affect. The only person in her family who never considered her objectively, which was the very reason not to mention Suzanne Cox. Finally the silence drifted into peace. "Can we look at the dress tomorrow?" she asked sweetly. "I'll tell you all about having my hand shaken. I have to write a column before I go home today and I haven't even gotten the information."

"Fine with me," he said, lingering on the phone.

"I've got to write something on anonymous phone calls," she offered. Her father seemed to know little about what she did, and occasionally but not effectively, she tried to tell him.

"Dirty?"

She hadn't even thought about the dirty kind. "Anything that's an annoyance," she said. "Tomorrow?"

She was hanging up the phone when she heard him call her name. "What?" she asked.

"I hope you're driving today."

"I am."

"If you ever need me to pick you up anytime, just call."

"I will, Daddy."

"I mean it."

"I know you do." His concern made her feel good, but she was right not to have mentioned Suzanne.

Under the table at the canteen Gisella's crossed legs jiggled at an incredible rate as they sat eating Campbell's Beanie Weenie. "She talked very aggressively," she told Molly, using one of her favorite words to describe women she didn't like. Molly had not gotten around to pointing out that both of them were aggressive too: they just had the talent or the weakness—she wasn't sure which—to hide it.

"The girl I saw wasn't aggressive. She hardly spoke."

Gisella paused a minute, pondering what Molly had accidentally said. "I thought she helped you," she said, her voice vaguely questioning as if she couldn't quite remember what Molly had written.

"She did. The man ran off when he saw her. I'd call that helping me."

Gisella pressed further. "What do you think she meant about errors in fact?"

"I told you I have no idea." Molly stood up to buy a candy

bar. "Is she really going to call me this afternoon?" she asked. "I doubt it. That was to get Charlie off my back. God, it's not even my story and I'm more involved in it than you." The remark hurt Molly's feelings, but Gisella didn't seem to notice. "Why didn't you want him to know what she said?" she asked bluntly.

Had the Good Samaritan mentioned that the man was black? She had a feeling Gisella might not volunteer such a detail, might wait to see if Molly told. "The man was black," she said in her most matter-of-fact tone. "Did she mention that?"

No, she had not, Molly could immediately tell.

"Why didn't you say so in the story?"

She had thought that Gisella would immediately *know* why, that she wouldn't have to explain. But Gisella was giving her a wide-eyed innocent look that might or might not be genuine. "Charlie thought it might sound racist," she said. The trouble with lying was how it forced you to lie again and again. Now she didn't dare admit that there had been something strangely hostile about the girl.

Gisella rolled her eyes. "That's the whole problem with the race issue. You can't mention that someone is black without that fact overriding everything else you say." Everybody had an opinion, Molly thought grimly. Jake thought everyone was a racist in his heart. Gisella thought no one ought to be. Charlie and she wanted to ignore race altogether.

"I guess I should have said he was black," she murmured. "I guess the newspaper shouldn't try to cover up what's actually happening." Then she changed her mind. "But isolated incidents tend to inflame. It doesn't *mean* anything that the man who threatened me was black." She felt her attitude beginning to waffle again. "Would he have approached me if *I* were black?" she asked in a quiet tone directed only to herself. That was not a hard question to answer.

Gisella listened to this one-person conversation with her lips pursed and her eyebrows raised. "Maybe Charlie was right," she said. Molly opened her mouth to remind Gisella that making the man white had been her idea before she remembered her lie just a minute before.

After lunch she found out from the public relations director of Southern Bell that harassing phone calls had become a huge problem for the entire Bell System. Besides obscene calls, there was also the type of silent harassment that Molly had experienced last night, as well as bomb threats and other anonymous threats. The problem had become so severe, the director continued, that a new way of tracing telephone calls—the diode—had been put into action two years ago. The diode was a transistorlike device that held a caller's line open so he couldn't disconnect his phone. The police had actually gone to someone's house because of what the diode could do and found sufficient evidence to arrest. Punishment for conviction was a $500 fine, six months in jail, or both.

Though pleased by what she had found out—Suzanne Cox's telephone calls were in violation of the law—Molly felt slightly ashamed as she stood before Charlie, who was just now eating his lunch. He edited while he ate, sometimes dropping shreds of lettuce from his sandwich on the story, which was only disgusting if he wanted you to do some rewriting.

"I talked to the PR guy at Southern Bell," she said. "It's pretty interesting."

"Oh, yeah?"

"I thank you for the idea."

He pulled out his handkerchief and wiped some mayonnaise off the copy. "Thought you would."

"I don't want to include any reference to me in this column," she said.

"You mean your call from the Good Samaritan?"

She nodded.

"Why not?"

"I just don't."

"Can't you give me a reason?"

"I think I wrote enough about her already." Always the most convincing excuse to give your editor: fear of overkill.

Charlie bit. "All right," he said.

She'd been wise to establish the ground rules for this column. Now she could write it the way she wanted. Already she had figured out that what offended city editors the most was if you wrote without telling them what you planned to say. If you explained yourself beforehand, you could choose almost any angle you wanted.

When she drove in the driveway late that afternoon, she saw Isabel's storm door open at the same time she opened the door of the You-Ass. "Your phone is about to drive me crazy," Isabel called.

She didn't have to guess what Isabel meant, yet she asked anyway. "What are you talking about?"

"It started ringing about noon and it hasn't stopped."

"At all?"

"Hardly at all."

"I'm sorry," she said, injury instead of penitence in her voice. She thought about the diode—were they being sufficiently harassed to ask for one? "I haven't been here so I couldn't do anything about it." Why wasn't Isabel more understanding?

Isabel glared at her instead of repenting, and Molly glared back. Shame enveloped her for treating someone older so shabbily. But since she was the same age as Isabel's children, since her parents were Isabel's friends, she expected a little motherliness from her. It didn't exist, she realized, watching Isabel's grim mouth. This was one angry adult against another. Landlord pitted against tenant.

"I'm sorry, Isabel," she suddenly said in a changed voice. "Really, I am." Hearing the faint constant ringing of her phone, she hurried to her front door. Through her tears she had a hard time finding her key. Finally she got to the telephone.

"Hello," she said in a breathless, angry voice.

"Molly?" It was her mother. "Are you sick?"

"No," she said sharply.

"What's wrong with you?" her mother asked, attacking back.

"Nothing," she almost screamed.

"Has that husband of yours given you back your car?" her mother asked, trying to pin the blame for Molly's mood. This attack on Robert would have pleased her last week; now, it did not.

"Would you make up your mind, Mother?"

"I've made it up," she answered huffily. "I wasn't upset at first when you told me what happened . . . but your father called me this morning . . . You could have been *killed*. It's obvious you need your car. Nobody's going to attack Robert." Her voice had moved into the hysteric ranges that she often used for simple emphasis. So her mother was concerned, but only because her father had told her she ought to be. "He's furious at me for not telling him," she continued in a subdued voice.

Molly knew she should leave it unsaid, but she couldn't. "I knew you weren't worried about me. The only reason you're acting worried now is because of Daddy."

"Sweetheart," her mother implored. Molly didn't answer. "Molly, honey." Still no answer. All at once the cajoling stopped. "This is ridiculous," her mother said, and, as was her habit when they argued, she hung up.

Molly sighed, totally deflating her lungs. Did she have enough energy to take another breath? Some of this must be her fault. She picked up her coat but dropped it again to the floor. Although she'd had a bath this morning, she started bath water and lay on the bed, her arms folded under her head. Today she had managed to upset her father, irritate her boss, and cause her mother to hang up on her. Plus, Isabel was angry at her, although it was for something she had no control over. So many people couldn't be wrong.

The phone rang—Mother calling back. Perhaps they could pretend they hadn't talked to each other yet, a device they often used to erase arguments. "Sorry," Molly answered.

The silent caller waited briefly and then hung up. Molly's heart quickened, the blood rushed from her face. She depressed the disconnect button, and the dial tone sounded on the line. She hung up and waited. It rang again. She picked it up, saying,

"This is against the law, in case you didn't know." The third time it rang, she barely lifted the receiver and then slammed it down. When the caller had hung up, too, she checked the line for the dial tone and then took the receiver off the hook. She waited a few minutes but Isabel's phone did not start ringing.

In the mail she found a nice letter from a man named Claude S. Ingold, who said he had bumped into her car last Friday and wanted to know if there was any damage. It was the first decent thing that had happened to her all day. She went outside to look, but the You-Ass seemed fine. She dialed Mr. Ingold's number and got his wife. She said thank you for Mr. Ingold's letter, but as far as she could tell, the car was okay. "Frankly, I don't think you could hurt that old thing," she added with a little laugh. She was fond of prissy Claude S. Ingold already.

On the other end Mrs. Ingold left her holding without a word. "Claude?" she called in a nasal voice. "Did you run into a little girl's car last week?" She paused for an answer that Molly couldn't hear. Mrs. Ingold continued yelling: "She said you wrote her a letter telling her to check and see if there were any damages."

Molly waited expectantly. "Mrs. Ingold," she finally called, trying to get the woman to return to the phone. "It doesn't matter, Mrs. Ingold," she hollered.

The woman came back on the line. "Miss?"

"All I called to say, Mrs. Ingold, is that my car is fine, and that I appreciated the letter."

"Claude said he didn't write any letter." The unsympathetic voice seemed to hover in Molly's head.

"Well, here's his name and phone—" She broke off abruptly. "I'm confused too," she said. Her heart was beating so fast that it seemed dangerous. "Never mind. I'm sorry to have bothered you."

"Could you give me your name again?" Mrs. Ingold asked.

Somewhat frightened, Molly quickly disconnected. She wanted a moment to think. Then she would call the Ingolds back and explain. She reread the typed, rather complex letter.

Claude S. Ingold was born on Mendenhall Street, where his

elderly mother still lived. Twice a week he took his lunch hour from Jefferson Standard Life Insurance Company, where he was an investigator, and fixed lunch for his mother at her house. As he was leaving Friday, he bumped into her Corvair with his Grand Prix. His windows had been so foggy that he couldn't see well. He'd asked his mother if she knew whose car it was, but she said the car was a stranger to the neighborhood. He knew that a note left on the windshield would probably blow away. So he took the license plate number and traced the car through the motor vehicles division in Raleigh. He himself had seen no visible damage to the bumper, but then—ha, ha—he hadn't seen the car to begin with. If Mrs. Carter found any problem at all, she was to contact him immediately. His insurance, as she might guess, was quite able to absorb any needed repairs.

She had been so interested in the fact that Mr. Ingold fixed lunch for his mother twice a week that she hadn't even noticed where or when the accident had happened. It was on Mendenhall Street, where Suzanne Cox lived. What this letter meant was that Robert had been to Suzanne's house on Friday. But not necessarily. At least, Mr. Ingold hadn't written the letter. He might not even have a mother living on Mendenhall Street. This was all made up, made up by Suzanne, except maybe Robert *had* been there, and this was the only way Suzanne could think of to let her know.

The phone rang. She'd forgotten to take it off the hook after talking to the Ingolds. She tuned out the noise, deciding not to answer. Suzanne was going to get tired of this sooner than she. For Isabel's sake, she hung her robe over the phone. What kind of waitress job did Suzanne have that let her bother somebody like this?

In the refrigerator she found a head of lettuce that was on the verge of going bad and decided to fix chef's salad for supper. The ringing began to irritate her. She needed to call her mother back: they usually talked not long after they hung up on each other. Although it was her mother's responsibility this time to call her, she wouldn't be able to get through. She had an intense craving to talk to *somebody*. Even Isabel. She might try explaining their problem in vaguely couched terms. Looking out the window, she saw that Isabel's car was gone. The ringing phone had kept her from hearing it leave. Maybe Isabel had gone to the sheriff's office to sign an eviction notice for her tenants.

Molly flung on her coat and hurried out the door, slamming it hard to push the endless ringing back inside. She hurried down the driveway to the street. Isabel's next-door neighbor, Mr. Whitworth, was standing in his yard watching his poodle circle a small patch of ground, but Molly walked as if she were exercising and couldn't stop for conversation. When she realized she was walking in time to the ringing phone, she immediately changed her pace.

Studying the house from the end of the driveway fifteen minutes later, she thought it looked quiet. Isabel was still gone; Robert appeared not to have come home yet. Halfway to her door, she heard the tinny sound again. Charging inside, she tore the receiver off the hook.

"What do you want?" she yelled angrily. There was no answer. She slammed down the receiver. When it had had a chance to disconnect, she picked it up again. The person was still there. She slammed it down again. At least she didn't have to listen to the damn thing ring.

In the kitchen she made up the chef's salad and put it in the refrigerator to become crisp. She checked the phone again. The connection remained unbroken. Hearing no one's breathing, she continued to listen. Through the faraway receiver she could hear traffic and people's voices. This must be a pay phone. Suzanne must have left it off the hook. Molly's phone would be tied up until someone happened along to hang it up, which might be in five minutes or two hours. She listened a few minutes longer, growing more and more certain that the person who had called her was gone.

Quickly putting on her coat, she ran out the door to the car. Then she returned to the apartment for a moment and turned on the television to an *I Love Lucy* rerun. She drove to Mendenhall Street, looking for a public phone. Perhaps Suzanne had used the one at university square. Driving there, she double-parked beside the movie theater, approached the booth, and found the receiver off the hook. With pride in her amazing sleuthing ability she picked it up to listen for Lucille Ball. On the other end Robert was saying, "Hello? Hello?" She could tell from the way he stopped talking that he knew someone was listening. "Suzanne?" he said in an angry yet tentative voice. She quietly hung up.

She was still exhilarated when she drove in the driveway. *Too* exhilarated, she realized, as Robert listened morosely to her discovery.

"Why didn't you speak to me?" he asked. He still wore his coat. Apparently he'd been to class, for his books lay in the middle of the floor. She leaned to pick them up, but he grabbed her arm roughly, pulling her up to face him. "I asked why you didn't speak to me."

"I didn't . . . I just didn't," she said lamely.

"I thought something had happened to you. The phone was off the hook. The car was gone. The door was open. The television was blaring." She averted her eyes. He grabbed her chin to make her look at him. "How you could hang up with me on the other end is beyond belief. It's *sinister*. Except that I thought it was Suzanne or that she'd come here and made you go somewhere with her . . . I don't know what I thought." He rubbed his eyes.

"I'm sorry," she said. She tried to feel sorry, but she hardly thought she needed to apologize for such a minor transgression. She returned his passionate gaze with an emotionless stare of her own. She believed that the letter from Claude S. Ingold was a hoax, but how did she know what else was false? Would Suzanne really go to these lengths with no basis? She got the letter from the kitchen counter, where she'd left it. "According to this," she said in a lording voice, "you went to see Suzanne on Friday."

"I did *not* go to see Suzanne on Friday." He snatched the letter out of her hand and angrily studied it. "That is a lie," he said. "Call up this jerk. Ask him if it's true. I'll bet you money that Suzanne wrote this letter. I'll call him. I'll call him right now."

"You don't need to call him," Molly said, chastened by his sincerity. "I believe you."

Robert went to the phone. "I'm going to prove to you once and for all that I'm telling the truth. That Suzanne Cox has made every bit of this up. That I don't know her from Adam." He began dialing the number.

"You don't need to," Molly said, moving closer so she could disconnect the call if she couldn't persuade him to hang up. "I trust you about this. I believe you." She put her arm around his neck.

He looked up, weighing her fervency. "No," he said. "This will prove to you that I've told the truth. I'm sorry you can't just believe me. But since you can't"—he paused to give her a critical look—"I'll give you the facts."

He dialed the last number, and Molly pushed the disconnect button. "I already called them," she said in a low apologetic voice.

His breathing seemed to come to a halt as he registered the knowledge that she had accused him of something she knew wasn't true.

"Just because the letter's not true doesn't mean you didn't go see her," she said, offering both her fear and her defense. She was being unfair, but at the same time she felt that underneath the skin of all this hid a splinter. If she summoned it to the surface enough times, one day it would pop through.

Robert looked incredulously at her. "What are you trying to do?"

"Trying not to be a fool." She added, "Like my mother." Robert thought tales of her father's exploits had been exaggerated. She looked for ridicule in his face but couldn't find it.

"I have not seen her," he said. "I swear I have not seen her except that one time on Saturday. I'll never see her again. I want you to stop punishing me for something I didn't do." He moved toward her, but she shook her head for him not to come any closer. "You want me, but you don't want me," he said, deeply exasperated. Picking up his books, he sat down at his desk to study, not knowing that supper was ready.

She looked disdainfully at the heart-shaped trivet that Robert had given her last Valentine's Day for what was then her hope chest. She chose instead an old potholder, which she placed in the middle of the table to receive the salad bowl. Perhaps small choices such as this—choices that Robert didn't even notice—would avenge her. The one thing she knew was that he had put himself in the position of being with a naked girl in her apartment. Did not using the heart-shaped trivet balance that? Did not identifying herself on the phone, not mentioning she'd called the Ingolds, make them even? Or would she herself have to be propositioned and turn it down? Had Robert *turned* Suzanne down? Would she ever know?

While they ate their salads, he told her that he needed to go to the university tonight to begin preparing for the opera auditions scheduled the week after Christmas break. "I'd like to borrow your car," he said.

"It's *our* car, Robert. You can drive it whenever you want," she said wearily. "But would you please stay home? I'm sorry I acted so badly. I've had a horrible day."

"You don't trust me to go over to a practice room," he said evenly. "Would you like to go with me? Do you want to wait in the car while I go inside?" His voice grew increasingly sarcastic. "Or would you like to sit outside the door and listen to me? That way you'll be sure I haven't sneaked out the back."

"I'll get over this," she said. "Just give me some time."

He came to sit beside her on the bed, taking her limp hand and rubbing it. He moved so close so quickly, when she should be giving the signals. She found herself kissing him. She didn't know when the kiss began or how long it had lasted. But their mouths were moving rhythmically with a rapt passion that she felt to her core. She put her arm loosely, as in friendship, around his waist, but as soon as it touched there, it tightened and pressed him closer to her. Thoughts of self-protection swirled in her mind. She would not let her dignity be unraveled. But her heart vaulted in her chest; her stomach swayed.

"I love you, Robert," she whispered. Did she say those words? Did he say, "I love you, too"?

All thought vanished as he pushed her slowly back upon the bed in the longest, most dizzying fall she'd ever experienced. She had thought she would not make love with him again until the splinter was removed or somehow absorbed by the body. It was a fall that transcended consciousness and made her only an animal. It did not distress her, this lust. It was a package that everyone carried. Her mind concentrated on his entrances and his exits rather than on the ambivalence she felt. But that was all right. Sex was just a bodily function, she thought, as a powerful climax seized her and shook her like a doll.

Chapter Nine

I T WAS not easy to follow someone when she was driving and you were on foot, so Suzanne had decided to stop following Molly this week before Christmas in favor of following Robert. He took the bus now, the bus she had taught him to ride. She watched as he jogged, books under one arm, down the steps of the big orange wheezing vehicle only about twelve feet away from the bay window of the Tristan and Isolde Café, where she sat. So he wouldn't notice her, she leaned toward her raised coffee cup. He turned his back on the restaurant, waiting to cross the street to the pillared brick music building, where the names HANDEL BACH BEETHOVEN MOZART had been set in a band of cement over the doors. She had never before studied him from the back for this long. He had a nice ass, trim but big enough to act as a genuine fulcrum for his long body. Some tall men seemed to have no ass at all.

She laid a dollar bill from her wallet on the table and stood up to put on her coat. Tomorrow, dorms were to close for Christmas vacation, and cars mobbed the street, students initiating their departure as early as possible. Tired of waiting for a break in the traffic, Robert walked out in front of a car, his flattened hand held up like a traffic cop's. Suzanne could see a pretty brunette driver shake a teasing fist at him. He crossed in front of the car and then walked around to the girl's window. Behind them someone honked. Robert leaned over to talk. This was a man who loved his wife: she mustn't forget.

She left the café as he was mounting the stairs to the building three at a time. On Saturday, while she'd waited for him to show up for her second lesson, she explored the music building, finding out where the theory classes were taught, the location of each teacher's studio, the names of some of Robert's fellow musicians. A half-hour late, Robert himself had furtively entered the building and sped across the foyer, pausing first at the hallway that led to the studio and then at the studio door. He did not see her in her hiding place. While he taught, she practiced guitar in an empty room, using a self-help book she'd bought at the university bookstore. In case the opportunity ever arose, she wanted to be able to show how well Robert had taught her to play.

His voice lesson, according to a schedule posted on the door of a teacher named Mrs. Loewenstein, was at eleven, but he had made himself late for it by stopping to talk to the girl. Through the milky glass panel of the studio door, she could see his outline and the outline of a grand piano. A stern but weary voice was addressing him: "*You* are your instrument, Robert." Surely this was Mrs. Loewenstein, but she could not identify the voice as either male or female. Suzanne sat on the wooden chair beside the door and took out a notebook to record the conversation. The voice continued: "If you don't stop smoking . . . if you don't warm up your voice before your lesson . . . if you don't give more of yourself than you're giving . . . I'm going to withdraw my letter of recommendation to Juilliard."

"Elizabeth!" he protested vehemently. Rather familiar, Suzanne thought.

"I've made up my mind. I can't in good conscience keep investing my energy in you if you insist on destroying your voice. The smoking has got to stop. Don't think that I don't know every single cigarette you ever put in your mouth." There was a long pause. Suzanne imagined them kissing, but when she craned her neck to look through the door, she could see only the single outline of Robert's body.

"They don't hold your hand at Juilliard the way we do here," she continued. "They would never even read your application without my telling them you have total dedication. I keep waiting for it, Robert. I thought this year would be your best. Especially now that you're married. Having a singing career takes more than talent. You don't seem to realize that."

"What if I said I didn't want to go to Juilliard?" His voice was petulant, almost sassy. So he didn't care about his music. Suzanne hadn't predicted that. Although she felt surprised, his not singing was all right with her. What did she really care whether or not he ever sang another note?

The teacher said, "I'd remind you that you say approximately the same thing at about this time every year. If I recall my first conversation with your mother, you've threatened to quit music your entire life."

"Why doesn't anybody ever listen to me?"

"So far you always change your mind." Mrs. Loewenstein's voice became more tolerant. "When something doesn't suit you, like stopping smoking, you think you can get your way by saying you'll quit music altogether. That may have worked with your mother, but it doesn't work here." Her voice grew sharp again. "I've spent three-and-a-half years teaching you what you need to know to succeed at Juilliard, Robert. I've cared about your career. But the only person who will care about it from now on will be you. Of course, I'll still *care*. But if *you* don't care, it doesn't matter whether I do or not. I find this hard to say, but if you don't want to continue your singing, you shouldn't." The location of Mrs. Loewenstein's voice began changing. Suzanne stretched in her chair to see what was happening. "That's enough talk," the teacher said briskly. "Take some time over the holidays, Robert. Decide about your smoking. Now warm up while I make a phone call."

Mrs. Loewenstein opened the door. Suzanne didn't have time to run, only to hide her writing pad and open her guitar book. "Are you waiting to see me?" the teacher asked, closing the door. Individual spit curls lined her cheeks. Her full lips were spread with a brilliant purple lipstick that shone neonlike against her white skin. Mindful of the needs of her larynx, she wore a wine-colored turtleneck dress.

"No, ma'am," Suzanne answered.

"There are plenty of chairs in the lobby," the teacher suggested. She looked frail, as if she had to protect not only her voice but her health. Suzanne stood obediently as she moved across the wide vestibule. Suddenly, Mrs. Loewenstein turned gracefully on very thin high heels. "What were you doing at my door?" she asked in the low voice that Suzanne still wasn't used to.

"Just sitting," Suzanne said. "Is it a private chair?"

Mrs. Loewenstein did not deign to answer.

The music building had a recital hall as its core with an outer circle of practice rooms from which issued a babel of sung, strummed, plucked, and fingered music. The general dissonance from the combined efforts of the musicians up and down the hall sent unpleasant shivers through Suzanne's body. She could not understand how someone could sing in a room next to someone who was playing the piano. She walked past the lobby area and down the hall to the room where she'd first met Robert. Through the peephole she saw a curly-headed, probably-male student playing Robert's piano, picking a note and then repeating the note with his voice.

Hands covering her ears, she walked the remainder of the hall quickly. At the end she had to enter the auditorium and walk behind the curtain to make the circle. Someone—she peeked out and saw an older man with a goatee and bushy eyebrows—was practicing on the master organ. The man, probably a professor, made a face in the direction of her interruption but kept playing. Suzanne grabbed the edge of the curtain and carried it with her the next fifteen feet. When she let it go, it made a frightening falling noise. The professor dropped his hands heavily on the keys.

"Would you mind?" he shouted, his voice like a giant's in the empty auditorium.

She hurried along, passing the left-hand corridor of screeching practice rooms, until she stood once more at Mrs. Loewenstein's door.

"More like this," she heard the teacher say. "Ahh-h-h menn-n." Like she had sand in her throat. Robert repeated. She found it interesting that he was learning prayers. Interesting and prudent.

Not wanting to be around when the next student showed up, she returned to the lobby, where several coeds were brushing their hair and applying lipstick. She ran her fingers through her hair and pinched her cheeks. No one spoke to her. Tomorrow she would introduce herself as a recent transfer student. At noon Robert stalked through the lobby, stopping to button his corduroy jacket before pushing through the heavy glass door. When he glanced toward the sofas where Suzanne sat with the other girls, she held as still as a lizard. In one quick motion he lit a cigarette and pushed through the door. It was so cold outside that if Mrs. Loewenstein should look out her window, the smoke from his cigarette might appear to be only the condensed breath of a hot-blooded young man. Could the teacher really tell how many cigarettes Robert smoked? That was a trick Suzanne would like to learn.

She followed him at a distance that might let her lose him, but this was not the time to be bold. He headed into the heart of campus, his head hunched down low, the hand that circled his books in his pocket. His cigarette curled inside the hollow that his other hand made. He walked alone, a bullish swagger in his step, not speaking to anyone. Once he kicked at the air. The sky was becoming overcast; snow was predicted again.

Could she convince him to visit her once more? Could she lock him in a room with her and prevail upon him to love her? If he knew how much she cared, what she could give him, how she would smother him with affection, he might decide in her favor. Part of him was growing inside her, she mustn't forget, so he belonged to her the most. Her gaze shot ahead, caressing his poor bent head, his shoulders, elbows, and hands; it swept his thighs, his calves, even his feet. She wanted to rescue him. Such love as this, foreign to the mundane world, deserved to be recognized. It was a love that ought to be announced.

He turned into the cafeteria, probably intending to nourish himself as a good singer should. She felt suddenly ravenous, which told her that their bodies had entwined in more ways than one. But she walked past the cafeteria to the student center, where she bought a turkey sandwich and black coffee out of vending machines. She should not be here. She should be walking at Robert's side, her arm in his. She should go to the cafeteria and take her rightful place. If he didn't want to go to Juilliard, he shouldn't have to. She bought a Hershey's bar and went outside to feast on the chocolate while he finished lunch.

He reappeared not long after she had finished licking her fingers, but he was with a girl, possibly the same one he'd met this morning on the street. Suzanne arose from the secluded bench, intending to claim what was hers, but then she sat down again. The girl, a flushed, excited look on her face, wore a full-length camel's hair coat with a scarf long enough to circle her neck and hang to her hem. Her long brunette hair fell down her back as fluid as a waterfall. She was so short that she had to tilt her head back to look at Robert. She looked like a miniature something, Suzanne could not quite decide what. She was shorter than Suzanne but not as slim.

She followed them until they turned into the semicircular path to the library. They looked at each other often but rarely at the same time. The girl climbed three steps—it took that many to get her eyes on the same level as Robert's—and threw up an awkward hand. Robert stepped backward, hands in pockets, not ready to turn his back on her. Suzanne paused behind a tree to pull her hat close around her face, but there was really no chance, absorbed as he was, that he would see her.

"See you tomorrow," the girl called brazenly when Robert finally turned around. He glanced back but promised nothing. A second later he began sprinting across campus in the direction of the music building, his flight as graceful as a giraffe's.

Suzanne watched until he was out of sight and then approached the building. She'd never been in a university library before. Was she required to have a student identification card? She pulled on the heavy outer door. Inside, a uniformed guard sat at a desk. She should act as if she belonged here. Steps rose to the right;

another pair of doors faced her, but more doors were intimidating.

At the top of the stairs she entered a hushed room crowded with long wooden tables, where students had spread themselves out to study. Her face burned in the presence of all these thick soldierly books. She felt her lips pressing into her teeth and noticed a wheezing noise in her head from trying to breathe entirely through her nose. Some kind of librarian at a desk about ten feet away seemed to be watching her. She stumbled toward the nearest table. Sitting down, she opened her guitar book.

Several minutes passed before she realized that the librarian at the desk was the girl minus her camel's hair coat and scarf. She wore wire-rimmed glasses now and a thick green turtleneck sweater. A silver cross hung between her plump breasts. The luxuriant hair lay on her shoulders like a cape. She was reading the thickest book Suzanne had ever seen.

Slipping out of her coat, Suzanne found the note pad and pencil in her bag. Next time she came here she would bring books. She doodled her name on a page and then began drawing hearts with arrows and appropriate initials. Her pencil lead was almost gone when the librarian took a fistful of pencils from her desk drawer and walked to a pencil sharpener attached to the top of a low bookcase. Suzanne got up and went to stand behind her.

"Go ahead," the girl said in a controlled library monotone.

"I can wait," Suzanne said.

"I insist." The girl stepped away. "This is just busy work."

Suzanne could smell her perfume and see the healthy flush of her skin. She sharpened her pencil and examined the point, thinking of it as a weapon she could use against the girl. She had seen Robert first: this chesty librarian was not going to steal him away. "Thanks," she said in a tone as dangerous as the point of her pencil.

"No problem."

She returned to her seat to listen to the rest of the pencils being sharpened. The notes she made were careful and organized, as if her thoughts had become solidified by the grind of wood and the presence of this girl. From her wallet she drew out a calendar.

If she had become pregnant in December, she would normally deliver at the end of August, or earliest, at the end of June. That was too far in the future. Actually she'd first met Robert in October. What had happened between them two weeks ago was the culmination of a long relationship, ended because she'd announced she was going to bear his child. Pregnant in October. Premature delivery in April. On her pad she listed the days of the week she would reach them by mail and the days of the week she would reach them by telephone. She selected at least one Saturday a month for a special surprise. Sundays—mostly because of her own superstition, Robert's singing of prayers, and the girl's cross—she decided they would all rest.

Late that night at work, when she was waiting for the next shift to arrive, the idea for a brand-new identity, Steve Briggs, sprang fully formed into her mind. Steve Briggs was her boyfriend, or had been until Robert Carter had come along, and he was willing to do anything to get her back. She began scribbling notes to herself about the history of their relationship. The ideas came so fast that she could hardly get them down. Suddenly, a man cleared his throat. She looked up from the stool where she sat and saw a check being thrust in her face. The man weaved back and forth as he pulled various denominations of money from his pockets.

"Just give me that ten,"she said impatiently. The bill had come to $12.97. "It's okay. My husband owns the place." The man looked at her as happy as if he'd said the secret word and won Groucho's hundred dollars. "Thanks for the tip," she murmured to his disappearing back. If she wasn't so occupied, she'd follow him out to the parking lot and demand that he pay the rest of the check. He could never prove that he wasn't a thief if she called the cops.

Steve Briggs, an auto mechanic who was saving his money to go to marine biology school, had been in love with her for years. But when she first met Robert back in October, she'd stopped sleeping with him. Molly should not view this as meaning that Suzanne was a loose woman. Steve, in fact, was the first man she'd ever slept with. They were engaged and planned to get married. Suzanne, moral person that she was, could not in good conscience sleep with two men at once. She'd been honest with Steve, explaining exactly how she felt about Robert, and he'd hoped that since Robert was a married man, the affair would blow over. Now, however, he was thinking of suing Robert for alienation of affections. Did Molly think that was an appropriate weapon to end this debilitating relationship?

The third-shift cook arrived, and Eddie, who'd been giving her a ride home ever since she started working at night, was ready to go.

"I'll walk," Suzanne said. She wanted to write the rest down while she had it so perfectly in her head.

"Whatever you say." Eddie wore sideburns and a slick curl in the middle of his forehead. It would be nice if it occurred to him that something might happen to her walking home this late. Not the way a boyfriend would worry—she didn't expect that—but perhaps a brother. Something might happen, and all these best-laid plans would be in vain. The third-shift waitress, Vada Gaskins, hurried through the front door, late as always. She carried a sleeping child in her arms.

"Eddie," Suzanne called, running outside. "Wait a minute."

His orange Volkswagen van rumbled at the front door when she exited with her coat and purse. The inside smelled of food, but then she realized that it was Eddie who smelled of his cooking. She'd had a narrow escape.

As the van glided like a boat over the bumps in the parking lot, she tried to make conversation. "What do you usually do when you get home?"

"Go to sleep." Eddie never seemed interested in talking. He showed a V-shape with his fingers, and she lit a cigarette for him. Their unarticulated agreement was that she paid him for the ride by giving him two cigarettes.

"I never can," she said.

"Maybe you drink too much coffee."

"That's not it."

She wished he was interested enough to ask what kept her

awake, but he wasn't. They completed the two miles to her house quickly, since after midnight all the traffic lights in the direction they were traveling began flashing yellow.

"Thanks," she said as she opened the door. He didn't even look at her, much less wait until she reached her steps. She watched his tiny oval taillights disappear and then walked up the stone stairs to her apartment. She took each step slowly, turning back at the last landing to look down on the empty, haunted street. This was not a rich enough neighborhood to have driveways and garages, so everyone—including visitors like Claude S. Ingold and Robert Carter and Steve Briggs—parked their cars along the street. In the daytime the cars sat with the inertia of a running stitch as if sewing the streets down. But at night the bluish-white street lamps made them look liquidy and alive the way still water looks in moonlight. Whenever she saw a car leaving, she imagined it was Robert going back to his wife once more. Would he ever make up his mind to stay?

No one ever believed it, but once could be enough. She felt sickest in the early morning hours . . . now, while she was toiling up the last steps to her apartment; now, after eight grueling hours of work. She couldn't afford to feel sick on the job, so she held back her nausea until she got home. She had to keep working, while he enjoyed the carefree life of a student. On day two hundred and seventy-nine of her pregnancy she'd still be serving pancakes, whipped margarine, and maple syrup. Where would Robert be?

She went immediately to bed, still feeling the sexual tension from riding home beside Eddie. Her bra brought subtle pressure to her breasts, and when she twisted her hips slightly, her underpants pressed against her clitoris. Tempting herself, she rolled over so that the warming pressure of the mattress could affect all parts of her—her stomach, shoulders, face, thighs. She moved against the always helpful springs in a slow rocking motion. Wasn't this exactly what she should not do? If the pressure inside her own body eased, how could she increase the pressure on Robert and Molly?

All parts of her were flush with desire, but she lay perfectly still on the bed.

When she could sit up in bed and not feel the longing ache between her legs, she telephoned Robert. Molly answered. An hour passed, and she called again. The same sleepy voice picked up. Why didn't he take a turn? Surely, if she tried once more he would answer. Molly, after all, was the one who worked. What was this, anyway? She had to be able to talk to the man she loved. Anybody who got in her way had better get out of it fast.

Chapter Ten

A FTER the ten-thirty deadline Molly directed Gisella to meet her in the ladies' room with their thumbs-together signal. She'd received a letter in this morning's mail from Suzanne's boyfriend—alleged boyfriend—and she needed an objective opinion. To get an opinion, though, she was going to have to tell Gisella something about what was going on. Today was her last day at work before the two-day vacation spanning Christmas Eve and Christmas Day that she'd been awarded as a result of her willingness to work both Thanksgiving and New Year's. Although she was used to two weeks of freedom at this time of year, she was excited about her first time off since she'd begun working. Except now, because of the letter, the excitement felt a little hysterical.

Gisella's rubber-soled shoes padded comfortingly behind her. Even the sound of her friend's gum did not grate as it normally did. Smacking gum was one of several things Gisella did to test the range of Molly's friendship. She also burped when she finished eating because Japanese people considered it a sign of courtesy. And she broke wind without embarrassment because of an essay Ben Franklin once wrote.

"Tell me," Gisella finally said.

"Tell you what?" Now that they were here, she realized she hadn't planned exactly what she was going to confide and what she wasn't.

"Whatever you brought me down here to tell me." The insistence in Gisella's voice waned. She was aware that whenever

someone pushed Molly to tell something—even something good—
she felt a helpless inability to open her mouth. There was a long
silence while Molly summoned forth what she wanted to say.

"One of Robert's students . . ." she began. "One of Robert's
students has fallen in love with him." She looked intently at
Gisella with eyes that warned her not to react yet. Gisella trained
her lips into an emotionless line, but her untended eyes opened
wider. "Robert hates her," she continued. "He canceled her lessons as soon as he realized what the situation was. But now she's
using the telephone to harass us." Gisella gave a look of recognition that related to Molly's recent column.

Molly took a deep breath. "I had to tell you all that so when
you read this you'll understand what it means." She pulled the
letter from Steve Briggs out of her purse but disappeared inside
a stall without handing it over. "The trouble is that this student
wants me to believe that she and Robert had an affair," she said
in a businesslike tone from behind the door. "But they didn't. She
came to her first lesson and tried to seduce Robert, but he turned
her down."

"Come out of there so I can see you," Gisella interrupted.

"I'm peeing. Anyway, he turned her down and she's angry. So
she calls and hangs up. And she writes us letters. And now her
boyfriend has written me. Read this," she said, suddenly offering
the Steve Briggs letter under the stall. The letter was snatched
roughly from her hand. She *knew* that she and Gisella were alone
in the bathroom. Still, she called in a suddenly fearful voice,
"Gisella?" Her friend answered by beginning to read the letter
aloud. "Don't do that," she called.

"Nobody's in here," Gisella said. Hastily flushing the toilet,
Molly came out of the stall, her hand beckoning for the letter.

"Someone might come in," she said. "Someone might come
in and ask what you're reading."

"Don't be so neurotic," Gisella said, turning so her body protected the letter. " 'Dear Mrs. Carter,' " she began again in a softer
voice. " 'I am Suzanne's boyfriend, or I was until your husband
got hold of her . . .' " Molly flushed deeply. She hadn't realized

how blunt the letter sounded. She wanted Gisella to advise her on the basis that this entire situation was a hoax, but how could she make sure Gisella believed that? Her friend continued to read in a neutral tone. " 'I can't do anything about them legally because we aren't married, but *you* can, and I would suggest that you do. Not that I want anything to happen to her, but if you sued Suzanne for alienation of affections, then you might get rid of her and I would get her back. I'd be glad to give you my ideas on this. How about next Tuesday at the Hilton Underground? I'll meet you there about five P.M. Sincerely, Steve Briggs.

" 'P.S. I've seen your picture in the newspaper, so I'll be able to recognize you.

" 'P.S.S. Maybe *we* might hit it off. Wouldn't that be interesting?' "

"Jeez-z-z," Gisella said.

"There's no such person," Molly said, taking away the letter and refolding it. Why hadn't she realized that before? "What I wanted to ask you was whether I should meet him or not, but there's no such person." The shock in her voice related less to this realization than to how thoughtlessly she'd spilled the beans to Gisella.

"Are you sure?"

"I thought he existed at first, but now that I heard the letter, I know he doesn't. 'Maybe we can hit it off.' Nobody *real* would say that."

"*Somebody* wrote the letter."

"Suzanne Cox wrote the letter." She offered Gisella the name for all her trouble.

"Do you think *she* wants to meet you?" Gisella asked.

Molly shook her head. "She might be there to watch what I do, but I think if she wanted to meet me, she'd call me up and schedule an appointment. This is just another red herring. Last week she sent me a letter saying she was a man named Claude Ingold who ran into my car when it was parked in front of her house. But that was just to make me think Robert had been to see her. When I called Mr. Ingold, he said he'd never written me a letter and he hadn't run into my car. He probably isn't even an insurance investigator," she added softly to herself.

"Maybe you ought to go anyway," Gisella said, her eyes dancing at the thought of adventure. "Maybe we ought to go together."

Molly glowered at her. "I wish you would take this seriously. It's not a joke. It's horrible. I might even have a diode put on my phone."

An amused look slipped onto Gisella's face, which she immediately forced away.

"Thanks," Molly said bitterly. Then she shrugged. Maybe the whole situation was funny. Maybe if she looked at it like that, she could stop thinking about it.

The bathroom door opened enough for Rebecca Rimmer, matriarch of all the reporters, to stick her head in.

"You two better get your tails back to your desks," she said, her pinhole eyes showing concern at the same time she was smiling. "Charlie and Garland are both screaming your names." Together all three hurried down the hall, which made Rebecca look as if she were on their side.

Even though the second deadline was near—Molly had no idea they'd been gone so long—several reporters took time to watch them move to their desks. Could people think they were trying to get out of doing their work?

"Sorry," Gisella called to all onlookers. Charlie leaned forward on his desk, using rigid fingers to prop himself up.

"Ladies," he finally said. Molly bent over her typewriter, not daring to look at anyone. Suzanne should be happening to Gisella, she suddenly thought. She would know how to handle her. But she did not really wish that on her friend.

After deadline Gisella stood at Molly's typewriter while she rewrote a headline that the composing room had sent back. "Can you go out to lunch?" she asked. It was always a special treat for Molly to leave, best arranged in advance, since she was allowed a thirty-minute break instead of Gisella's hour.

"I'd better not." She tore her new shorter attempt at labeling the investigation of the murder of an elderly woman out of her typewriter. The thought suddenly occurred to her that if something happened to Suzanne Cox, she would be the likely suspect.

"Look, if they can't understand when someone has a personal crisis, screw 'em," Gisella snapped, almost reclaiming her attention. But she could not keep from thinking of this new possibility: Suzanne Cox could arrange her own death, and Molly, the woman with the motive, would go to the electric chair. "I'll tell Garland it's important," Gisella said.

Inside the wire room, where Garland was checking for updates on major stories, Molly saw her friend explaining about her "crisis," but the clattering machines drowned out whatever she was saying. She sat transfixed by fear. She needed an alibi for where she was every minute of her life. Finally, Garland got rid of Gisella by nodding.

"I think you're pushing my luck," Molly said as they waited for the elevator.

"I'm making your luck," Gisella boasted.

She did not want to go on this lunch, she did not want to be "helped" by Gisella, she did not want Gisella to draw any conclusions other than the ones Molly had drawn herself. And not all of those. She wanted Gisella to believe the story as she told it, to offer advice based on the fact that Robert had had no relationship with Suzanne, to respond as an innocent—which was the way Molly wished she could have responded. She *had* been an innocent until that first moment when she realized Robert could be somewhere she didn't expect. How could her belief in him crumble at such simple knowledge? Was it because her mother did not believe in her father?

Over lunch at the Lotus, an inexpensive Chinese restaurant frequented by newspaper types, she confided the story that she wished Gisella to believe: Robert was being victimized by a woman perhaps on the verge of craziness. Gisella did not ask why Suzanne was doing all this, only listened. But as she talked, why, why, why hammered in Molly's brain. Why would Suzanne do these things if nothing had happened?

"You're telling *me* to believe Robert, but *you* don't?" Gisella asked when she had finished.

"I believe him," Molly said fiercely.

"You don't." Her friend's voice was gentle but insistent.

"I do," she answered, but her voice faltered.

"Have you told me everything?" Gisella asked.

Molly nodded. Everything except the fact that Robert had gone to Suzanne's apartment. And that he had turned down her own advances that night in favor of studying.

"Then why don't you believe him?"

"I don't know."

"Are you sure they only saw each other once?"

"That I'm sure of."

"Wouldn't you consider it unusual to go to bed with someone you'd known thirty minutes?" Gisella's voice teetered on the verge of chastisement. "In a music studio?" she added.

Molly had not considered what a dogged questioner Gisella could be. She offered her more obvious holdout: "They went to her apartment." Gisella's eyes flashed. "Let me explain. She asked him to look through several old boxes of music to see if it was any good. And he agreed to. Innocently," she added. But there was more. "She took off all her clothes," she mentioned in an ironic tone. "And at that point Robert left." Now Gisella knew every fact but one.

"So what's your worry?"

"No worry." Her tone supported her words, but she was about to cry.

"Do you not believe him?"

"I believe him." Tears fell. "Logic tells me not to though," she added, forcing herself to explain. "Why would Suzanne make up all this stuff about somebody she doesn't know?"

"Maybe she's just very creative."

"She's more creative than me," Molly said bitterly, blowing her nose in her napkin. "I can't even keep up with the tricks. She fools me every time." Which wasn't exactly true. She had found the receiver Suzanne left off the hook, and she'd figured out immediately that when their line was busy, Suzanne was calling Isabel. Fortunately, Isabel was leaving today to spend Christmas with her son and his family. Tonight their friends from college were stopping through Greensboro on their treks home, and Molly would be able to leave the phone off the hook.

"What does Robert say about all this?" Gisella had finally understood how upset she was and adjusted her demeanor appropriately.

"What I've told you—that nothing happened."

"I mean, he loves you? wants to stay married? all that kind of stuff?"

"Of course."

"Well, then, I think you ought to forget about it."

"It's hard to when she calls us every day."

"She can't call you forever."

"I guess not. I'm still going to get a diode put on my phone." She glanced at Gisella to see if she still thought it was a silly idea, but her friend's expression didn't change. "I should probably send her letters back unopened."

"I'd keep those," Gisella said. There was something lawyer-like—her husband, Gray, was a lawyer—in her tone. "I wouldn't open them, but I'd throw them all in a box somewhere. Don't read them though." Gisella's voice grew steadily more authoritative. "Try to ignore her as much as possible. Then one day she'll go away. Didn't you just say so yourself?"

Molly looked up questioningly.

"You wrote it in your telephone column. Don't try to talk to a prank caller. That's how he gets his kicks. You shouldn't respond to anything she does."

"You're right," Molly said, wondering why such sensible behavior was so difficult to carry out.

They were cracking fortune cookies when a young man in a down jacket and wool beret approached the table. Molly glanced up, but he was unfamiliar, probably one of Gisella's many unusual friends.

"Miss?" the young man said to her.

She looked up again, shading her eyes against the glare from the front window.

"Don't you write a column for the paper?" He offered his

hand—the only thing she could remember about him later was that it was dirty—but hers held half a fortune cookie.

"Yes."

"I thought so," he said, turning to leave.

"Who?" she called faintly.

"I'm impressed," Gisella said.

"That was weird," Molly answered, presenting a false smile that her friend did not immediately detect. Her skin tingled; the inside of her body felt hollow with fear; she did not want to attempt to take a breath. Sliding deeper into the booth, she tried to concentrate on the good sense Gisella had just made but couldn't even remember one of her points. Could the young man be Steve Briggs? He was certainly male, not Suzanne in disguise. *Could she have a boyfriend?* Molly felt as if she had two brains. One continued her after-lunch banter with her friend. The other tried to fit this sudden apparition into the puzzle. Gisella asked what her fortune said.

" 'You write an interesting newspaper column,' " Molly kidded, trying to make the young man into who he said he was, trying to erase her own growing confusion.

"Mine says, 'You need to get back to work and finish your fascinating story on heating bills on Country Club Drive.' "

There were tomorrow's and Christmas Day's inside pages to lay out for the sake of those who had to work on the holiday. Before settling down at the desk, Molly called her man at Southern Bell to thank him for his help with her column. She was about to say a nervous goodbye when he began talking. She'd explained it well, he thought. There'd been a noticeable increase in reportings of illegal phone calls since the column appeared.

"Is that good?" she asked, attempting a joke. It must mean more work.

"It's good," he assured her. "We like for offenders to be prosecuted. When they are, the newspaper always gives us lots of publicity, which in turn helps keep abuse down."

Keeping the abuse down was something she certainly believed in. She said, "The reason I was interested in this subject to begin with is that I've been a . . . um . . . victim." Her ability to say the word "victim" pushed her on. The man sighed.

"Did you guess?" she asked, wondering if she always let her feelings show even over the telephone to perfect strangers.

"Not really," he said. "I mean, your questions were pretty emotional. Want me to put a diode on your phone?"

"Is it too much trouble?"

"Not at all." He paused, holding something to say.

"Did you want to tell me something?"

"Only that maybe you can get a real story out of this."

"A real story?"

"I don't know what your problem is. It might be too personal. But you might want to write about it when it's over."

"Maybe so." She wished now that she'd called Southern Bell's security department unintroduced. "I might be able to get another column out of it, but I might not."

The man said it was up to her and that he would alert the security department that she was going to call.

She didn't finish her work until five, which was all right with her. She knew that when she finally left, she wouldn't have to come back for two whole days. After riding the bus for a week, Robert had kept the car today to buy groceries and a Christmas tree, which they planned to decorate tonight as part of their reunion with Pat and Mark. Because of their limited means, she'd suggested that they dine on either spaghetti or hamburgers, but she thought he would probably come home with steaks. That was the penalty she paid when she didn't have time to do the shopping. When she left, waving especially fondly at Allie, since it was Christmas, she didn't see the You-Ass. But parked in front of the building was another familiar car, Pat's Volkswagen, the car that they'd driven to Canada in the summer of their junior year. Both doors of the car opened. Pat got out and so did someone she didn't know.

"This is Wesley," Pat said after they screeched names and hugged each other's necks. Her friend had lost weight and cut her blond hair, which had been waist length, like Molly's. She

wore a suit; she'd probably left Richmond straight from her job
and hadn't had time to change. She looked well beyond her
college years. Molly had come to work today dressed unusually
casually so she would look like they'd looked in college. Wesley
wore trousers instead of jeans, and a tweed jacket. He had thin,
flyaway hair, deep-set almond eyes, and a pointed nose.

"Hi, Wesley," Molly said, making it clear that she wasn't much
interested in him. Maybe that was rude, but they didn't have
room for him and they didn't have enough money to buy a perfect
stranger a steak. She hadn't known how much she'd missed Pat
and college until this very minute. Holding her old roommate at
arm's length, she thought how certain choices make the rest of
your life inevitable. Which didn't seem fair. It would be nice if,
when your life changed to something you didn't like, you could
wind it back and make a choice that would put you somewhere
else. If she went back to age fifteen, for example, she'd probably
never have married Robert. She would have gone to boarding
school to get away from her parents and never have met him.

"How'd you know to come pick me up?" she asked.

"Robert went out to buy another steak for Wesley and sent us
after you." Molly tried not to let her smile fade. Her parents
would probably give them money for Christmas, which would
help their strained finances. Then she remembered that she'd
insisted on *not* receiving money from them, not wanting Christmas to become too "useful."

She conversed exclusively with Pat until she realized that both
of them thought she was being rude. What was wrong with her?
Mostly, she was disappointed that she wasn't going to have Pat
all to herself the way Robert was going to have Mark. They
couldn't talk about old times without everyone feeling that Wesley
was being left out. They couldn't ask their friends' opinions about
Suzanne Cox. Although she and Robert had agreed last night
not to spoil the reunion by telling about Suzanne, Molly expected
that the very fact they'd agreed so easily would make them catch
each other's eye tonight after a few beers and tell after all. With
Wesley around, that wouldn't be possible.

Agreeably, Wesley squeezed into the back seat so she could ride beside Pat. She craned her neck to speak to him. If she was going to be mad at anyone, it ought to be Pat, who had brought him without letting her know. "Who are you, Wesley?" she asked in a sort of friendly version of "Where are you from?" and "What do you do?"

Who were both these people? she suddenly wondered, looking again at the new skinny Pat dressed in the tasteful wool suit. Although she was still driving the same car they had screamed at and kicked all the way to Canada, she was making money. A $3,000 raise, Molly recalled the most recent letter saying. She remembered when Pat carried a backpack instead of a purse. Now on the dash lay a sleek leather clutch that matched her glossy high-heeled boots.

Wesley had told who he was, but she hadn't listened. Robert would have to be enlisted to ask the same question later. "That's great," she murmured in the small void that followed. She knew she should ask him something else, but she just didn't feel like it. Instead, she and Pat started naming college friends and telling what news they had of them.

Wesley taught religion at Virginia Commonwealth University, they found out over dinner, when he began describing how he decimated students' religious beliefs first semester and restructured them second. Mark had not showed up nor had he called, so they decided to eat without him. She had mentioned trimming the tree while they were waiting, but no one had shown even the mildest interest. She wasn't even sure she wanted to decorate her first married Christmas tree with someone she felt hostile to. For she felt hostility toward Wesley. She'd found out from Robert that Wesley had given him money for his steak, and so for a while she'd tried to be extra nice to him. But now she was listening to what he actually had to say.

"Jesus Schmesus," he called from his end of the table. Robert thought that was funny.

"First semester anyway," Molly said.

Wesley looked challengingly at her. "How can you say that

indoctrination is the same thing as belief?" he asked. "If religion is only a habit, it doesn't mean anything. You've got to question it, *abuse* it, *deny* it . . . before you can really possess it." His eyes flared with conviction rather than passion.

"You've got to *stop* believing something before you can *begin* to believe it?" Molly parroted. "I don't believe you. I don't believe that what's destroyed can be built back better than before. I think you lose something forever, a sort of innocence in your belief that makes it special." She was thinking of her relationship with Robert now. A relationship with a husband could not be destroyed and then restored to health; neither could a relationship with Jesus. It was possible, she supposed, that either relationship could weather a question or two. Standing up, she said to Pat, "Let's do the dishes." Normally she would expect everyone in this recently equal society to help, but she hoped to have Pat to herself for a few minutes.

"You're giving up," Wesley accused.

"I'm not giving up. I don't see any point in arguing with you. You're not going to convince me, and I'm not going to convince you." She busied herself stacking the dishes.

"Have you run out of arguments?" he persisted.

"No," she said impatiently. "I've run out of interest." In the hope that no one would notice how severe her remarks to Wesley had become, she continued quickly, "Pat says you two are getting married next Christmas." They had had one five-minute interlude to talk when they went into the bathroom together.

"Oh, she does, does she?" he asked, his nose seeming to drop as he gave a broad grin. Pat looked smitten-eyed at him.

"If she can keep you hooked . . . ?" Molly supplied, but he didn't notice her bared teeth.

"That, and if my divorce comes through the way I expect."

"How old are you?" Molly asked, genuinely shocked that he could be old enough to have been married once already. Pat had not mentioned that Wesley was married. She looked at her docile, reverent roommate, who, she suddenly realized, was sleeping with a married man, and her heart turned cold.

"How old do you think I am?"

It had been a reflexive question to which now she didn't even want the answer. "It doesn't matter," she said, which was better than what she wanted to say—that she didn't care. He seemed unaware that he'd offended her. She placed the dishes in the sink, deciding not to do them after all, and walked to the wall where the phone, in deference to their guests, hung off the hook. Isabel's phone had been ringing all evening, but only she and Robert had noticed. She replaced the receiver, not caring if it began ringing now or not.

The others joined her in the living room, Robert taking the phone back off the hook, Pat and Wesley sitting in the wing chairs. She thought of mentioning the tree again but did not. Perhaps Wesley would say that they really ought to get on the road tonight. The room had been quiet for several minutes. Suddenly she realized that Wesley was occupying the silence, as well as Robert's and Pat's attention, with a soundless performance of his own. From various pockets of his tweed jacket he drew out a satin handkerchief, a leather pouch, and a folder of cigarette papers. She had not smoked marijuana in college, but that had been wise and mature. Now, six months later, she was in a world where it was immediately apparent that smoking grass was a mark of sophistication. Did each person know what to do when the funny cigarette was passed to him? Robert's face looked eager; Pat's, dreamy; Wesley's, beneficent; her own, she knew, was skeptical.

"Merry Christmas to our host and hostess," Wesley said after he took one long draw and passed the brightly burning ash to her. Not knowing how to inhale and not wishing to learn now, she took a short whiff and passed the joint on to Robert. She expected Wesley to protest or try to correct her style, but his eyes were closed and his face was pointed toward the ceiling, his sharp nose like a miniature steeple. Her hatred of him diminished: all she could think of was how much this resembled communion.

Pat and Wesley wanted them all to sleep in the bed, not for sexual purposes but because making the pallets at this point was just too much trouble. But that way no one would really rest. By herself she set up the cots she had borrowed, Robert having fallen asleep spread-eagle on the Oriental rug. Isabel's phone was still ringing, but she'd grown used to it by now. After she lugged Pat and Wesley to their feet, they moved amiably where she wanted them to go. She put the phone back on the hook again, imagining that by now even Suzanne had given up. Robert was not a guest, so she let him stay where he was. But when she turned out the lights, he struggled up off the floor and onto the mattress beside her.

A few minutes later their phone began to ring.

"Go answer it," she muttered, although she knew the ringing was affecting only her. "Robert, do you hear me?" He moved his pillow on top of his face. The phone had rung twice, was about to ring again. "Do it," she ordered, but he didn't move.

She got out of bed. She wasn't brave enough to say it aloud yet, but under her breath, so that if he was listening, he could hear that she'd said *something*, she murmured, "I think I hate you." She found the phone, answered pleasantly for the sake of her guests, and then said for everyone to hear, "Wrong number." When the line disconnected, she let the receiver dangle to the floor.

"What did you say to me?" Robert whispered when she got back in bed. He was sitting up now. "What did you say that you didn't have the *courage* to say out loud?" He grabbed her wrist, twisting it painfully.

She maintained her silence, feeling the righteousness of an angel of the Lord.

Chapter Eleven

A POSTCARD, ostensibly from Steve Briggs, came to the office on Tuesday: "Remember our date this afternoon." Molly wondered what the office secretary had thought when she read it. She was tempted again to meet this stranger. She felt that he must exist, that he was the young man who had approached her at the Lotus. No other possibility made sense.

Gisella stopped by her desk after the morning deadline. "Going?" she asked, not having forgotten what today was.

"I haven't decided."

Bobby Cranford, an alert freckled middle-aged man who sat beside her, looked up. "Going where?"

"To lunch," Molly answered dryly. At Gisella she shook her head. It was impossible to laden newspaper air with too much mystery. No reporter could limit his search for news to what he was actually assigned. Earlier, Bobby had asked who was writing her all those odd letters, though she'd received only two. Gisella walked away.

"Maybe," Molly sent after her. Gisella returned, bending over the typewriter, her eyes stretched disbelievingly.

"Really?"

"I'm not sure, but I might." She rolled half a sheet of paper into her typewriter. She was telling for reasons of safety: someone should know where she'd gone in case something happened to her. She motioned Gisella beyond earshot of Bobby. "You can't go with me," she whispered. "But I feel like I have to go. I have to find out what he wants. If he even exists. That guy at the Lotus wasn't just a coincidence." Curiosity gleamed in Gisella's eyes: she had not made the same connection herself.

"Let Gray go with you."

Molly shook her head. "Nobody's going with me. Nothing's going to happen. What could he possibly do to me in the basement of the Hilton?" Her own words seemed to assure her of the facts. "Why would he want to hurt me, anyway?"

From the copy desk she heard Garland clear his throat. Three stories slid across the desk toward her empty chair. "Later," she said to Gisella, who rolled her eyes. "Really, your position here is a little more secure than mine." At her place she found a continuation of the Charles Manson murder trial she'd been reading about for the past two weeks. She began editing, quickly sucked into those faraway California events. She enjoyed being a spectator, she thought, much more than she enjoyed participating in the world, which said a lot—not good—about her. Today, investigators of the murders had taken the witness stand to describe what they had found the next day in Roman Polanski's mansion.

"This belongs in the *National Enquirer*," she announced a few minutes later. Garland sucked his pipe skeptically. "I'm serious," she said. "I'm cutting this. You can only have twelve inches." He'd asked for twenty. It was the first time she'd ever censored something. "The rest is offensive to common decency," she proclaimed. Before she handed the long story over to Garland, who held out his hand to read for himself, she impetuously drew the "finis" sign and the squiggly line that indicated the remaining copy was to be cut. "You won't disagree," she said, rolling paper in her typewriter to try a headline.

When he finished reading, Garland spiked the story and took a long draw on his pipe. He'd made no adjustments to her editing. She slid her headline across the table, BRUTAL NIGHT DESCRIBED. "What did you think?" she asked.

"I wish I hadn't read it," he said.

"Trust me next time," she kidded.

"Next time, I will."

Later, when she was sitting at the bar waiting for Steve Briggs, she considered his remark. Had she not shown good judgment before or had there just not been a test? Next time he would trust her, which should please her. She'd shown an awareness of what should be put before the public and what shouldn't. At least she seemed to be in the right line of work. She was helping maintain a civilized world, not as a censor of the truth so much as a censor of unnecessary horrific details.

Her two-day vacation had revitalized her, she knew. After Pat and Wesley had left Christmas Eve morning without a word about when they would ever see each other again, she and Robert had gone to bed together, a long satisfying experience reminiscent of their two love weeks after they were married but before she'd started work. Although in the middle of a kiss she'd remembered she hadn't taken the phone off the hook, he wouldn't let her up to do so. Amazingly, it hadn't rung. Nor did it ring all day long. Once, Robert left in the car for an hour—"my secret," as he termed his trip to buy her present—and she hadn't felt the slightest suspicion. When he came home they decorated the tree with the special ornaments that her parents had given her while she was growing up. Something had left in Pat's Volkswagen besides Pat and Wesley. Or maybe she just felt grateful she wasn't about to marry a clod like him.

That evening they'd gone to her parents' for dinner and to exchange gifts, a new tradition, because Christmas morning they were driving to Raleigh to see Robert's mother. The before- and after-dinner sherries, the softly lit candlelabra on the mantel, the generous gifts—more generous than ever before—all contributed to her feeling that here she was safe. She was glad, when she went home to sleep in Robert's arms, that the feeling carried over. Christmas Day with Robert's mother, a sturdy yet soft-spoken woman with styled hair and the same insistent blue eyes as her son, was as comforting. They ate a rich stew, exchanged simple gifts, and took naps. For the first time Mrs. Carter was as attentive to her daughter-in-law as she was to her son, which warmed Molly. It was so unlike what she was used to from her own mother, and, in a way, quite pleasant. Gisella had told her that Suzanne would get tired of harassing them, and she was right. Still, she was going to meet Steve Briggs.

They were alone in the bathroom again, drinking Cokes and eating cheese Nabs, when she decided it was necessary to ask Gisella to swear that neither she nor Gray would make an appearance at the Hilton Underground.

"Only if you'll promise not to leave with him," Gisella said.

"Do you think I'm crazy?"

"A little. I think you'd do anything to stop what's going on."

"She *has* stopped," Molly said. Did two days constitute a stoppage? "All I want to do is see what he wants."

"What if he suggests that the two of you go talk to Suzanne together?"

Molly hadn't thought of such a possibility. If Steve Briggs turned out to be a sensible man, it might be a sensible idea.

"You'd *do* it," Gisella crowed.

"Not if he was crazy," Molly insisted.

"You think you're qualified to judge?" Gisella asked, her voice at a new haughty pitch. "You think you can *tell* when somebody's crazy?"

"I think I can." There was an air of cool superiority in her voice that even she could detect. "It's *easy* to pick out crazy people." She thought of the Manson "family" and the black man walking down the street in winter without a shirt on. She also thought briefly of the Good Samaritan, but that was only a hunch. As a matter of fact, she realized, she felt almost expert at picking out crazy people. Gisella continued to look at her incredulously.

"You know," Molly said, caught up in this newly recognized talent of hers, "whenever I read those articles about what a nice boy Richard Speck was, how he just kept to himself, was a little quiet—trying to figure out how to get six nurses in a room so that he could kill them—I never believe the people who are being interviewed. They had *never noticed* Richard Speck. Or they were afraid to notice him too closely. They were afraid of what they might see." She paused. "I don't believe it. I don't think you just suddenly *go* crazy. I think if you're crazy, you're always crazy, and if somebody even half observant gets to know you, they'll be able to *tell* you're crazy."

"You are dead wrong," Gisella said. "I'm not going to let you go to a bar while you're thinking like this. I swear I'm not. Look, I'll get there before you do. I'll sit in a corner. Gray can go with me. We'll pretend we don't know you."

"I'm not going anywhere with Steve Briggs," Molly promised.

"But you might. The way you're talking, you might."

She gave a strange, knowing smile. "No, I wouldn't. I think he's crazy."

"Don't look like that," Gisella said.

Molly made a looney face. "Why? Do you think I'm crazy?"

"Yes," Gisella squealed. She turned on a faucet and threw a handful of water at Molly. "Do you think *I* am?"

"Damn you," Molly said. She jerked some paper towels from the dispenser to blot her skirt. "Stop it." Gisella was always getting out of hand.

"My true identity is Suzanne Cox," Gisella said, flapping her arms at her sides like wings. "And I'm after your husband." She bent over in heaving laughter.

Molly grabbed her shoulders and pulled her up straight. "You are *not funny*," she said. She drew back her hand, let it fly forward until she saw the shocked, sane face before her. But she could not stop the slap, only the force of it. Gisella eyed her warily.

"It was *your* fault," Molly said. "You say things you shouldn't say." Gisella went to the mirror to brush her shaggy black hair, but Molly knew she was really looking at her pink cheek where she'd been hit.

"You could *tell* me instead of hitting me," Gisella said.

"I *have* told you. I tell you every day that you're saying too much. What if you *are* Suzanne Cox. How do I know you aren't?"

"I won't dignify that with an answer."

"How do I know anything?"

"Two minutes ago you claimed to know it all," Gisella said drily.

The reemergence of her friend's normal tone made Molly suddenly burst into tears. "I'm so sorry I slapped you, Gisella. Please forgive me. I'm not my normal self." Her last words made the tears come faster.

Gisella hugged her distantly.

Molly's tears dried up so suddenly that she couldn't even fake them. Was she crazy? Would Gisella think she wasn't truly sorry? "I know you can't totally forgive me now, but will you eventually?"

Gisella nodded, the hurt, which she kept trying to hide, still evident in her eyes. "I'll try to be more careful about what I say," she offered.

"No-o-o," Molly said. "I don't want you to do that. Please say whatever you want to say. I can't stand it if you aren't yourself. Okay?"

Gisella nodded.

"If you want to kid me, I'll just learn how to take it," she said bravely, forcing a smile upon her pinched lips. "You see, I can do it. I can laugh at myself even in the most dire circumstances." She attempted a small chuckle.

"Keep trying," Gisella said. "Maybe in ten years you'll have it."

Molly arrived at the Hilton Underground just before five o'clock. Whatever job Steve Briggs had would not put him here before now, she thought. She wanted to settle herself in an out-of-the-way corner that would afford her a view of the entire room. Red and black paisley carpeting covered not only the floors but the walls, making the room feel like one big dirty floor. She felt lucky that she'd happened to wear a pants suit today, only recently allowed at work, instead of a miniskirt. A couple of men, who had the worn look of regular hotel guests, turned all the way around on their barstools as she crossed the room. They sat, their feet hung on the middle rungs, their knees wide apart, and watched her. The bartender, a blond with cheeks ruddy from a bad complexion rather than good health, walked over, unwillingly it seemed, to take her order.

"Can you make those two men turn around?" she asked.

He glanced over his shoulder at them. "Not really," he said. What kind of chick was this, he must be wondering, who sat as far as she could from the nearest available men and asked that they not look at her?

The men watched her as she drank her beer and stared at her napkin. It was hard to swallow with those four eyes on her neck. If she were Gisella, she would know how to make them leave her alone.

Gradually, the bar began to fill up. Four men and two women, who looked as if they had come from the same office, took a table near hers, which gave her a feeling of relief. Three women entered and perched on barstools, showing their legs to the two men who'd been watching her. Several couples snuggled in the darker corners, and a number of single men stood near the cash register.

Molly ordered a second beer, although it would probably have been more prudent to stick to one. She hadn't decided how long she would wait for Steve Briggs, but as time passed with no sign of him, she decided she would leave at six. So far, no one had sat particularly close to her, but it wouldn't last. If she wasn't a pickup, why was she here?

"Mind if I join you?" The voice belonged to a not unattractive male with dark, parted hair and thick black eyebrows that seemed to overbalance his small frame. He was not the young man she'd met at the Lotus.

"Is your name Steve Briggs?" Molly asked hastily. "I mean, I'm supposed to be meeting someone by that name."

"So I'll be Steve Briggs," the smooth voice said. He pulled out a chair. He had the kind of pouty smile one sees on male models. "But you're not really him?" she persisted.

"Let's put it this way. I'm him unless somebody else comes along with the same name." Molly shook her head. "That won't do?" the cool voice asked. She kept shaking. He stood up as smoothly as he'd approached her. If anyone was observing him, he would have scarcely looked rebuffed at all. More as if Molly had been turned down by him. She was inclined to explain, he seemed so nice. But he seemed so nice because that was the way people operated in places like this. That was the way people met and went home to bed with perfect strangers: people who sometimes were crazy enough to murder you if you didn't somehow get their number. She thought of Gisella's worries and then she thought about this man who would like to be Steve Briggs. She hadn't observed him long enough to determine whether or not he was crazy, but from what she'd seen, she guessed he just wanted to get laid.

The general din in the bar picked up, as most of the customers neared the end of their second drinks. She idly watched the young man who wasn't Steve Briggs as he wandered among the tables looking for someone who might appeal to him. There was something purposeful about his movement: whomever he met was not going to be met by chance. When last she saw him, he was standing in the outer lobby putting on his overcoat. She expected he would find another bar. This particular happy hour, in an odd deal of the cards, had ended up nearly all male. No one new had come in for some time now, so there was no Steve Briggs. Despite several entreaties by the barmaid, who had finally arrived, Molly did not want another beer. Before long, she would have to deal with the rest of the men who hadn't found companions. It was probably time to leave.

She drained the last of the suds in her glass. Of *course* there was no such person as Steve Briggs. No man would want a woman like Suzanne as his girlfriend. She left her money on the table. As she passed the two men on the stools, her head bowed demurely, one of them muttered, "Stuck-up cunt." Her heart faltered in her chest. Her face flamed. No one had ever called her that before. Her feet became unwieldy blocks, and she concentrated all her attention on them so they would keep moving.

Meekly she mounted the paisley stairs, the relief that there was no Steve Briggs not so important to her anymore. She felt tainted somehow. She wished she had not come here. There was a rustle of movement behind her. Molly turned. Gisella, her expression sheepish, came across the lobby.

"Did he show up?" she asked in a stage whisper.

"I told you there's no such person," Molly said in a distant voice. She stretched out a hand to Gisella, forcing a smile. "My protector," she said, feeling distressed all over again about what had happened that afternoon in the ladies' room.

"I wish he'd shown up. I really do." Gisella's eyes blazed hot with excitement. "Did anything happen?"

"Nothing," Molly said. She wasn't ready to tell about being called a stuck-up cunt. She glanced down the stairs. "Nobody's down there but a bunch of old men on the make." She laughed ironically. Gisella deserved more, though, for trying to watch after her. "You may be right about not knowing who's crazy and who isn't," she offered. She had not been able to peg positively the young man who stopped by her table.

Gisella looked pleased. "I'm glad you finally figured that out." She looked unwilling to leave, but Molly turned toward the door.

"Nothing happened, but I'll tell you every single detail to-morrow. I had two beers," Molly added for a joke.

"I don't want to wait until tomorrow," Gisella moaned.

"Then I'll call you after we eat," Molly said, which she knew she wouldn't do. She didn't want Robert to know that she'd been trying again to verify his story.

Chapter Twelve

"I SABEL wants us to come up for some iced tea." Instead of recradling the telephone receiver, a naked Robert perversely let it drop from his grasp so it banged against the counter and then swung by its cord near the floor. She had just walked in the door from work. He'd telephoned her at the office twice today at times he was supposed to be in class, so she knew he'd cut. He hadn't been able to remember what he was calling about. Now she realized why. He stumbled toward the torn-apart bed, where it appeared he'd spent the day.

"Why didn't you tell her no?" she asked, trying to think about this unwanted invitation rather than Robert's condition.

"I couldn't think of an excuse." His voice was thick like his morning voice. While hanging up her coat, she felt a quick rush of sympathy for him: maybe he was sick. But if he was sick, he wouldn't be smoking. An ashtray filled with butts sat on the floor beside his bed.

"Call her back and tell her I'm exhausted."

"Call her yourself. But she has something to tell us that we'd better go hear."

"What?" she asked. She repeated the question again, this time heatedly: "*What?*" Robert scrunched his pillow around his ears. She walked to the bed and jerked it away. "What does she have to tell us?" she asked, sensing another betrayal. "What have you told our *landlady?*" She spoke the word "landlady" in a derogatory tone, hoping Isabel might hear. She was angry with Isabel for whatever she knew. She was angry that they lived in such proximity to a friend of her parents. "Tell me," she demanded. Robert covered his ears with his hands. He lay on the bed like a log.

Suddenly she stopped asking. In a stiff removed voice she said, "You know, Robert, the one who deserves to lie around is me, not you. It's me she calls. It's me her boyfriend writes to. It's me she wants out of the way. For you, she just feels 'love.' " She dropped the pillow on the bed. "Does Isabel know? Tell me the truth. I'm not going up there until you tell me what she knows."

"I don't know what Isabel knows. I just know she has something important to tell us. I could hear it in her voice."

"Have you been talking to Suzanne?"

He hesitated. "Sort of. Not like I normally talk to people. She's been calling me to say that she loves me and would I please come see her. She sent me a postcard—*me*, not you," he added, fishing around in the drawer of his bedside table.

Molly took the card, which said, "I'm after your balls, baby, and when I get them I'm going to grind them up and feed them to my cat." The message was typed. It looked as if it might have been typed on Molly's typewriter. But she wouldn't mention that now. "That's nice," she said. "That's very classy. I think if I were you, Robert, I would pick nicer friends."

Ignoring her sarcasm, he said, "Not exactly the words of a lover. Would you say?" His bare back propped against the headboard, he pulled the sheet to his waist. His looks suddenly startled Molly, the way they hadn't uncovered. His blond hair was a wreck; he hadn't shaved. He looked beaten.

"Why did you hang around here today?" she asked in a kind voice. "Why didn't you just go to class and ignore all this?" The words had a familiar ring.

"I cut," he said, swinging out of bed. "Do I have your permission to cut class once a year?" She'd thought the question gentle enough not to anger him, but she'd been wrong. He stepped into his underwear and then into the still-belted khakis he'd dropped the night before beside the bed. "We've got to go see Isabel. We don't have a choice. Come on."

"You go," Molly said.

"I want you to come too."

"Have you arranged for Isabel to tell me something that you're scared to tell me?"

"I told you I *don't know* what she wants."

"Then why do I have to go?"

"Because I said so."

"I've stopped taking orders." She walked briskly to the bathroom, which was the only place of escape in this crummy apartment. Robert followed her to the door as if he might try to drag her upstairs, but she quickly locked herself in. She turned on the shower so he couldn't hear anything. Maybe he would think she was going to kill herself.

The shower noise prevented her from hearing what Robert was doing too, and when she finally came out, he was gone. She ran on tiptoe to the door. The car was parked outside. She just didn't want to have to listen to Isabel tell her to forget about Suzanne.

After a while she began to realize that if she didn't go upstairs, they might decide to keep something from her. She washed her face, skipped putting on fresh makeup, and hurried up Isabel's steep side steps. They saw her through the picture window as soon as she saw them. Before she had a chance to knock, Isabel greeted her at the door, a false smile on her face. "Hello, dear," she said. Molly thought of her parents again. Could she ask Isabel not to mention to them whatever she knew?

She took the twin couch opposite Robert. Isabel sat in a chair halfway between. "What's wrong?" she asked, striking what she thought was the same false note Isabel had struck. She noticed that Robert had a piece of paper in his lap. He stretched it across the coffee table toward her, but she ignored him. Isabel's eyes momentarily lost their cheerful guard. In a formal motion Robert placed the paper on the table in front of her.

"What's this?" she asked, her voice suddenly high and haughty. "Another letter?" Boiling tears strained to be free. She told herself that she was not going to cry in front of Isabel and withheld them. Reaching across the table, Isabel took away the letter with her large adult hands.

"It's okay, honey," she said. "It really doesn't make any difference." Already she was folding the letter. It disappeared inside her jacket pocket.

"Give me that," Molly said hysterically. She reached into Isabel's pocket, immediately horrified that she could do such a thing, and withdrew the letter. Isabel did not try to stop her. "I'm sorry," she said quietly, turning her back. She felt deeply ashamed, knowing that Isabel would think her behavior reflected not just on herself but on her mother. "I don't want to stay here," she said, beginning to weep. "I want to go home."

"Maybe you should take her," Isabel suggested to Robert.

He stood dutifully. "Come on, Molly." He walked straight to the door, looking out at the winter darkness that had descended. Isabel nudged her arm. The unread letter in her hand, Molly joined him at the door, unable even to say goodbye.

They walked single-file down the steps, but instead of going to their door, to the single room that so mercilessly bottled them up with each other, they walked in tandem out to the street. She thought he must want to talk to her outside, where the openness might have an inhibiting effect on what she might ask or say or do. But at the end of the driveway, before they could step out into the neighborhood, he said uncomfortably, "Let's go back home." They turned and walked silently into their apartment. Robert slowly circled the room, turning on lamps. She began making up their sour, tangled-looking bed, holding the letter between her chin and her chest while he leaned against the wall. She knew that this bed ought to stay made up forever.

"That is one of nine identical letters," he began slowly, "sent to all our neighbors."

With great deliberation she tucked the spread under the pillows. She worked on each side of the bed until she had formed a perfectly round roll with each pillow. When she finished she stood up, her back to Robert. "I guess I might as well find out what the rest of the world knows," she said.

"They all brought their letters to Isabel. I told her we would move out if she wanted us to."

"Move out?" she asked, turning to face him. "I'm not going anywhere. Why did you say something like that? Now I know she'll call my parents." He didn't answer.

Her face hot and tense, she unfolded the letter, expecting to read more about Robert's balls. But it was much worse:

An open letter to the Forest Street neighborhood:

All of you really must congratulate your neighbor at 309½, Robert Carter. He's expecting. He's been rather quiet about it. Modesty must be overwhelming him. Or, perhaps he isn't passing out cigars because it's his girlfriend who's going to have the baby instead of his wife. Fine fellow, that Robert, a credit to any neighborhood . . .

The letter was unsigned.

Molly lowered herself slowly to the bed, unable to speak. She found Robert's aware, unemotional eyes. But she also saw in them the battle weariness of someone who doesn't know where the next attack is coming from. Her breathing grew quiet; her body passive. This was no longer a question of love, she thought, for she finally knew that Robert could not love Suzanne. This question was bigger than love: it involved another life. One thing she was immediately sure of, even before she found out any more, was that she would never have a baby herself. She couldn't bear to think of such a thing.

"It's another lie," Robert said. "It's just a harder one to take."

She felt her mouth opening and closing but heard no sound. A strange sort of wail filled the room. Eventually she realized it was her voice calling Robert's name. He curled his body around her limp one on the bed, holding her. "Did you make someone else pregnant?" she asked. It seemed so much more intimate than just screwing.

"No, honey. You know I didn't. All she's trying to do is drive us apart."

"She's not driving us apart," Molly said in a low, controlled voice. "We are apart. We're so far apart that we may never get back together again."

"Don't say that."

"It's true," she said, shrugging her shoulders. Making even that slight physical response was unpleasant. She let her whole body go limp again. "I don't love you right now." It was hard for her to believe that she could be this honest.

"Of course you love me."

"Robert, I don't love you. I don't know what that says about me: that I can stop loving you without knowing one way or the other about Suzanne. Maybe it's not being sure that I know the truth. Maybe it's the idea of her being pregnant. That's so much worse than what I thought you did."

"I never did anything."

"You must have. She couldn't make up a baby."

"You *do* love me," he said, pressing his rough beard to her cheek. She didn't want to hurt him again, so she did not reply.

They lay together on the bed for a long time, both trying to understand the new words that had passed between them, while they listened to the pattern of Isabel's movements in the kitchen above as she prepared her supper. Molly tried to imagine being alone. If she didn't start loving Robert again, that was how she would be. She would not stay married as her mother had. Nor would she ever let herself be vulnerable again. The best way not to be vulnerable was never to be involved with anyone.

"I think we should call Suzanne," she said in a studied thoughtful tone.

"Why?" He sounded open to the suggestion.

"I want to know why she sent that letter to our neighbors."

"I can tell you that."

"I'm interested in what *she* has to say. And I want you to call her and ask."

"I don't want to."

She struggled out of the position on the bed they had held for so long. "Then I will."

"*I* will," he said, defeat and pride in his voice. At least he would not allow her to lower herself by calling Suzanne. "It's not going to do any good. But I'll call her if you want her called."

He picked up the phone and began dialing the number. Seeing her pained expression, he explained, "I know her number the same way I'd know if I had cancer." That could possibly be true, she thought, giving him a slight smile.

Before the first ring, he hung up. "I don't want to talk to her," he said. Molly lifted the receiver, but he pushed her away and began redialing. Someone answered.

"This is Robert Carter," he said in a formal voice. "I'm calling to ask why you sent those letters to our neighbors." Molly could hear the shrillness of the reply, but not the exact words. "Sure, Suzanne," he interjected sarcastically every few seconds. He shook his head as if he couldn't believe what he was hearing. "This is such bullshit," he said to Molly and Suzanne at the same time. He was losing patience. "Goodbye, Suzanne," he said loudly. He hung up.

"She says . . ." He paused, composing himself. "She said that her neighbors also have received letters announcing that she's pregnant, and she wanted me to thank *you* for sending them. She said I should check the letters our neighbors got against your typewriter at work." Robert smiled a sort of crazed smile. "She said she was going to sue us for defamation of character."

"Does that mean she's not pregnant?" She felt a sort of guarded relief.

"I guess so." The relief in his voice sounded tentative too.

"It *must* mean she isn't," Molly said. Suzanne's idea of accusing her was rather clever, she thought.

A strange look crossed Robert's face. "You haven't written anyone, have you?"

"What?" she cried.

Robert suddenly laughed as if he were kidding, but he hadn't been.

"I won't answer that," she said. She was reminded of how his not answering her questions made her suspicious rather than confident. "I have not written Suzanne," she said. "I would never write anyone. I would never have anything to do with a person like her." The reminder—that *he* had had something to do with her—hovered uncomfortably between them.

"Can anybody get to your typewriter?" he asked.

"They'd have to know their way around. But the building's always open. I guess she could go there early in the morning and nobody would ever notice her." Shifting tones, she said, "She wouldn't dare. Would she?"

"I don't know. I don't know her any better than you do."

Over supper he wanted to talk about what they were going to say to their neighbors. He thought they ought to try to explain the letter; she thought they should not. "We shouldn't dignify an anonymous letter," she said. "What would we say?"

"Maybe Isabel could say something."

"Don't worry, she'll say plenty."

"Is that mean?" He put his fork, laden with a bite of hamburger steak, on his plate. "I can't eat this," he said. Molly pushed away her plate too.

"Did it sound mean?"

"Sort of."

"I think she'll defend us the best she can. Isabel likes my father," she added ironically.

"*Everybody* likes your father," he said.

She let the comment pass. "Did you tell Isabel everything?" she asked.

"No." With his fork he began fiddling with his food again. "I told her that Suzanne was crazy, that she'd done the same thing to about a hundred other guys in town—"

"Is that true?" Molly interrupted.

"It's just a guess."

She let Robert take her plate to the sink, although she was still hungry. Eating did not seem appropriate. For the first time it seemed that he might be willing to explain things to her, to establish that link of logic she knew was missing.

"I need to tell you something," she said, using "tell" instead of "ask" for the moment. "It's not that I don't love you, but I just don't know what to think. What do you expect of me? What do you think I ought to do? Am I supposed to pretend nothing happened? You don't. You stayed away from school. There must be a reason. Did you know she was going to send that letter? Have other things happened that you haven't told me?" Robert's face told her that she had stumbled onto something. "Has something happened over at the university?"

"I didn't want to tell you," he began. "My professors got a letter yesterday similar to the one she sent to this neighborhood. Only she changed the wording to say I was a fine credit to the university community. *Those* letters were given to Elizabeth, who called me in for a conference."

"Oh, no," Molly said. It appeared that Robert had been under siege just as she had, but unlike her, he had tried to keep the worst parts to himself. "What did Elizabeth say?"

"Nothing. The conference was about whether or not I had decided to stop smoking."

"Have you?" As much as she hated cigarettes, she couldn't believe he'd stopped smoking and she hadn't noticed. She remembered he'd had a cigarette in his hand when hanging up the phone with Isabel.

"I'm trying. She didn't say anything about the letters. Just handed them to me. I didn't look at them until I left her office. That was why I cut today," he finished in a sober voice.

What a fool she'd been, Molly suddenly realized. Robert was telling her the truth; he'd always told her the truth. She had put her marriage in jeopardy for no good reason. There was no need to be cowed by lies, to be unable to hold up her head in the face of untruth. She retrieved her dinner plate from the counter.

"This is the last time," she said. "The last time for all time. I want you to tell me what happened that afternoon once more, and I'll never mention it again."

Robert said, "You asked me what I thought *you* should do," he said, but surrender filled his eyes. "I want you to love me. And if you love me, I want you to do what the love tells you to do." Robert's clichéd phrases had moved her in college as they were unable to move her now. But could she blame him for not being able to express himself in an original way? "Love me as I love you." She wished he would just stop talking.

"Why didn't you want to make love to me that night you saw Suzanne?" she asked. She had already decided that a logical answer could be that the idea of making love that night had too many echoes.

Robert looked confused.

"You remember . . ." she said. Of course, he remembered, she could tell by the blush that crept up his neck. He was surprised that *she'd* remembered.

"I don't know."

"I tried to seduce you. You said you had to study." He had come back from seeing Suzanne with a totally changed view about the You-Ass, too. As if he was making up for something. "It was the same night you offered the car back to me." She made the statement as if it was a charge.

Maybe she would never get the truth out of him. Or maybe he would end up admitting to something that he hadn't done just to end it all. Prisoners of war did that all the time. "I still don't feel like I know exactly what happened."

"Molly, you know the truth." His voice was almost desperate.

"Just listen to me," she said. "Say we wipe the blackboard clean. We never mention Suzanne Cox to each other again. No matter what she does to us. We ignore it all."

"Suits me." Robert always took things literally.

"This is just a supposition," she reminded him. "Say we got married this afternoon. Can I trust you for the rest of my life?"

Robert hesitated slightly before answering, "Yes."

"You don't sound positive."

"I'm trying to be honest. I *think* you can trust me."

"You're not sure?" She must have confused him with all the other questions. "I'm asking you if from now on I can trust you."

"I know what you're asking," he said, folding his hands on the table before him. He sat taller as he said, "If you really want to hear the truth, I don't know whether or not I trust myself."

She looked at him in disbelief.

"I-I must be crazy. There's something wrong with me." He slumped in his chair; his clasped hands fell apart.

Molly rose slowly, standing over him. "Do you realize what you've just said? Do you mean that you can't promise to be faithful to me after all this?"

"I'm not saying I'll be faithful or unfaithful," he said, misery in his voice. "I'm only saying that I'm an unknown entity—even to myself."

"Does this mean that you screwed Suzanne Cox?" Molly asked in a chilling voice.

"You said you wouldn't ask that again. No, it doesn't mean that. But we're starting fresh. That's what you said."

Later that night as they lay beside each other in the dark, not touching and not sleeping, Molly tried to think through what he'd admitted. What she wanted from him was a promise of fidelity after this one minor—in the realm of their lifetimes— indiscretion. For she had decided that he *had* screwed Suzanne, not out of love, but out of some sort of lust. She had decided somehow that she could accept this fact, although she had never been able to accept it before. But she could accept it if she was sure it would never happen again. Robert had said that he didn't know if he could be trusted. Of course, we can trust you, she'd instinctively felt like saying. She wanted to try to talk him out of feeling the way he felt. But such a course had the danger of establishing a base from which he could lie. She somehow had to accept what he'd said as the real Robert, unless this was some sort of strange self-hate.

At two in the morning the telephone rang, and Molly, still wide awake, hurried to answer before it woke Robert. It was probably Suzanne, but just in case it wasn't, she sent up a quick prayer for all the people she loved. The caller hung up. At two-thirty the phone rang again, and they both sat up, but as always she was nearer.

"Next time I'll answer," Robert murmured.

The telephone didn't ring again although she lay there waiting for what seemed like hours. All through the night she thought: he is willing to endure this torture rather than make an absolute commitment to me. Every aspect of her life felt tinged with melancholy. Her father and mother's relationship was the true reality; what she'd expected for herself was only immature idealism. This was Robert's gift to her in the aftermath of Suzanne Cox: grinding, unadulterated honesty. Maybe she hadn't wanted to know the truth. Near morning she decided he must be punishing himself. He loved her: he said so over and over again. Didn't he realize he would lose her if he could not promise to be faithful?

Chapter Thirteen

FROM the second floor balcony where she always stood, Suzanne watched the glossy black hair—as alive as a cat—move through the lobby. Hoping to go unnoticed, the owner of the hair chose to hug the circumference of the large room rather than striking a diagonal across it. Tonight she had hit upon the idea of blowing her nose as she walked. People rarely stopped someone so engaged. Other nights, the girl had studied a book or rummaged through her purse to avoid meeting anyone. The anonymous creature—Caroleen York, daughter of Mr. and Mrs. E. G. York of Lake Waccamaw, North Carolina, freshman piano major, third-ranked in a high school class of sixty-five, recipient of numerous Girl Scout awards, member of the Lake Waccamaw United Methodist Church choir—always arrived first. Robert, since he had "complications," in other words, a wife, was always late, although Suzanne thought he would be late regardless. *He* hid from no one, always choosing the diagonal as he raced across the green and white checkerboard floor in squeaking tennis shoes, *not* on his way to practice singing. Was it possible he didn't suspect he was being observed? Could anyone be followed for a month and not realize it? Could he want *her* to report him to Molly?

Jemma was gone from the pancake house, a victim of some skillful innuendo, so Suzanne had become the nighttime hostess. She'd hired an extra waitress for the nights she was gone, which made the nights she went to work a breeze. The extra waitress covered the cash register whether Suzanne was there or not, so all she did now was drink coffee, smoke cigarettes, think of things she would like to eat, and call Robert. None of the girls had any thoughts of reporting her. Whenever she called in sick, they assumed she was out with Bennie.

For a whole month nothing had changed. Robert met Caroleen for lunch, walked Caroleen to class, talked to Caroleen on the library steps, screwed Caroleen—or so she assumed—on the wooden floor of his practice room, which undoubtedly had become less uncomfortable with the arrival ten days ago of a quilt under Robert's arm. It was the quilt—a bit of color in a gray series of arrivals and departures—that had made her realize how bored she was. She'd been too interested in it: who made it?—Robert's grandmother or Molly's?, what bed was it stripped from?, who else had it offered warmth or padding to? She'd imagined a whole series of communications with Molly regarding it. Which might be just what Robert wanted her to do. In short, she was trying to make something out of nothing; this was probably the reason she'd planned tonight's diversion. Not that there were actual plans. She'd met a guy, a student here, who attracted her in a sort of perverse way. She thought he was queer, and if he was, could he do it with a girl? Maybe when Kearns arrived, they would knock on Robert's door and introduce themselves. She would try to notice if Robert turned Kearns on.

She thought Robert had stopped taking voice lessons. He never arrived on campus before noon, so after that first week, she'd stopped her own early arrival at the Tristan and Isolde and slept late too. When he got off the bus now—the bus she had taught him to ride—he went straight to the dining hall, always emerging with Caroleen at his side. He didn't go near the music building until night, when all the professors were gone. On campus he was always smiling, but whenever she telephoned him at home, his voice was gruff and angry before she even said who she was.

She had hung around the music building for so many weeks now that she had come to be regarded as another student. Her name was Dorothy Johnston, she'd said. A flute major who'd previously attended Stratford College in Danville, Virginia, before she'd drunk a beer in front of an upperclass informant. She let it be known that she didn't have much interest in the flute, which was the reason no one ever saw her with her instrument. She didn't really have to have a career, she'd explained, because she was one of those children born with a million dollars in the bank. She was getting a degree to satisfy her father, a self-made man who had dropped out of school in the fifth grade.

Her stories were what had attracted Kearns, a drummer who spent his nights playing jazz at a college spot called Mickey's and his days smoking grass. Suzanne had confided that a similar schedule appealed immensely to her. She had arranged to meet him on the balcony tonight to discuss their future.

She leaned over the banister to give herself a clear view of the triple front doors. Caroleen had been waiting twenty minutes. How could Robert be so insensitive? There he was, finally, with Kearns right behind. He headed across the lobby, while Kearns removed his glasses to clean them. Kearns was not handsome and he was much thinner than Robert, but he was tall and tallness took away her breath like nothing else. A man seemed so in control when he was tall, so strong, so dominant. Her own smallness became emphasized, unlike the way she felt when she had a boyfriend her own size. She didn't want to look like pals with the man she was screwing. She wanted to look like lovers. Taker and taken. She wanted people to wonder how they did it. If her mouth met his breast, her foot, his knee. Kearns had thin lips and a pale complexion. His chest stuck out effeminately as he climbed the stairs, but she thought he would do.

"Do you have a car?" she asked, leaning over the banister so he could see down her dress. For a month Robert had followed the same schedule. What else did she need to know?

"Yes," he answered hesitantly, as if he was afraid he was going to be asked to give without getting. He lifted his shoulders and then dropped them. Why the hell was she flirting with him?

"Do you fuck boys or girls?" she asked, angry with herself.

Kearns grinned. She was allowed to say "fuck," she knew, because she was assumed to be rich and, therefore, reckless. Or maybe he viewed her as one of the "boys." "Why do you want to know?"

"Curiosity," she said, an open sneer on her face because of the obvious answer.

He climbed the last few steps to the upstairs lobby where they were alone. It was eight-thirty in the evening, the middle of a practice hour. He stepped toward her, putting his hand on her waist, and then he slid the hand up to cup the underside of her breast. Neither of them took their unwavering gaze off the other. He did not smile at her pretended astonishment.

"Want to go home with me?" she asked, taking his hand away and sliding along the banister until her body touched his.

"More than anything in the world."

Her breasts tilted upward, her hips tightened, her mouth opened. She could close her eyes and imagine that this man was Robert. She saw a bulge in Kearns's pants and reached teasingly but didn't touch.

"Let's go," he said. She checked his watch.

"I need to stay for about ten more minutes," she said. "I'm spying on somebody. Two people, actually."

"What for?"

"Curiosity."

"You're a very curious lady," he said.

"It's how you find out what you want to know."

But he was ready to go. She could tell by the portentous air around them, by how he looked dissatisfied and maybe even uninterested if he was going to have to wait. The magic of this moment could vanish. She glanced at the diminishing bulge in his pants. *Would* vanish, no question.

"Let's go," she said impetuously. She moved toward him and pressed her breasts just below his belt, barely seizing the tail of that disappearing moment. The tension between them flowered again, was tight and promising. They tripped down the long stairs like girlfriends. Suzanne felt her jeans moving against her.

They drove, one hand each on each other's private parts, to her apartment. She giggled when after he parked he wouldn't let her out of the car. Then she broke loose from his hard kiss, opened the door of his Mustang, and rushed up the outside steps. She turned on the porch light so he could see the way, left the door ajar, and then, in her bedroom, stripped quickly, dropping her clothes on the far side of the bed. She turned on the lamp that had a scarf draped over its shade.

Kearns called her by her made-up name when he came in the door, but she didn't answer, only lay carefully on the bed so that even the springs wouldn't summon him. "Dorothy?" he called again, anticipation in his voice.

Her name wasn't Dorothy. He didn't even know whose apartment he was in. Typical play-around man. He seemed to stop in the living room, probably to take off his jacket and a rakish cap he'd produced from a pocket just before they left campus.

She lifted her head from her pillow. For some reason she lay naked on top of her bed covers. What time was it? Had she fallen asleep and missed work? Her nipples were at attention. Chills ran through her shoulders. There was a noise in her living room. She sat up. Someone was in her living room. But she had locked the door. How had anyone gotten in?

Steps—confident, swaggering steps—moved toward her bedroom. She drew her knees toward her shoulders, hiding as much of her nakedness as she could. The doorway filled with the gaunt, tall figure of a stranger whose lips looked hungry. He wore a white cableknit sweater and jeans and he slipped out of his shoes while she watched.

"Who are you?" she asked in a childlike voice. Men were unlikely to rape children, she thought.

"I'm the doctor," the man said, smiling. "What's the problem, little girl?"

"You don't even know my name," she said snidely.

"Dorothy," he whispered. "Dorothy Johnston."

"Wrong," she said.

He looked a little surprised. "All right," he said with some bravado. He had unfastened his pants but held them around his waist. "What's *my* name?"

Suzanne looked at him in a humoring way. "*I* certainly have no idea. Shall I guess?" She eased her legs straight on the bed, looking at the three lines whose intersection marked her irresistible vortex. Her nipples were less shriveled now, but she was still chilled. Her flesh longed for the imprint of his hands.

"Me Kearns, you Dorothy," he said for a joke.

"Kearns who?"

"Kearns Harris. I play the drums, remember? You invited me home with you."

Suzanne looked astonished. "I've never seen you before in my life," she said. "My name is *not* Dorothy. My name is Suzanne Cox."

The stranger gave her an uncertain look. He rezipped his fly and threaded his belt through the buckle.

"I thought you were going to rape me. I thought you were going to nail me to the wall." Her voice alternated between alarm and coyness. She suddenly rose up on her knees, her nakedness like a painting he could touch. "You *are* going to nail me to the wall, aren't you? Kearnsy? Kearns-whoever-you-are?"

He shook his head. He began tucking his shirt carefully into his pants. "Not like this," he said. He turned his back on her and walked into the living room.

"Kearns!" she called in a normal voice. "Kearns Harris! It was a joke. Come on back." She felt his hesitation all the way from the living room. "Kearns!" She didn't want to leave the bed where she was so happily settled. "Kearns?" He still didn't answer. When she reached the living room he was buttoning his jacket with the same pained expression on his face.

"It was a joke," she said.

"It may have been."

"Please, Kearns." She flung her bare arms around his jacket, her breasts brushing the rough wool fabric, but he pushed her away.

"I've got to go," he said.

She began to unbutton his jacket, but he grabbed her wrists and held them. He seemed no longer to notice that she was naked, that her body was his for the taking.

"I'm leaving now," he said. "I want you to stop trying to make me stay." Behind his glasses his green eyes were placid, unseeing.

"I'll scream," she threatened.

"No, you won't." He changed his hold on her so that one of his large hands shackled both her wrists. Without trying to be gentle, he turned her half around and smacked her ass with the flat of his palm. She lay sobbing and injured on the bed as he slammed the front door behind him. Her skin stung where he'd been rough with her. But most of all her chest ached. She'd wanted him like she'd wanted no other man but Robert, but he'd rejected her.

She pulled her nightgown from under her pillow, her anger seeming to grow instead of subside. This was Robert's fault. Because Kearns reminded her so much of the man she loved, she hated him. Masturbating now might help how she felt, but she refused to give Robert that pleasure. She believed that there were no real secrets in the world. For example, although Molly might not "know" yet that Robert had made love to her, he did in a very real sense *know* it. It was more than intuition. It was a sort of omniscient knowledge that all people had, if they recognized it. If she provided her own sexual release, Robert would sense it and laugh.

With her nightgown on, she'd begun to warm up. But the tension that she hoped was only from being cold had not eased. Perhaps never again would she be able to enjoy a normal relationship with a man. Perhaps she had become frigid, and, if so, she was going to sue Robert. The courts were her only answer she was beginning to realize. There would be the paternity suit, of course, and now this frigidity suit, which was probably a psychological question that the courts had never before considered.

She'd mentioned nothing about her baby to anyone for so long, and suddenly she wondered if everyone but she had forgotten about the little thing. Molly's parents had never answered her letter requesting funds, and Robert refused to discuss child support. He'd accused her of trying to blackmail him, but there was no blackmail in the facts.

When he answered the telephone he sounded ebullient as if

he'd just socked it to Caroleen. It was unfair for him to continue having everything that he'd had before, while her life was essentially ruined. He hadn't been content simply to hang on to Molly but had added a mistress—while Suzanne, who was four months pregnant, though scarcely showing at all, was unable to let a man touch her.

"Don't hang up," she said, her voice rasping over the lines. Robert let out a long bored sigh, which infuriated her.

"What do you want?"

"I need to talk to you about our baby."

"I had nothing to do with any baby," he said. At least he hadn't hung up.

"Caroleen," she said.

"What?"

"Caroleen."

"What are you talking about?" he asked, but she could hear the muffled panic in his voice.

She also heard Molly in the background. "Just hang up on her," she said.

Foolishly, in view of what she'd just conveyed she knew, Robert kept talking. "You're a nut. Do you know that? You ought to be put away."

"*I* ought to be put away?" She laughed harshly.

In the background Molly said, "Let me talk to her."

"She's all yours." Robert's voice was suddenly distant from the receiver. He *must* want her to tell Molly. But this was an opportunity she hadn't had a chance to evaluate.

"Suzanne?" Molly said.

"The one and only."

"Just listen," Molly said patronizingly. "You might as well stop all this. Nobody believes you, so you might as well leave us alone. We aren't going to break up. We're very happy together, and nothing you can do or say . . ." Molly's voice faltered. She was handing the phone back to Robert. "I can't talk to this person," she wept to Robert. "I just can't."

"Goodbye, Suzanne," Robert said.

"I need to talk to you. About Caroleen."

"No." Why didn't he sound more afraid?

"Either talk to me or I'll see you in court," she screamed, finally unable to contain herself.

"Let me know the date," he said. In the background she could hear Molly making requests: "Tell her to stop calling Isabel. Tell her to stop writing me letters." Robert covered the phone.

"Tell your stupid wife to fuck herself," Suzanne said. Robert hung up.

When she called back, the line was busy and then busy some more. She called Mrs. Gant and Molly's parents and hung up on them. That was all she would do tonight. She was tired. Maybe a bath would help or a glass of warm milk for the mother-to-be. Perhaps she ought to relax her self-imposed rule and masturbate. Pregnant women wanted to do it and do it because they knew they couldn't get in trouble, a second time anyway. As long as she could stand it, though, she was determined to wait for Robert, now that Kearns was gone.

Chapter Fourteen

FEELING for her glasses on the bedside table, Molly sat up, carefully holding her feet poised above the cold floor until she could see well enough to stick them directly into her bedroom slippers. It was still dark, only seven o'clock according to the glowing dial on her bedside table, on a Saturday morning. The doorbell rang twice more, insistently.

"We have company, Robert," she mumbled, sticking her sleepy arms into her robe. "You might want to put something on." Her voice stiffened with sarcasm, since she already expected this early morning visitor to be more harassment, perhaps even Suzanne herself. Robert lay motionless beneath the sheet.

She cracked open the door. Outside stood a man wearing a thick down jacket who smiled at her. "Maybe we're early," he said. He moved slightly aside, and she saw people beyond him. Several strange cars were parked in the driveway and out on the street. "Or maybe we've got the wrong house." He looked up toward Isabel's door, which was also dark, and pulled a copy of the morning newspaper out of his back pocket. Molly noticed her own newspaper on the doormat at his feet.

"We can't *all* have the wrong house," a nasal female voice behind him said.

"Maybe if you told me what you want?" Molly asked timidly. From inside, Robert called to her to shut the door.

"Honey, you're having a garage sale," the brawny man in front of her said. "The paper says you have a roomful of Stanley furniture."

"It does?" Molly opened the screen and bent quickly to pick up her own paper.

"Molly!" Robert yelled.

"Could just *you* come in?" she asked the kind-faced man. "I'm sorry," she said to the rest of the people. "There's not enough room for everybody. Also, my husband's"—she grabbed a word— "sick."

"You don't need to look at your own paper," the man said, following Molly to the kitchen table. "I got one open right here." She saw him looking around their small living quarters. "Where's all the furniture?"

"All what . . . ?" she said and then stopped.

"I'm a used-furniture dealer. So's all them others except one lady, I believe, who was just looking for a good sofa."

Robert sat up in bed and lit a cigarette. One side of his bushy blond hair was mashed flat. "We don't have any furniture for sale," he intoned.

The kind man looked over in his direction. The doorbell rang again. "That's probably somebody thinking I'm getting it all," the man said. He looked around once again. "But it don't look like there's much to get."

"I didn't run this ad," Molly said. "My father works for Stanley and we have a few pieces, but nothing for sale."

"Our furniture's not for sale," Robert said irritably.

"Who he?" the man asked with a quick grin. This was not his fault. Molly wished Robert would realize that.

She said, "A lot of things like this have been happening to us lately. Don't mind him. He's just upset."

From the bed: "You're damn right I'm upset. It's seven o'clock in the morning. Would you mind leaving?"

The man paid no attention at all to Robert, who did look rather ineffective, obviously naked under a sheet pulled to his waist. Still, Molly felt the need to explain.

"It's not his fault, Robert. He was simply answering an ad. I'm really sorry," she said to the visitor. "Do you think you could explain to everybody for me?" He sighed and led her to the door;

outside the size of the group had doubled. "My God," she muttered.

"You ought to put a sign on your door," the man advised. "There's bound to be more coming, if there's this many here now." He turned to face her, reaching toward but not quite touching her hand. "Don't worry. They got thirty more yard sales to go to today. This one just looked the best."

"It's cold, Molly," Robert called. He began coughing, but it was only his cigarette cough.

The man leaned toward her. "If that's your husband, he's a real pill," he said.

"He's just upset," she repeated, maintaining the blandest of expressions.

"We all are," the man said, and then he turned his back so she was finally able to close the door.

Molly rested her forehead against the smooth paint of the door jamb. "You shouldn't be so mean," she said in a muted enough monotone so that no one outside could hear. "He's getting rid of a dozen people for us. Besides—"

"Besides what?"

"You're only mad because somebody woke you up. You don't even care that all those people came here for nothing. *Do* you?"

"As a matter of fact, I don't."

"They weren't *all* dealers," she went on sadly.

"So?"

"So, I'm humiliated."

"You don't even know them."

"It doesn't matter," she said, draping her arms around the proud back of one of the wing chairs. "They know me."

"I'm so tired of listening to this," he said.

"Find somebody else then. Call Suzanne. I'm sure she'd love to hear from you. Or maybe she hears from you all the time."

Robert scrambled naked out of the bed, but as he reached the telephone, the doorbell rang again. At her desk Molly scribbled a sign with magic marker that said the newspaper ad was erroneous. When she finally answered, a nicely dressed woman in a gray shearling coat was tiptoeing down the driveway. She looked vaguely familiar, possibly a friend of Molly's mother. Perhaps Molly should be polite and explain in person to the woman, who had now reversed her path. Instead, she hurriedly taped up her sign and closed the door.

Robert came out of the bathroom.

"You know I don't want you to call her," she said, her anger already dissipated by how defeated she felt. "Take the phone off the hook. Our number's in the paper, too."

"I'm going back to bed," he said.

Slipping out of her robe, Molly climbed between the sheets. She put her arms around his chilled body, trying to lure her mind back to some sort of thoughts of affection. This wasn't Robert's fault either, she forced herself to admit. A long time ago it was, but not now. Or was it? How long would he be accountable for what Suzanne did? A strict examination of the facts might say forever. A charitable one would set him free. Robert began coughing, and she relaxed her embrace. When he stopped, she held him close again. This time, protective feelings welled in her, which was a sort of love, wasn't it? "You said you were going to quit smoking," she said in a babying way. She tried to think about this bigger thing: Robert's health was more important than anything that had happened so far.

"I will when I'm ready," he answered.

They lay in the semilight, listening to furniture seekers trudge up the driveway, stop to read the sign, and leave. She ought to call Isabel and explain what was going on. Around eleven she arose and made French toast without turning on any lights. They ate and then went back to bed. People still occasionally came and went, but no one rang the doorbell. It was as if they were in some secret hiding place.

At one o'clock Molly awoke to find Robert quietly dressing.

"I've got to go practice for the opera," he said in a thick scratchy voice.

"When are tryouts?" she asked, hoping to sound interested.

She knew he had been practicing regularly, expecting a major role. She contemplated their rescued wing chairs while he answered, "Next week." If, in fact, a note to prospective customers was taped to their front door, then this morning's events had actually happened. "Will you drop me off at the shopping center?" she asked. Then, "Never mind. All I really want to do is drink a little tea and listen to some records."

"Sounds tempting," he said, "but I feel stir crazy. When I come home, we'll go to a movie. Look in the paper and pick one out."

She saw the newspaper that contained the ad. Yes, Suzanne had advertised a yard sale at their house. What would she do next?

"I'll probably be gone most of the afternoon."

She dragged herself out of bed to turn on the radio. "By the way, do you think we should be keeping records of what she's doing to us?" she asked.

Robert grimaced. "That's the trouble with you. She's all you ever think about. If you would ever reach the point where you don't care, all this would stop." He looked accusingly at her. "Until then, count on being awakened, count on being harassed at work, count on her inviting strangers to our house."

"She's not all I think about," Molly protested.

"Why did you let that man in this morning?"

"I was trying to be nice to an innocent bystander."

"No, you weren't. You were trying to be a martyr. You were prolonging the agony as long as you could."

"I was *not*," she cried. "I was being considerate." *Had* she gone to undue pains to explain? Had she *allowed* herself to be humiliated?

"Suzanne's whole point is to upset you." He reached into the closet for his jacket. "Your whole point is to let her."

Molly shook her head. "Her whole point is to make us split up," she said.

"What for? Why all the energy? She knows I hate her guts." Robert grasped the doorknob, ready to leave.

"Why doesn't she bother *you?* Why *me* all the time?"

"She can't upset me," he said. "I don't care what she says or does. But you do. She could tell you all sorts of lies about me now, and you'd believe every word."

"That's not true."

"Wait and see."

"I don't believe *anything* she says, Robert."

"I hope not." He looked intently at her, his eyes like thumbtacks pinning up her promise.

"When will you be home?" she asked. Although she tried to make the question casual, those words spoken aloud sounded suspicious.

But Robert's thoughts were out the door: only his voice remained for her to hold on to. "Let's plan on going to the five o'clock show and then having Italian at Deno's."

"Deno's has gotten so expensive."

"You need it," he said. Her unnoticed smile faded. "See you about quarter to five." He returned momentarily with the mail. "I'm not even going to look at this. What I don't know can't hurt me," he said instructively. "You hear?"

Molly knew that the correspondence lying on the small carved table near the door contained something from Suzanne. When the You-Ass's motor turned over, she thumbed through it, finding a postcard, another Madonna and Child, addressed to Robert. He was right: this unfolding evil had mesmerized her, created a willing actress in the play of her own demise. Would a psychiatrist advise her to answer the phone with a steady hello, never slamming it down?, to meet anyone named Steve Briggs with perfect equanimity?, to close the door in some furniture dealer's face with no explanation?

Postcards were a popular form of correspondence for both Steve Briggs and Suzanne Cox, it seemed. To send them you paid only six cents, but what you got was a message available to the entire world, including the mailman, the landlady, and whatever furniture buyers might flip through your mailbox. Turning over the card, she read:

Robert,

    You know I work every *night. Is it too much to ask to be left in peace in the daytime when I sleep? I just can't cope with the phone calls. They are driving me half out of my mind. Tell Molly I'll do anything if she'll stop.*

Love,
Suzanne

    It was as though she was laughing, the thick sound that came from her chest, but there was no pleasure either in the sound or deep inside her body where the laugh originated. It hurt, this laugh, the way trying to inhale hurt, but she couldn't stop her heaving chest. How absurd, even insulting, she thought. How almost comical. She was innocent. Who would believe otherwise? A small fear, like a lone cloud, pushed into her mind, but she pushed it out, going to her desk and drawing out the fine engraved stationery that she'd used to say thank-you for her wedding presents. With a fountain pen, suiting the solemnity she felt, she wrote in neat script:

Dear Miss Cox:

    I would never stoop to call you on the telephone anonymously. Such activity is reserved for more desperate minds than mine. I also wish to inform you that a diode device has been placed on my telephone and on the telephone of my landlady. Perhaps you will now refrain from your unlawful use of the telephone system. Your letters, including the recent red herring, have been turned over to the U.S. Postal Service and to a lawyer.

Truthfully,
Molly Carter

    The finished letter disturbed her beyond all of its untrue claims. Although she'd wanted to sound intelligent, she thought she sounded pompous instead. Furthermore, wouldn't Suzanne love to have a sample of her handwriting? Taking a fresh sheet of paper, she copied the letter over, this time using print instead of cursive. But, when she finished, she realized that a printed letter made her appear as fiendish as Suzanne. She could type the letter, she guessed, but she would have to use her office typewriter. Perhaps she shouldn't answer the letter at all. Say the correspondence wound up in a court of law. Molly's sounded more intimidating, as she had fully intended it to, but Suzanne's sounded more injured. How could the truth be discovered if both parties claimed the same injuries and produced identical evidence? Perhaps Robert was right that the best course of action was no action at all.

But, say she mailed the letter. Suzanne could decide to install her own diode device and then set Molly up. All she would have to do would be to drop by once or twice a day and telephone herself from Molly's place of business. No, someone would have to be at her house to answer, thus tripping the diode. Steve Briggs would have to help, if there was a Steve Briggs.

Molly stuck the letters inside her desk, deciding for the moment not to decide. Before she left the apartment again, though, she would burn her samples. Suzanne might be going through her garbage. She got out the letters. What if she forgot them? What if Robert discovered them? He might even think that she had been secretly harassing Suzanne this entire time.

The doorbell rang—someone who didn't believe the sign—while she was standing at the sink with the letters and a pack of matches. She hurried to the window and saw the profiles of her parents. How could she open the door at two-thirty in the afternoon still wearing her bathrobe? She had the right to take a lazy day, she supposed, or better, a sick one.

She tucked her uncombed hair behind her ears to give herself a neater look. "What a pleasant surprise," she exclaimed, opening the door. Her father was gazing up the bank at Isabel, who had come out of her door to say hello. Her mother, wearing a dress-length poncho and black boots, swept into the apartment. Dad, in his own physical impeccability, followed, ending Isabel's inquiries.

"We wondered if you were still alive," her mother said. "And

I see, *hardly.*" She referred to the fact that Molly was not dressed.

"Hi, sweetheart," her father said, brushing his cheek against hers.

She felt a sudden extraordinary warmth for her mother's gruffness, her father's placidity, that made her wonder why she hadn't sought them out sooner. Who cared about her more than they did? Who but your parents always loved you no matter what? Impulsively she threw one free arm around her mother's neck, the other, around her father's, and pulled them close. Neither minded being close to her, but she could feel them straining away from each other.

"It will take me one second to get dressed," she said, letting them go. "I've had a lazy day." Her mother rearranged some bobby pins in her bun as if Molly had jarred it loose. Suddenly Molly remembered the postcard on her desk and the two versions of her answer, lying in the kitchen sink.

"Why dress now?" her mother asked wryly. "It's almost bedtime."

"You don't mind?" Molly asked. If she disappeared into the bathroom, they might discover her letters while browsing about.

Her parents stood stiffly, looking around, as did Molly for a moment. The bed wasn't made, breakfast dishes were still on the table, Robert's underwear lay on the floor by the bed.

"Take off your coats," Molly said, touching the nape of her mother's poncho. "I'm sorry for this mess. It doesn't usually look like this."

"It usually looks worse," her mother said. She'd been serious, but now she grinned as if she'd been joking.

"I'll get rid of these," Dad said. With one black wing-tip shoe he swept Robert's underwear under the bed. Molly needed to regain some sort of control: it was as if they were a search-and-seize patrol. Her father walked toward her desk, his attention caught by Suzanne's postcard, which was turned picture-side up. Her mother, halfway out of her poncho, asked for Molly's help. Passing her mother by, Molly went after her father, her hands reaching to his shoulders to take his coat.

"Help mother," she whispered. Her father moved hastily in her mother's direction, but she had managed to take off the poncho alone. She gave them both her long-suffering look. Molly seized the postcard and threw it into her desk drawer.

They weren't really nosy. It was a longtime family habit to reacquaint themselves with the place she lived each time they visited. It was her habit to do the same at their house. "Looking for something?" her mother often asked her, a line she'd never been able to bring herself to say to them.

Her mother walked toward the kitchen, passing by the sink to study the favorite cartoons and editorials Molly had pasted on the refrigerator. Molly stuck the unburned letters in the pocket of her robe. Thank God they had arrived before she struck the first match. She would never have been able to explain the odor of fire.

"Will you two please come sit down and talk to me?" she asked. "Mother. Father," she added sternly. And then suddenly they were sitting in the wing chairs, the Stanley wing chairs that had not been sold today.

"What is that strange sign on your door?" her mother asked. Her hands were folded in her lap; her legs crossed at a sharp angle, showing off their shapeliness.

"Oh, *that*," Molly grimaced. "A mix-up. The wrong address was put in the paper."

"The wrong name, address, *and* telephone number?" her father asked. So they'd seen the ad.

"It was a composing room slip-up," she started, shaking her head over all those crazy mistakes the composing room made. "You see, Robert had an ad in the paper for new guitar students, and the address got transposed with an address where somebody was selling some Stanley furniture." She grinned idiotically, fluttering her hands slightly.

Neither of them smiled back. Their eyes were heavy with sympathy, parents watching a child fail. Her father opened the front of his jacket. Molly saw a letter sticking out of the inside breast pocket. She felt her false smile, her bright gestures slip away.

Together they came to the bed where she sat listlessly, her head bowed, her hands silent. Her father put his arm around her; her mother rubbed one hand. She smelled the fragrances each of them used.

"Let's have it," she said.

She could not help but focus on their six side-by-side knees: her mother's stocking-covered ones, her own unshaven ones sticking out of the robe, her father's blue-trousered ones. Cradled in her father's blunt fingers was yet another letter. Her mother's hands lay folded in jeweled reverence. Dad jiggled one knee, sending tremors through the mattress, not realizing he was making them all incongruously bounce until Molly lay a restraining hand on his knee.

"We'll *tell* you what it says," he said, tucking the letter back into his pocket.

"Carroll," her mother instructed. "It would be easier on everybody simply to let her read it. She'll want to read it anyway."

Her father reproduced the letter, sliding it into her lap. She guessed she was expected to open it in front of them and respond appropriately. But for the first time here was a letter that she didn't care to see. Could she say that? The matches still lay by the sink. Neither of them would prevent her from burning the letter. Then, if she ever wanted to know what it said, she would have to ask.

The confident hands that pulled the fragile onion skin out of the envelope seemed not to belong to her. There was still dread, but it was the kind of mild dread one feels about the evening news as opposed to the bomb. Suzanne's letters were inevitable: nothing they pronounced could upset her anymore. Eventually everyone she loved would know about Suzanne. There was some comfort in her helplessness to prevent it. She unfolded the letter to read what would not upset her.

> Dear Mr. and Mrs. Covington:
>
> I am writing to you because I don't know where else to turn. You see, I am pregnant by your daughter's husband. I already know what a mistake it was to get involved with

*Robert, but when I first started seeing him, I didn't realize
he was married. I actually thought he loved me until the
day I told him that part of me and part of him had made
a permanent connection.*

*I don't want to hurt Robert or your daughter. I care too
much about him to do that. But I have tried to communicate
to him the fact that I must have some money. I work as a
waitress, so you can imagine what my income is. Since
Robert doesn't work, the money must come from somewhere
else, which is why I am writing you. Please let me know as
soon as possible if you can help me out. The baby, in a
sense, will be your grandchild.*

Thanking you in advance, I am

Suzanne Cox

Molly's throat thickened as if it were going to close and suffocate
her. She swallowed hard several times. "Grandchild," she said
aloud, her mouth twisting in disgust. "How ridiculous. There
isn't even a baby." Was it too complicated to explain? Would
her parents understand that Suzanne had written letters to her
own neighbors? Was there a baby or not? Fresh shame and un-
certainty filled her. If she wasn't pregnant, why was Suzanne
asking her parents for money? Had she asked Robert for money
too?

"How could she do this?" Molly asked, crumpling the letter
in her hands. The easy way the onion skin succumbed made her
want to destroy more things. Like the lamp or Robert's stereo.
But her parents were here, both trying to put an arm around her.
She stood, shaking herself free of their touches, moving away
from their pity.

"You aren't going to give her a dime," she said, angry tears
springing to her eyes. Her lungs seemed to have shrunk, pre-
venting her from drawing even one real breath. She sat on a
chair, her face in one of the corners so she wouldn't have to look
at them.

"We're not worried about the money," her father said. "We're
worried about you. Are *you* going to give her some money?"

"What are you talking about?" she asked.

"Why are you trying to sell your furniture?"

"I'm not," she said instantly.

Her mother said, "I can't bear to think that you would sell the things we've given you instead of asking for money." She stretched her arms toward Molly. "Honey, we love you."

Molly stared at the long beautiful arms, knowing that the refuge they offered could only be temporary. Still, she longed for someone to take over.

"We also want to know what's going on between you and Robert," her father said.

"Let me tell you the whole story," she said, letting her exhaustion show in her eyes. "First of all, I was honestly not trying to sell our furniture. This woman, Suzanne Cox, put that ad in the newspaper just to harass us. Of course, I have no way of proving that. I'll probably even get the bill for the ad." The very company she worked for was being used against her. Of *course*, Suzanne could figure out how to accuse Molly with the diode.

"Between Robert and me things are pretty good," she continued. "He says that he didn't have an affair with Suzanne, that if she is pregnant, he isn't the father. She took one guitar lesson from him in December, and according to him, she's probably mentally ill. He doesn't want us to split up or anything."

"Do you?" her mother asked.

"Of course not. This kind of thing happens all the time. Women accusing perfect strangers of rape. You know, the preacher and the fourteen-year-old. Who knows whether the man did it or not? But . . . Robert says he didn't. And I believe him. I really do." Her parents avoided looking at each other. "What do you two think?" Molly asked. She felt strangely righteous, thinking how superior her relationship with Robert was to theirs.

"I agree with you," her father said. The lines in his face seemed to deepen, making him look just past his prime.

"I agree when there's a doubt like this," her mother said. "But I would not agree to a future filled with the same thing. You'll just have to decide if you can trust Robert over the long haul."

She began searching her purse for her cigarettes. "Otherwise, I'd get rid of him now."

"Kate!" her father said sharply. "What a horrible thing to say. This is your daughter, not one of your bridge friends. Don't pay any attention to her, Molly. If Robert says he wasn't unfaithful, he wasn't. You can't say you'll give him one more chance. He hasn't taken his first chance yet."

The father with whom she'd almost always been aligned suddenly seemed a representative of men rather than his own individual self. "I'm not going to stay married to a run-around," she said evenly. "I mean, he's not one now, but if he turns out to be, I'm going to divorce him."

"That's understandable," her father said. "At least you have an open mind." Her mother cleared her throat, but her father chose not to look in her direction.

"Who is this Suzanne Cox?" her mother asked. "I've always hated the name Suzanne. Sounds like a pig. Soooozannne."

"Grind her into the dirt, Kate," her father said sarcastically.

Molly threw up her hands. "Would either of you like a Coke?" she asked.

Her parents lowered their voices, but continued arguing.

"If you don't stop, I'm not going to tell you another thing, and I'm going to ask you to leave." She went to the kitchen, and by the time she returned, her parents had moved back to the wing chairs, leaving the bed for her. She handed each of them a glass.

"I've known about it since right before Christmas," she said, feeling suddenly expansive. The story was so horrible: it felt good to be able to tell someone, especially two people so sympathetic to her. "She's written everybody in our neighborhood. I'm surprised Isabel hasn't told you." Molly looked at them closely, but both faces were blank. "She calls us all the time and then hangs up."

"That's what those calls are all about," her father said.

"What calls?" Molly asked.

"We've been getting some late calls. No one says anything. Then they hang up."

Her mother said, "And I thought it was someone for him."

"Could you focus on me a minute?" Molly asked.

"Sorry, darling," her mother said, but she continued to give Molly's father one of her challenging looks.

"Really, I'm not going to talk to you unless you keep yourselves out of it."

"All *right*," her mother snapped.

"That's about it," Molly said, amazed that so many weeks of misery could be summed up so quickly. "Of course, that thing today. Also, Isabel is always mad at us because when we take our phone off the hook, she gets calls." Molly shrugged. The problem sitting before her in the persons of her parents diminished the seriousness of her own situation. Her mother would *die* a betrayed woman. She would not.

"Maybe I can talk to Isabel," her mother suggested. She finished her cigarette and pulled out her compact to repair her lipstick.

"Don't. Not yet. I don't think she's still mad. Just a couple of times when her phone rang all night. She shouldn't have to endure this. She's not even related to me." Molly smiled ruefully. "The only people who really have to deal with this are you two and Robert and me."

"And Mary Ruth," her mother said absently.

"Mary Ruth?" Mary Ruth was Molly's eight-year-old accidental sister.

"She called her once, I think. She told her that she was in love with her brother-in-law. Mary Ruth wasn't even sure what a brother-in-law was."

Molly's stomach took another dive. "I'm sorry. God. I wish I could do something."

"What *are* you doing?" her father asked, appearing refreshed by his Coke.

"Nothing. Waiting. What can I do?"

"What if there's a baby? Is she going to sue for support? Have you asked a lawyer about the legal ramifications."

"There isn't a baby," she said.

"I'd still find out," he said in a warning tone. Had he ever been in a similar situation? Molly wondered. She lowered her eyes when she became aware of the anger in them. She did not know enough to blame him so mercilessly. As a sort of punishment, though, she considered asking him who was a good lawyer for this type of problem.

"Mother, do you think we ought to get a lawyer too?"

"If there's a baby involved, I would say yes." Her mother was still of the mind that she should get rid of Robert.

"But there isn't," Molly reminded everyone. A long silence followed.

"Does anyone feel sorry for the girl but me?" her father suddenly asked. Molly could tell it was something he had not intended to say.

"No," she and her mother answered simultaneously. "Well, maybe," Molly added. In her more humane moments, she knew that Suzanne must be a miserable person.

"I don't," her mother said. "I feel sorry for Molly."

"I would hate to be having a married man's baby," Molly said. Christ. "I mean . . ." She decided to let it drop. Now they knew that she wasn't as convinced as she'd pretended. It had slipped out of her mouth when she was feeling sorry for her mortal enemy. "It's a relief that you know," she said. "Thanks for showing me the letter." Maybe they hadn't noticed her slip.

"Actually it was our second," her father said. "We got another one right before Christmas, but I threw it away. Don't ask what it said. I don't even remember. But then Isabel called us about the ad—"

"You didn't tell me that," Molly said sharply. The inability to sustain a lie ran in the family.

"I wasn't supposed to."

Her mother stood up. "By the way, Isabel's not mad anymore. She's just sorry all this is happening. She thinks she's hurt your feelings, though, and she's afraid to come down. So if you get a chance . . ."

Molly nodded wearily. Yes, if she got a chance she would try to make Isabel feel better. She'd minister to anyone caught up in something unpleasant, make their hurt go away. Who was going to minister to her? "Sure," she said. "I like Isabel. I just think she won't face up to things." Her father looked quizzically at her, but she didn't have the energy to explain.

They were ready to leave. Unlike when she went to see them, there was nothing to do here but talk, and talking so intensely for so long was draining. Visiting them, she could roam their huge house, observing her mother's constant rearranging, looking in her closet for new shoes, of which there was almost always a pair. She could go to her growing-up room that so far hadn't been turned into the upstairs den her father wanted, and now, for a while at least, probably wouldn't be. She would never move back in with them, but it seemed ungracious and perhaps inappropriate to say so now. In a few days she would ask how the plans for the den were coming, so they would know she wasn't expecting them to save it for her.

"Will you come back soon?" she asked.

"Only after we get a visit from you," her mother said coaxingly. "You *and* Robert."

"You aren't going to hate him, are you?" The fear had been uppermost in her mind for weeks, but somehow in the conversation she'd forgotten it.

"Of course, you come first," her mother said. "As long as you're happy, we are." That was what they were supposed to say, but did they really feel it?

"Daddy?" she asked.

"I'll do my best," he said stiffly. The man who felt sorry for Suzanne Cox was, interestingly enough, antagonistic toward Robert.

"You said I should be *trusting*."

"That's what I said *you* should be, not *me*."

"Please be nice," Molly said, meaning that he should be nice to her as well as Robert.

"He's always nice," her mother said. She lifted her carefully painted eyebrows. "Almost always."

"Where is he, by the way?" her father asked, all of them noticing the choice of the pronoun.

Molly looked at her watch. Four-thirty. They were supposed to catch the five o'clock showing of a movie she had not selected or dressed for. "Good grief. He'll be home in just a minute. He's over at the music building practicing. We're going out to a movie and to eat." Saying that he was out practicing made her feel insecure again, but telling their plans for the evening remedied her worry. Just like a young couple in love: a date for the movies and dinner.

It hurt her to see them hurry to leave as if they wanted to get away before Robert arrived.

Chapter Fifteen

"WHOSE BABY?"

The question came from the desk next to Molly's and referred to a pink bubble-gum cigar lying in the roller of the typewriter that she'd just uncovered.

"Whose baby?" Peter Leo asked again. He was the investigative reporter she sat next to now that she'd become a reporter herself.

"Somebody's wife in the composing room," she answered. She picked up the cigar, thinking that it was likely a coincidence rather than the symbol of a baby girl, and dropped it in the trash can. Maybe it had been left for Rusty Eanes, the reporter whose desk and job she'd taken.

"I'll take that," Peter said.

"You don't want it," she hastily insisted.

Peter dipped his skinny boyish arm into the trash can, retrieved the cigar, removed the cellophane wrapping, and wiggled it in his mouth like Groucho. She tried to suppress her alarmed expression. Was there any way to poison a bubble-gum cigar? Peter chewed contentedly as they walked into the managing editor's office for a staff meeting.

It was April, the month of her twenty-third birthday, and until the appearance of this cigar, which might not mean anything, she felt as President Nixon did about ending the Vietnam War: "cautiously optimistic." The last contact they'd had with Suzanne, apart from the fake garage sale, was the day they'd both talked to her. Perhaps hearing their voices had made Suzanne realize she was hurting real people. Perhaps the call had shown her that they were united against her, that nothing she could do could drive them apart.

Robert had pulled himself together, too, beginning the next afternoon after the garage sale and her parents' visit. He'd walked in the door only moments after they'd left, ready, as he'd promised, to go to Deno's and the movie she hadn't selected. She'd thrown on her clothes in between the time she heard the tires crunching on the driveway and the time he walked in the door. She did not mention Suzanne the entire evening. Instead, she got him to talk about the opera, which he said was going very well.

Their relationship had grown warmer in the sense of caring, though not of sex. She was willing for frequent lovemaking to resume, but out of some sense of shame Robert seemed to be denying himself, as if she had had some kind of surgery, and he was giving the incision time to heal. She had decided that she could live with her question about what he had done with Suzanne. She even thought his worry about his ability to be faithful would go away. They just needed time to forget.

"Would you be willing to work on that project, Molly?"

Hearing her name jerked her to attention. "Yes," she answered without hesitation. She had no idea what Charlie had asked her, but she had learned years ago how to answer without hearing the question.

"Do you have any ideas about how we should approach the subject?" he persisted, giving her no clues. He perched on a stool in the middle of the conference room, swiveling to address various of the *Record*'s ten reporters.

Gravely Molly answered, "I'd like to give the project some thought if I may." She hoped Gisella could tell her what she'd missed.

"Sure." Charlie grinned impetuously, glad he hadn't been able to unnerve her.

On command, other reporters began mentioning their pet ideas for stories. Peter wanted to investigate a judge who was allegedly taking payoffs. Gisella wanted to write a series of character studies on the various neighborhoods in town. Rebecca, the ranking female reporter, a short challenging woman who wore ankle-length skirts and jogging shoes, said that she wanted to do a profile on the mayor.

It wasn't easy to turn Rebecca down—she was the type of reporter who would write the story anyway, "encouraging" Charlie to run it because she'd expended the energy—but Molly thought Charlie ought to say no. Rebecca had been covering this same mayor for eight years: how could she find out anything new?

"We haven't had a profile like that in a while," he hedged, looking around for help. "What does everybody think?" All faces were blank, unwilling to tangle with Rebecca.

"Peter?" Charlie pushed.

"What's the question?" Peter had the spunk to admit he hadn't been listening.

"We're talking about a profile on the mayor," Charlie explained, patient primarily because he needed Peter's help. "Do you think it's a good idea?"

Peter turned up his palms. It made no difference on earth to him what Rebecca did.

Since this was only her second staff meeting, it was too soon for her to participate, but Molly did want this newspaper, every aspect of it, to be the best. "I think we can do a profile," she began tentatively. Charlie's bottom lip edged out. "But I think somebody who doesn't cover City Hall regularly should write it. We need a fresh look at that guy." Charlie nodded. A couple of reporters stirred, but no one was willing to back her up.

Rebecca said evenly, "I suppose you want to do the schools *and* the mayor." So the unknown assignment had to do with schools. "Such energy."

"No!" Molly protested. "Not at all. You can do the schools. You can do the *mayor*. I just think the idea of long-term beats doesn't always work. I haven't been a reporter, but I *have* been reading what all of you write. After awhile, everybody tends to lose their freshness." She hadn't wanted to accuse Rebecca alone, so she'd accused everybody. Would all the reporters be angry at her?

"You'd be fresh at anything," Rebecca murmured. "I mean, it's a given." She wrote a note to herself on her pad while Molly blushed furiously.

"I'll shut up," she said. Charlie was lighting a cigarette, the ostensible reason he hadn't said anything yet. He reminded her of a weak teacher she'd had in college who in the interest of class discussion often let discussions become personal attacks.

"That's an interesting idea," he said.

What's an interesting idea? Molly wondered.

Smugly Rebecca continued, "Just *where* are you going to get a better story? From someone who has background on a subject or from someone with so-called fresh ideas?"

"I didn't say better," Molly insisted. "I said different. I think it applies to all of us, not just you." She looked at Gisella and Peter, but both of them watched the corners of the room, waiting for a discussion that didn't concern them to end.

After a moment of embattled silence, Charlie succumbed. "You can do the profile, Rebecca. Give me a date when it will be ready before you leave today." Placid in victory, Rebecca made more notes on her pad. Charlie flipped to a new section of his notebook.

"Wait," Rebecca said suddenly, waiting until all eyes were upon her. "I've changed my mind." She looked around the circle. "I think Molly should do the profile."

"I don't want to do the profile," Molly said. Would Charlie please rescue her? "I don't have any idea how to do it." That admission should make Rebecca feel better. In fact, though, she probably could write an interesting story about the mayor.

Rebecca drew into silence, her small nose pointed in the air. "You can learn," she said.

Molly stared at Charlie, mentally commanding him to help. *He* was the one who didn't want the profile.

"I want *you* to do the interview, Rebecca," he said in a tired voice.

"Don't you think we need a fresh look?" she asked, only barely mocking the word fresh.

"*Please*," Charlie said in the same tone he would have said, "Shut up."

"Whatever you say," she answered in a pliant, yet foreboding, voice: *next* time she would not be so easy to deal with.

Molly paid close attention to the rest of the meeting but chose not to offer any more ideas. She reminded herself that she didn't know what kind of emotional attachment one might develop for a certain beat. In a sense the mayor *belonged* to Rebecca. Maybe one day she would feel that the environment belonged to her. She sensed that there should be no emotional attachment to beats at all, but she also sensed that such impartiality was impossible.

When the meeting was over, everyone left to go look for news except Gisella, who was on special assignment for a week. Not wanting to discuss the meeting with Charlie, Molly had hoped they could leave together. Genuine support of a boss's position was permissible, but she had no interest in becoming Charlie's handmaiden. She certainly didn't want him to thank her, which he wouldn't do if she was with Gisella. As he emerged from the managing editor's office, she dialed her friend's extension.

"I thought you were right," Gisella said immediately. She began taking notes as if conducting an interview.

"Why didn't you say so?"

"I will sometime. I thought if I said something today, everyone would think we'd discussed Rebecca beforehand. I hoped that Peter would back you up."

"Why is no one willing to give Rebecca an opinion?" Molly asked. Charlie stopped ten feet away from her desk, as if waiting to talk to her, so she drew out a legal pad and began doodling.

"Because she's been here so long."

"What difference does that make?" Molly asked.

Gisella was silent for a moment. "To tell the truth, Rebecca knows a lot."

"Oh."

"I know how you feel," Gisella continued, trying to soften the praise, "but she's a good news reporter. She never lets a personal relationship interfere with what she writes."

Automatically Molly asked, "Do I?" She thought of the columns she'd chosen not to write over the past few months because of what Suzanne might find out about her. But Gisella didn't even know about them.

"I think you're untested."

"Oh," she said again, feeling not quite so clever as she had half an hour ago. Charlie started out the door in the direction of the canteen. "I'm going to leave while he's gone," Molly said quickly. She had received an anonymous tip yesterday that a chemical company was dumping untreated by-products into South Buffalo Creek. She had planned to investigate tomorrow but decided to go now instead.

"Better hurry," Gisella said.

Charlie saw her from the far end of the hall, throwing up his hand as if to stop her, but Molly pretended not to see him. She dared not wait for the poky elevator, so she took the steps. At each landing she felt a heightened sense of embarrassment. She thought she recognized her problem: because of her recent troubles, she'd begun to feel wise. Smart-ass, Rebecca might say. She thought that if her suffering had brought answers to *some* questions, she knew the answers to all questions. The worst sign was how smug she'd felt talking in the staff meeting. She could now give advice on how to hold a marriage together, how to maintain the proper space between parents and husband, how to leave work problems at work and home problems at home. Why shouldn't she know what was good journalism and what wasn't? She'd been a reporter for less than two weeks, that was why.

She felt worse and worse, and by the time she reached her car, she was crying. When she saw Rebecca tomorrow, she would apologize. Beg her to believe that she didn't know what she was talking about. If Rebecca refused to forgive her, she would try to win her friendship slowly, first by asking her advice, then by taking it. How does one handle a friendly source? Did she ever feel that she was being used? How does a reporter find out more than the powers-that-be want her to know?

The You-Ass handled strangely as she backed out of her parking place. She pulled up the emergency brake and got out. The right front tire was flat. Poetic justice, rewarding her egotism. She knew as much about newspaper reporting as she knew about changing this tire. She ought to change it herself just to drive home the point.

She managed to find the spare under the carpet in the trunk and succeeded in assembling the jack, but she wasn't strong enough to pump the car up. She pried off the hubcap, knowing that it meant nothing unless the tire was off the ground, but at least someone could see she was trying. She looked around the empty parking lot, not seeing any—she thought wryly—Good Samaritans.

Reluctantly she dismissed the idea of calling her father, who she knew could solve this problem, in favor of calling Robert. Although he was on the way out the door to biology lab, his voice became less dismissive when he learned what the problem was.

"I wish I could do something, but I don't have a car," he said. "Why don't you call your father?"

She knew what she wanted Robert to do. She wanted him to make a sacrifice in her honor: to cut lab, walk here, and help her out. She'd *tried* to change the tire. It wasn't as if she'd thrown up her hands.

"My father is a busy man," she said. "He doesn't have time to come change my tire."

Robert did not respond.

"What am I supposed to do?" she asked.

"Call a gas station. Somebody will be glad to come change it for you."

"I'll do that." The neutrality of her tone only meant that she was furious.

"If you can't find any help, call me back," he said. It was an absurd thing to say, since he wouldn't be there. She hung up without saying goodbye.

Although it made her feel totally stranded, she decided not to call her father. Not calling him did not mean that she was martyring herself, as Robert would insist, only that she was taking responsibility for her own problems. She returned to her car, determined now to help herself. She managed to jack it up, but she could not budge a single one of the lugs that held the tire in place. Straining against them made her eyes tear.

She walked to the gas station instead of phoning to prove that walking was not beneath her. A young man named Mike, according to the patch on his shirt, drove her back to the parking lot.

When he knelt to examine the tire, his eyes grew wide as if someone had just jarred him awake. "Somebody's done took a knife to this tire," he said, almost excitedly. A section of long hair fell over his eyes.

"A knife?" She looked around the parking lot, wondering if from some driver's seat someone might be watching her. Was this a juvenile delinquent or Suzanne? "What kind of knife?"

"Lady," Mike said exasperatedly. He knelt to the tire again. "Pretty big one," he said. "Look here." She knelt beside him, which she could tell made him nervous. "See that stab place? That there's the width of the blade." The slit was about an inch-and-a-half wide. "Hate to have one of them chasing me," he added.

Molly stood up. "Can it be fixed?" she asked briskly. She felt strange, almost queasy. All her previous fears seemed like ashes in the wind. She hadn't realized what a small irritation the phone calls and letters had been. The attempted sale of her furniture seemed insignificant.

"Nothing but a miracle could fix that tire," Mike grinned. "You a lucky lady," he added.

Instantly, she was on guard. "Lucky?"

"They only slashed one," he said. "I seen cars where they slashed all four."

"Oh."

Even Mike had to strain at the lugs, which should have made her feel better.

Chapter Sixteen

ALL DAY long she had watched the sky outside her bedroom window grow heavier and heavier until the bottoms of the clouds seemed to graze the rooftops. The sky ached to drop its load; she ached with it. The telephone calls, the letters, the clever surprises seemed childish to her now. In these six months the only thing that even began to illustrate the depth of her passion was when she stabbed the tire of Molly's car yesterday. She'd planned simply to loosen a valve. Why, on the way out the door of her apartment, had she turned back? Why had she tested each knife against her wrist to find the sharpest one? She'd told herself it was for self-protection in case someone surprised her in the act.

The black valve had been hard between her fingers when she'd decided that it wasn't enough to let out some air. She wanted to do damage, to hurt Molly the way she'd been hurt. Still squatting, she had drawn the butcher knife from her purse. In a two-handed thrust from between her legs, she stuck the knife into the tire. The actual puncture flooded her with relief. The rubber tried to hold onto the knife, but she wrenched it away. She felt as if she'd killed something. How would it be, she wondered, to drive the knife into Molly's ribs or to turn it on her own womb. Such thoughts, of course, were only fantasies. A block away, the knife concealed inside her purse, she caught a bus home.

She had awakened this morning in pain. Yesterday's fierce movements had begun the chain of events she'd been awaiting. When she had swung her arms, she had started that mysterious process of birth. The baby was turning now, poising her head at the entrance to the birth canal. Coming early, she would be a small baby, but that would make delivery easier on both of them. It occurred to her that whether her delivery was easy or difficult mattered not at all to Robert and Molly, which made her hate them more.

She was not the hysterical type, so as the pain had accelerated through the day, she'd remained calm. She felt contempt for all the women in the world who had faced birth by themselves, who had known that when they returned home they would be alone still, who knew no father would ever show his face. Why had they let themselves be trapped like that? She had bathed, carefully shaving off her thin pubic hair to avoid that humiliation at the hospital. She'd packed a small suitcase with a nightgown, slippers, and toiletries. She called Bennie to tell him that she would be out of work for a week. When he wanted to know why, she said that she was having a mastectomy, which even he knew the meaning of.

"What hospital are you going to?" he asked.

"Cone."

"I guess you'll want some privacy," he said in a tone more hopeful than questioning.

"I will," she'd said, a combination of pride and disdain in her voice. Bennie did not want to visit a woman who'd lost a breast. "For a few days. Then you can come see me." She managed to keep the sound of her grin out of her voice.

"You know Ruth quit," he said. Ruth had quit? "I've been running the cash register myself, but I'll try to make it by."

Suzanne suffered a sudden pain. "Where'd she go?" she asked.

"How would I know?"

"Does she have another job?"

"I didn't ask her a thing."

"She hasn't moved, has she?" He didn't answer. When he got tired of answering questions, he simply stopped talking. "Dammit, Bennie."

"Good luck with your operation," he said.

She hung up without saying anything.

Ruth gone? If Ruth had left, nobody would remain in this whole town who cared about her. Why hadn't she waited just a little longer? Eventually they would have worked the same shift again. They might even have moved in together.

She dialed Ruth's number. When Ruth finally answered, she sounded as if she'd been asleep or maybe drinking, except that she didn't drink.

"Why'd you quit?" Suzanne asked.

"Suzanne?" Ruth's mind sounded far away. "Is that you?" The warbly voice rose as if she were hearing from a long-lost lover.

"This is me. Bennie said you quit."

Ruth broke into a long wailing tirade during which she called Bennie a lying son-of-a-bitch. "He fired me," she finally enunciated angrily.

"He couldn't have fired you."

"Ask him," Ruth sneered.

"He can't do that."

"He can't?" Ruth asked pitifully. She must be drinking.

"What have you been doing today?" Suzanne asked.

Ruth hesitated. "Looking for a new job." Fresh sobs made her voice ragged again.

"You have not."

"All right, I haven't," she said angrily. "What do you care?"

"Just curious," Suzanne said coldly.

"Well, 'curious' yourself to hell," Ruth said. Suzanne waited for the phone to slam down, but Ruth kept holding it, sniffing heavily as if she was trying to pull herself together. "Suzanne," she said, hiccupping. "Why did you call me?"

She tried to think why she had called Ruth.

"You haven't called me in four months, and the week I get fired, you call up acting like you're my friend again."

In a careless voice Suzanne said, "I wanted to wish you luck."

"Thank you very much." Ruth paused. "And may I wish you luck too."

"Are you leaving town?" Suzanne asked.

"Why would I leave town?"

"I just wondered."

"You know I don't have anywhere to go."

There was a long silence.

"Goodbye," Suzanne said.

"Goodbye to you."

Suzanne held on to the phone a few more seconds before hanging up, as did Ruth, but neither of them spoke again.

She needed to free the line anyway so she could call a taxi. It was four-thirty, time for her to go to the hospital. Like most people, Ruth always seemed better in her imagination. She checked once more that she had the things she needed and then telephoned United Taxi Service.

"I need a cab to take me to Cone Hospital," she said.

"Is it a 'mergency?" the colored female dispatcher asked.

"I wouldn't call it that."

"I was wondering if you needed a ambellance," the voice said.

"Must you inquire about my health?" Suzanne asked coldly.

"I must if you wants one of my taxis to die in," the woman retorted. Suzanne was about to hang up when the dispatcher asked the name of her street.

She gave her address and hung up, not waiting to see if she'd been understood. If a United taxi came within ten minutes, fine. If not, she'd call another service, or perhaps she'd call Robert. Could even he refuse to take a woman in labor to the emergency room?

Within minutes the cab was honking on the street below. Suzanne walked with stateliness down her steep wooden stair and then down the cement steps of the house. The milky eyes of the driver watched as she descended, but he made no move to take her suitcase or guide her to the car. When she'd settled into the shiny brown plastic seat, she found his eyes, which were viewing her apprehensively through the rearview mirror.

"Where to?"

"I don't think you need to ask."

He mumbled something to himself and threw the gears into

drive. Small-town taxis didn't have plastic dividers between driver and passenger, and she knew he was wishing they did. He opened his window for the fresh cleansing air, driving with his shoulders hunched up around his neck as if to ward off her germs.

She groaned.

"Yowsa!" the cab driver said. He stepped harder on the gas, taking a light that had just turned red.

"*Slow down,*" Suzanne exploded from the back.

He hit the brakes, throwing her forward. She clutched the back of his seat, thinking of all the hands that had been there. She'd be sure to wash up before delivery. Sitting forward, she was closer to him, and when she groaned again, he jumped so visibly that she was scarcely able to carry the sound through. He turned to see why she was so loud. She sat as close behind him as a ghost.

"Sit back. Please sit back," he said, his voice fervent as if he were praying.

"It's the plague," she said. "It's the black death."

He stopped for red lights now, but no longer waited for them to change. If he began to speed, the ghost behind him moaned, so he slowed down again. Finally, they turned into the double lanes to the hospital.

"Emergency entrance," she managed to eke out.

He took the turn with howling tires, dropping rubber as he skidded to a halt in front of the door. He jumped out of the taxi. She waited for him to open the door for her, but he stood instead by his left front fender, lifting wet cottony eyes toward the heavens.

She gathered her purse and suitcase, climbing slowly out. The car rumbled fitfully beside her, its engine missing without any gas feed. The driver shuffled backward as she approached him.

"How much do I owe you?" she shouted.

"Nothing!"

She thrust $2.00 into the air between them.

"I don't want your money," he said. Before she could force it on him, he circled her and jumped into the waiting vehicle.

She walked into a rather tumultuous scene. The waiting room was clogged with about fifty people: the injured, who were moaning or weeping; and their relatives, who were trying to offer comfort. A woman whose clothes were as bloody as Jackie Kennedy's was waiting for her child, whose finger, Suzanne quickly found out, had been nipped off by the scissors hinge of a suitcase. A man who had smashed his hand through a pane of glass held it wrapped in the tail of his shirt. The woman beside him held her forearm over her eyes as if she, too, were injured. An extremely pregnant woman, breathing heavily, half sat and half lay in a chair, an older woman clasping one of her hands.

Suzanne placed her suitcase under a chair and asked the mother covered with blood if she knew the location of the ladies' bathroom. The mother, a woman with dark delicate features, only looked past her shoulder. A friend standing beside her told Suzanne to go ask a nurse. After giving them a look of intense irritation, Suzanne approached the pregnant woman to ask the same question.

"Down the hall to the left," the woman grunted.

"Thanks," Suzanne said. She turned away and then back. "What's the problem?" she asked.

The older woman glanced up sharply. "She's trying to deliver too soon," she said in a clipped tone that asked for no further questions.

"She looks pretty fat to me," Suzanne said.

The pregnant woman, her eyes as vacant as marbles, held up three fingers.

"That's triplets," the older woman translated.

"I see," Suzanne said. She thought of telling the pregnant woman that the fittest would survive, but it was premature to cause a commotion. "Good luck," she said. Only the daughter attempted to return her smile.

She started for the bathroom, her purse swinging on her arm. Today, even without the benefit of earlier investigation, details were falling into place for her. First, she'd had a free ride to the hospital. And now, she discovered, the bathroom was what she'd hoped for but never expected: room for just one and a lock on the outside door. She glanced over her shoulder. No one seemed to be on the way here.

A round light on the ceiling lit the room. She pulled the chain of another fixture above the mirror and the new, brighter light shone on her face. In the medicine cabinet she found Band-Aids but no pills. She was feeling worse now. So hot. Her skin was as pale as paste. Pearls of perspiration appeared on her forehead and then ran together like a puddle. More sweat formed small pools under her arms. Her stomach hurt. She put her hands on it as if to caress it, but then she turned her hands into fists and pounded them against herself. She focused on the mirror again. Her face disappeared. All she could see were her eyes, her harsh dark eyes. She breathed faster. Chills shook her. Drumming her fists once more against her stomach, she felt movement, the slow painful movement of birth.

The baby was coming. She used her muscles and the hands on her stomach to start pushing it out. Push, breathe. Push, breathe. Her head whirled dizzily. She needed to sit down. Stumbling to the toilet, she pulled down her pants and strained. Push, breathe. Stay conscious. Push, breathe.

When it was over, she lay her head quietly on her knees. Her arms and legs hung from her body like lead. The wetness all over her skin began to evaporate into the hospital air. The beat of her heart slowed.

When she stood, she pulled her underpants tight against her crotch and turned to gaze into the deep water. Finally she reached for the handle. Closing her eyes, she pushed it firmly until everything that was in the bowl had drained out into the world. She was a mother.

Someone was knocking at the bathroom door. Suzanne slowly washed her hands. The knocking grew insistent. A voice called, "Are you all right in there?" She activated the blow dryer, which drowned out the knocking. After a second cycle she unlocked the door for a large-busted nurse with an overwrought expression on her face.

"Are you all right?" the nurse asked, obviously relieved that she wasn't going to have to break down the door.

Suzanne smiled wanly. "Cramps," she said. "But I'm okay." The nurse looked past her into the bathroom.

"Another patient says she's been waiting outside this door for thirty minutes."

Suzanne shuffled against the door to push it closed. "Tell her I didn't hear her knock," she said.

"Just so you're all right," the nurse said. She touched Suzanne's arm. Unprepared, Suzanne recoiled before bringing her muscles under control.

"I never felt better," she said, but the nurse clasped her elbow as they walked down the hallway. Suzanne looked at her name pinned on her left pocket. Jane Hunter. Now she even had her own nurse. "I need to call a cab," Suzanne said. "Can you direct me to a phone?"

The nurse walked with her through the waiting room to a closet where phone conversations could be made in private. The pregnant lady in the orange peignoir had made no progress except that her mother had stepped away. The man whose hand was mangled had evidently reached one of the examining rooms. His wife continued to cover her eyes, perhaps not wanting to be identified. The mother whose child had lost part of a finger now held him as she spoke with the doctor. His bandage was bigger than his tiny hand.

"Shall I wait?" Nurse Jane asked her.

"Don't be ridiculous," Suzanne said. In the telephone booth she dialed United and requested a driver to come take her home.

Chapter Seventeen

THE NEWS she'd been half expecting, on account of the bubble-gum cigar and the slashed tire, came in a telegram delivered to the office. Wondering if one were allowed to refuse Western Union, Molly reached for the envelope, but the bold-eyed messenger lay his clipboard on top of her hand and said, "Sign this first." She scribbled a version of her name, which he scrutinized before leaving.

The full early-morning news room waited while with feigned enthusiasm she slit the envelope, scanned the message, and stuffed both into a zippered pocket of her knapsack. She leaned close to Peter, affecting shyness toward the rest of the room. "My mother is so ridiculously proud of me," she said. The ears at nearby desks seemed satisfied, and typing resumed around the room.

"It's nice she cares," Peter said. His sad expression, a consequence of the heavy bags under his eyes, summoned a similar look from her. With great effort she gave her mother's thoughtfulness an appreciative smile.

She held her mind in total check, turning mechanically to the three stories in the morning paper she'd been assigned to rewrite. This first edition, which was sent to outlying areas, went to press before any new local news had a chance to develop. Therefore, it was filled with stories like this one beside her typewriter, an Irving Park robbery for which she had to figure out one more interesting lead.

Charlie had complained all week that she'd taken too long on her rewrites, but she did these in record time. Pasting them up, she summoned the copy girl to deliver them to his basket. Until today she'd felt shy about asking someone to fetch and carry for her. Now it seemed an easy way to avoid notice.

She continued to direct her mind toward not thinking. Knowing what words were printed on the telegram did not automatically admit them to her life. She would postpone the knowledge, the way people in World War II postponed admitting what the Germans were doing to the Jews. Could failure to act have, on a smaller scale, dire consequences? What could she do at this point anyway?

While she waited for Charlie to check her work, she cleaned off her desk. She was about to cover her typewriter when she realized what a giveaway that would be. Charlie's phone, which had been ringing constantly, rang again. "Yeah?" he answered. Swinging the mouthpiece aside, he asked in a voice that lumbered around the news room, "Who can take an obit?" She felt him look in her direction, but she was holding her telephone receiver and writing notes on a legal pad. If she had to record someone's demise right now, unless it happened to be Suzanne's, she thought she'd become hysterical. Nobody volunteered as usual, so as usual he picked. Not her, thank God.

Her stomach began to pain her as if it had been cut open and exposed to something cold. The early deadline was near, the reporters' work done for this edition. Rebecca stood up and then Peter, leaving to find new stories. Molly rose too. She'd been working all week to define and develop the rather nebulous environment beat so that she'd have somewhere to go when everyone else left. Her legs suddenly folded, sitting her back down in her chair. Across the room the copy girl, the only person to see her legs disagree with her mind, grinned at her. Molly stood up again, a stark look on her face. Perhaps the copy girl would conclude that she had some horrible degenerative disease. She gathered her things. She had never cut class deliberately in college: today, April 10, she was walking off her job.

Out in the hall Rebecca, wearing a fake fur jacket over her blue-jean skirt, was still waiting for the elevator. Peter had disappeared. "What's cooking?" she asked, her eyes crinkling with friendliness. This was the first time they'd spoken since the staff meeting. Molly had not yet figured out how to properly apologize.

"I thought I'd ride around and look at some of the new developments," Molly said. "See what precautions, if any, the builders are taking to prevent erosion." Fabrication, she noticed, was becoming disturbingly easy for her.

"On deadline time?" Rebecca asked. She jabbed the elevator button three times.

The idea hadn't sounded totally appropriate to Molly either, but it was the first thing she'd been able to think of. Afternoons, not mornings, were usually used for such leisurely exploration.

"I'm just getting to know the beat," she said lamely. "You know." The elevator was stuck on the second floor. "Charlie said it's okay," she added without thinking, knowing at once that she'd fallen into Rebecca's trap. Like the good reporter she was, Rebecca had remained silent, letting Molly talk more than she should. "This elevator is ridiculous," she suddenly exclaimed, starting for the stairs.

"Good luck," Rebecca called after her.

As she bounded nimbly toward the street, she considered whether to answer. At the first landing she called, "Thanks."

She drove the You-Ass over to the university. When she passed the Baptist Church, she felt it looming to her right. It was an unwieldy institution just like marriage. It did not exist for true need or else she would feel drawn toward it instead of repelled. Robert had a lesson with Elizabeth Loewenstein at eleven o'clock, but he would have to miss it.

She parked the car a block from the music building, hoping not to see anyone she knew. She felt alienated from the student family, all of whom seemed so innocent and unexposed. Hurrying up the tall steps, she realized she hardly looked like a student anymore now that she wore actual skirts, stockings, and stacked heels. Maybe she looked like a woman. Maybe she looked like something in-between. She stumbled on a step and the small scare brought tears to her eyes. Robert was a father. What did that make her?

She stood outside Miss Loewenstein's office beside the wooden chair where she used to sit waiting for Robert to finish his voice lesson. It was not quite eleven, and he hadn't arrived. She let herself remember those Thursdays of her senior year, how, listening to him sing, her heart beat so fast she thought she would faint. More than once, Miss Loewenstein had emerged from her studio to give Molly, the fiancé, a compliment about Robert's voice. She did not allow herself to think what this most recent development would do to their future.

Elizabeth emerged from the studio, her coat over her arm, but instead of heading to her office, she started out of the building. It was unusually close to lesson time for a coffee break.

"Miss Loewenstein?" Molly called. The slim figure turned like a dancer, her disdainful expression vanishing as she recognized Molly.

"I'd thought about calling you," the velvety mezzo-soprano voice began, "but I wasn't sure I should interfere." She withdrew her keys from her purse and started toward her office. Molly followed, standing mouselike as Miss Loewenstein opened the door. Light from two very tall windows temporarily blinded her. She had forgotten that Elizabeth had seen letters from Suzanne. No wonder she'd felt so uneasy about coming here.

"I'm looking for Robert," she said. "Doesn't he have a lesson now?" Elizabeth hung her coat on a freestanding wooden rack and motioned for Molly to do the same. Books, sheet music, and records lined both side walls of the small room and wound around the door they had just entered. The teacher motioned her to the tattered upholstered chair where students sat during conferences. She opened her date book, flipping back through the weeks. After she found what she was looking for, she shut the book with a snap.

"If you think I don't know about Suzanne Cox, I do," Molly said, fingering the plaid of her skirt as she spoke.

Miss Loewenstein's flat painted eyebrows rose questioningly. She tapped a pencil eraser against her famous neon lips. "I'm not aware of Suzanne Cox," she said ponderously, as if trying to fit this piece of information into what she already knew. But she *must* know. She'd received the letters. Flushing, Molly half rose, but Elizabeth motioned with a conductor's signal for her to sit back down.

"I'll pass Robert," she began, her heavy lips stroking the words, "but only under certain conditions. I've never given a student special treatment before and I never will again. It's too much of a strain. Too much of a strain." She shook her head: the heavily sprayed hair didn't move. "I don't lie," she continued softly. "That is, I never have before. I had an inquiry from Juilliard this week. They want to give Robert a scholarship. I said he was the most talented student I'd ever taught. They know me, you know. They respect what I say. You must get him here to see me. He has one more chance, and that's all."

Molly was confused. Juilliard wanted to give Robert a scholarship, but Miss Loewenstein was considering failing him. She stiffened with anger. "Do you think that's fair?" she asked, trying to keep the trembling out of her throat.

"I think it's generous," the perfectly modulated voice said.

"His personal life shouldn't make you flunk him," Molly cried, nearly hysterical. "I don't care *what* he's done." Did she mean this or did she only fear losing the chance to go to New York? Molly could see only Miss Loewenstein's glowing lips through the huge tears that had welled in her eyes.

"I know nothing about Robert's personal life," the teacher said, so quiet that Molly instinctively leaned forward to hear. Miss Loewenstein was leaning close, too, probing Molly's face. "I'm flunking him because I haven't seen him in a month. I'm flunking him because he gave up his role in our opera."

"What?" Molly said. The sharpness of her voice startled them both.

"Robert quit school, dear. I thought you knew. He quit at the end of February. Everyone in the department has tried to talk to him, but he won't show up for an appointment."

"Why didn't someone call me?" Molly asked. She was not a mother but a wife who was supposed to know things like that about her husband. "I guess Robert didn't tell me because he was ashamed," she said quietly, her throat paralyzed anew.

An uneasy silence descended. She had to leave before she lost control. If Robert wasn't in the opera, if he wasn't taking voice lessons, if he'd quit school, where did he go all the time? He must be visiting Suzanne. But if that was true, why did she keep sending all her messages? She blinked rapidly, managing her tears. Miss Loewenstein drew back, settling in her chair. She had to find Robert. If necessary, she would beg him to see Miss Loewenstein. What would they do if they couldn't get away from here? How could they go to New York with no reason? Robert had been offered a scholarship to Juilliard. Could anyone turn that down?

She sat straighter in the old chair, tightening her ankles and the muscles in her arms to stall the physical collapse she was beginning to feel. "This has been quite a shock," she said pleasantly. She tucked her feet together, preparing to stand up. Surely Miss Loewenstein wouldn't force her to stay a second time.

"I can imagine," the teacher murmured. With a pencil she was drawing little feathery notes in a lined notebook. She was considered an excellent composer of lieder. Was she writing a sad song about Molly and Robert?

"I don't quite know what to do," Molly said.

Miss Loewenstein stopped her doodling. "You may not be able to do anything."

"Would all his other teachers take him back?" She should at least find that out.

"If he was willing to make up the work . . . and to explain. I could use whatever influence I have," she added, which was considerable, since she was head of the department. "Dr. Hoyle may be a problem." Dr. Hoyle, a teacher Molly had never met, was the director of the opera. "He was forced to find a replacement from another college."

She didn't want to leave until she had some sort of guarantee for Robert, but all the questions she was trying to repress kept assaulting her brain. She could not listen to them and address Miss Loewenstein at the same time. "You've been kind," she said, standing.

"Not kind. Hopeful."

Molly tried to express in her face the appreciation she felt for the truth Elizabeth had told her, but each time her eyes crossed the teacher's calm ones, she blinked rapidly. "Can I thank you when I'm less upset?" she managed.

"You don't need to thank me at all." Miss Loewenstein's face suddenly swam through Molly's tears. The tone of her voice shifted from teacher to student to woman to woman. "Are you *really* all right?" she asked.

"I'm fine," Molly said. But she didn't pretend to smile. What she meant, and what she knew Miss Loewenstein understood, was this: that she had the power to move herself out of the office, down the steps, into her car, and home. After that, she didn't know.

There were flowers on their front stoop when she arrived, and for a moment she thought that Robert knew what she'd discovered and was already trying to make up. She wished he'd stop wasting money on meaningless gestures. When she drew closer, she saw that the flowers were Shasta daisies dyed pink and arranged in a little vase the shape of a baby shoe. She did not bother to read the card, which was addressed to Robert alone. With a trembling step she walked to the back corner of the house, where Isabel kept the trash cans. She lifted the lid and smashed the arrangement, flowers first.

She bent to pick up the discarded trash can lid, not for herself but for her duty as a tenant. Blood rushed to her head. She felt weak enough to faint. If she collapsed here behind the house, would the search be begun in time to find her before she froze to death? She didn't really want to die, but it seemed so much easier than the alternative. Her chest quivered, trying to find enough air for just one more moment of life. She leaned against the wall of the house, closing her eyes. Tears eased down her cheeks.

A car, probably Isabel's, drove into the driveway. Hidden from view by a thick holly tree, Molly did not open her eyes, only listened while Isabel walked briskly up the cement steps, her ring of keys chattering in the lock, the front door opening and then shutting. For an unknowable amount of time Molly leaned against the house until the natural world, only interrupted by Isabel's arrival, began to breathe again. Then she opened her eyes.

Before her lay an acre of untouched woods. A similar stand had existed behind her house when she was growing up. As a child, whenever she wanted to be alone, she would disappear into the woods, where she knew of two trees fully connected to each other by a section of living trunk that lay on the ground. This natural bench was where she sat and listened. There was so much to hear, once she had become an accepted part of the animate landscape. She had heard animals moving and the wind blowing and water bubbling in the creek. She had heard coolness and heat and she had heard the seasons change. She had heard things that made noise and things that didn't.

She breathed deeply now, sucking in the sweet smell of enormous nature, listening to and hearing life. A first trace of green sprinkled the trees like dust. She hadn't even noticed. She couldn't freeze to death if she tried. Now that everything had come into perspective, she was ready to think about Robert. It was the only time she ought to think: when her mind was clear like this. She did not hate the baby. That was one thing she had decided. She did not hate the poor, pitiful, premature, clinging-to-life baby. She did not even hope that it died. She did hate Robert for quitting school and not telling her.

What day was this? What time? Molly tiptoed on gravel to her door. Inside, the clock said twelve-fifteen, only fifteen minutes before the final deadline. She owed it to Charlie to tell him she wouldn't have a story for second edition. She dialed the number. "Charlie?" she ventured.

"Where are you?" he asked.

"At home." She didn't have the imagination to lie.

"What are you doing at home?"

She sighed. "I called to tell you that I won't have a story for second edition."

"Do you have any suggestions for this fifteen-inch hole on B-1?" he asked.

Molly was silent. "I'm sorry," she whispered.

"I'm going to transfer you to Gisella, and I want you to dictate a story."

"Charlie, I can't!"

"Of course you can."

"What can I possibly say?"

"Why don't you tell what you've been doing the last two hours?"

"It wasn't on purpose."

"Did you *tell* me?" He was shouting. "Did you walk up and tell me that you needed to leave? Have I ever said you couldn't go somewhere when you needed to? Huh? Have I? Answer me. Don't answer me. But don't you dare hang up. You and Gisella . . . you two make me a story."

"I can't do this," Molly cried as the connection was made with her friend.

"Rebecca reported you," Gisella whispered.

"I *should* have asked him," Molly said.

"Not today, you shouldn't have." Gisella rolled paper in her typewriter. "Uh-oh. Start giving me your story. He's already motioning for it."

"I don't have a story," Molly wailed.

"Shut up," Gisella said. "You're going to make one up. I'll help you. Come on. Think."

They were both quiet. "I can't," Molly said again.

"Goddamnit, Molly. Shut up. I mean it. This isn't the time to feel sorry for yourself."

"You sound so mean."

"Listen, Molly, if we can't write this story, we're going to lose our jobs. I really believe that. Now, think."

Molly sobered. She would resign today, as soon as she got back to the office, but she couldn't jeopardize Gisella's position.

"We're going to have to write something funny," Gisella said. "We're going to have to write about your first big mistake as a reporter. Go ahead. Reel it off."

"Okay, okay. Okay, give me a by-line." She had an idea. She had a precious idea.

Gisella typed her name.

"Ready?" Molly asked.

"You concentrate. I'll get it. Don't ask me anything. Just give it to me."

"Okay, here: 'I'm a big-time reporter now.' " Molly's voice ached with the irony of it all. Her second and last week. " 'The transfer came a week ago, when your former environment reporter, Rusty Eanes, took a job in the not-exactly-greener fields of Philadelphia . . .' "

"Good," Gisella prompted.

"What next? *Help* me."

Gisella was silent. Molly imagined her hands poised over the keys. This had to be *her* story.

" 'Today I wished I *was* in Philly. There at least they have foul odors to smell, illegal chemical dumping to monitor, and regular fish kills.' New paragraph.

" 'I did what I thought I was supposed to do. Peter Leo stood up, and then Rebecca Rimmer—' "

"I wouldn't give *her* any credit," Gisella interrupted.

"Shut up. '. . . and then Rebecca Rimmer, and then I did too. I didn't think it was going to be *easy* to find a story my first time out, so I wanted plenty of time. I got in my Unsafe-at-Any-Speed Corvair, which is an environmental problem that I guess I *could* write about, and I drove around town. It was a very quiet day in Greensboro, in case any of you didn't notice. No ambulances crossed my path, no one jumped off the parking garage, nor was this the day another branch bank was robbed. I would have liked to have found an environmentally related story, but have any of you seen such a clear sky? No temperature inversions. No nothing. I even checked several construction sites, and all the bare earth had been thatched and seeded. There were holding ponds where chemical companies dump their wastes. Even the lake out at Country Park looked reasonably clear.' "

"Did it really?" Gisella asked.

"Just type. 'As time began to evaporate, I decided I'd take anything. I even drove through the college campuses. It was business as usual there, which means some of the students were

studying and some were goofing off.' " She was proud of this dig.
" 'This was Greensboro today, folks. Spring is coming. New life
issues all around us.' " She liked even that irony. " 'The most
civilized of North Carolina cities' "—would Charlie use that?—
" 'was spending her day mopping, taking deposits, playing cards,
eating lunch, deciding sales strategies, buying and selling stocks,
nursing babies, learning multiplication tables . . . you name it.
Maybe nothing "newsworthy" at all happened here today. Maybe
if it didn't, we're lucky. But, P.S., if anyone knows of any environmental problems that I failed to sniff out, I'd appreciate a
call.' "

Gisella whizzed through the last sentence. Molly hung on as
she counted lines. "Is nine inches enough?" she called haughtily
to Charlie.

"It'll do," he yelled back. "Tell Molly to bring her sweet little
self back to work."

"Did you hear him?" Gisella asked.

"Me and everybody else," Molly said, the excitement of deadline composition suddenly extinguished. Perhaps it was just as
well Charlie had ordered her back to the office. If she found
Robert now, she had no idea what she'd say.

"Don't worry about it," Gisella said.

"I'm going to get fired, aren't I?"

"No. You came through."

"I wouldn't exactly put it that way."

Chapter Eighteen

M OLLY pulled in the driveway after six, having made up, despite Charlie's stiff protestations, the two hours she'd missed in the morning. Although he said he was pleased with her invented story, she couldn't bring herself to thank him, but only to say she was glad she'd been able to fill the space. She offered to quit, but he told her not to be ridiculous. "You'll beat this," he said softly. She gave him a dark, penetrating stare to prevent him from telling her what *he* knew about Suzanne.

When she'd rounded the corner to the canteen, where Gisella waited, she gave her friend a cheery smile and said, "Thanks for saving my life." She bought a ham-and-cheese sandwich and began chatting about Rebecca's bitchiness, Charlie's unreasonable demand, and the excitement of composing a story together on deadline. Gisella's dark eyes grew more and more insulted.

"You're not going to tell me where you were," she finally stated.

"I was at home," Molly said disarmingly.

Gisella gave her a sideways look. "*Why* were you at home?" she asked.

"I can't tell you now." She sucked in her trembling lower lip between her teeth, her cheerful façade crumbling. She wanted to confide in Gisella, but not until she had a chance to think things through. She didn't want to have to say, "Robert quit school" without being able to provide a context. She knew that he'd allowed her to believe that he left every night to practice for his role in the opera. Could he be seeing Suzanne Cox all this time? Could he *love* Suzanne Cox? Did he feel fatherly obligations? Why had he quit school? Worse, why hadn't he told her that he'd quit? Had this whole mess with Suzanne so drained him that he'd just given up? He hadn't seemed particularly drained lately; he seemed happy.

At least all the mistakes Robert had made could still be remedied. He could return to school and then he could go to Juilliard. He could return because Molly had finally *done* something instead of waiting for everything to be done to her. Not that she'd directly chosen to see Miss Loewenstein, but the result was the same.

She pushed opened the door of their apartment. Robert stood at the stove, stirring a can of water into some condensed soup. Barely looking up, he said, "I wondered if you were coming home." She noticed how well-fixed he was: a fresh shirt—she'd not ironed lately, so he must have done it; a new shave; hair drying from a recent shampoo. His eyes had an absent look.

"You need the car?" she asked casually. She felt enraged and amazed at the same time. How could he not sense that she'd discovered the truth? Robert, who had always claimed to be able to read her mind through her eyes, was not even taking the time to look at her. She felt an absolute distance from him, as if, in truth, they had hated each other for years. "If you need the car," she said, pausing, "you can have it, of course."

Finally noticing her tone, he looked up sharply, his eyes pinning her for observation. It was their transparent blue that had first attracted her the day they had both been waiting outside the dean's office for an appointment. But he had told her what beautiful eyes *she* had. All she could think was, So do you, but she had used her beautiful eyes to say so instead of speaking the words.

"What's wrong with you?" he asked. Accusations begged in her throat, but she contained them. "Don't start bitching," he threw carelessly at her. He pulled two slices of bread out of the bag. A container of pimiento cheese sat on the counter. Supper for one.

"What are your plans for this evening?" she asked in a businesslike tone.

"Opera practice," he shrugged. "I may be a little late."

Mesmerized now, she asked, "Why may you be a little late?"

He cut his eyes at her as if the question were out-of-line. Being a dutiful son, though, he would answer. "Some of the kids at school are going out for a beer."

"Girls?"

"Not that I know of."

"You look awfully nice for guys," she said.

"You're welcome to join us. We'll be at Mickey's."

But with only one car—unless he offered to pick her up—there was no way for her to get there.

"What time?" she asked, going through the motions.

He slapped his sandwich together with vague irritation. "I guess about ten-thirty. Whenever practice is over. Are you really coming?"

"Do I have to tell you for sure?"

"How are you going to get there?"

"I may walk." She turned her back on him to end the conversation and dropped her coat, purse, and work sack on the bed. It was two or three miles to Mickey's, but he was not offering her a ride.

She listened to Robert's spoon rhythmically dragging the bottom of his soup bowl. He popped the tab of a second beer. How blatant could he be? He *knew* she knew he wouldn't drink before a rehearsal. She noticed a letter on his bedside table from Suzanne. "You didn't open this," she said, picking it up.

Glancing over his shoulder, he said, "I have no interest in what that woman has to say." It seemed not unlike his attitude toward her.

"You also received some flowers." His eyes swept the apartment for what he might have missed. "I threw them away."

"What for?"

"Why did I throw them away?"

"No, why'd she send flowers?"

"You're now a father," Molly said calmly. "As of yesterday at about five-thirty in the afternoon."

He left his dishes on the table and started for the door. "I'm going to be late," he said. In an altered instructional tone he added, "It hasn't been long enough."

"Very premature. But alive." She held the unopened letter out to him as far as her arm could stretch. She almost felt as if she herself had written it.

"Don't give me that," he said contemptuously.

"It's a girl."

"How do you know?"

"She sent pink flowers. The card is in the trash can. It may explain more."

"What else do you want to know?"

"Mother and Dad say—"

"You told them?"

"No. They already knew. They've been getting their own letters and phone calls. Suzanne's asked them for money." He might as well know every single indignity. "I'll bet *your* mother knows too."

Robert pulled his windbreaker out of the closet.

"I wish you wouldn't leave," she said, meaning to be sarcastic but not succeeding.

"I can't stay here. Living with you is like being with Suzanne."

"Where are you going?" she asked.

"I *told* you where I was going," he exploded. He snatched up the keys from the bed, where she'd dropped them, and stormed out the door.

"See you tonight," she called, letting the words fall ambiguously: whether she would see him at Mickey's or back here.

When the car was gone, she briskly opened the letter, knowing now that she needed every single fact. "Truth" obtained from Robert was too vague, too contradictory, too compelling—she *wanted* to believe what he said. Suzanne had written the following:

> Dear Robert,
>
> We have a little girl. Although she weighs only a couple of pounds, she's alive. God knows, if she'd died, I couldn't have lived with the guilt. I love her so much that my heart feels like it's going to burst just looking at her. You should see her in her Plexiglas world all naked and struggling for

every breath. I have nightmares about her dying without ever being held by me.

I want you to see her. Now that you've quit school, you have plenty of time. Don't deny yourself the pleasure of knowing your own daughter. Suzie looks exactly like you. Think about it, please. I love you both and I want more than anything for you to know each other.

Fondly,
Suzanne

Suzanne had known Robert had quit school before Molly had. What did that mean?

Molly cleared Robert's dishes off the counter and ran them and his pot under the hot tap, watching each item as if it meant something. Then she fixed herself an omelet. Normally she made many false movements in the kitchen, but tonight each effort was deft, no wasted motion, as if she were a cook on television. A piece of bread for toast jumped out of the bag into her waiting hand. The cheese grater sat atop a tangle of utensils in the drawer. She prepared an entire meal, including a pineapple salad, in eight minutes. In the refrigerator there was a bottle of wine, the cheap sweet kind she still liked in spite of her mother's entreaties to upgrade her taste. She might as well have some.

By the time she finished her second glass she felt pleasantly light-headed. The sweetness counteracted the throw-uppy egg and cheese taste, and then acted as dessert. She'd never drunk a whole bottle of wine. And before she did, she wanted to make one thing clear to herself. The purpose of what she was doing was not to get drunk, but to enjoy herself. She wasn't going to roll over and die just because her husband had quit school without telling her, was now a father without her being the mother, and was going out tonight with the "boys." She had her dignity to maintain. She was only providing her own entertainment.

The dishes clashed rather loudly against the sink, but she expected that. With ladylike steps she walked toward a chair. She held up the bottle: not much left. There was a bottle of good wine on the bottom shelf provided by her mother in case she and Robert ever had company. She doubted she would drink it, too, but she might.

She suddenly remembered the flowers Suzanne had sent and how she had wasted their beauty for something that wasn't their fault. Walking outside, she noticed that Isabel's car was gone. She hadn't heard her leave, had even entertained the notion of borrowing the MG when it was time to go to Mickey's. Now she would have to take a taxi.

With none of Isabel's lights on, this side of the house was dark, but if someone had suddenly whispered at her back, she wouldn't have been startled. The vase of flowers was smashed upside down as she'd left it. Isabel had added no garbage of her own. She lifted the broken container. It would probably be prudent of her not to let Isabel find this. Many of the flowers appeared salvageable, only slightly limp after their seven waterless hours.

Although Molly didn't really want to read the card pinned to the ribbon, she thought that perhaps it might have some value at some point. For now, though, she put it in the pocket of her jacket. The flowers would die and what could she show a lawyer or a judge or even God if someday she needed proof. Proof of what? The baby? Suzie herself was proof of that.

It was so quiet out here, but then she focused her ears and heard wild music in the trees. She felt the woods beckoning, but they were only a place to hide. She wasn't really afraid; it wasn't that far to school. Her only fear was that she might get so sleepy that she would lie down alongside the road. Then someone might find her, think she was dead, and call the police. She did not *ever* want to make the police report. She took the disheveled arrangement into the apartment and laid it in the kitchen sink. She sprinkled water on the petals. She did not know where he was, but she was going to find him. Carrying a flashlight, she stepped into the dark night.

When she reached where her street joined a thoroughfare, a pair of headlights turned in. A neighbor, she guessed. Perhaps even Robert or Isabel. Molly was only strolling, if anyone asked.

Maybe Robert had come to take her to Mickey's. That would make her happy. The car slowed when it saw her, but the occupant was no one she knew. An older man—old enough to be her father—let down the passenger window of his Ford Fairlane and asked if he could take her somewhere. He had a small feminine nose and wore granny glasses as if he was hip.

"If appears that we're going in opposite directions," Molly said politely. Then she yelled, "Get out of here, you creep." She aimed her flashlight at his eyes and ran down the street. Finally she was beginning to understand the difference between good manners and good sense. It was hard to run. Her legs felt sluggish, and although she wasn't sleepy anymore, her head hurt.

Along both sides of the street sat modest houses with burning porch lights for the possible stranger in trouble. Molly walked briskly. At first the heels of her shoes rang out against the cement, but then she set her feet down more carefully so as not to announce her approach.

What should she do if someone appeared ahead on the sidewalk? First of all, hope that the person intended her no harm. Realistically, though, she should take some diversionary action. She could turn up the sidewalk of whatever house she was passing as if it were her own. But what if the person turned in too? She could cross the street. Or get into an empty car and lock the doors.

No one *asked* to be mugged, but some people looked more muggable than others. You could be a woman or be old and be as unapproachable as a weight lifter. It had to do with how you carried yourself, what you were willing to let happen to your body. Her encounter with the black man was obviously an exception. Molly shoved her hands into her jacket pockets to make herself look as if she were in contact with a weapon. If circumstances warranted, her hands were saying, she could draw out her pistol and shoot.

Only the few blocks before the university, once occupied by Greensboro's Victorian society and now by a tribe of Lumbee Indians, were truly run down. In the daytime the porches of the

Lumbee houses were filled with young braves who catcalled even the old ladies in the neighborhood, but now, as she approached, the houses were dark. Lights from the student square ahead brightened the sky. She turned one last corner and saw the music building, the movie theater, the shops and restaurants that catered to college tastes. Students were everywhere.

Her fear of the dark left her, but without a moment of relief an entirely new fear made her blood race. Parked a hundred yards ahead of her was the You-Ass. She should be glad to see it. She didn't understand why she was not.

Footsteps came running up behind her, and she was momentarily startled into the other fear, but it vanished as soon as her mind made all the connections. There were too many people around to be mugged. A heavy young man dressed in corduroy pants and a flight jacket huffed past. He kept running, crossing the street between two moving cars, passing the You-Ass and then a beer joint at the top of the hill. She had not really thought that the car would be here. She'd expected to have to search for it, perhaps even call a taxi to ride first past Suzanne's house and then on to Mickey's. A kicking dread filled her.

Outside the pool of light, the way home loomed. A man in a red Ford Fairlane roamed the streets. Lumbee Indians might drag her into one of their dark houses and rape her. She crossed the street, preserving her life by looking in both directions. The You-Ass was at least familiar to her. She glided toward it, not stopping, but passing closely enough so that she could run her fingers along its side chrome strip. She continued up the street. At the corner, she crossed to be on the same side as the music building.

The steps rose before her as monstrous as a pyramid, but she took them without slowing. She braced for the familiar wooden door. When she was a senior they actually used to turn off the lights in his studio and make love. It was safer than parking down some strange road. She couldn't imagine making love anywhere but a bed now. And never in the dark.

She could see a bit of brightness at the keyhole and a strip of light shining under the door, so if Robert was in there, he wasn't

screwing someone. Noise came from all the studios, mostly so-
prano noise. Certainly, she could not hear Robert's voice. The
peephole was covered, but it could be the same wad of tape from
last year. She put her ear to the door, but before she could really
concentrate, she stepped away. She couldn't bear for someone to
catch her doing this. The hall past her was empty. Back in the
direction she'd come from, though, there was a girl leaning against
one of the massive interior columns that held up the roof. The
girl held her hands close to her face as if she were filing her nails.
She didn't seem to see Molly.

She could knock. She could knock and disturb the artist at
work. She could knock and show Robert that she'd followed him
here. But if she knocked and he answered, she would only have
to listen to him again. His explanations were what she was trying
to avoid. To find out the truth, she thought she was better off
simply observing.

In the foyer the girl filing her nails had disappeared, but still
Molly retreated from the door. She would wait in the shadows
outside Miss Loewenstein's studio. When Robert left, she would
simply confirm that he had been here. Maybe he was keeping
his voice in condition on his own.

The foyer was empty except for books, coats, and scarves piled
on the three sofas. Molly could hear voices on the catwalk over-
hang near the recording studio. As soon as she sat down, she felt
the wine again, although she'd thought that the walk had exercised
it out of her body. The chair was uncomfortable, something she'd
never noticed before. A couple came down the center staircase,
stopping at the sofas to pick up their possessions. Molly knew
neither of them, but the sight of people made her stomach trem-
ble. She stood up, needing to pee. If she left, even for one minute
though, she might miss him. Someone else started down the
stairs, but halfway down, the person turned and started back up.
More students appeared, this time out of Robert's hallway. Molly
turned so that she was almost facing the wall. She knew two of
them, but they didn't notice her.

The hall grew quiet again, and her need to go to the bathroom subsided. Perhaps Robert would never come out. Perhaps he wasn't even here. How late was she willing to stay? She had to leave for home at a reasonable hour. Especially since she was walking. Comforting though the presence of the You-Ass was, she didn't have its keys.

When she saw Robert, it was as if she were watching him from a future time. He was someone with whom she'd once been intimate but had not seen in years. He had not aged the way she had. His still youthful body moved with sensuous, enchanting grace across the foyer. His face was handsome, lively, a face that magnetized her body and soul. In her imagination her arms reached out for him. If they embraced, they would fit together as if God had carved them. Why had she ever given him up? she wondered. He appealed to her as much this minute as he ever had, even while he held open the door for Suzanne—a much more attractive Suzanne than she'd ever expected—who stood on tiptoe to lift her face to his as she walked under his arm.

Molly felt the contortions of her face—her open mouth, her angled head, her eyes hooded by grief. The silence that the couple left behind pounded at her. She felt that she did not exist; perhaps she had never existed. Strange footsteps—the same ones she'd heard earlier—moved halfway down the stairs and then retraced their path, holding her motionless and awakening her to the truth. She could hear; she existed. When the footsteps were gone, she approached the wooden doors. Both ahead and behind, things frightened her, but she resolutely put her shoulder to the door. The pair had vanished. Across the street sat the You-Ass, empty. The lamps that lit the steps to the music building also illuminated her, and she stepped hastily to remove herself from their reach.

Chapter Nineteen

S UZANNE told Bennie over the telephone that the doctor had
sent her home to recuperate.

"That's terrific," he said. He was punching numbers on the
cash register. The drawer opened with a loud zing. "Look, I told
Adele about your operation. 'That's nine and one makes ten.
Thank you, ma'am, and come back.' Adele said she hadn't ever
heard of anybody so young having a"—Bennie let his voice drop—
"masectomy."

"Mas-*tec*-tomy," Suzanne corrected.

"Whatever. Anyway. She's coming to visit you. I'll call and
let her know you're already home. Uh. Look. How're you feeling?
I meant to get to the hospital, but with Ruth gone, I've been tied
up. You doing okay?"

Suzanne was silent.

"You still there?"

She waited a few more seconds. "What do you think?"

"Well, it's good you're out."

"Good for who?"

"For you, dummy."

"Oh. I thought it might be good for you."

Bennie paused. "Look, Suzanne, you said you were through
with ole Bennie. I ain't no jack-in-the-box."

"You mean yo-yo."

"That's right. I'm not a yo-yo. Hold on," he said. This time
he laid down the phone to take the customer's money. There was
a third checkout, and then he picked up the phone again. "Look,

it's pretty busy here today. I know you'd like some company, so I'm going to call Adele . . ."

"Bennie."

"What?" he asked, a touch of nervousness in his voice.

"Don't you let Adele come over here. Do you understand?"

"She wants to come, Suzanne,"

"I don't want her, and if you send her, I'll tell her every single thing we ever did together." She paused. "Plus some."

"How am I going to tell her you don't want to see her?"

"That's your problem."

"Maybe I can say you're embarrassed or something. But that won't work forever, Suzanne. She's made up her mind to see you."

"I need some loving, Bennie," she interjected in a low wheedling tone.

"What about your . . . bandage . . . your . . . ?"

"My what?"

"Isn't it too soon?" The dirty louse was stalling, scared of a woman lacking one of her tits.

"I wanted you to visit me in the hospital," she said. "You don't know what it does to you. It makes you want to fuck everything in sight."

"No kidding." There was honest amazement in his voice. "Are you all bandaged up?" he asked. Maybe if he didn't have to see anything, he could be interested.

"Sure."

"I mean, I don't know what it looks like."

"You won't have to look now."

The idea of having to look *sometime* made him hesitate again. "I don't know. It seems like you ought to be sore."

"That's right. I'm aching," she said.

Now that she had gained his interest, he kept talking to her while he rang up the next bill. He was figuring out loud: who could he get to operate the cash register this afternoon, how soon could he be at her house, did she need food or anything?

"What I'd really like is some flowers," she said. She decided against suggesting that he call Ruth to come in until she found out more about what had happened.

"Why, sure. Of course. I'd already planned flowers. I mean, anything besides. Anything to eat?"

She told him huskily, "Nothing but you."

"Now look," he said, lapsing back into his original hesitancy, "if Janet doesn't show up today or something, I can't come. Nobody else is smart enough to handle the money."

"She'll be there."

"I think so too," he said, almost halfheartedly.

"So I'll see you at five then?"

"Yes," he said, barely audible.

"You won't be sorry."

He wanted to say he hoped not, she could tell, but he stopped himself.

He arrived at five-twenty—she'd already called the pancake house twice—with potted white chrysanthemums and a bag of groceries. She was reclining on the living room sofa in a nightgown and a robe, the trunk of her body wrapped in gauze. "I bought us some steaks," he said in a brave tone.

"Wonderful." She tried to sound enthusiastic. He didn't look quite as good as she'd expected. His shirt was the one he'd worked in all day. And he had his own ever-present detractions—things she'd forgotten about: his pancake belly, the brown slimy teeth, and those stubby ungentle hands that liked to squeeze her harshly everywhere. Below the waist only today.

"You got a grill?" he asked, emerging from the kitchen where he'd taken the groceries. He held the pot of flowers directly in front of his face. Very romantic, Bennie. On the other hand, she didn't have to look at him for a few seconds.

"No."

"I'll get you one next week." His nervousness about her condition seemed to have disappeared. He was behaving as he had when they first became lovers: boyish and a bit dimwitted. "For you," he said, handing her the pot and allowing his face to show.

The chrysanthemums were slightly past their prime, as if bought at a grocery instead of a florist.

"They don't smell," she said.

"They're not supposed to smell." He stuck out his fat tongue playfully at her and then got the idea that he was going to kiss her. He leaned across the sofa. The brown of his teeth was repelling. She tilted her head back and closed her eyes. Bennie's tongue roamed around in her mouth, while his arms hung stiffly at his sides.

"Whoa," she said, pulling away. He'd started rocking rhythmically on the balls of his feet. The crotch of his pants bulged, and his breath came in short gasps. He came around the sofa to sit beside her, one horny guy. The impassioned face moved toward her again, and his hands slid slowly into the folds of her robe. As soon as they disappeared under the pink quilted fabric, though, they came as alive as fish thrown back to the waves, squeezing her legs, grabbing the satin of her gown. They pushed up around her hips to her waist and back down again.

Desire like a scream welled within her. Her breasts longed to be crushed under his fingers. Her vagina ached for the penetrating thrusts that Bennie had the gift to give. Consciously, she tightened her thighs against each other.

"Oh, baby, baby," Bennie moaned. His hands were digging between her legs like an animal. He set his wrists against each other and levered her legs open. Deciding not to fight, she let his thumbs dig into her.

"What's wrong?" he asked, pulling his hands out of those great depths. "What did you do to yourself?"

The pause angered her. "Nothing," she said. He looked uncertain. There was supposed to be something wrong only with the top of her. "I shaved," she said, grabbing both his hands and pulling them back to her. "It's really nicer. It's like a little girl." He looked at her strangely as if she were another species.

"I liked it better the other way," he said. His head tilted in the air; his eyes gazed down his own cheeks.

The length of the sofa was behind her, so she lay down, slowly untying her rumpled robe. Her head rested on the sofa arm. She lazily dropped one slipper at a time to the floor. The robe became the sheet of their bed. Now, when he looked, he could see how the flattening effect of the gauze gave her the appearance of being sexless. She let her knees drop apart a few inches. With her hands at her waist she began inching up the ankle-length gown. It rose past her calves and then to her knees, and then Bennie, sitting on the other end of the sofa, began to watch. Just before the gown lifted past her thighs, she stopped its slow rise. He raised his eyes to hers commandingly. His mouth hung open slightly. He returned his gaze to the bottom edge of the gown, and obediently she raised it the last few inches, showing him the bareness of a little girl. He fell on her as if famished. She tilted her pelvis so that he could get to her best and came quickly, only the beginning, a thrilling tickling sensation that brought her backbone alive. Bennie felt it happen and leered at her.

He rose from the couch and stood over her, unbuttoning his shirt, unbuckling his belt, dropping his pants. She lay with her legs apart. He didn't take his eyes off her pink skin. His body was the shape of a machine, his penis the lever that made it operate. She took hold of the lever, using it to raise herself from the couch. The gown fell back in place to her toes. He noticed the bandage then, she thought. His gaze dropped to the sofa.

"Lie down," he said. He put his hands on her small waist, and his thumbs nearly met at her navel. She felt like a child.

"I want to show you," she said. Her husky voice, heavy with satisfaction, pretended to be seeking permission.

"Later," he said. "I won't mind it later."

"You'll mind it less now."

Ignoring her, he lifted her until her feet no longer touched the floor. With his leg he brought her feet skillfully out from under her and lowered her again to the couch. She drew the gown up quickly this time, pulling it over her head before he could stop her. Except for the bandage, she sat naked, arms by her sides, her youth apparently crushed.

"Poor Suzanne." He stepped back. "I gotta take a leak," he

said suddenly. She would lose her edge if he masturbated. Like a nurse she jerked away the adhesive. One end of the gauze fell to her waist.

"I don't have to look at this," Bennie said, but he stood mesmerized as she began dropping the circumferences of the thin white fabric. "You shouldn't ought to be taking off your bandages, honey," he said, his voice growing superstitious. "You might get an infection."

"I already had an infection," she said tonelessly. "That's what I had the operation to get rid of. I had a *cancer* infection, Bennie."

His eyes rolled back in his head, horrified. His body, attractive as all bodies become in the throes of passion, again appeared misshapen and ugly. His skin was a yellowish white, a reminder of his stained teeth. His penis, shriveled to nothing, seemed deformed.

He waited as if under a spell while the last layers dropped to the floor. His eyes, glued to her, showed the pain of seeing. It was as if he felt he owed it to her. When she stood naked before him, his face became utterly confused. He did not look at her eyes for confirmation, only at the unharmed diseaseless breasts that swelled out of her body toward him.

After a long silence, she said, "I wanted to see if you really loved me." Kicking away the gauze, she stood with her breasts at proud attention, watching pointedly while his penis grew again. He did not move his eyes above her neck, so when she beckoned him with her fingers, she did so at a height he would notice. She lay down on her robe on the sofa, as if he had commanded her, turning her hips so her legs crossed sexily. She cupped her hands under her breasts, lifting them to his watchful gaze.

His huge body fell upon her, and, as if he were giving a sort of primitive thanks, he pummeled her healthy breasts with his hands and teeth and mouth. Finally, he pulled himself up on her body so that his penis lay in her cleavage. He moved back and forth only a few times before his sperm shot into the indentation of her collar bone.

Bennie broiled their steaks in the oven and made French fries, but she declined to eat, saying she was tired. She needed for him to leave so she could bathe and dress for Kearns, whom she was to meet at the music building at nine.

"Did you go to the hospital at all?" Bennie asked, his mouth in a half smile to show that he could take a joke just like anyone else.

"Of course, I went to the hospital. My nurse's name was Jane Hunter," she said, but she would not explain any further. As soon as he'd speared his last bite, she took his plate away, which they did at the pancake house when there was a waiting line. Almost reflexively, Bennie stood up to leave. Before he reached his car, she was in the shower washing his odor away.

Over the telephone late last week she had told Kearns a new made-up story of her life, which included an incestuous rela- tionship with her father, and he'd agreed that by telling it, she'd managed to explain a lot about her behavior. He asked to see her again, but this time they would go to his place, a dormitory room that, for a premium fee—his parents were rich—he occupied alone. They had some unfinished business that he expected would take all night.

She'd argued uselessly that her apartment was safer, freer— she had a private john; he shared with the guys next door—but he'd said no. She could not think how he might be tricking her. He'd be the one in trouble if she was caught. The idea of screwing Kearns all night in a men's dorm with all those inexperienced bodies around made her breathless. If, by chance, Kearns lacked the expertise he claimed, she might simply slip into someone else's room. She told him yes.

She didn't arrive at the music building until eight-thirty, some- time after Robert and Caroleen usually came. Dropping her over- night bag at the sofas, she started toward Robert's studio, just to make sure it was business as usual. For the first time she felt vaguely repelled by him and Caroleen; her mind was on Kearns, who seemed so promising. She tried to imagine his dormitory room and how uncomfortable the bed would be and what would be on the walls. She expected giant posters of nude women, maybe even nude men because she still thought that Kearns went both ways.

Suddenly, she saw a girl standing at the door of Robert's studio, her hand to her ear. Without seeing her face, she knew who it was. She backed quietly away. Molly might see her and put it together with the other time she'd unknowingly seen the same face. She wasn't ready for that to happen.

Suzanne climbed the stairs. Molly came out of the hallway, an air of listening about her as she crossed the lobby to Miss Loewenstein's door. Her face wore the undecided look of fear. She seemed reined in, not wanting to destroy her own ability to hear by bolting. At the top step Suzanne paused.

The downstairs and upstairs lobbies grew quiet. Suzanne cleared her throat and imagined that Molly could hear her. She tried to think of some way to summon Robert and Caroleen out of their love nest. A shout of fire might not convince them. A real fire would do the job but seemed hardly necessary, since they would produce themselves soon enough anyway.

She expected Kearns any minute. And if he hadn't been willing to wait before, in the face of such mystery, he certainly wouldn't wait this time. She crossed the catwalk and headed down the far hall to the section of floor she thought lay directly over Robert's studio. There she sprawled trying to hear them, but the floors of this building were much thicker than the walls. Sitting up cross-legged, she removed one of her shoes. With its thick hard heel she beat out a Morse Code message to them: S.O.S. S.O.S. Love, Suzanne. She repeated the message five times.

Not for fifteen minutes, as if they hadn't heard her warning, did Robert and Caroleen emerge from the hallway. Suzanne stood above but in full view of them. Molly sat thirty feet away on their same level. Although they did not touch, they walked closely enough to make touching unnecessary. They saw no one but each other.

At the sight of Robert, Suzanne felt moved to scream out, "Murderer." She thought of her poor dead baby, the physical pain she'd endured, his heartlessness. She wanted to point at him from the balcony, scream out her story, drape herself over the banister until even Molly begged her not to jump. But she would save all that for another time. Tonight was Molly's to rage and claw and tear.

They were nearly outside, and still Molly had made no move. Robert opened the door into the dark night, sending a cold draft up the stairs. Caroleen ducked under his arm, standing on tiptoe to press her cheek to his as she passed. Then, unscathed, they were gone. Where was Molly? Could she have left without Suzanne knowing?

When she was halfway down the stairs, the chair in front of Miss Loewenstein's door creaked. Suzanne retraced her steps until she could see but not be seen. Like someone lost, Molly moved forward, stopped, moved again. She struggled with the wooden door as if it were an actual burden, which made Suzanne shiver with contempt.

The hesitating figure was only halfway down the outside steps when Suzanne, her overnight bag slung over her shoulder, opened the door herself. Molly hadn't even tried to catch them. Across the street in front of the coffee shop sat the empty Corvair. Robert was evidently walking Caroleen to her dorm. Molly crossed the street to the car, slid into the passenger seat, and ducked low. Suzanne followed closely enough behind that she could have shut the door for her. Instead, Molly's favorite Good Samaritan kept moving. When she passed the car, she stared through the windshield, drumming one set of fingers on the long front hood Molly looked at her without recognition.

Inside the coffee shop she took the window table, which seemed providentially to have been left for her. She ordered coffee, laying a dollar on the table in case she had to leave quickly. In time she saw Kearns climb the cement steps to the music building. His spidery legs made her laugh. Seconds later he reappeared, scanning the college horizon for some sign of her. She took a long sip of her coffee.

Kearns went away, and then Robert arrived. Molly had crawled into the back seat where she could no longer be seen, so Suzanne was the one who observed his jaunty, whistling approach. He lit a cigarette before he opened the car door, and the match bathed his face. Suzanne fell in love with him all over again.

Seconds after he folded into the car, he whirled around, discovering his wife. When he pulled away from the curb, the car burned rubber. Suzanne calmly finished her second cup of coffee. Leaving the dollar, big-spender that she was, she climbed for the last time the steps to the music building and rang up Caroleen on the house phone.

When the babyish voice answered, she asked, "Are you aware that Robert Carter is married?"

The girl said nothing.

"Before you hang up, you should know that his wife, as of tonight, is very much aware of you." Just so Caroleen would know she was telling the truth, Suzanne added, "Remember touching Robert's cheek when you left the music building? Molly saw you do that."

She replaced the receiver without the usual sense of rage she felt toward Caroleen and started home. The night was crisp and clear, and the stars shone like Morse Code dots in the sky. The heavens might be one great message if one only had the key.

At the pay phone by the movie theater she called Kearns, but he told her he had no intention of seeing her again. Before he could hang up, she shouted some stinging words about schedules and people who had to work all the time versus those who got to play. Then she slammed down the phone. She'd have to consider him later.

From her apartment she dialed Robert and Molly. They hadn't arrived home yet, so she let the phone ring and ring and ring until finally they did answer.

Chapter Twenty

T HE ARTIFICIAL light of the student square made Molly totally visible to passers-by, so she decided to wait for Robert in the more shadowy back seat. Locking the doors for safety—he would simply think that he'd locked them himself—she climbed over. By curling fetally, she was able to ward off her growing chill. Knowing how sleep blurred a clear mind, she fought against dozing so no sense of his possible innocence could take root.

Fifteen minutes later he pulled at the handle and then fumbled for his keys before swinging smoothly into the car. He was smoking a cigarette from which he took two quick puffs before extinguishing it in the ashtray. The very movement of his elbow made her want to weep.

She spoke his name, but he was already turning, feeling her presence at the same time she announced it. Without a word he angrily turned back around and started the car. She touched his shoulder and he flinched.

"You said Suzanne was ugly," she said softly, intending to speak obliquely, since he was behind the wheel. When he was angry, Robert used the car as a sort of weapon, slamming on brakes or squealing around corners to make his points. *Had* that girl been Suzanne? She'd assumed so, but now it occurred to her that she was someone else. Suzanne was in the hospital, wasn't she?, with a newborn.

"What are you talking about?" he asked. He was headed toward downtown not home. At a corner he took a right turn that made the tires sing. "You followed me," he said.

She realized that he was stalling. He had no idea how much she'd seen or whether she'd seen anything. "You're going to get stopped," she said calmly, unable to keep herself from adding, "I'm not paying for the ticket."

He stepped hard on the gas again. This was dangerous.

Leaning forward, she said in a saner tone of voice, "Let's go home and talk." To her relief he turned the car around. After several blocks she felt confident enough of his driving to climb into the front seat. He even reached out a hand to help her. His face was composed. She could tell that he'd decided to wait, to see what she'd reveal. She knew everything. Where should she start?

"How did you get to school?" he asked.

"I walked."

"That's not a safe thing to do."

"I know that better than you."

They turned down their street, Molly remembering the bottle of wine that Robert would blame for her actions. He might even claim she'd been seeing things. She felt a sudden intense nostalgia. Had she the choice now, she thought she would have fallen asleep with the bottle to her lips. She would have waited for the truth, not sought it out. Maybe.

It took effort to get out of the car. Isabel's lights burned, making her think of the audience they would have if they started yelling at each other. The basement looked like a cage. Robert guessed correctly that she had failed to lock the door and stalked into the house ahead of her. The phone was ringing, but he only lifted the receiver and set it back down. He held up her wine bottle to the overhead light and then tossed it a dangerous distance into the trash can.

"I see why you came over," he said.

"No, you don't." She was tired of wearing clothes, but undressing seemed too intimate. Not for Robert though. He undressed except for his boxer shorts and lit a cigarette. "I walked because I didn't have a car," she said. "I wasn't drunk." He would not listen. "I *wasn't drunk*," she insisted.

He put his hands on his hips. "I didn't say you were drunk. I said you were braver than usual because you'd drunk a bottle of wine. Or don't you remember just a few months ago"—his voice took on a patronizing tone—"when you were too frightened to walk to work in broad daylight?"

"Some things you have to do; some you don't."

He went into the bathroom, and without shutting the door, took a leak. Next he brushed his teeth. He clearly seemed to be getting ready to go to bed. She waited in one of the wing chairs. Without looking at her, he walked out of the bathroom and over to the bed.

"Are you actually thinking of going to sleep?" she asked.

"What else do you want to do?" He straightened the sheets, unmade from the night before.

"I want to talk about tonight"—he began shaking his head—"and about your new baby and about a conversation I had with Miss Loewenstein today."

"There is no baby," he said, shaking his head more firmly.

"I'm not going to stay married to you like this."

"Like what?" he asked, as if he truly did not understand what she meant.

She was ready to make firm accusations, wanting more than anything to know whom he'd been with tonight—was it Suzanne or someone else—but she restrained herself. Was the baby a hoax? Why had he quit school? Would he now agree to return? He sat on the edge of the mattress watching his cigarette burn down. She didn't know what to say first. The bold outlines of his collar bones made her stomach feel bottomless. Shamelessly, she wanted to touch his smooth skin.

"Robert," she said, rising from the chair. Her voice held a mixture of hurt and forgiveness and love. If he would just explain everything . . . Tears glistened in her eyes. She sat beside him on the bed, so carefully that the springs hardly registered. When he put his arm around her, she moved closer. Dropping her head against his shoulder, she pressed her nose into his skin, thinking fleetingly of a world that existed without the past. The thought of her own faithless father—she dared not think of her mother—entered her mind, and her brimming eyes dried, some unknown force steering her back to reality. Tonight's scene at the music building unfolded anew before her eyes. She sat up straight, withdrawing her shoulders, her arms, her hands, her existence from Robert's grasp.

"I saw you with a girl tonight," she began in a low careful voice. "I was sitting on the chair outside Miss Loewenstein's door when you finished practicing." Practicing? "Or whatever you were doing."

"That was Caroleen York, who is my accompanist," he said with dignity. The tension in his body passed through the bedsprings into her.

"What do you need an accompanist for? You're not a student anymore." She felt the way she imagined a private investigator must when he finally knew enough about a case to ask the right questions.

"I figured Elizabeth would butt in," he said, his face clouded with irritation.

"Elizabeth did not 'butt in.' I saw her when I came to find you at your voice lesson to tell you about Suzanne's baby. You have quit, haven't you? That's the truth, isn't it?"

"Temporarily," he said. "I had to. Elizabeth was trying to tell me what to *eat*." She'd heard this same silly complaint ever since she'd known Robert.

"They want to give you a scholarship," she said, smiling a hopeful smile. It *was* good news. It was very important news.

"Who does?"

"Who do you think? Juilliard. But you have to be back in all your classes by Monday." The news did not seem to excite him at all. She herself felt only a mild excitement, but it was because of all the other things she'd found out. Watching his closed face, she said, "Rather petty of them."

"What?" he asked from faraway.

"Rather petty of them to insist that you graduate."

The ice-blue eyes that she had loved for so long penetrated

hers as if to do harm. She turned aside her gaze. "I'm not going to Juilliard," he said.

"You're not what?"

"I've changed my mind." He smiled weakly at her. "I'm not going to be a singer."

"You don't mean that."

"Yes, I do."

Fear as immense as the ocean swelled in her chest. He was tormenting her, angry that she had not trusted him over these past months. Or he was going through one of his phases. Or he meant it.

"What were you doing tonight with Caroleen?" she asked.

"We were copying music."

"Robert," she commanded.

"Okay. We were talking. Caroleen is my friend. I haven't had one in the last six months."

"You mean she's your girlfriend." The label hurt coming out of her throat.

"Friend, Molly. I'd even thought about inviting her home to dinner, but I knew you'd think something exactly like this." He paused to light another cigarette. "What kills me is that none of this would have ever happened if it hadn't been for Suzanne. You'd never have followed me anywhere and seen me acting friendly with a girl I know."

"You're lying to me. I watched you walk through the lobby." Even now Molly reconsidered what she'd seen. There was no way she could be mistaken, yet she wanted to be positive. The scene rolled through her mind, as exact and painful as it had been in the flesh. They did not touch, but they walked as if they were intimate. She had never seen Robert with Suzanne Cox, so she wasn't sure what to think about them, but she had registered Robert and Caroleen with her own eyes.

"I am not lying."

Tears streamed down her face. The only truth you could ever count on was what you saw for yourself, so almost everything she claimed to know was suspect. "Can't we talk about Juilliard?"

she asked in a faltering voice. "It's what we've been hoping for."

"What *you've* been hoping for."

"It's our chance to leave here. To leave this whole mess."

"You've never listened to me, have you?" he said in a suddenly expansive tone. "Juilliard has always been my mother's dream, not mine, and you don't even know it. All you want is a chance to work for some big newspaper."

"Of course, I want to work for a big newspaper. But you were going to Juilliard when I met you. You haven't spent five years singing just because of your mother. Sure, I want to work for a big newspaper. Sure, I want to move away from here. Don't you? Or do you want to stay here so you can screw your guitar students?" She was leaving out Caroleen. "And your so-called accompanist." He slapped at her, but she jumped out of the way.

"This will kill your mother," she said.

"It's *my* life, not my mother's life. I won't be chained to a career I hate."

"You're stupid, Robert." Her voice was shrill, out-of-control. "You're an idiot."

"Caroleen doesn't think so."

"Does *Caroleen* know about your baby?"

"There is no baby."

She tried to breathe, but no air would penetrate her lungs. She was not crying, but her face was wet with tears. All these months she, too, had thought there was no baby, but then the telegram came and she knew it had to be true. "Maybe we ought to go to the hospital and see," she said evenly. "Especially if we're staying here in Greensboro. She's so innocent and dependent that we couldn't hate her. She'll be just another person brought into the world under less-than-ideal circumstances."

"I'm going to say this one more time," Robert said, his jaw locked with finality. "There is no baby. If there was a baby, it would not be mine. Do you hear me?"

"Of course she's yours," Molly persisted. "You've got to face your responsibility. You can't walk away from a living baby like you can an acceptance from Juilliard. I know you didn't mean for it to happen, but Suzie's here, and we have to deal with that reality."

"You're crazy," Robert said. "You've gone fucking crazy."

"It can take only one time to make a baby," she intoned. "Really. I know that's hard for anyone to believe. Especially since we've never made one in all the times we *did it* without any protection."

"Don't do this, Molly," he said, but the emotion in his voice had worn itself out.

"Don't do what?"

"Nothing. Never mind." But he gathered himself for one last plea. "You're destroying everything. You've got to stop."

"What have *I* destroyed?" she asked, innocence and righteousness in her voice. He looked helplessly at her.

She felt as if she were in a womb of aloneness: only she existed for herself in any honest way. She was the only person she could ever believe in. She couldn't even trust Gisella. She took a deep breath. "I want a divorce," she said quietly.

"You don't want a divorce."

She looked uncertainly at him. His eyes did not break from hers. "There's no other choice." Why *wouldn't* he want a divorce if he was in love with another woman? They were young. They had no children. There was no reason not to go their own ways. Robert turned back the covers. "We can't sleep in the same bed tonight," she said hastily.

"Oh, come on."

"I mean it."

"You mean what?" he said in a pouty, sexy tone that tried to dismiss everything that had been said.

"Stop it," she said, moving out of his reach. Why would he lie? Why would he lie? Why would he lie? tumbled over and over in her mind as if it had become the rhythm of her life.

The bed was like a river that Molly swam alone in the dark. Robert lay on a pallet on the floor, breathing easily. She could make out the darker black of the opening to the bathroom, the white column where the phone hung, and the shadowy furniture that stood guard above his invisible body. She felt torn by this separation, a separation especially intense because he lay so near.

"Robert," she called with just enough volume to pass through his curtain of sleep. But he wasn't asleep. Soundlessly—she saw his outline rather than heard him—he arose, gliding like a thief toward the bed. He lay down in a pool of moonlight beside her, his bare back turned. He had come not for her but for the comfort of the bed. His broad expanse of skin seemed like a field of snow. Her hands moved instinctively to make a mark, but just as instinctively, pulled away. She imagined that like the tragic Greeks she'd studied in college, she was being prideful. Robert didn't have the right to touch her first: she must touch him.

She started at his neck, where the tight skin could be loosened by her fingers, and moved down his backbone, her fingers kneading the indented center and wandering to either side. Goose bumps formed on his skin, went away, reformed. Like an expert, her hands moved; within their small perimeter, but nowhere else, she felt a radiant desire. When finally he turned to her, his body hard and alive, they were two nameless people who wanted nothing more than satisfaction. It was not unhealthy, she told herself after they had assumed separate positions in the bed. It was a simple willingness to acknowledge the difference between body and soul.

She viewed it no differently late the next morning when she awoke. Bright sunshine scooted through cracks in the curtains. When she opened the door for the newspaper, the rich blue sky and the fragrant spring air momentarily charmed her. Robert slept with his head under his pillow, his bare body covered by the sheet up to his hips. Had they not made love last night, this sight might have moved her. But she felt cleansed of desire, able to deal with him today on one basis.

She cooked simply, bacon and eggs. Intending to call a halt this morning to all undue special treatment, she set the two hot plates on the table and sat down. To her surprise Robert rose, stumbled to his robe hanging on the bathroom door, and came to the table.

He ran his fingers several times through his blond curls. He tied the sash of his robe. His boyish face seemed older this morning, or perhaps he hadn't slept well. But Robert was never unable to sleep.

They ate in tandem, noticing each other's need for salt and pepper, butter, jam. Molly started to comment about the weather but then decided not to. The telephone began ringing while they were taking their last coincidentally synchronized bites, but Robert waved her down when she started to answer it. This refusal to answer the phone was beginning to annoy her: what if it was something important? But she sat to appease him. The caller hung up after the fourth ring, meaning it wasn't Suzanne after all. If it rang again, she was going to answer no matter what he said.

She took their plates to the sink and brought coffee to the table. While she poured, Robert broke the silence by asking, "What could you expect?" His voice was clear, not at all as if these were the first words he'd spoken today. His clever blue eyes seemed to snag and hold hers.

Molly smiled the kind of smile she used when he initiated an argument in front of her parents: a broad, amused, lying smile that attempted to deny the essence of what was being said. She bought time by putting sugar and cream in her coffee. The implication was that Caroleen was his girlfriend after all.

"I don't know *what* you expected," he rephrased. His tone had a sense of history, as if because he'd been found out, the affair was over. She should never have made love with him last night. He'd interpreted it as meaning he was forgiven. But in spirit he was not her husband: she'd just been an easy lay.

"What are you trying to tell me?" she asked sharply.

"I was lonely and you gave me no succor," he said in a Biblical tone.

"Are you having an affair with Caroleen?" she asked.

"Not really."

"Yes or no."

"We are very close friends."

Molly put her face in her hands, listening to his words echo over and over again in the suddenly tense air. When the silence became unbearable, she stood, turning her back to him, one knee on the seat of her chair.

"You've been a jealous, suspicious bitch," Robert said softly. "You've followed me, you've driven me to do things I would never normally—"

"You have a *girlfriend*, Robert," she interrupted. "How can you call me suspicious when what I'm suspicious of is a fact?"

"I'm not talking about Caroleen," he said in the same unruffled tone. "I'm talking about Suzanne Cox."

"You're blaming *me* for Suzanne?"

"Not for what she did, but for not believing what I told you about her. For making this go on and on. For the letters, for the phone calls, for all the other things she's done. I wanted to ignore her, but you decided it was important. That it meant something when it meant nothing."

She stopped him to add some truth to the story: "So instead of loving me and trying to help me understand and get over it, you just took up with someone else."

"No, I didn't. Not really."

"I saw you. I saw you. How many times do I have to tell you? I *saw* you." Tired of standing, she sat down in her chair again, her shoulders drooping.

"It was your imagination," he argued. "You've always seen more in things than were there. Isn't that true? Tell me exactly what you saw, and I can explain all of it."

She opened her mouth to describe the familiar movie that moved through her mind at fast forward. But she had already done what her profession insisted upon: looked at the film from every angle. She was not the hysterical victim of a bank robber or rapist. Even in the most frightening experience of her life— her encounter with the black man—she'd still been able to observe objectively. She knew that Robert and Caroleen looked at each other with love.

"There's no *reason* for me to lie," his smooth voice was saying. "I like Caroleen. I'll admit that. But all we were doing was talking. That's all we've ever done."

"Your arm was hooked through hers," she accused.

"I don't think so." She remembered it wasn't true. "She touched her cheek to yours."

"If she did, she was just being friendly," he said. "I walked her back to the dorm, but only to finish our conversation. *You* know how long I was gone. You were in the car spying. Five minutes?"

"Is she afraid to walk at night by herself?" Molly asked.

"I don't know why I bother," he muttered.

"Do you need to 'copy music' again today? Would you like to borrow the car?" she asked brightly.

"Go to hell. Just go straight to hell."

"All I want is the truth, Robert." Her voice became plaintive. "I saw how you were looking at each other. It all fits. We've hardly made love for weeks. We haven't spent any time together. You've been going to the music building night after night. To be friends with Caroleen. Do you think I'm a fool? It's perfectly clear: you're in love with somebody else."

"I am not," he said fiercely.

"You don't love *me*."

"Yes, I do."

"No, you don't."

"I do. You have to believe I do."

"It's not enough. Love is not enough. You've got to respect me. You've got to be willing to give something up. You just can't have whatever you want. We're married."

"I didn't know it was jail."

She put her head in her hands. "Don't you want a divorce?" she pleaded. "Don't you think each of us should just start all over?"

"No. No. I want things to stay like they are."

"They can't. They'll never be the same."

"They can be."

She asked, "How?," but it was not a question—only "no" in a different form. She left the table and methodically made up the bed. Robert and she were perpendicular lines. Couldn't he see that? They had crossed paths once, and now, through an inevitable law of geometry, would never cross again. Suddenly she was sobbing in great choking gulps over which she had no power at all. She buried her face in Robert's pillow, absorbing his musky scent.

He lay beside her, his lips moving against her bare neck, not kissing but whispering to her skin. Finally, he spoke words. "You *do* love me, don't you?" But his question was not a question either.

She shifted slightly in his direction, the strain in her muscles relaxing so that she curved more naturally against him. "I never said I didn't," she said in a voice heavy with truth.

He fell asleep lying next to her on the bed only moments after extracting her inverted confession of love. Hearing his regular breathing, when he was supposed to be comforting her, fanned the smoldering bitterness in her heart. She was becoming aware one by one of the many ways he'd deceived her. For weeks he had slept every morning while she slaved away at the newspaper. Whenever she'd telephoned to wake him for his eleven o'clock class he'd pretended to be on his way out the door. Each night he had opened his books to study. And, of course, he had gone regularly to his studio. The true distance between them widened with each new awareness rather than narrowing because Robert had reminded her that she loved him. She wondered if he'd been with Caroleen a few times or many times. Did the number matter?

His arm lay across her like a piece of angle iron. As soon as she could, she slipped out from under it and began dressing. He did not awaken when, with the normal amount of noise, she let herself out the door.

She headed in the direction of the only hospital with an intensive care nursery, feeling an eagerness that was not really strange. Now that Robert was not going to Juilliard, she ought to improve her home territory. She did not understand how someone who didn't know her could be her enemy, so in the past few months she had often thought of going to Suzanne's door to talk things out. Visiting the baby seemed like a safer alternative.

A smiling Gray Lady manned the huge, horseshoe-shaped reception desk that blocked easy passage to the bank of elevators. She beamed at Molly, her cheeks rising in wrinkles to nudge the bottoms of her glasses frames.

"Suzanne Cox," Molly whispered. She cleared her throat and said the name again.

"Cox, Suzanne," the woman repeated, her smile diminishing as she clicked her fingernails through the plastic file cards.

"Maternity," Molly whispered as the woman drilled twice through the C's without stopping. There was a moment of uneasy silence. Before the woman could speak, Molly said, "Actually, Suzanne's gone home, but her baby's still here. Intensive care nursery."

"I don't have any Coxes at all. . . The baby should have its own listing."

Molly leaned forward to try to examine the cards herself, a puzzled look on her face. "I was here yesterday, and they were both in the file. I don't understand. The baby is my niece," she added, feeling her heart go cold at the claim.

"Could the baby have gone home?" the lady asked.

"Oh, no," Molly said. "She was very premature. I talked with my sister this morning. It's going to be at least a couple of more weeks."

"There must be a mixup in the files then. Just go on up." The woman smiled her same cheeky smile which Molly tried to return. She felt faint. Until this minute it had not occurred to her that she might encounter Suzanne. What if she were in the nursery holding Suzie?

She took the elevator to the third floor, emerging into the maternity waiting area. The room was occupied by three lone smokers, two women and a man. Danish-style blond furniture was scattered in no visible arrangement around the room. On the wall opposite the television was a bank of phones. Molly hesitated before heading toward them. She checked the time: one o'clock. Where was Suzanne usually at this time of day? She didn't even know when her shift began.

She dialed Suzanne's apartment first, not knowing if she would simply hang up or apologize for a wrong number. Suzanne might know her voice. She didn't have to make a decision. The phone rang and rang without answer, and with relief Molly hung up.

There was one more number to try, the pancake house, and if Suzanne wasn't there, she might not go to the nursery at all. She dialed the number, feeling less nervous, although without doubt someone would answer this ring. She was simply going to ask if Suzanne was working today. They needn't call her to the phone.

"Hello? Pancake house," a shrill voice said. Was that *her* voice? Molly felt frozen to the receiver. Her eyes closed as she tried to rehear the voice.

"M-May I please speak with Suzanne Cox?" she said. Her body was shrouded in sweat. Her heart beat in her throat so she could hardly talk.

"Molly?" the voice said, vague accusation in its tone. Then, more loudly, "Molly Carter? Is that you?"

She felt her last shred of dignity drain away as she, lacking the courage to answer or confront, quickly thrust the receiver from her ear. For a moment she held it poised over the shiny silver hook. Behind her an elevator door opened, emitting a chattering group of people. Suzanne might even guess she was at the hospital. In terror Molly hung up the phone, both hands curling around the black receiver. She leaned her forehead against her thumbs. She felt the prayerfulness of her position, but all she could think of to whisper was, "I'm sorry." She knew she was talking to God. She felt no better than her accuser, no better at all. *Is that you, Molly Carter? Is that you?* She couldn't even own up to who she was.

Without thinking, she pushed the elevator button but then hurried past the opening doors. She had been here to see babies before, but now she was confused about which direction to go. Down one hall she saw several people, the elevator crowd, peering through a glass window.

Her steps were tentative but firm as she approached. She had just proved to herself where Suzanne was, so she had no worry about meeting her face to face. The group adjacent to her chattered among themselves, constantly moved to better vantage points, waved at a baby who was asleep—not Suzie Cox, since a blue tag identified the crib.

Two nurses monitored six babies, all of whom were hooked up to various fluids. She strained to read the names on the pink tags, but they were too far away. The sight of the babies' helplessness told her she was right in coming. How could an infant hurt her? How could she feel anything but pity for the poor little things behind that glass wall?

The family headed to the lounge for cigarettes, leaving her alone at the window. She tapped gently on the glass. A nurse with muted red hair that was swept perfectly into place signaled for her to wait. She changed a glucose bottle and exited the unit, stripping off her mask and gown. In a room adjoining the nursery, she opened a sliding glass window into the hall.

"Whom would you like to see?" she asked, her deep brown eyes expressionless. A baby might be dying; a nurse had to steel herself against involvement. Suzie Cox might be dying.

"Suzanne Cox's baby," Molly said.

"We don't have a mother by that name." A questioning look crossed the omniscient features. "You're not the first person who's asked. But there's been no mother by that name or a baby with that last name in the hospital at all. Not in the last month anyway." She brought questioning eyes to Molly's. "Have you checked the other hospitals?"

"No."

"Is the baby you're looking for premature?"

"Yes."

"Then it would have to be here. This is the only premie facility. But we don't have it."

"It's an illegitimate baby," Molly said softly. "Would that make any difference?"

"That's what the young man told me," the nurse mused. "No difference at all."

"Was he tall and blond?" Molly ventured. The perfect, knowing face eyed her intently. "I'm sorry," she said quickly. The nurse's face softened, the rebuke in her eyes gone. Molly leaned toward the open window, her eyes asking, her hands touching the window ledge in their own personal appeal.

"I didn't notice," the nurse said. "I really didn't." For a long moment her eyes withstood the plea in Molly's, and then she closed the window. Molly watched as she put on a fresh gown.

She stood before the window a long time, watching movement instead of things, focusing on the purposeful sway of the white uniforms and the fluids that carried life through the tubes. The need to cry pulsed upward through her body, but she forced herself to breathe quickly. Organic knowledge crowded her chest, her head, her heart. She did not feel she had been delivered. She did not feel relief and joy. She only felt an amazing ache for the world in which she lived both as sinned against and sinner. There was no baby at all. Just like Robert had told her. Just like she had always known.

Chapter Twenty-One

Too Mickey Mouse for a *real* detective, but a hair glued across the crack of a door worked, Suzanne discovered, as she found the one she'd placed on Robert's studio last night intact. She'd anchored one end of the hair to the door frame and the other to the door with clear fingernail polish. Now she broke it loose. This hair could identify her. Robert and Caroleen must be seeing each other somewhere else. In the daytime, not at night. Although she'd been sick with the flu all week, Suzanne had telephoned the dorm every evening, and Caroleen's baby voice, ever waiting and hopeful, had answered. Not an ordinary "Hello." The voice overflowed with vulnerability, a willingness to be smashed by whatever the caller might say. So far Suzanne had said nothing; she suspected that Caroleen must think the caller was Molly.

She had time to have a cup of coffee in her old haunt, the Tristan and Isolde, before Caroleen went on duty at the library. Something about that woman disgusted her more than anybody she had ever known. Her luxuriant black hair, for one thing. Unfair hair. Hair that was more alive than anyone deserved. Without it, Caroleen would have actually looked mousy: she was too short to be considered womanly. She'd always be "cute," sort of like Louise Sherrill. Her huge tits in truth made her look dumpy, although no man would ever think so. Suzanne wondered what Caroleen's parents would think about her screwing a married man her first year away at college.

The restaurant had no customers. Students either slept or starved in the mornings, not yet aged enough to need a coffee fix to pump them alive. The only person she would probably see from her window seat was Kearns, who had a ten o'clock class in the music building. Kearns: her great missed opportunity. She held that against Robert and Caroleen, too.

His glasses and big nose led him up the street right on time. She stood up, but then she sat down again. It was too late for them now. Nothing she could do could convince him that she really loved him. Unless, of course, she in some way sacrificed herself for his sake. When all this with Robert and Molly and Caroleen was over, she might sneak into his room one night and surprise him. She might follow him home over summer vacation. She might travel on foot to his hometown, arriving bedraggled and joyous like a long-lost pet. The wooden door of the music building closed behind him, forever separating them. Did he long for her the same way she longed for him? Love forgave. She knew that, but did he?

She had unfinished business. The coffee was old, anyway. Her waitress had disappeared for at least ten minutes. Although Suzanne normally left payment on the table, this time she rang the bell at the cash register. The girl came from the back to take the money, her face flushed as if she'd been caught at something. She had shoulder-length streaked hair and heavily made-up eyes, uncharacteristic of a college girl. Suzanne peered past her through a tiny plastic pane in the kitchen door. The girl glanced over her shoulder to see what she was looking at.

"The coffee sucked," Suzanne said.

"What?" the girl yelped, already rattled by her curiosity.

"I said the coffee wasn't fresh."

"Oh." The waitress had a studied look on her face. Someone in the kitchen knew how to handle this situation, but should she ask? "I guess you don't have to pay," she said. "In fact, you *don't* have to pay. If the manager gets mad, I'll make *him* taste the coffee," she added in a friendly manner. "I know it's not good, but they always use last night's until someone complains."

"Someone did," Suzanne said. She laid a quarter on the counter.

"You don't have to pay," the girl repeated. Who would pay when they didn't have to? her eyes asked.

"Take the money," Suzanne said.

The girl shrugged, disappointment in her face. She was pulling nine cents in change out of the drawer when Suzanne said, "Keep it."

She arrived at the library ahead of Caroleen. She felt at ease now, walking through these doors and up the steps. In addition to the long rows of tables, where she used to sit and observe Robert's girlfriend, there were private desks at the end of each row of shelves. She chose the one from which she had a side view of Caroleen's desk. The library had only a few patrons this morning. The room was cool from last night's temperature plunge. Suzanne pulled her sweater tighter around her and rubbed her freezing hands together. She took her mind off Robert and Caroleen long enough to will her blood vessels to expand.

They walked in together at one minute to eleven. Caroleen's face was drained except for a splotchy red patch on each cheek. Robert appeared gruff and determined. Walking to her desk, Caroleen pulled out her chair petulantly. He stood in front of her, leaning forward, spreading his hands on the desk to get closer to her. She looked with embarrassment around the nearly empty room, not noticing Suzanne.

"Don't," Suzanne saw her whisper.

He stood up straight. Caroleen gazed at her desk and then pitifully up at him. He reached for one of her hands, but they were in her lap and she didn't move them. He turned around, placing his hands on his hips, and she shyly lifted her eyes. He glanced over his shoulder and grinned at her, and, as if she couldn't help herself, she grinned back. Then her somber face returned. She shook her head slowly, as if telling him he couldn't *keep* her smiling. He turned his palms up in the air as if he were giving up, and then walked away. At the doorway to the stairs, he looked back. Her eyes had filled with tears, which she let him see before she folded her face in her arms. He came back to her desk, walking behind it to squat beside her. They huddled like two refugees.

Suzanne looked around, an offended expression on her patron's face. No one else was paying attention to the love-birds. This was a library. For shame, she thought. Angrily, she marched toward them. She was barely ten feet away, but neither of them noticed her. Then Caroleen jerked upright in her chair. Her frightened eyes found the unknown face. Robert's hands were on her knees. There were wet spots on her beige skirt where her tears had fallen. Aware through Caroleen only of the motion behind him, Robert rose, waiting for the intruder to pass by. But Suzanne walked directly up to the desk, her face white with fury.

"What's going on here?" she asked. At the sound of her voice, Robert turned, his face registering a disbelief that Caroleen didn't see. Evidently, he had not told her about them.

"Nothing," Caroleen said. "I'm sorry if we disturbed you. Really I am."

"Robert?" Suzanne said.

His head bowed at the sound of his name.

Caroleen looked from him to her. "Are you Molly?" she asked in a terrified whimper.

"Am I Molly?" Suzanne echoed witheringly. "Tell this sweet girl who I am, Robert."

"Please get out of here, Suzanne."

"This is hardly fair, do you think? Corrupting an innocent child her first year away from home. The lovely daughter of Mr. and Mrs. E. G. York, 314 Hammel Drive, Lake Waccamaw, North Carolina. It was different with me, Robert. At least I was all grown up."

Robert grabbed her wrist. "I could kill you," he said, ragged, naked rage in his voice. She tried to break his hold but failed. His thick blunt nails dug into her skin. She grabbed at his face. They were on the verge of slugging it out.

Caroleen had slunk back into her chair. "Stop," she begged. "Please stop."

To spite her, Suzanne stomped on one of Robert's feet. A second later she found her arm twisted high behind her back. Robert's hand was at her throat. She let her body go limp. "Let go of me," she ordered.

"What's going on?" Caroleen asked in a stricken voice.

Abruptly, Robert pushed Suzanne away from him so that she stumbled into the desk. "This is a crazy person," he said. "You can't listen to her."

Suzanne held her wounded wrist at her waist. "I'm the one he was screwing before he started screwing you, honey."

"That's not true," Robert said. He walked behind the desk to be close to Caroleen, but she shrank from him. "Go with me now," he said in a soothing humble voice. "Come on. You've got to." He cupped his hands around her shoulders, guiding her toward him, but she began to struggle against him.

"You can't treat me like this," Caroleen said.

He strengthened his grip on her shoulders. "Stop fighting me," he said. "We've got to talk. Away from here. Come on." He let go of her, hoping that she would come voluntarily, but she sat back down, staring warily at Suzanne. Robert moved toward her again.

"Leave me alone," she cried in a wildly insistent voice. "If both of you don't go right now, I'm going to call security."

"Caroleen," Robert begged. She picked up the phone.

"I insist that you leave," she said, her face white from her glimpse of the abyss. "Both of you."

"I'll call you," he said.

"I don't want you to." She lifted her face slightly, angling it for a touch that she would not allow him to give. Her eyes showed the terror of truth.

"Shall we?" Suzanne asked, offering her arm to Robert. He flung back his hand as if to slap her into oblivion, but she kept herself from flinching. Caroleen began dialing. "You are such a man," Suzanne managed. "Such a fine upstanding specimen of the human race."

Robert started for the door in an angry run. She followed. As they clattered down the stairs, the officer who checked at the front door for stolen books called out, "Hey," before he saw that neither of them carried anything at all.

Outside Robert broke into a gallop, but he could not get away. She stood at the top of the marble steps where one day not so long ago a glistening black fly about to be trapped by a dirty spider called, "See you tomorrow," in a sickeningly innocent voice. "Robert Carter," she yelled at his running figure, her hands cupped around her mouth. His name bounded off the curved rotunda, filled the ears of hundreds of students changing classes, and traveled on into the pitiless world at large.

Chapter Twenty-Two

As soon as they put the second edition to bed, she was going there to apologize for her telephone call Saturday and to get the facts. She'd been toying with this idea for weeks, and then this morning when she awoke, the decision was made. She did some rewrites, took some obits, and made some calls. This afternoon she was supposed to write a column, but she was without an idea. Maybe something would come to her on the way to Suzanne's.

When she arrived home from the hospital Saturday, Robert had had supper ready, but yesterday morning he left to take a walk that lasted five hours. He was not surprised when she told him there was no baby. He had been saying the same thing all along. When she asked, he admitted that he had been to the hospital. It relieved her to hear something corroborated. When he came back from the walk that she was sure had taken him to see Caroleen, she left in the You-Ass without speaking. She went to visit her parents, who weren't home, she sat on one of the stone bridges in Fisher Park and hurled pebbles in the creek, she considered taking in a porn movie at the Star Theater to reinforce her melancholia. When she imagined that Robert was sufficiently worried, she drove home. He had called her parents looking for her, and since they were worried too, she had to call them with a lie. The rest of the evening she and Robert moved around the basement without speaking, but it was as if each of them was living here alone rather than angry at the other. When they both went to bed at the same time, it was purely coincidental.

This morning Gisella had asked her to go to lunch, but she'd declined, saying she was having lunch with Robert. "Just for a change," she commented when her friend raised her eyebrows. As her relationship with Robert had deteriorated, she had become dishonest with Gisella. Why she had blabbed at all she didn't know. She would give anything to have pretended from the beginning that the letters, the ads, the phone calls were the work of some crank, to have shown by her calm façade that she herself was untouched by this craziness, a craziness only on the outskirts of her life. She believed now that everyone would have gladly accepted the falseness. Instead, she had six people, including Garland and Charlie, who watched her, who expressed pity with their eyes, who on occasion asked, "How are things going?," as if it were the most ordinary question in the world.

This time she told Charlie she needed an extra-long lunch hour. He said he appreciated her letting him know. She offered to make up any lost time this afternoon; he said that would be fine.

She parked the You-Ass a block away from the statuesque Victorian house that she thought contained Suzanne's apartment. The sun beat through her windshield, warming the car enough so she felt a slight sense of lethargy. Her stomach was either nervous or hungry, maybe both, and she wished she had stopped somewhere for at least an apple. On one hand, she felt uneasy about meeting Suzanne, but on the other, she wondered what could possibly happen. Suzanne was just another person. A rather strange person who'd pretended to have a baby but hadn't. But still a person. At least that's what Molly thought. At any rate, she wanted to see and judge for herself. She could no longer accept Robert's assessment.

Long cement stairs led from the sidewalk to the porch, and then a second set of steep wooden steps wound around a corner up to Suzanne's door. As she climbed, the breathlessness caused by her fear turned into a real breathlessness; the sharp edge of her nerves dulled slightly. It was lucky that Suzanne hadn't had a baby. These steps would be hazardous both for someone pregnant and for an infant. She stopped a few steps from the top, wanting to regain her composure. Behind her, the gray painted stairs fell away dangerously. She would take care not to antagonize her enemy at the doorway.

Suddenly she grew aware that someone was walking up the steps behind her. She saw first the top of a head with thin brown hair that allowed scalp to show through. Then she saw knees rising and falling like pistons under an old-fashioned pleated skirt that hung like a sack on the girl's thin hips. Her skin was pale, almost bluish. She could not yet see Suzanne's face, nor had Suzanne noticed her. She felt a moment of superiority, the unobserved observer. But then the slowly rising head flinched as Suzanne saw the unexpected feet.

"It's Molly," she said quickly, not wishing to startle. She wouldn't mind if Suzanne fell, but she didn't want to be the cause. The eyes jerked upward, locking when they found hers. "You're the Good Samaritan," Molly blurted. Suzanne's face was strained and perspiring, the skin around her eyes wrinkled and tired. Her jugular area looked almost hollowed out; the tendons in her neck looked like something you could grab. She appeared older than someone their age.

She did not speak or even slow her steady climb. Molly moved back against the railing to give her room to pass. When Suzanne reached Molly's step, she seemed suddenly to expand across its entire width. She pushed at Molly, her elbows extended like wings. The wooden banister came against Molly's buttocks like a crutch. She grabbed behind her with both hands to keep her balance.

The fear of being crowded off the step, if it had been real, lasted only a moment, and then Suzanne moved on. A set of keys appeared in her hands, and she passed through the screen and wooden doorways hardly breaking stride. From the fifth step down, Molly tried to see into the apartment. A voice from an invisible location demanded that she come in. She hesitated, and the voice repeated, "I invited you in."

She was less afraid now that she had seen the not abnormal

face, the face that once before had made her uneasy but not paralyzed her, but she wished Suzanne would reappear. The screen door stood open an inch because of a warping in the wood. She had expected to see a room filled with cartons because of Robert's original description of clutter, but the room was bare except for a hooked rug, a black and brown striped sofa, and an old wooden chair that had once sat in a room being painted. Nothing at all hung on the dingy walls. Suzanne materialized in the middle of a doorway, apparently the doorway to her bedroom, where once she had seduced Molly's husband, if, in fact, that was what had happened. Through the other door Molly could see a kitchen.

She opened the screen door wide enough to slip inside. Suzanne stared at her, kept staring. Molly could not match her frozen, angry face, could not even keep herself from averting her eyes. There was no reason to feel embarrassed—all she'd done in six months was make one anonymous phone call—but she did.

The girl sauntered to the middle of the room, beyond the sanctuary afforded by the doorway and the bedroom. She stuck out her chin as if daring her visitor to fight. Molly took a step forward, slowly bringing her second foot under her. She had no idea what might lurk in this room to ambush her. Could Steve Briggs be hiding behind the couch?

Her hostess chose the wooden chair, leaving the sofa so that Molly would have to cross in front of her. Affecting confidence, she propelled herself across the room. She perched on the edge of a cushion, sensing imaginary arms and legs wrestling in the air over her head. She thought she smelled the odor of lovemaking, released by the cushion when she touched it. Still, watching the chiseled face before her, she was finally convinced that, about Suzanne anyway, Robert had told the truth.

"I suppose you want to know about Suzie," Suzanne said. She gave an inward smile as if lost in reverie for her daughter. Although she had stopped perspiring, a residue of oil kept her skin shiny. Face-to-face, Suzanne seemed less angry and more suffering. She had an ordinary upturned nose and full, rather nice lips, but her eyes were slightly bulbous or else they did not have enough flesh around them to sit naturally in her face. "She's such a pretty thing," Suzanne continued. "That may upset you, but it's the truth. She has Robert's looks."

"Does she?" An eerie glow suddenly entered the room, but it was merely a change in the position of the sun. Molly looked at the ardent face, wondering what reception the spoken facts would have. She was certain of what she knew. Seeing Suzanne's frailty made her surer. "There is no Suzie," she said. Her voice, which had felt timid coming out of her throat, sounded with power in the air between them. Suzanne blinked rapidly. "I went to the hospital. You haven't had a baby." Molly relaxed her gripped hands. Suzanne sat forward slightly, her body tense as if she might spring out of her chair. She assumed a knowing expression, as if she had suddenly been struck by the obviousness of her lies. "Isn't that the truth?" Molly pushed.

"There was a baby," Suzanne said in a low fierce voice. "Not a *live* baby." Her voice rose threateningly. "If you want to see her, I'll drive you out to the city dump. That's where my little Suzie is."

"I don't believe you," Molly said quickly, coldly.

"You don't believe me because you didn't have to see her. You didn't have to look at the bloody mess." The glint in Suzanne's eyes seemed to pierce her. "I couldn't afford her, so I aborted her," she said self-righteously. "It's as simple as that."

Molly felt hollow inside as if her vital organs had suddenly been scooped out. Involuntarily, she whimpered. She could not help but visualize the six bits of life she had witnessed in the premature nursery. "It wasn't Robert's baby," she cried out.

"Are you sure of that?"

Molly could not say she was sure.

"What I had to do has haunted me," Suzanne whispered. "And because of it, I've haunted you. I'm not ashamed of anything I've done. I would do it all again and more." She placed her fingertips together, gazing over them. Molly could not turn away now; she had to bear this. "You've deserved it all. You more than Robert. The same thing has just happened to a girl more innocent than me, and you've done nothing. Robert still shares your bed. He no longer shares mine, as I'll readily admit. But he screws one Caroleen York. And I don't care whether you believe me or not."

Molly's face caught fire. "They're only friends," she said shakily. She expected Suzanne to laugh at her; already a sneer filled the vulturish face. "He needed someone to help him endure all the things you've done to us. I wasn't able to," she said, feeling the beginning of a sense of self-hatred. She lowered her eyes, raising them again quickly when she heard Suzanne's chair creak. "They're friends," she repeated, but the words rang naïvely in her ears. Suzanne didn't answer, didn't have to answer in order to jeer her.

"You had an abortion?" she asked weakly. She recalled praying once that Suzanne would miscarry, more concerned about her own security than a life. What kind of despicable creature was she? Suzanne nodded. "I'm sorry," Molly said. "I'm truly sorry you had to go through something like that. He's not with Caroleen anymore," she felt compelled to add.

Suzanne smiled, a naked gleam in her eyes. "I just left them," she said. Molly's heart seemed to stop. "They were at the library together. Having a fight. I think Caroleen is ready to dump him. She didn't know he was married until I told her."

Molly stood up and so did Suzanne. "I don't believe you." But what Suzanne said seemed more real to her than anything else she knew. Like the perfect newspaper reporter, Suzanne had all the details.

Suzanne only smiled.

Molly started toward the door. "The reason I came here was to apologize for calling you on Saturday," she said briskly.

"What about all the rest of the things you've done?" Suzanne's voice was intense, agitated. Her eyes glittered strangely.

"I haven't done anything else to you. Honestly, I haven't."

"I could put you in jail for five years," Suzanne cried, her body jerking as she spoke.

"What are you talking about?"

"Phone calls, letters. You want to see them? I've got a stack a foot high. In your handwriting, on your office typewriter, your stationery."

"You know you don't. You know that's not true. If you have letters, you wrote them yourself. Experts know the difference. You can't pretend you're me." It made her sick that Suzanne had actually sat at her desk at work.

Suzanne put a shaking finger to her lips to stop Molly. "Maybe you've simply forgotten what you did. Maybe you've blocked it out." A sudden connection brightened her face. "*I* blocked out the idea that I had an abortion," she said in a consoling tone. "And then I remembered. I remembered one day when I saw Robert and Caroleen in the cafeteria together. It can happen. People do things and forget they've done them all the time."

"I have fifty letters from *you*," Molly cried, but her mind was drawn again by the mention of Robert and Caroleen. *Did* Suzanne know the truth?

"Maybe you're right." She looked steadily at Molly. "I myself have a tiny backward-slanted style of writing. I've had it all my life." None of the letters Molly received had been written in such a hand. Suzanne continued: "Maybe neither of us wrote any letters at all. There could be a third party interested in each of us—"

"Steve Briggs?" Molly interrupted sarcastically.

"Who?"

"Your so-called boyfriend Steve Briggs."

"I don't have a boyfriend."

"Who are *you* suggesting?" she asked.

"I have no idea. Some friend of yours."

"None of my friends would do anything like that."

Suzanne was perspiring heavily. Her eyes had become brighter, angrier. She rushed abruptly for the kitchen, and Molly felt her own body poise. Drawers and cabinets began to open as if she was looking wildly for something. Molly slipped toward the door.

"Don't leave," Suzanne called.

She turned at the new hysterical tone that wavered in Suzanne's voice. Her body seemed to drain of blood. Suzanne held a butcher knife. Molly was afraid to turn her back to run.

"I'm cutting up some fruit to eat," Suzanne said. "You look hungry."

Returning blood warmed Molly's face. "Thanks, no," she said, trying to smile. "I've got to get back to work. I can't eat anything." The idea of sharing food with Suzanne seemed crazy. "Do you know the time?" she asked in as ordinary a tone as she could. A feeling of faintness, which she could not allow, surged through her shoulders. Suzanne might kill her while she was unconscious. With enormous concentration she breathed slowly to clear her head.

"I don't have a watch," Suzanne said, although she was wearing one. The hand holding the butcher knife dropped to her side. "I'd better put this up before I cut myself," she said, flashing it between them again. Molly remembered her ruined tire. A moment later Suzanne reappeared.

Molly felt that somehow she had made Suzanne put the knife away. "*Would* you stop harassing us?" she asked quietly.

"I haven't done anything."

"*Please*, Suzanne."

Suzanne began walking toward her, and Molly moved graciously but quickly through the screen door. Suzanne seemed not to notice her haste. The door was between them; Molly turned.

"The abortion cost five hundred dollars," Suzanne said.

Molly's lips met in a narrow line. "We don't have any money."

"Your parents do."

"We're not giving you any money," Molly said. She turned around to leave. Behind her she imagined the knife reappearing, dancing in her enemy's hands. Or Suzanne could have a pistol, even a small rock. She took the first two steps calmly. Then the screen door creaked as if Suzanne was opening it, and fear took hold of her. Molly fled, leaping the steps three at a time, bobbing her head in case Suzanne was aiming a weapon at her. She had the sensation of bullets whizzing by either side of her. She imagined the knife burrowing into her back. If she was extremely lucky, it would simply sail by, clattering harmlessly down the steps.

All at once she was past the curve. No footsteps were following. She took the rest of the steps one at a time so that she wouldn't break her neck. When she looked behind, finally, the house stood against the silver sky like a mountain. For a moment she thought she heard insane laughter, but when her ears concentrated, there was only silence.

Chapter Twenty-Three

WHEN Suzanne arrived at the pancake house late Monday afternoon, Ruth had been there for hours sitting alone in a booth. According to Jan, one of the waitresses, she had spent the day circling want ads in the newspaper. She'd eaten three meals and finished two pots of coffee. For advice Jan had tried to reach Bennie—Suzanne raised her eyebrows at this—but he'd been on the golf course. Although she hadn't worked with Ruth, she knew who Ruth was, so she hated to call the police. Ruth hadn't done anything except stay here an unusually long time. Plenty of odd single men did the same thing. Ruth hadn't been drunk when she arrived, just strange-looking. Jan figured you could sit here and drink coffee from opening until closing and it wouldn't be illegal.

"What do you mean, 'strange'?" Suzanne asked. Ruth had glanced up when she came in the door but failed to recognize her.

"She was crying," the waitress said. "I can't describe the rest."

"Try," Suzanne said.

"Oh, I don't know. Her eyes were sort of unfocused. Like one looked one way and one looked the other. She got better once she ate." Jan pulled a pack of cigarettes from her skirt pocket and lit one. She was big-boned, taller than Bennie. Although she wasn't ugly, her face had a fleshy piggish look to it. She must not know that Bennie didn't like his waitresses to smoke in uniform. "She's been asking for you," Jan continued. "I tried calling you, but you weren't home. She keeps looking in her purse. I don't think she has any money."

"Could you wait until you're out of here?" Suzanne asked abruptly.

The sudden change in tone caught Jan off guard. "For what?" she asked.

"To smoke."

Jan looked at her watch and then at the clock over the cash register. "I'm off duty, man," she said.

"You're not off duty as long as you're in uniform."

"Says who?"

"Says me."

Jan took a long defiant drag. "Go to hell," she said softly. "I know all about your fake cancer."

A young couple with two small boys came in the door. Suzanne lifted menus out of the rack beside the cash register. In a quick gesture of intimacy she leaned toward Jan. "I had a miscarriage, but I couldn't tell him *that*," she said, her softened eyes seeking Jan's sympathy. "Cancer was the first thing I could think of."

Confusion, then worry, settled on Jan's face. Suzanne led the family to a table well away from Ruth. In her periphery she saw Jan put out her cigarette and squat by the shelf under the cash register, where she applied lipstick and drew a brush through the crown of her shoulder-length hair. She must be on her way to meet Bennie, but she lingered at the cash register.

"Give Bennie my love," Suzanne said when she came back up front. Jan's mouth dropped. "And would you tell him that I've rehired Ruth?"

"Can you do that?" Jan asked.

"Sure. And you probably can too. Soon." She glanced over her shoulder at the young family, who appeared ready to order. "Excuse me," she said, sliding off the stool.

A few minutes later she had a chance to sit down across from Ruth, who, despite all the coffee, seemed close to being asleep.

"Yes?" Ruth said with forced alertness.

Suzanne reached across the table top and pinched her wrist. "Wake up," she said.

"I'm awake," Ruth insisted. "Suzanne? Are you finally here?" Ruth smiled, showing her small gapped teeth. Her dyed brown hair had grown out, revealing an inch of gray roots.

"You can have your job back," Suzanne said.

"I can?"

"Unless you don't need it." But it was obvious that Ruth did need it. Her clothes, though not spotted, carried both a layer of grime and an odor that perfume could not disguise.

"I'm getting married," Ruth announced. "I'm getting married, but I need the job, too," she hurriedly added.

"Can't have both," Suzanne teased.

"Aw, Suzie."

"Don't call me Suzie either."

Ruth's eyes rolled. "Okay. I'll call you Suzanne Cox. Or Miss Cox, whatever you want. Madame Cox. Queenie Cox. Her majesty Suzanne."

"Who are you going to marry?"

"I am your most humble servant, Ruth Crowder. At your service." She bowed her head, showing her ridiculous two-toned hair. "The medicine man. I'm going to marry the medicine man."

Suzanne dug her fingernails into Ruth's wrist.

"Why did you do that?" Ruth shrieked.

"Quiet down," she ordered. The light over the kitchen door said that the family's order was ready. "I've got to deliver some food." She squeezed Ruth's wrist, not using her nails. "Now keep quiet." Ruth was still examining her injury when Suzanne returned. "I didn't hurt you," she said. "What are you on?"

"On?"

"What did the medicine man give you?"

"The medicine man," Ruth said, grinning foolishly. "I'm getting married, and I came to ask you to be my maid of honor."

"You're not getting married. Don't be a fool."

"I am too. Too too too." Ruth sashayed her shoulders proudly.

"Nobody would marry you," Suzanne said impatiently.

Ruth finally opened wide her eyes. "They would," she said, her chin thrust into the air. "And somebody will marry you, too, Suzanne. You just have to act nicer." Ruth's eyes went half closed again.

Suzanne slipped out of the booth. She checked first the family, who needed milk, coffee, and butter. Then she telephoned the three waitresses who hadn't showed up for their shifts. Ruth was not going to be any help. Marie had cut her toe and would be late, but she'd be there. No one else was at home. It would have to be the two of them, she guessed.

She called the police and told them that a woman had passed out in a booth in the restaurant from either booze or pills, probably the latter. Did she know the woman? the police asked. Barely, she said. They were particularly interested in an address for her, which Suzanne said she could provide.

Two policemen arrived fifteen minutes later, standing benignly at the cash register as if they were customers. Suzanne was busy seating a group of six. Marie hurried around the restaurant in one rubberized shoe and one bedroom slipper. Ruth had awakened and poured herself a cup of coffee.

"That's her," Suzanne said to the policemen, nodding in Ruth's direction. The two were older and younger versions of the same type of man; dark-haired, large featured, and kindly looking. The older one was thinner than the younger.

"Why don't you ask her to come to the door?" the young man suggested.

Suzanne gave him a timid look. "What if she has a fit?" she asked.

The older man leaned around the cash register to appraise Ruth. "She doesn't look much like the type of lady who would do something like that."

"She's been acting awfully strange," Suzanne said.

By now the two young boys had spotted the police uniforms

and began waving and squealing. Hearing them, Ruth turned to look. She waved at the boys as if she were Miss America.

"I think you ought to go ahead and *do* something," Suzanne said, her voice reaching into a higher register.

"I'll talk to her," the younger man said, walking gently in Ruth's direction.

"How long did you say she's been here?" the other man asked.

"Hours. I think she keeps sitting there because she doesn't have the money to pay. She's eaten three meals."

"All we can do is ask her to leave, you know. She hasn't committed any kind of offense."

"You can't arrest her?"

The policeman looked strangely at her. "Do you *want* her arrested?"

Ruth must remind him of his mother. Or maybe his wife. Why was he making things so hard on her, the law-abiding citizen? "Not particularly," she answered. "I just thought not paying for your meal was against the law." Now she wished she had checked Ruth's purse while she was asleep instead of relying on Jan's intuition.

The younger policeman returned. "She doesn't want to leave," he announced. "She says she's still hungry."

"Is she planning on paying?" Suzanne interrupted. What was the point of having cops? she wanted to ask.

"She said you were her daughter, and you'd be glad to pay." The older policeman looked at her with fresh curiosity.

"I am not her daughter," Suzanne said. "That is a pure lie. My parents live in another town. She's not old enough to have a daughter my age. She only looks old because she's hopped up on something. Probably heroin," she added. The vehemence of her answer seemed to convince them, but, enraged, she stalked back toward Ruth's booth. There was a growing air of un-settledness in the restaurant. Marie gave her a beseeching look, which she ignored. She heard one of the policemen follow-ing her.

"I am not your daughter," she said to the foolish, drunken face

that greeted her. She stepped back, giving the policeman room
to join her. "Tell him that I'm not your daughter."

"Aw, Suzie," Ruth said. "You don't want me to get married,
do you?"

"Is this domestic?" the young man asked.

"Sir?" Ruth said.

"No, it isn't," Suzanne said sharply.

"Maybe you two should go home and settle your problems,"
a soothing voice said.

"She isn't my mother," Suzanne repeated. "Can't you hear
me, you dumb cluck?" A moment of silent amazement descended
on the restaurant. Suzanne took Ruth's arm and began pulling
her out of the booth.

"Stop it," Ruth said, resisting feebly.

The policeman moved conciliatorily between them. "Let's be
ladies about this," he said. Ruth glanced up gratefully.

"If you won't do anything, I will," Suzanne said furiously. She
tightened her hold on Ruth, shouldering the policeman away.
Ruth's face twisted into tears. The young man's hands returned,
this time with authority, easily separating them. Ruth examined
the loose flesh of her arm, where Suzanne had bruised her. She
rubbed the skin vigorously and then dabbed at her face with her
napkin.

Suzanne felt herself coming back into control, although the
policeman continued to restrain her. Ruth began to clamber out
of the booth, her newspaper and purse clutched in both hands.
When she lost her balance, falling toward them, the policeman
released Suzanne in order to catch her. Free, Suzanne grabbed
the check and marched to the cash register to add up the enormous
bill so that everyone here would know exactly what had happened.
Still hungry? How could she be?

The policeman guided Ruth past the cash register. "Pay for
this, will you?" he asked his partner, who had calmly watched
the entire scene. "She doesn't have a dime." Just as Suzanne had
thought, although it seemed to make no difference.

As if he were helping his own mother instead of a perfect

stranger, the older man offered her a ten-dollar bill. "I want you to be pleased with the outcome of this," he said with only the faintest trace of irony.

Suzanne spoke stiffly: "I'm responsible for what goes in and what comes out of this cash register. I don't see why you don't understand that." He touched his hat as he started out the door.

"Before you go, I'd like your name," she said with flippant antagonism. She held a pencil between two fingers like a cigarette.

"Officer Courts." His eyes, noncommittal until now, bored into hers.

"And the name of your partner?"

"If you're going to complain, complain about me," he said.

"You aren't the one who manhandled me."

"Neither one of us did," he said, turning to leave.

"I can find out his name by calling the station," she said.

"That's right," he acknowledged before the door shut behind him.

Now was catch-up time. She took orders from the three tables nearest where Ruth had sat, briskly flipping her order pad so that no one would delay her by asking questions. They all had eyes and ears. Let them draw their own conclusions. She hurried to the kitchen with the orders, put bread and butter on every table, and poured at least thirty cups of coffee. Everyone seemed to realize that she and Marie were trying, except for four women dressed in warmup suits who walked out a few minutes later. At the time, Suzanne was taking an order from a young man who'd arrived just after the policemen left with Ruth. She kicked her foot in the direction of the departing women. "Rich bitches," she commented, watching his face. He hesitated before laughing with her. The light in his eyes found hers. He had a large grin that captured the entire lower half of his face.

"You shoulda been here earlier," Suzanne said. "We had this woman drunk in a booth. The cops came and treated her nicer than they treated me. One of them even paid her bill for her."

"I wish one of 'em would pay my bill for me," the boy said. He tossed his head, and his mane of black hair shook together and then split down the middle.

"You got plenty of money," Suzanne said. "Y'look like you do anyway." She shook her head naughtily at herself. "Gimme your order," she said. "I know how to get carried away talking."

"That's okay," the boy said. "I don't ever talk much."

"I got other people waiting."

"Go find out what they want and come back, pretty," he said. "I can wait."

The hick had called her pretty. "You better give me your order now or you'll be here all night. I'll come back when I have the chance," she said in a thick but efficient voice.

He had his fork poised playfully in his hand when ten minutes later she delivered a plate heavy with pancakes and sausage. "Wasn't I right to tell you to order?" she asked before she had to hurry away.

She gave him as much special attention as she could, considering how ridiculously hard she was having to work. If he were her boyfriend, she would enlist him to bus tables. Finally, everyone had been served and no new customers had come in for a while. She assigned Marie to the cash register and went to talk to her new friend.

"Can you cook this good?" the boy asked with a satisfied grin. It sounded something like a marriage proposal.

"Better," she said.

"You look like a girl who knows how to cook, but I bet you don't eat none of it."

"Sure I do."

"It don't show."

"I really don't have nobody to cook for," she admitted, giving the restaurant a sweeping glance so that he would have a chance to examine her.

The boy wadded his napkin and threw it on the table. "Gotta go." She stood up, angry at his abruptness. "Wait a minute," he said. "I wondered—I wanted to know if you'd . . . if you'd like to go out on a date with me. Whenever you have your night off," he added, as no answer was forthcoming. "I could take you to some real nice restaurant."

Without smiling, Suzanne looked him over.

"I shouldn't have asked," he said, pulling himself out of the booth. He was taller than she'd expected: his belt buckle was at the level of her breasts. "I wasn't trying to pick you up. I could call you on the phone and ask you politely."

The sap was asking her on a real live date. She was touched. "I'm off tomorrow night," she said. She wasn't, but she would arrange to be. A man across the room held his coffee cup in the air, signaling her. "Why don't I give you my telephone number. I'll be at home all morning." She pulled out her order pad.

"What's your name?" he asked shyly. "Mine's George Oakes."

She hesitated only a second, considering giving him someone else's name and number, Molly's or even Jan's, but she was sick to death of Molly and she hadn't fully decided about her plans for Jan. "I'm Suzanne Cox. Pleased to meet you." She scribbled down her phone number. The man across the room had gotten up to find his own coffee. It was up to George Oakes to remember her name.

"Do you like fish?" George asked. He stood studying the phone number. She wished he would put it away.

"Fair."

"I like anything," he said quickly.

"Why don't we talk about it when you call me?" She did not turn to look when she heard Marie ring up his bill, only slanted her waitress's body at a more provocative angle.

She was on the phone with him before dawn the next morning, listening to him explain to her fuzzy "Yeah?" that he'd had to call so early because he started work at seven. She pulled the covers tightly around her neck.

"I woke you up, didn't I?" he asked.

"Probably," she murmured. "At least I find myself in the bed." There was a long silence. "Are you still there?" she asked.

"Yes," he said in a low voice. She couldn't decide whether he was awed or frightened. The idea of lying in her bed with him tonight unexpectedly warmed her.

"I've been thinking I'd like to cook something for you," she said.

"Oh, gosh."

"I'll give you a list of ingredients, and you can buy them on the way over," she continued matter-of-factly. "Do you mind doing that?"

"No, but—"

"I'm in a restaurant six days a week, you know. I'd really like to eat at home."

"I hadn't thought about that."

"Call me when you get off work and I'll tell you what I'm going to need." George was silent. "All right?"

"I don't know if this is proper or not," he said solemnly.

"I don't mind cooking for you," she insisted.

"That's not what I mean."

"What do you mean?" she asked, finally giving him his opportunity, but he couldn't find the words to explain.

She allowed herself to sleep until nine and then couldn't remember if she'd dreamed about George or if he'd really called. She lay in bed looking at the ceiling, feeling the sun warming up the world. Torturing herself, she rolled to the cool side of the bed, George's side. She must have talked with him because she remembered how cold it had been before daylight.

When she arose, she dusted the table in the living room, reversed the couch cushions, and checked to see if she had any beer. If George drank at all, that was what he would drink. Then she wanted breakfast. She already knew, but just to be sure, she called the pancake house. Yes, Bennie was there.

At the restaurant, she joined him while he was being served in high fashion by his new favorite. He looked at her in disbelief and then grinned, realizing that she had come to claim him. Perching her elbows on the table and folding her hands under her chin, she looked coy and fragile the way big-boned Jan could not. She ordered from her rival, who glared in silent fury. "You'll treat, won't you?" she asked Bennie before Jan had a chance to leave the table.

"All my sweethearts get to eat free," he said, sweeping his eyes magnanimously across them both. Suzanne smiled, but Jan did not. There was a big crowd this morning, so Jan would not be able to hover over them. She pulled out a cigarette, which Bennie did not offer to light.

"Why didn't you tell me you were horny?" she asked, her amused eyes watching his forehead.

"I didn't know you cared. Give me one of those," he said, pointing at her cigarette. She gave him her own, a blot of lipstick on the filter, and lit another for herself.

"Didn't you think you'd start a war?"

"You're on different shifts," he said carelessly. "At least when you don't change things on me."

"Not anymore," she said. "I want to go back to day work. Starting today. In fact, the main reason I'm here is to tell you I'm taking off this afternoon and tonight."

"Thanks for all the notice."

"You're welcome. Did you know that nobody except Marie showed up last night? You can hire the dumbest bitches I've ever met. Anyway, I worked twice as hard as I should have had to, so to make up for it, I'm taking tonight off."

"You don't get a lot of high-class girls wanting to work here," Bennie said scornfully. He knew he couldn't make her work when she didn't want to, so he insulted her instead.

"You got me."

"That's what I mean."

She pulled his cigarette out of his mouth and broke it in half. "Buy your own next time," she said.

"Give me another cigarette."

"No."

He curled his ankle around her leg, moving it up and down. "Come on," he said.

"Come on where?"

"Give me a goddamn cigarette." He was heard by the people sitting behind him, who shifted in their booth.

"When we get to my place," she whispered.

"You really want to do me in with Jan, huh?" He leaned across the table, his whole face reddening with lust.

"Course not," she said in little-girl talk. "I just want to do you in." At that moment Jan slung her plate to the table. The bacon and eggs looked as if they'd been dug out of the garbage. "Thanks a lot," Suzanne said. "It looks like shit."

"Looks cold, Jan," Bennie said. Jan gave him a betrayed look. She must think the battles of love went by some kind of rules.

"I'm not hungry anyway," Suzanne said. Jan grabbed the plate from in front of her, and some of the scrambled eggs slid off onto the table. "Oops." Suzanne braced herself for a face full of eggs, but Jan only hurried toward the kitchen.

"You wait," Bennie said, rising from the booth to follow Jan. At the door he looked back at Suzanne, proudly pointing his trigger finger at her.

Jan emerged from the kitchen first, her purse and a cigarette in hand. Her angry eyes found Suzanne, who smiled smugly, but instead of approaching the booth, she went to the cash register and began taking money out of the drawer. Bennie caught up with her, covering her hands with his as unobtrusively as possible.

"I'm not coming back here," Suzanne heard Jan say. "So you just pay me now."

Bennie looked unhappily at her. He couldn't understand why she didn't behave the way Suzanne did. "What do I owe you?" Suzanne thought he mumbled. He counted out the amount she named into his own hands. Holding it, he whispered something to her, but she answered with a loud "No." He talked some more but she shook her head. Finally she took the money and started in Suzanne's direction, but evidently thinking better of it, she turned around. When she passed Bennie, she hit him in the stomach with the back of her hand. A sorrowful look crossed his face as he watched her rear swing out the door. He closed the cash drawer and tidied the rack of menus before he returned to Suzanne.

"Now what am I going to do?" he asked.

"About what?" He was all hers again. The triangle had been

so much more interesting. But Bennie wasn't exactly subtle enough to carry one off. That was one thing she'd liked about Robert: his ability to keep two women—three, if she counted herself—equally unhappy and happy.

"I don't have enough girls to work this afternoon."

"Not my problem," Suzanne said.

"What's wrong with you?" he demanded.

"Nothing. Not one thing."

"You *got* me, didn't you? So how come all of a sudden you're treating me like hell? Will you do me a favor and work this afternoon?" He asked the question hopelessly, knowing that she wouldn't.

She shook her head. "If I could, I would. I have an important engagement."

"Yeah," he said morosely. "You're screwing me this morning and some other jerk tonight." He looked toward the door where Jan had vanished. "Come on," he said moving brusquely out of the booth.

Suzanne didn't move. "I'm hungry," she said.

"You said you *weren't* hungry." His eyes shone pitifully. He sat back down hard, and his cushion screeched. "I don't want to make a scene," he said. "But you better get up now."

She returned his angry stare. "Not until I eat."

Jan was not absolutely gone for good until she'd been away from here a week, Suzanne knew, so after Bennie had treated her to a fresh breakfast, they went to her apartment, where they made carnal love without even removing their clothes. That way it was over quick.

While he lay on her bed asleep, she halfheartedly telephoned Molly, but after just one ring she hung up. It was over. She had done all she could do for them. She had found out what Robert was and then slowly, painstakingly presented the evidence to Molly. The only thing that surprised her was how long it had taken Molly to come see her. She had even had to go so far as to have a baby. Then up the steps came the reporter sleuth, proud that she'd discovered there was no baby at all. Had Molly realized yet that whether Suzie existed or not made no difference? Robert was who he was. Forgive him though she did, it was not for Molly to do the same.

After a while she roughly shook Bennie awake and drove him out of her apartment. Then she cleaned the bathroom for what's-his-name, George.

Chapter Twenty-Four

S EEING Isabel's blossoming rhododendrons as she turned into
the driveway made Molly think about how, for the first time
in her life, the work she was doing would not end in May. Spring
had always been the time when the little top that spun inside her
chest began spinning faster and faster. Exams were coming, and
that top represented her last push. But the newspaper had no
exams. It just kept on and on, day in and day out, history-in-
the-making in all its seeming irrelevance because she lived too
close to it to recognize the trends. Her top had been picking up
speed for the last month. But there was no vacation to look forward
to. She wondered if Gisella, who was a year older and had begun
work a year sooner, ever had the same claustrophobic feelings
she was having, trapped by something that didn't let you off the
hook every nine months.

Inside the apartment she bit into a cold apple from the refrigerator, grabbed an oatmeal cookie, and hurried back to the You-
Ass, which she'd left running. Not that it was any big deal, but
as Suzanne had promised, Robert wasn't home. She shouldn't
judge him based on this one moment: he could be taking another
walk. The fuschia color of the rhododendron blossoms, always
garish when some artist tried to imitate it, almost implored her
attention.

Until today she'd never entertained the concept of working
forever. She had known she would take a job after college, but
the never-endingness of it, now that she had recognized spring,
astounded her. She was astounded, too, that she was even able

to focus on something new. Not half an hour ago she had fled down Suzanne's steps, filled with a greater terror than she'd ever known. In comparison, her encounter with the black man hadn't even frightened her, but then her back had not been turned. Still, this other matter, this spring fever, kept crowding her mind. Had Gisella longed for freedom that first May after she'd graduated? How had she overcome her desire to quit work? Had she considered going to graduate school forever?

A sense of personal shallowness filled her as she turned the You-Ass in the direction of the office. Rebecca Rimmer would be glad to remind her that work did not end in May and begin again in September. Perhaps she was spoiled, but she was also very tired.

She turned into the parking lot of the historical museum. Every day now she parked somewhere different. And if she drove somewhere for lunch, she parked in a different place from where she'd parked that morning. Did that mean she was crazy? How long would one slashed tire determine where she parked? Speaking of crazy, though, was anybody? The black man, maybe, but wasn't he simply a victim of poverty? Suzanne Cox, maybe, but weren't her actions legitimate? Herself? Not really, but could she judge? Now that she'd met Suzanne she might start parking in front of the building again. But, then again, maybe she wouldn't.

She wondered if it wasn't spring fever she was feeling after all. Maybe she simply wanted to stop being a newspaper reporter. The truth was, she didn't feel quite right anymore about examining other people's lives. She had done it when she was twenty-two, but now that she was twenty-three she didn't think she'd be able to ask the mayor how he felt about his father being murdered. "Get a comment," Charlie had told her the day the two thugs had robbed and shot him. Rebecca had been on vacation. "A comment?" she'd asked, maligning not only the request but the word he'd used to make it. He'd spent twenty minutes convincing her that obtaining a reaction from a public figure had been a newspaperman's job since time began. She'd agreed to ask the question a month ago, but she'd never be able to today.

She slipped into the news room, where only Gisella and Peter remained. April afternoons were times to find interesting assignments outside the office. But she had a column to write. As jobs went, she supposed this one was best for the freedom it allowed. But not for the exactness of behavior it required. It wasn't fair to seek out lies and indiscretion and immorality on the part of others when she or someone she was close to was guilty of the same things. Charlie would argue that since she wasn't a public figure, no one cared, but how long could you hide behind that?

Suzanne had accused her of being characterless. Was she? She had delayed making a decision about Robert because she didn't know enough facts. What had he done? Would she ever know? Did it matter? What Charlie had said about her responsibility as a reporter was a "fact." So maybe she was growing less attuned to facts than she used to be. Maybe facts weren't important at all. Her *feeling* was that it was wrong to ask the mayor about his father. Her *feeling* was that Suzanne had never even been pregnant. Her *feeling* was that Robert was more than friends with Caroleen. It had occurred to her when she was leaving Suzanne's to go talk to Caroleen, too, but as she'd nosed the You-Ass out into traffic, she realized she didn't need to. She was not interested in one single other fact. What did she have to know in her mind that she didn't already know in her heart?

Gisella appeared not to have noticed her come in. But while she was simultaneously editing and pasting up a story, she dialed Molly. "How was lunch?" she asked, continuing to edit. This phone talk was a habit: no boss was even here to frown that they were wasting time.

"Fine." Molly wanted to discuss spring fever, feelings versus facts, but she knew if she ever started talking, she wouldn't be able to hold anything back. Gisella looked across the room, her dark eyes chasing Molly's. Molly felt as if she were hooked up to one of those telephones of the future where you could see and be seen by the person you were talking to.

"Don't you trust me anymore?" Gisella asked.

"Of course, I do." She faced the wall so that this would be a real phone call. She would never be able to bring herself to tell Gisella about Caroleen, too, so how could they talk at all? She could take only so much humiliation. If Gisella knew everything, she might begin to wonder what was wrong with Molly. "I've burdened you too much already," she said.

"Molly the martyr."

"It's not that."

"What is it?"

"I don't know."

"Anytime you want to talk, I'll be glad to listen."

"I appreciate that. I really do."

They hung up. For a while Molly was aware of every move that Gisella made, moves she knew were not made to attract her attention. Gisella had returned to her own world, which made Molly want to reach out again. Maybe it was beneath Gisella to force the truth out of her, just like it should be beneath her to try to force the truth out of Robert. If someone didn't want to tell you something, you shouldn't demean yourself by begging him to. When you lacked facts, you relied on your judgment. It was what court judges did all the time. When they didn't know enough or when facts were contradictory, they just guessed.

Charlie's desk top, as management urged, was perfectly clear. This place never looked the way a newspaper office should. Also, she couldn't tell whether or not he was gone for the day. On the other hand, a neat desk top could work in her favor. Who would know when she left this final time whether she was in the bathroom, at the canteen, on assignment, or shopping at Montaldo's?

She waited until Gisella was talking to Peter before she picked up her phone and dialed. Her mother answered on the first ring. "Mom?" she said. Somehow, she'd expected her not to be at home. In her typical ironic tone, her mother acknowledged that yes, indeed, she was who Molly thought she was. She also reminded Molly that "Mom" was her least favorite form of address. "Mother," Molly said pointedly, "I've got the afternoon off. You won't believe this, but I'm tired of looking like a college student."

"Thank the Lord," her mother said.

"Would you like to take me shopping?"

She was not going to let her mother spend any money on her. She would simply admire whatever clothes they saw and say she'd think about them. So the trip wouldn't be wasted, she would try to get her mother to buy something for herself, never a formidable task. They agreed to meet at the store in fifteen minutes, Molly walking the block from her office, her mother driving in from Irving Park. The question of whether her mother was well enough dressed to go shopping was not necessary.

She bade Gisella goodbye with a casual wave, not letting herself see the questions in her friend's eyes. Someday she would tell her the whole story, just not right now. She knew how boring it was to listen to someone's problems month after month, how doubly boring it must be if that person was doing nothing to make things better. On the other hand, Gisella's feelings might be honestly hurt. What reason did Molly have to suddenly close her out? The poky elevator drove her crazy. While it was giving her time, she ought to go back and tell Gisella not to worry.

As if anticipating her return, Gisella was staring at the door, but Molly knew she always stared into space when she was trying to think of a lead. "In case you're worried about me . . ." she began. A grin crept onto her face, although she wanted to look serious. How could she smile? How could she smile when everything was so awful? It must be a smile of insanity. "In case you're worried about me, I'm sneaking out to go shopping with my mother. She's been wanting to spruce me up for years."

Gisella did not smile back. "Has something else happened?" she asked.

"Nah," Molly said uncomfortably. "I just want to ask her a few things. A few things you don't know about," she added hastily. But the assumption that Gisella didn't know about *everything* made her grimace deeper at Molly. "It's the kind of thing you're *lucky* not to know about," she offered, but she could not betray her mother by saying more. "I've got to go. I'll tell you everything eventually. I promise."

"That's nice to know," Gisella said, but Molly could tell she didn't mean it as sarcastically as it had sounded.

She skipped the elevator this time because now she might be late. Waving at Allie, she pulled her jacket only across her shoulders, letting her hair stay caught beneath. She was tired of this long hair, tired of having to wash it all the time, tired of defending it against her mother's criticism. It hung heavily from her scalp. She wasn't going to buy any special clothes, but she might get a haircut. For nobody's sake but her own.

She passed the side door to the Montaldo's shoe salon, a claustrophobic room filled with saleswomen who always seemed to be sizing up one's stylishness, and traveled to the end of the block so she could enter by the front door. Here was another sign that she was nuts: her paranoia over having no style. She wished she didn't know about style. Then she could be like Rebecca Rimmer: oblivious to condescending eyes. The narrow cosmetics department was a worse choice than the shoe salon, she suddenly realized. Had she put on any makeup this morning? She couldn't remember. Newspaper reporters didn't wear makeup, she reminded herself, thrusting her pale cheeks forward. She was so busy looking as if she didn't care what she looked like that she failed to notice her mother sitting on a tufted sofa near the stairs that led to clothes for women under thirty.

"Molly?" her mother said, the same way Molly had said "Mom?" on the phone.

"Yes, it's me, your daughter," she answered. They drew close together, touching but not hugging, grinning at their inside joke.

"It's nice to see you, honey," her mother said. She wore a raspberry-colored linen suit that she'd probably had on all day yet was without a wrinkle. The kind of makeup she used made her skin look luminous and touchable. Her eyebrows were plucked into narrow, wispy lines. Although she was tall and striking, she could appear quite vulnerable.

"I just want to look today," Molly began. "I don't want to buy anything. Show me what you think would look good on me."

She touched her mother's elbow lightly. "Then we'll find something pretty for you," she added.

A silence settled between them as they ascended the stairs.

"What's Daddy doing today?" she asked, wanting them to chat so she could slip in her questions unnoticed.

"He's at work."

"Oh, yeah," she said. "It's just that I'm off for the afternoon, so I guess I think everyone else is." What an idiot she sounded like. "Where have you been all day so dressed up?"

"I went to garden club this morning. And then I had lunch with Betty Jane. I feel so sorry for her. She always attracts the kind of people who tell her all their problems." Like Gisella and me, Molly thought, feeling glad that she hadn't told her friend anything else. "And Betty Jane's such a dear. She feels a responsibility to listen. Nobody ever wants any advice, she says. They just want somebody to commiserate, to tell them, yes, your life is really crummy, the crummiest I've ever seen. Everybody wants to feel like they're the *worst* worst off. For some reason nobody like that ever comes to me. I guess I ought to be glad, but I've always felt that it must mean I'm a bad listener. But I don't *want* to hear about people's problems. We've all got them. I like to *enjoy* my friends, *forget* about what's wrong when I'm with them." The passion in her mother's voice suddenly vanished. "It still makes me feel funny that I never know any of the dirt." She gave Molly a quick intimate grin.

"You're lucky," Molly encouraged, except she knew she would be hurt if no one ever confided in her.

"Probably," her mother said. Her eyes suddenly lit up. "I called your father. He said to buy you anything you want."

They weren't rushed when they got to the top of the stairs, primarily because her mother was known as one of Jessie's customers. Her mother began scanning the floor like a professional. She started in the direction of the dresses. "Let's browse together for a while," she said, "and then I'll put you in a dressing room and Jessie can bring in the things we like." Molly remembered the parade of clothes coming in and out of the dressing room for that college weekend when she'd allowed her mother to dress her. She even felt a slight shiver about that never-worn-again backless navy dress with the bib top and long sleeves.

"I'm not really ready to try anything on," she protested.

"It's almost May, Molly. We're buying late as it is. If we find something we like, we need to go ahead and take it, believe me."

How could one new dress hurt? It would please them so much, and if she worked on her mother, maybe it would even be something she was willing to wear. "Okay," she said.

By now she realized that they wouldn't be able to talk until later: her mother was flipping through the racks with near vengeance. Molly heard her murmur that they'd come too late; still, she selected five dresses that she handed to Jessie, who had quickly appeared. Molly went through a rack of pants suits, but they were all too duded-up with sequins or silver studs to suit her taste. She sidled over to where her mother was still pulling out possibilities. How *did* she know what would look good and what wouldn't? Not even colors had any special pull for Molly, although she knew, after years of being told, that blue looked good on her. If she was to dress a little better, she needed this help.

She allowed her mother to buy her two reasonable-looking shirtwaist dresses but refused the denim pants suit with an eagle outlined in beads on the back of the jacket. "You *love* blue jeans," her mother insisted.

"Not like this."

"Please try it on," her mother begged.

"I'll think about it, but really, Mother, I couldn't go anywhere dressed like that."

"Where's your imagination?" her mother asked, throwing her hands to the sky. "Don't answer that," she added quickly. But Molly was answering anyway. Her mother interrupted, "I know you use your imagination every day. You don't have to explain that to me again. I know you think the clothes you wear say nothing about your creativity." She seemed to have finished, but then, not able to help herself, she added, "But they do. If you're imaginative, you're imaginative in all aspects of your life. You wear interesting clothes, have interesting knicknacks on your shelves, see interesting people."

"Mother!" Molly said heatedly.

Her mother looked sadly at her. "I'm right," she said.

"Okay, you're right." How had she gotten involved in this?

"You don't believe I'm right."

"Yes, I do."

"Well then, why aren't you interested in how you look?"

"I am, Mother. I don't want to spend too much of Daddy's money. I don't go many places. I don't need anything else."

"Promise me you'll think about the pants suit. And for heaven's sake, stop worrying about your father's money."

She promised, knowing that she was going to regret this stage she'd set forever.

They walked the three blocks to Meyer's Tearoom for dessert and coffee while Molly studied her mother's finely formed figure with her peripheral vision. She wished she could stop her mother on the sidewalk without her knowing, stand right in front of her and examine every inch of her face: the expression in her eyes, the message on her lips, the information provided by her cheeks and forehead. Did her mother's serene expression only mask hidden pain? Did she view herself as a tragic figure? Was she sorry for the life she'd chosen or not?

Molly wondered if she should approach her directly. Ask the exact questions she wanted answers to. Did you ever consider leaving Daddy? If so, why didn't you? What convinced you to stay? Was it laziness? Was it fear for your financial security? Was it me? Did you love him no matter what he did? Can a husband be untruthful and still love you? How deep is that love?

Her mother never walked leisurely but like a model, though unconsciously, causing both men and women to let their eyes drift after her. As had always been the case, Molly felt like a child, an adopted child to be exact, walking beside her. Although their identical long legs kept a synchronized cadence, no one would ever take them for mother and daughter.

"How's the work on the den coming?" she asked.

"We've delayed it," her mother said, not looking her way. "We're not sure we want one anymore."

"You've wanted one for years," Molly exclaimed. She didn't want them to make room for her. She didn't want it to be easy: walk out of Isabel's house and back into her own. "You haven't delayed it because of me?" she asked in a small voice.

"For you? No," her mother answered abstractedly. "We didn't think you'd come home no matter what happens between you and Robert."

"I wouldn't," Molly said. She felt funny that they were deciding this for her, so she added, "I mean, I might for a couple of days while I looked for my own place." Her words surprised her, although she'd said them to keep the option of the den open to her. She hadn't decided to leave Robert, had she? No, she was here for answers. How easily did one give up a marriage? Was it a sign of character to stay or to leave? How had she always viewed her mother? As weak or as strong? She would like the den to be available even though she would refuse it.

Her mother preceded her through Meyer's revolving door, where the smells of things to buy—perfume and leather purses in particular—assailed them. Walking immediately to a counter, her mother shot a tester spray of Chanel No. 5 on to one wrist, rubbing it against her other wrist as if she were mixing blood with her best friend. Molly trailing, she traveled to the counter of costume jewelry, something she never even bought.

"Come on," Molly said, tugging her arm in the direction of the tearoom. "They might be about to close. Come on," she repeated. Her mother had the capacity for mixing the wheat and the chaff like nobody she'd ever seen. Nothing seemed more important than anything else. Looking at costume jewelry had the same pull as discussing her daughter's unclear future.

As a child she'd been taken mostly to two places outside home for food: the drive-in at the Irving Park Delicatessen, where her mother and her mother's friends had parked close together—all the children in the back seats—to talk across the open windows like a party line, and here, the tearoom, which served special treats, ice-cream pie with hot fudge sauce, strawberry parfaits, and flaming baked Alaska. The former trips were a way for the mothers to escape the monotony of home. The trips to the tearoom were where Molly began to learn to do what her mother and her mother's friends did: engage in conversation that was rewarding but not necessarily vital. This afternoon, the tearoom was almost empty, and a waitress dressed in crisp black and white told them to pick a place to sit. They took a table, her mother choosing the inside seat. Circling the room just behind her head was a two-foot high mirror so that customers who faced the wall had their own view of the rest of the room. From where she sat, Molly could see a multidimensional view of her mother's head: the perfectly arranged French twist, the graceful neck, the face that from every angle was handsome.

"You say you're leaving Robert?" her mother asked after the waitress had taken their order.

"Oh, no. I was just telling you to do whatever you wanted with the den."

"So you aren't leaving Robert?"

"I don't think so," she said. Would you? she wanted to ask. But if she asked the question, she had to be willing to provide some details. With long graceful fingers her mother lit a cigarette and took a deep indelicate drag. What Molly wanted was to listen to what had happened to someone else without telling what had happened to her. Her mother was her only source; probably no one under thirty, including Gisella whether she knew it or not, knew anything about infidelity.

"How are you and Dad getting along?" Molly asked nonchalantly.

Her mother jerked her cigarette out of her mouth, holding it at a sharp angle beside her head. "How are we *what*?" she repeated. Molly hadn't anticipated that her mother might not want to answer her questions. The familiar green eyes looked at her, actively adding up what she thought her daughter was getting at. "Clothes," she said in an ironic voice. "I should have known."

"I like the dresses," Molly insisted. "I wanted them." She felt badly that she'd tried to trick her mother. "Well, actually I didn't want them, but now that I have them I'm glad."

"Let me guess why we're here," her mother said. "You are trying to make a decision about Robert?"

Molly nodded.

"And you want my advice?"

Molly nodded again. She felt the color rising in her cheeks.

"But?"

"I don't want to spell everything out. I just want you to give me some advice . . . based on your own experience."

"My own experience," her mother mused. The desserts arrived, Molly's cheesecake, which could be lingered over, and her mother's lime ice cream. "What experience are you talking about?" she asked, her eyebrows arched protectively about her face. Molly watched the changing angle of the spoon she was using to stir her coffee.

"Nothing," she whispered. Although her mother had never discussed her relationship with her father with her, she had made overt references to their problems ever since Molly was in junior high school. Now she pretended not to know what Molly was talking about. It must be the same for everyone: some things were too humiliating to speak about directly.

As her mother ate her ice cream, the tense lines in her face gradually faded. In a quiet voice she said, "I can't discuss my relationship with your father with you. I think you can understand why. And I really don't want to hear about you and Robert. Someday, maybe, but not now. If you've got to talk to somebody, find a friend, but not me, and I would not recommend your father." She took an almost ceremonious bite of ice cream. With a different kind of intensity, her eyes sought Molly's. "We're taking the Booths to the lake house next weekend, and I can't wait." Seeing Molly's stricken face, she said, "Honey, I'm just running my mouth, so we can change the subject."

"Okay," Molly said slowly. "But I do have to tell you one thing." Her mother's face had an inflexible look about it. "Robert dropped out of school. We won't be going to New York next year."

"That does make it impossible, doesn't it?" her mother said before quickly lowering her eyes to her coffee. In an almost inaudible voice she said, "That *is* all I'm going to say. I'm sorry I said that."

Eventually, they began to chat until conversation came easily again, the same way she'd always returned to a horse that had thrown her when she used to ride in high school. When they passed the costume jewelry counter on their way out, Molly remembered she'd left the Montaldo's bag beneath her chair. By the time she returned with it her mother had bought what she said was an excellent copy of a jade necklace, which she'd noticed on their way in.

She walked her mother back to the Montaldo's parking lot, giving her an understanding hug that she did not really mean. She wondered whether at some future point she would think her mother had been wise or had let her down. Right now she didn't know. At least she'd gotten one reaction: "That does make it impossible." But did her mother mean their marriage or Robert's future or everything?

She went straight to her car instead of back to the office, deciding not to make up the time she'd missed. What she'd really wanted from her mother, she was beginning to realize, was to be told what to do. Not that she'd spent her life relying on her mother's view of things. But this one time, she really wanted an opinion. Her decision about Robert, however, could not be based on what her mother believed in or based on what anyone believed in but her. What did she believe in? Facts? Feelings? Did she believe only what she saw? Only what she intuited? Did either way ever offer the whole truth? Was there such a thing as "the whole truth"?

She tried to call on what she knew. There was the world of experience, the twenty-one years she'd lived within the framework of her parents' marriage. Her mother had chosen not a perfect life but the life that made her happiest. Maybe. Molly didn't really know that. There was the bigger world of real life, which she was learning about as a reporter. Wasn't she, for example, better off than 95 percent of the world's population, even though her husband omitted telling her some things? A case could be made that she should be satisfied with personal freedom and plenty of food to eat. There was also the world of herself. But if she didn't know what she believed in *now*, when *would* she know? How old did you have to be before you knew exactly what you thought about things?

She didn't think she'd expected Robert to be perfect. All people made mistakes, herself included, but most of them admitted them, even on occasion asking forgiveness. She wasn't as good as God, forgiving whenever the sinner decided he was ready to repent. But for the past four months she would have accepted any explanation Robert had offered. He wouldn't admit he'd done anything wrong.

When she turned into the driveway at five-thirty, he was again not home. She resisted the many urges that hammered in her mind: the desire to drink wine, the desire to call Caroleen's dorm and request her version of the truth, the desire to confess all to Gisella, the petty but real desire to ask her father what do men want? She remembered that no one person, no two people even, ever represented an entire group. Besides, what did she really know about her father? Her mother had certainly not confirmed anything. She resisted the desire to cry, the desire to blame herself, the pulling desire to confront Robert's accusation that she had sent him to Caroleen. She hadn't sent him to Suzanne. Nor had she had anything to do with the terrible mistake he was making about his education.

She put the Montaldo's bag in the bottom of her suitcase and then threw in the other spring clothing she owned, since before long it would be truly warm. She would operate out of her parents' den-to-be for a few days until she found a place of her own. Robert would have to go to work if he was to continue living here. It occurred to her that he should have gotten a job weeks ago.

On the practical side, she expected Robert to ask if she would loan him the You-Ass and coax her own transportation out of her parents for a while. But that would be an endless situation. She did not want to have to badger him to get it back, so, no, she would not loan him the car. The You-Ass belonged to her. Her father, whom she loved and forgave, had given it to her.

She wondered if she should go ahead and leave, get things *started*, as Suzanne would, but she had to face him sometime. She was not going to try to explain it to him. Words would not do what she wanted. Words would slide away from the truth, perhaps toward facts, perhaps toward lies, but always away from the truth. Just his saying that he loved her would move her as it always had. Just his reminding her that she loved him would make her think things were different than they really were. She would always love him after a fashion.

One thing she would say, whenever he came home, was that she was not leaving him because of Caroleen or even because of Suzanne. She was leaving him because of him. She was going to look into his tantalizing blue eyes, those eyes that had always seized her very soul, and say so.

About the Author

CANDACE FLYNT's highly praised first novel, *Chasing Dad*, appeared in 1980. She lives with her family in Greensboro, North Carolina, her hometown. Her stories have appeared in *The Atlantic Monthly, Carolina Quarterly*, the *Greensboro Review*, and *Redbook*.